Tame the Heart

a Runaway Ranch novel

AVA HUNTER

Cover Design: Okay Creations
Editing: Lilypad Lit
Formatting: Champagne Book Design

Also by
AVA HUNTER

Playlist

Oh Sarah | Sturgill Simpson
Paradise | John Prine
Actin' Up | Miranda Lambert
Wasted on You | Morgan Wallen
Aw Naw | Chris Young
You Are in Love | Taylor Swift
Dirty Looks | Lainey Wilson
Wishful Drinking | Ingrid Andress & Sam Hunt
Bluebird | Miranda Lambert
Way of the Triune God | Tyler Childers
Sun to Me | Zach Bryan
Slow It Down Cowboy | Anna Bates
Sleeping on the Blacktop | Colter Wall
Life Ain't Fair and the World is Mean | Sturgill Simpson

To Billings and Red Lodge and Cook City and Dunn Center and Telluride and Deadwood, and all the small towns that made me.

What is it you plan to do with your one
wild and precious life?
—Mary Oliver

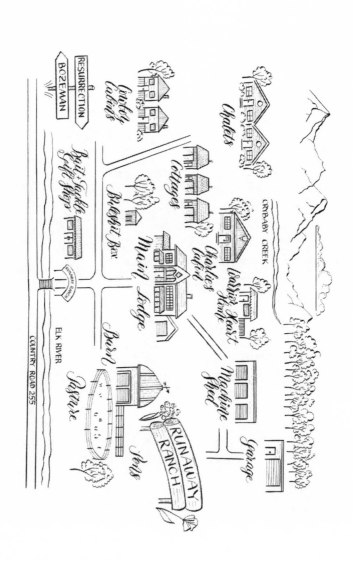

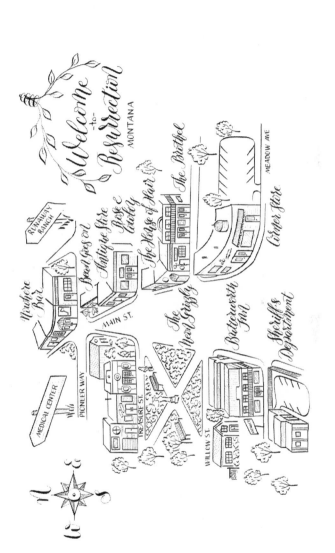

Welcome
-to-
Resurrection
MONTANA

RINAWAY RANCH

Snedgeord

Antique Store

Pose Alley

The House of Hair

The Brothel

Water Barn

General Store

MEADOW AVE

MAIN ST.

MEDICAL CENTER

PIONEER WAY

The Mean Grizzly

Butterworth Inn

Sheriff's Department

TREASURE ST.

WILLOW ST.

Tame the Heart

the

a Runaway Ranch novel

Ruby

HEARTS, FLOWERS, AND SUNSHINE ARE SOME OF my favorite things.

My heart especially. It is wild and weird and wonderful and currently pumping at around 180 beats per minute.

Maybe it's the car I'm spinning around in, or maybe it's because it's my normal. Probably both. Apparently, birthdays are meant to have many awful and wild surprises all at once.

With a tight grip on the steering wheel, I slam my eyes shut as the sound of screeching tires over the rain-slicked road echoes in my head. Over and over like a fun house tilt-a-whirl ride, sending my stomach lurching into my throat. My heart hammers in my ears like it's made of gunfire. Finally, the front of my sunny VW beetle hits a telephone pole with a wicked crunch.

My eyes fly open as the power to the block goes dark.

I gasp, seeing I've stopped feet from Bloom's Blooms, the white-shuttered flower shop my father and brother own.

Oh, no. No, no, no.

They'll never let me out of the house again.

Be safe is what my dad said today when I left the house. It's always *be careful, be safe*, it's never *have fun.*

Overcautious is what my big brother Max calls it. I call it *overprotective.*

Needing oxygen, a life preserver, an escape hatch—because in five seconds all of Carmel, Indiana will come running—I open my door and fall to the wet cement. I gulp humid air and take in the damage. Crumpled fender. Smoking hood. Strawberry milkshake all over my dash, and I groan because I really wanted that milkshake. Still, the rain falling from the sky is pleasant, and I'd give anything to stretch out in snow-angel position and listen to the gentle soundtrack of rain.

I don't even get five seconds before the front door to the flower shop slams open. My dad and my older brother run out, their faces harried. Dad has his pruning shears in his hand, which means I've caught him in the act of what he calls "sweet talking" wild roses.

Shit. They'll never believe it wasn't my heart.

Everything is always about my heart.

Because why wouldn't it be?

I squint at the shrubs to my right and catch the disappearing end of a bushy red tail.

I smile brightly. At least one thing has gone right today. "Ruby!"

Suddenly, my brother and my father are on their knees in front of me, their hands everywhere like no one has lectured them on personal space.

"Ruby Jane, are you okay?" Ted Bloom booms in a voice that has my stomach clenching. It's always that same sad tone. It's always my middle name. To remind him of my mother.

I lean back against the car and puff a lock of hair out of my eyes. "I'm fine, Dad," I say with a bright smile. Making my father worry is like burying an ax in my heart. I always want to reassure him I'm okay. "Not even a scratch."

My father's hands fold around my shoulders. "Hospital."

I shake my head, taking in his craggy face. "No more hospitals." I meet his tired eyes. "I'm not hurt. I swear."

Max's blue eyes narrow like he thinks I'm lying. "Did you have a flutter?"

A *flutter* is what we call one of my fainting episodes. Whenever my heart rate skyrockets, my body floods with adrenaline, which causes me to pass out. This year I've only had one "fluttering" incident. I'm not in orange alert territory yet, not until I faint behind the wheel or in the shower.

I sock him in the arm. "No, asshole."

"Then what happened?"

"I swerved to avoid a squirrel."

Max looks horrified. And disgusted. "Jesus, Rubes." He makes it sound like avoiding helpless animals is a bad thing.

Tilting my head up, I try to find the bushy red tail again. Black smoke clogs the sky.

I quirk an eyebrow, impressed. It's the most action I've had in this lifetime. "Oh man, I smoked the car, didn't I, Max?"

"The car? You're worried about the fucking car? You could have died!" Max whisper-hisses, and it's like the words drop into the perfect Tetris position to make sense.

I could have died. Today.

"Huh," I say brightly. "I could have. That really sucks."

My brother stares at me like I'm nuts. My father looks like he's about to have an aneurysm, because I can see the classic Bloom vein throbbing in his temple. I'm saved by old Mrs. Hester, coming out of the American Legion and asking him why her daylilies always die so fast. Instantly, an argument begins.

If I had my phone, I'd hop on it and try to calm the quarrel with a peace-sign emoji. But I can barely hear what they're saying over the din of the gathering crowd complaining about the power outage.

That's when I look up and spot the squirrel in a tree, chittering away with another squirrel. Without warning, hot tears flood my eyes.

It's the stupidest thought, but it rocks me.

Even the squirrel has more of a life than I do. It has a best friend, or better, a lover.

It has more than me.

Once again, Max's words flood my ears: *You could have died.*

I could have died.

Which is not new information.

I could have met my maker today, and what would I have to show for it? What would I have written in my gratitude journal from the afterlife?

That I, Ruby Bloom, am grateful for my very planned schedule? That my father and brother hovering is one of my favorite sports? That my favorite words are: *Planned. Orderly. Safe. Vegetables. Oatmeal. Hospital. Medication. Syncope.* That even though I work for a luxury travel agency, running social media and content marketing from the comfort of my bedroom, I've never set foot outside Indiana. That I've only had sex once in my life with a man who sounded like a carburetor when he came and who I scared half to death by fainting when it ended.

Maybe all men sound like a carburetor, not like I would know what good sex is. I've never even been handled rough. Never had an orgasm. Never been in love.

I blink then. It's like an unexpected sucker punch to the face. The *what-ifs.*

What if I have two good years left? What if I die and have never lived?

What if I go my whole life without love? Without good sex?

My heart, agreeing with me, hammers like it wants to beat its way out of my chest.

I close my eyes and imagine my heart running off, away from my body. Where would it go? What would it do?

For so long, I thought I was happy, when all I've been is happily unhappy.

I've spent my entire life living quiet and safe for my father, but the right thing feels so . . . wrong. So sad. So boring.

This world is beautiful, and I'm watching it pass me by.

I let out a strangled squeak. I feel my throat closing up, panic attack style.

And that's when it hits me.

I'm not afraid of dying. Others are.

"Ruby?" Max's voice floats.

"Today's my birthday," I tell Max.

"Yeah, Rubes." He sounds worried. "I know. We got a cake inside that's melting."

I'm melting.

I'm too hot, sweating when the rain just keeps falling. My father's on the phone and now I can hear the ambulance, which just makes me want to curl up and . . .well, not die, exactly, because I've already been there done that today. More like sink into an abyss of exhausting existential despair because I wish everyone would let me be.

Let me live.

"You okay?" Max asks. "Rubes?"

In answer, I push away from the car and lie down on

the wet cement. I spread my arms out. A pebble grinds itself into my shoulder while the May rain seeps through
my dress, chilling my bones.

I place two fingers on my throat. I've lived with SVT
long enough that I can monitor my heartbeat. I track the
rapid tick of my pulse, and it sounds like—

More time. More time. I still have more time.

"Fuck." Max hovers over me, hands in his shaggy blond
hair like he's ready to tear it all out. I can see the soft blue
of his eyes, matching mine, matching our mothers. "Where
does it hurt?"

I stare at the squirrel, now squeaking in a tree above
me. The sun is brighter. Intense. My brother's panicked
voice rattles in my head. Out of the corner of my eye, my
hair, a bright strawberry blonde, mixes with the rainwater,
and slowly turns a muddy red-brown.

My heart speeds up its beat.

I rest a palm over my chest and sigh. "Everywhere."

1

Ruby

ONE MONTH LATER

TIME TO CALL MY BROTHER AND GIVE HIM proof of life.

I park my new Buick Skylark, a behemoth of a car, at the gas pump and crunch across the dusty parking lot of the Gas 'N Go to find the one pay phone that's been around since the seventies. Although I have a cell phone, there's something about using a pay phone that feels very road trip.

I've finished my last part-time shift at Rita's, a sleepy mom-and-pop Mexican restaurant in downtown Winslow, Arizona. It was a relaxed waitressing job, but the tips were good and the exertion minimal. I've kept my remote job at the travel agency, managing their social media account, but I like the boots on the ground style of working locally. Everyone needs a helping hand and if

I can be that person, I'll step in. Diners and bars are easy part-time gigs that let me move on when I want to.

And trust me, I've been moving on.

A week after my near-death-hit-and-run-squirrel experience, I went to my cardiologist one last time, then left Indiana. The last month I've seen and done things I've never experienced. I got a tiny tattoo of an EKG line on the inside of my ring finger in Charleston. Danced in the second line in New Orleans. I've seen houses on stilts in Galveston and had the best pie of my life in Key West.

For the first time in my twenty-six years on this earth, I feel alive.

Like I've fixed a hole inside of me I didn't know was leaking.

I am greedy and feral and in love with this life. And I want to see more. See it all. Take risks.

Sometimes—and I can never tell this to Max—I don't want to go back home.

I want to keep running and never stop.

As I drop a coin in the slot, a man in ripped Wranglers tips the brim of his dusty cowboy hat to me as he passes by. Rugged and weathered lines crease his tan face, giving him a wise and magnetic appeal.

Fascinated, I beam at him and wave. Then I tuck the map I purchased at the gas station under my arm, pick up the sticky receiver and dial numbers I know by heart.

Max answers with a curt, "Come back."

I gasp, smiling at the sweet way he tries so damn hard to charm me. "Never."

"Where are you?"

"You know I can't tell you that. Super-secret sister business."

Not that my father or brother have any legal pull if they track me down. I'm an adult of sound mind and body, but they have the powerful ability to make me feel guilty until I come home, which is why I'll keep my whereabouts off-limits.

If I'm gone, it means my father and brother can get back to their lives. No more worrying about me, no more obsessively hovering. They're well-meaning and want to protect me, but being away from them is like a heavy weight lifted. I can live.

And so can they.

Max lets out a long-suffering sigh. I close my eyes and rest my forehead against the glass.

I can't win. Either way, I can't win. I hurt them when I'm there, and I hurt them when I'm gone.

A shadow enters his voice. "I worry."

My eyes pop open, and I rush to reassure him. "Don't. I have pepper spray. And I haven't had a flutter since January, you know that. I'm taking all my medication, and I have weekly Zooms with my doctor. See? I'm on the straight and narrow." I gape as a gorgeous black Cadillac passes through the parking lot. "I do not plan to go hog wild. I plan to live, Max."

And damn the consequences.

"What if you're alone and something happens?"

"I'll find a hot cowboy to give me mouth-to-mouth."

"Hardy har har."

I can see Max's sullen scowl over the phone. He worries, but he shouldn't. By now, I know the signals my body sends me when it's close to shutting down. I sweat more than humanly possible. Rapid heartbeat and shortness of breath accompany the pounding sensation in the neck and chest. To ensure I don't keel over, I have to pay attention to small bodily rules. Light on alcohol, light on caffeine, light on exercise.

Extreme stress, exhaustion, exercise—best-case scenario, I faint.

Worst-case scenario, my heart stops.

"What're you doing for work?"

"Waitressing."

"Yeah, well, make sure you turn it down a notch so your heart doesn't explode."

I roll my eyes. Death doesn't scare me like it does my father and my brother. Being angry at my heart and condition never helped me in life.

Since my diagnosis, I've been told I can't do this, or I can't do that. No riding bikes with the neighborhood kids. I had to give up the dance class I loved so much. All because my dad and brother were worried about the *what-ifs*. It didn't matter if they didn't know whether it would affect me. They just assumed it would, and for the betterment of my health, sheltered me. I spent my life not knowing what I could do. Not knowing who I am.

Now it's my destiny. My choice. My *what-ifs*.

In fact, I would rather rip my life apart than live in fear that someone—or something—will take it from me.

Just like I have rules for my heart, I have rules for my new life. A to-do list scrawled in my journal that I'm continually adding to. While Max rambles all the negatives about my trip, I write each happy thing I plan to accomplish on my cross-country road trip in the dust on the glass side of the phone booth.

Ruby Bloom's To-Do List (so do it!):
~~1. Get a tattoo.~~
2. Have sex. Good sex.
3. Stay up all night and see the sunrise.
4. See a California sunset.
5. Swim in the Pacific.

Say yes.

Say yes to everything, because for so long others have said no.

Except regarding love.

I am temporary. I don't get to let anyone love me. I've seen where it got my father and mother.

Gingerly, I run my finger over the delicate opal and silver cuff bracelet on my wrist, the most precious thing of my mother's I own. She made it herself, affixed opals that look like the sky, ocean, and sand onto the ends. Hammered the silver until it pebbled. That was back when she was a beautiful starving artist in Malibu, the summer before she met my father and fell in love with him and his purple roses.

Max's growl intercepts my daydream daze. "I want you to come home."

I stick my tongue out at my reflection. "This is my life, Max. Don't take it from me."

"Goddamnit, Rubes." Exasperation cracks in his voice. "I'm not trying to do that. I'm trying to keep you safe. Keep you around."

"I will be around," I say, even as my lungs constrict.

"You'll probably be sick of me when I come rolling back into town, ready to kick your bony ass."

He chuckles. "How long you think you'll be gone?"

"Why? You miss me?" I ask, watching the man with the cowboy hat exit the Gas 'n Go with an ice-cold bottle of Coca-Cola. He goes to his pump, taking a long sip as he funnels unleaded into his lowrider.

"Hell no. I hate this job of yours."

When I graduated from college five years ago with a degree in marketing, I started up my family's small business social media account. Built it up from two followers to a healthy five thousand.

Over the line, I hear the slam of a keyboard. "I don't know how you do it. Everyone bitching about something when all they are is just fucking flowers."

"They're not just flowers, Max." I instantly smile. Flowers are safe. Soft. But they prick when ruffled. "They're bright sides."

Everything has a bright side. Even with my condition, even when assholes on social media tear up the comments, you can always make it better. You can always survive it.

"Here's a tip, Max. Don't feed the trolls. And smile."

Get a life. Go date a girl. Go have good sex.

"I don't smile," he grumbles. Then, in a resigned voice, he says, "So far, what's been your sunflower on this trip?"

Our long-time game perks me right up. "Hmm." I decide not to tell him about riding the mechanical bull in Nashville. "I saw a merman at an alligator farm and petting zoo. It was incredible and terrifying in all the best ways."

"Oh, yeah?" There's a smile in his voice. "Where was that?"

I laugh. "Nice try. I'm hanging up now. I love you. Tell dad I love him too."

I end the call and exit the booth.

With a hopeful exhale, I stretch my arms out and tilt my face to the sun, drinking in its warm rays. I love the southwest. I love the wicked sun and the dust and the palm trees sweeping the glossy blue sky, letting me know I'm alive. I love wearing tank tops and flip-flops and feeling half-naked and wild and free. This rugged country is not meant for everyone, but I have lived here for a week and survived.

And next?

Beach or mountains. But how to choose?

An idea comes to me.

"Excuse me," I say, rushing up to Mr. Cowboy Hat to intercept his empty pop bottle. "Can I have that if you're done?"

He blinks and lifts the brim of his cowboy hat to see me better. "It's trash, *senorita*."

"It is, but it's my trash."

He looks puzzled as he hands it over to me. With a bounce in my step, joy blooming inside me, I head to my car and spread the map out on the sun-warmed hood. I place the bottle on top of it. And I spin.

It's not a game, but living a life I don't have to take seriously feels like one. I can ramble and roll and have hopes and dreams, too.

As I watch the glass bottle's tip go 'round and 'round, I wonder about destiny.

You can only do so much, my Dad would constantly remind me. *Watch your triggers. You wouldn't want to pass out on the treadmill, would you?* Doctor Lee might warn. *You're psychotic for even doing this*, Max would tell me. *You can have a good life despite your heart, or a bad one because of it*, my Aunt Jonnie used to say. *So, choose, toots.*

I choose the good life.

I choose *my* life.

All these little white pills in my purse, this tattered map, my twenty-dollar sundress, this beauty of a bucket list. They will all get me to some wild, wondrous adventure I cannot yet imagine.

The bottle stops.

It points north. The tip of it lands in a state that shakes me awake inside.

My heart shivers, a familiar sensation of hope taking root in my soul.

Montana. The mountains.

Cowboy Hat steps up, his eyes crinkling in a beguiling grin. He holds out his sunglasses. "You need these, *señorita*, to have a little fun."

I meet the man's smiling eyes and warm tears of gratitude fill my own. Cheap plastic gas station shades have never looked so beautiful. I clutch them to my heart. "Thank you."

He nods.

I lower myself into the car and take a deep, slow breath. My mother once said, years before she died, years after everyone warned her not to have that last baby, "*Honor your heart until you become it.*"

Well, my heart is open wide.

And I intend to use it.

2

Charlie

FLIP-FLOPS. THEY'RE WEARING GODDAMN FLIP-*flops.*

    I stare at the tourists, bright-eyed blonde sisters, giggling in a corner of Runaway Ranch's lodge as they select a walking stick from an iron umbrella stand. A local carpenter whittled the rods of smooth wood, fashioning the heads of each stick into a furry woodland creature.

The girls giggle some more.

Christ. Their tiny shorts and thin tank tops aren't even appropriate hiking attire. I note the absence of water bottles or canteens and cringe. They'll die out there on the trails.

This is a working ranch, not a goddamn glamping experience.

I almost erupt when they dig into the bucket of ice-cold PBRs we leave out for our guests. Great. They're gonna get drunk and fall down the side of the fucking waterfall.

I close my eyes and breathe out through my nose.

What a fucking mess. It's been a week since the ranch opened for the season and already we have guests going rogue.

I listen closely to their conversation, catching *Crybaby Creek* and *hot cowboys*.

The girls choose a walking stick and head for the back door.

I reach for the two-way radio on my hip. "Colton."

"What's up, boss? How can I help?"

I massage my brow. Colton's a new hire fresh out of high school who dropped into the ranch at the beginning of summer looking for work. We hired him on the spot. Young and eager to please, he has the energy and enthusiasm for odd jobs around the ranch that no one else wants to do.

"Don't call me boss." If anyone deserves the title, it's Davis, my oldest, bossiest brother. "Listen, we got two newbs headed down to Crybaby Creek in flip-flops."

Colton cackles. "I'll keep a watch on 'em."

"Thanks." After a beat I say, "And intercept the goddamn beers."

"You got it, Charlie."

"Call me if you need anything."

"Roger dodger."

I turn my radio to channel four and holster it.

As I walk through the great room, I flip a wave to Tina, our Guest Services manager. She's at the front desk, her dark brown curls bobbing as she chatters away with a group of eight about their reservation. I lift my chin to a small group of tourists snapping photos of the deer antler chandelier that hangs in the lodge's entryway.

The lodge—or the Main House, as we call it—is 5,000

square feet of rustic style. It's the most striking part of the ranch, embodying the spirit of the Wild West with vintage rodeo artwork, high-beamed ceilings, and plush leather couches. The great room is the centerpiece of the lodge, where guests relax or book activities. On one side is Bar M with cowhide bar stools and the best local moonshine around. On the opposite, the entrance to the chow hall, saloon, and gift shop. But the lodge wouldn't be complete without the gigantic windows that offer a 180-degree view of thick pine forests and stands of aspen.

I drag a hand over my beard, watching the guests pour in. Summer season means tourists. Not my favorite part of the ranch, but it's a living. I prefer the quiet of fall.

Solitude.

Silas Craig, our chef, pops out of the kitchen as I approach the front doors. "Hey, Charlie."

I nod. "What's on the menu tonight, Chef?" We serve all meals buffet-style in the chow hall, except for our farewell campfire dinner.

"Beef stew. Cornbread. S'mores. People love that shit." He smooths a tattooed hand over the front of his apron, a lopsided grin on his face. "Drop some off at the house for you tonight?"

"Appreciate that," I tell him. Having our own on-site chef has its benefits. Three months a year, no cooking necessary.

Good people. All of them. No matter how big or small, every season, our team handles what the ranch throws at them. From guest services to wranglers to cattle foremen, after five years in business, the ranch employs ten percent of our small town.

Still pissed about the girls in flip-flops, I slam out the

front door and pound down the steps, having a near miss with a kitten scrambling its way into a grove of bushes next to the lodge. Breathing deep, I stand there and take in the rugged backcountry of Montana.

Blue skies that break every boundary in nature. Jagged mountain peaks that dare the most adventurous to conquer them. The late afternoon June sun beats down on me, at that perfect angle that even my dusty cowboy hat can't shield me from its furious rays. Summer in Montana is a piece of paradise.

Our property sits at the base of Meadow Mountain, framed on both sides by dense national forest. Off in the distance, the custom metal *Runaway Ranch* sign hangs over the entrance to the ranch. 17,000 acres of untamed wilderness.

Once upon a time I'd call Georgia my home, but not anymore.

Resurrection, Montana is where I hang my hat. And damn, I love it.

Boots crunching gravel, I head out across the grounds, mentally logging some things that need fixing. Broken fence post. Overgrown weeds. I pluck a pair of pliers from the ground and toss it into a flower bed to retrieve later.

To me, this life is church. Making sure our employees and guests feel like family. Inspecting the ranch. Working from sun up to sun down. Driving cattle. Breaking horses.

Ranching, horses, and rodeo are part of my blood. I was born and raised on it; my parents ran one of the most successful horse breeding farms and training facilities in the United States. Ten years ago, I competed on the rodeo circuit with my younger brother Wyatt.

At twenty-four, I had everything.

The woman I loved, my titles, prize money, a future mapped out.

Until suddenly, I didn't.

My fiancée's death unraveled my whole life and exploded everything inside of me.

I did whatever I could to run from Maggie's memory. I drank too much. Cursed God. Tried to sell every damn horse I owned until my father talked me down. It was around six months after her death that I knew I couldn't stay in Wildheart. At every corner, memories burned of me and her. The creek where we'd kiss until the sun came up. Our family's rodeo ring where she died. If I saw one more sad smile from her mama at the grocery store or found another one of her hair ties in my truck, I was going to throw myself off the Jackson Street Bridge.

I needed a new memory. I needed a new place.

I had to move my boots on this fucked up broken ground that was my life or else I'd fall apart.

So, I got lost.

I found Resurrection.

On a whim, I bought the ranch.

But I learned it didn't help much. For the first five years, I stumbled through life without her. I was a walking heartache with a bad Jim Beam habit. I can't describe how much I missed her. How desperate I was to hear her voice, to feel her skin, to catch that shock of red hair that was her calling card, and my salvation.

Eventually, my brothers, all scattered to the wind, followed me.

Wyatt was the first. Two weeks in and he was busting down my door.

"You ain't doin' this alone," he said, and he stayed.

A year later, Ford joined us, and a year after that, our brother Davis.

It was Davis's idea to turn this overgrown plot of land into a working ranch.

"Listen," he said in that hard-ass, no-nonsense military way of his. "You can mope the rest of your goddamn life, but the rest of us, we gotta make a fucking living."

So, it's what we did.

Runaway Ranch, my brothers, and Resurrection saved me.

Sometimes I'm still pissed off about it.

The deep buzz of the two-way radio cuts through the silence of the outdoors, and I reach for it.

"Charlie?" Davis's deep voice crackles through the speakers. "You there?"

"Yeah, I'm fuckin' here," I say with an edge.

"What's up your ass?"

I watch a cowboy hat-clad family of five squeal and point at the emerald-green horse pasture. The sound grates at my skin and I grit my teeth, feeling the irritation building in my bones.

"There's too many people here."

"We need people," Davis barks back. "They pay our bills, remember? You're the one who had to buy a fucking ranch."

I rub my brow, disgruntled at the reminder.

"Besides we might not have people here much longer."

I frown. "What're you talking about?"

"Get your ass over to the Bullshit Box and I'll tell you."

Christ. Now what?

"Wyatt. Ford," Davis says before there's another crackle

on the radio channel me and my brother's all share. "Get your asses up here, too."

Redirecting my course, I veer right, heading for the Bullshit Box, a tiny corrugated metal home that we use as our business headquarters. Since it's situated in the center of the ranch next to the lodge, it allows us to do our office work while monitoring comings and goings.

When I step through the large garage-style door, Davis's Belgian Malinois rescue, Keena, tearing up a box in the room's corner, spazzes, then barks at my appearance. After roughing her fur, I clock Davis at the computer, wearing his standard attire of a tight navy USMC T-shirt, blue jeans, and boots. He has a video paused mid-action. The stiff hunch of his broad shoulders tells me he's in alert-mode.

At thirty-five, Davis is as opposite as he can get from his twin Ford. In looks and personality. Tall and muscular, Davis, a veteran marine, is quiet and intense—no-nonsense and take-charge—with a determined set in his dark brown eyes.

As co-owner of Runaway Ranch and head of security, as well as heading the Montana Search and Rescue operation in Cascade County, Davis handles the safety of the ranch. Anyone who tries to make it past my older brother better have a death wish or a prayer.

Davis, not taking his stare off the computer screen, says, "You hear our sister's ready to pop?"

"You got me up here for that? Emmy Lou?" Our baby sister is pregnant with twins and expecting any day now.

I shake off the worry threading through me, focusing on what's got me stuck inside when I could be out on the land. Since Maggie's death, I've fought against being an overprotective bastard about my family. That feeling of whatever can go wrong will, and there's nothing I can do to stop it.

"Nah. Soon as Wy and Ford get here, we'll get into it." A vein pulses in his temple. "Security system is down. Been trying to get it back up all day. Got a new one on the way." He pushes back from the desk and looks at me. "Bigger and better."

I sigh. It's not a surprise. The ranch's security has been shit ever since we got here. But we all decided together—only cameras on the lodge, the barn, and the gates. Spooking the guests or invading their privacy by having cameras aimed at the cabins didn't feel right. And boxing us in with electrified fences strikes me as bullshit.

My back molars grind together as I sit on the edge of a desk and scan the space. The office looks like a bomb's gone off. Unpaid bills scattered across the desks. Illegible chicken scratch scrawled on purchase orders that'll make them a bitch to file. A box of ammo sits too close to a space heater. On one side of the small room hangs a dartboard used to settle arguments and divvy up chores no one wants to do.

"Who's in trouble?" I ask, keeping a close watch on Davis. My play-by-the-rules brother is the definition of calm. But I've been around him my entire life, and I know when he's pissed off. He's got that Montgomery tick in his jaw that gives everything away. "Ford or Wyatt?"

"Who's saying it's not you?" he demands.

Before I can respond with words and not the middle finger I'm giving him, Wyatt lopes through the open door. "Hey, cocksuckers," he drawls, greeting us cheerfully. He's covered from head to toe in dust, having landed back in town today fresh off the Calgary rodeo circuit.

Wyatt, at thirty-two, is two years younger than me. While all the Montgomery men share the same tall height and broad shoulders, Wyatt and I resemble each other more than the twins do. Same crooked grin, same blue eyes. A two-time world-champion saddle bronc rider, Wyatt works at the ranch part-time training cowboys during the off season.

Davis runs a careful eye over Wyatt. "Anything broken?"

I snort. If broken bones or gored body parts bothered Wyatt, he would have stopped riding a long time ago.

"Just my last record."

I roll my eyes. *Cocky motherfucker.*

Wyatt glances at me and whistles. "Good lord, Charlie, you look like a busted mule. Ain't you took a break since I left?"

Defensively, I cross my arms and grunt. "I don't need a break." I fight the urge to remember the last time I left the ranch for fun and not going into town for supplies.

Wyatt drops into a chair and kicks his dirty boots up on the desk. "Can we get this over with so we can start drinking?"

My little brother hates any business talk. He'd much rather be out riding, or starting fistfights, but for me, that's where I excelled. Despite the cowboy in me, during my time off from the rodeo circuit, I earned my business degree. Between negotiating vendor contracts and managing expenses, it's come in handy more times than I can count.

"Get your fuckin' boots off the desk," I snap at Wyatt as I push a mound of papers his way. "And clean this shit up."

"Charlie's right," Davis barks.

"Assholes. The both of you." With a grumble, Wyatt

yanks his boots to the ground with a heavy thud and half-heartedly stacks the papers in a neat pile.

A second later, Ford strides in, automotive grease all over his hands.

He grabs a chair, spins it around and plops down next to the desk. "You summoned?" he says to Davis.

Davis looks annoyed, and I hide a smirk. Pissing off Davis is always satisfying, and the one who can push Davis's buttons the best is Ford, his fraternal twin.

Ford, a retired professional baseball pitcher for the Phoenix Renegades, has the same lean, ropy build as Wyatt. The same adrenaline junkie attitude. There aren't very many people in the world who love their job, but Ford's it. When we give him a weekend off from fishing or riding, he's mad about it.

The only brother missing from the ranch is Grady, the youngest and the baby of the family. Six years younger than me, he took off for Nashville last summer to try to make it in the music industry with a little help from our brother-in-law and Brothers Kincaid bassist Jace Taylor.

"Good," Davis says with a curt nod. "You're all here."

They sure fucking are.

Ten long years now and I've never been able to get 'em gone.

If it weren't for my brothers, I'd still be losing my damn mind.

One by one, they came to put my sorry ass back together. And goddamn, I have my guilt.

They gave up their lives to rebuild mine. Now they're stuck here.

Sometimes I feel like I made a mess of everything.

Sometimes I wonder if we'd be better off without the ranch so they can all get back to their own fucking lives.

"You ready for this?" Davis's sharp drawl reverberates around the Bullshit Box as he pulls up YouTube. "Hang onto your hats."

With a powerful punch, he hits play. A few seconds later, the video begins, and I step closer to the monitor. Recorded by an unseen guest, the video shows Ford, who runs our outdoor activities and excursions, with a group of guests on one of his daily rides. His languid instructions cut the morning air as he shows how to mount his gelding, Eephus.

"Oh, shit." Ford perks up. "That was yesterday."

Davis gives his twin a dry look. "And there's nothing wrong with it?"

Ford's expression is the definition of confused.

My stomach twists. Shit. It's bad.

The platinum blonde woman in the video, dressed primly in black shorts and a white polo, yanks on the bit in the horse's mouth as she goes in for a mount and fails. Whoever is filming the video laughs.

Ford, flashing his usual charming grin and a mouthful of white teeth, swaggers over to her. "Listen, ma'am, seeing as you're having some trouble, if you'll let me help you out—"

"I know how to do it, sir." Her tone bleeds with arrogance. "I've ridden my whole life."

A muscle ticks in Ford's jaw, but he keeps an easy posture, watching as she gets one foot in the stirrup. That's when Eephus trots away.

For a long second, the woman hangs there, screeching as she tries to get a grip on the saddle horn. Then, in what's a really fucking stupid idea, she whips the horse with the reins. Hard.

Wyatt hisses a shocked breath.

I'm not far behind him. Anyone who knows horses and loves them like we do knows it's a fucking cardinal sin. She's not helping the horse focus his attention, she's hurting him.

The woman tries to pull herself up on Eephus, fails miserably, and falls to the ground with a splat. Eephus trots off.

And then the Ford in the video laughs.

The Ford in the Bullshit Box laughs too. He and Wyatt break into wild cackles.

"Goddamn," Ford crows, slapping his knee. "It's even better the second time around."

I'm about to ask Davis what the fuck he's so worked up about, when the Ford in the video looks down at the woman in the mud puddle and barks, "C'mon, lady. Get your spoiled fucking ass up and let's ride."

Gasps sound from the guests. The woman cries. Ford stands there, arms crossed, staring at her with impatience and amusement.

Davis pauses the video.

I swear under my breath before I slowly turn my face to look at Ford. "You told her to get her *spoiled fucking ass up?*"

"This is a working ranch, little brother." Ford stares me down, daring me to argue with him. We're only a year apart, but he and Davis pull rank when they want to piss me off. "It ain't glamping. Our guests aren't getting sunshine and rainbows. They're getting cowboys and dirt and dust and if they don't like it, they can go back to New York or L.A. or wherever the hell they're from."

"She didn't get hurt," Wyatt says, worried eyes flicking to mine. "They all sign a contract. They can't sue us."

"They can't," Davis interjects. "But this is all over TikTok. It's going viral on social media."

I scowl. "What the fuck is tick tack?"

Wyatt snickers. "Tik*Tok*. Social media, man. Way of the future."

After a few clicks on the computer, Davis has a new browser up.

TikTok.

"Here . . ." He shows us the original poster's account. *Lassomamav76.* "Read the goddamn comments."

All 2,483 of them.

We all lean in.

#boycottRunawayRanch

Your downfall is imminent.

Thanks for showing us your true colors. GROSSS.

#cancelcowboys

Absolutely disgusting thinking you can treat human beings like this!!!

Anger surges through me as I read the flood of backlash. It's all foreign as fuck to me. Technology isn't worth my damn time, not when I have a ranch to run and animals to take care of. I couldn't give two shits about the type of people who run wild at the mouth without caring who they hurt or have no interest in getting both sides of the story. Gossip is all they care about. Revenge. Keyboard warriors with fucking sticks up their asses.

Ford drags a hand through his dirty blond hair that curls behind his ears and along the nape of his neck. "Cantankerous fucking Karens," he mutters.

"Shit." Wyatt rears back from the comments like

they've reached through the computer screen and slapped him across the face. "They want people to boycott the ranch. Those fuckers."

Davis jerks his chin at the social media posts. "*We* should've been doing this social media shit from the beginning."

I rub my temple at the harsh admonishment. My older brother is always the semi-frustrated voice of reason.

"I talked to Tina." Davis's gruff voice is sober. "We've already had four cancellations."

My ears ring at the sudden seriousness of his words, and I lift my eyes heavenward.

Fuck, this is the last thing we need.

It's our first week of the season. We're not a success, but we're surviving. Every year, we put our blood, sweat and money into our land and our animals, and now one trigger-happy woman is ready to burn it all down.

The idea of losing guests, respect, money, already has me tired.

I give one last look at the video and then shut off the monitor.

Fucking social media.

Davis narrows his eyes at Ford. "I'm not thrilled with you right now, asshole."

Ford snaps open his mouth, but Wyatt shoves up out of his chair, no doubt ready to fend off an argument. While my younger brother's always ready to start trouble, he also finishes it. "C'mon, y'all. Let's get a drink."

I rub a hand over my beard, a list of problems to tackle already running through my head.

Wyatt raises a finger. "I know that look. You ain't gettin' out of it. It's Friday night, man." He jerks his chin at Ford and scoffs. "Would you believe this guy? Only hangs out with his horses when he has three perfectly good brothers."

I let out a resigned sigh when Ford claps my shoulder and propels me outside. Keena follows, trotting loyally beside Davis. My brothers won't back off, so I guess I gotta give the fuck in.

I meet Wyatt's eager face and give a nod. "We going to Nowhere?"

Wyatt hoots. "We're going to Nowhere."

3

Charlie

THE VEIN IN MY TEMPLE THROBS IN ANNOYANCE as the waitress slams a round of ice-cold beers down on our table. The jukebox cranks out outlaw country amid the booming rabble of the Choir Boys, a law enforcement motorcycle club pounding shots in the corner.

Coming to Nowhere was a bad decision. By now, everyone in our small town has seen the video. Lucky for us, they're on our side. Unlucky for me, everyone wants to offer their opinion and sage advice.

Scoot, our resident prepper, leans in like he's got all the secrets of the universe. "I tell ya, I tell ya, I tell ya what, Charlie, man, you gotta screen these people. They're looking to cause trouble, so you gotta prepare. Take their phones at check-in. Institute curfew. I'm telling you, man, panic rooms."

"That so?" Davis grins, an ice-cold beer at his lips. "Tell Charlie some more. I don't think he gets it."

I shoot my older brother a glare, and before I can tell

him to come up with his own fucking solutions, Wyatt drops back to the table with a round of shots.

Beef, a burly bartender with a shaved head and a long black beard, leans across the bar. He waves a bottle of vodka around like a mallet. "Wyatt, you see this sign?" He gestures at the chalkboard hanging on the wall next to a signed photo of Clint Eastwood. Scrawled across it in threatening red chalk is DAYS WITHOUT A FIGHT— 50. The exact amount of time Wyatt's been on the rodeo circuit. "I'm warning you, you ruin my streak and I'll kick your ass myself."

It's the law of the land every weekend. Riotous and violent living. We drink. We fight. We do it all over again. We'll be doing this till the day we die.

Here, in Resurrection, the Wild West still lives.

Rowdy and rough and situated at the end of Main Street in an old building that used to be a pharmacy, Nowhere is the local's bar. The last stop before you raise hell. You want to drink someplace safe and secure, you hit up the Spur which is located in the historic Butterworth hotel.

Outsiders are unwelcome.

A fact I know from experience. My brothers and I were met with resistance when we moved here. Now, ten years later, we've paid our dues and we're as local as can be.

"No fights tonight." Settling in to play town bouncer, Davis points a finger at Wyatt before swinging it to me. "That means you, too."

Wyatt and I exchange a smirk. While Wyatt's the first one to start a fight, I always back up my little brother. Which gives Ford and Davis no choice but to join in. Not that Davis puts much heart into it. His grumpy ass usually looks bored swinging a fist.

"We're in enough trouble with that video anyway," Ford adds.

Wyatt arches a brow. "Sounds like a *you* problem, Ford."

Ford scowls at the reminder. It's the last thing my older brother needs. More bad press. Another video to haunt him.

"We're all in the shit with the fucking ranch." Davis scrapes a hand over his dark hair before rubbing his shoulder, where he took a bullet in the Marines. An injury that left him unfit to serve and sent him straight to Resurrection to babysit my sorry ass.

"You hurting?" I ask in a low voice.

"Not too bad." Davis crosses his arms, refusing to let even an ounce of emotion slide across his face.

"I'll say it once, I'll say it again," Wyatt says. "What's good getting shot, if you can't talk about it?"

Davis scowls at Wyatt's never-ending curiosity of his injury. Our brother never told us what he went through in combat. Not that Davis would open up to any of us.

"Drink this," Ford insists, brown eyes clocking his twin. He slides a shot of tequila Davis's way. "Best kind of medicine."

Davis grunts and accepts the shot.

I can feel them communicating in their secret twin language.

Wyatt knocks back a shot. "I was good for two damn months," he grouses. He may be a party animal, but when it comes to the rodeo, he doesn't fuck around. It's the only thing in his life that gets him to heel.

"Now I'm not saying I'll be a saint. Because if the Wolfington brothers show their ugly faces, I'm gonna knock their loud mouths out." Anger flashes in Wyatt's eyes. "I know my horse is on their goddamn property."

Davis and I let out the same long-suffering sigh.

The Wolfington brothers have been the bane of our existence since we moved to Resurrection. They're pissed Stede McGraw sold his land to a boy from South Georgia when the locals were chomping at the bit to get it. In retaliation, they stole a roan of Wyatt's worth more than a small fortune and never returned it. Now we've entered some petty rivalry that, if Wyatt has his way, will last longer than the Hatfield's and McCoy's.

Ford groans in exasperation. "Let the horse go, Wy."

Wyatt ignores him and rubs his hands together in wild glee. "This is gonna be my twentieth bar fight, man."

"Didn't you hear?" a husky, familiar voice drawls. "These days, Wyatt has a new setting called Neanderthal."

An irritated expression overtakes Wyatt's face as Fallon McGraw approaches the table. Feisty and venomous, Fallon's the wild child daughter of ex pro bull rider, Stede McGraw.

"Better than your setting." He ticks off a checklist on his fingers. "Unbridled mayhem. Hell on wheels. Shit stirrer to the nth degree. Category five bi—"

Davis pounds on the table with his fist, ever the moral barometer. "Knock it off, dipshit."

Looking pleased at Wyatt's compliment, Fallon grins. "Trying to romance me with sweet talk, Wyatt? This soon?" The corner of her mouth lifts. "Keep to the skills you excel at."

Wyatt manages a dry laugh, but I notice the clench of his jaw.

Though Fallon and Wyatt are in separate divisions on the rodeo circuit, for years, they've had an idiotic competitive rivalry for who can take top prize every year. Most days, they're at each other's throat, but Wyatt needs to get his head checked if he thinks he's fooling anyone with his *I can't stand her* act.

Ford grins, finger-gunning Fallon a salute. Having known her for ten years now, she's the little sister we love to annoy. "Ballbuster's back in town."

"Got in today, along with Wyatt." She holds up her middle finger wrapped in white gauze. "Only broke a finger."

"Best finger to break," I add.

"Next time, I'll give that horse a carrot so you break your neck," Wyatt says, crossing his arms and slinking down in his seat.

"Still got four more lives, baby," Fallon quips.

Ford arches a brow. "What happened to the first five?"

"Mind your goddamn business."

"Ask one simple question and cowgirl gets pissy," Ford mutters.

Fallon sidles around the table like she's taking inventory on which one of us to stab with a fork, and then she settles at my side. I can feel Wyatt's gaze blazing a trail to her. "Daddy wants to talk to you tomorrow, Charlie."

I blow out a breath through my nostrils, wishing I could be anywhere but here. The day keeps getting better and better.

Fallon chuckles and rests a tattooed hand on my shoulder. Her sleeve of bright tattoos could light up the bar.

"Relax. It's not about that video. Although . . ." She narrows her eyes and swivels her gaze. "Ford, you could deal with learning some manners."

Ford grunts and makes a jerk-off gesture.

"Where's Stede at tomorrow?" I ask. "Corner Store or hospital?"

A cloud enters Fallon's hazel eyes. "Hospital." She lifts her hand and wiggles her fingers the best she can and takes off toward the jukebox. "See ya, assholes."

"Christ." Wyatt shudders, his stare on Fallon as she joins a circle of girls pounding on the jukebox. I snort at the hangdog look in his eyes. "She's like the female reincarnation of George Jones."

"What do you think Stede wants?" Ford lifts a hand to signal for more shots.

I grunt. "Not sure. Find out tomorrow."

"Want me to go with you?" Davis asks.

"Nah," I say, not wanting him to worry. My brothers have done enough. "I got it."

My job. My ranch. I handle it.

"So, who is Charlie goin' for tonight?" Wyatt's jovial drawl pulls me away from my thoughts.

I look up from my beer to see my brother wiggling his brows as he scans the sea of women.

"No one," I grunt, swerving a wry eye around the bar. It's all local girls you couldn't pay me to touch. Too much drama, too much work.

Even though it's been too damn long since I've been laid. Two years at least.

These days, after long hours spent working on the ranch, all I have the energy for is a hand job and a cold shower.

For a long time, losing Maggie was like chronic pain. Over the years, it's become a numb feeling I've accepted. A routine. I've never thought about moving on, not because I can't, because I don't want to.

My heart's never been in it since Maggie died. My dick, sure, but love? I'm not looking.

Because fuck loving another person I could lose.

Fuck falling apart all over again.

I have my brothers to worry about.

Family is all that matters.

I groan as Wyatt continues his get-Charlie-laid tirade. "Don't worry. I already picked few out for you, Charlie."

I take a sip of my beer even if I don't want it. "I'm too old to drink like that."

Ford sits back in his chair and laughs his ass off. "You mean, you're too grumpy."

"Aren't you off tomorrow?" Davis points out.

Wanting to shut them all up, I give Wyatt a menacing glare to enforce big brother status. "You're one to talk. Aren't you seeing Sheena Wolfington?"

Wyatt twists a hand through his shaggy light brown hair, his gaze snapping to Fallon, who's so far across the room she isn't even breathing the same oxygen. "Dude. Shut the fuck *up*."

"Dickhead," I mutter.

The cacophony of the bar increases. The Choir Boys bellow obscenities and battle it out in shuffleboard. Through the window, I watch the sky turn dusky as the sun dips below the horizon.

That's when three things happen at once.

Number one. The jukebox sticks. Merle Haggard

croons a wobbly refrain. Fallon swears and pounds on it with her fist.

Number two. Lionel and Clyde Wolfington saunter into the bar.

Wyatt gets out of his chair. From behind the bar, Beef yells out a warning, jabbing his finger at the sign which doesn't stand a fat fucking chance.

Number three. The front door swings open again, and sunshine spills into the room.

I blink. Not sunshine. A girl.

She's delicate and small in a bright yellow sundress that hits high on her slim thighs. Big blue doe-eyes. Bee-stung lips. Slight, elfin features. Thick, silky hair the color of rose gold hangs down to her shoulders. In her hands, she holds the cardboard "HELP WANTED" sign Beef put up ages ago after his chef attacked him with a can opener.

On a dime, the mood of the bar turns. Though it doesn't slow its pace or stop its conversation, all eyes are on the girl. An offender, a stranger in Resurrection.

It's like someone dropped a wildflower onto a gravel road.

"Immediately no," Ford announces, leaning low on the table as if to track her.

His concerned eyes sweep to Davis, who's suddenly on alert. Wyatt, oblivious, banters with Lionel.

I shove a hand through my hair, then scrape it down over my beard. My mouth goes dry. *Fuck. Be lost. Turn around.*

But she doesn't.

All I can do is watch the girl cross the room, elbowing her way through the crowd, only a faint trace of apprehension in her eyes. She looks calm and composed—shoulders back, expression even—as if she's walked through hell every day of her life and doesn't give two shits.

"Ballsy." Davis sounds impressed.

Ford lifts a brow. "Ballsy is right."

Wyatt, realizing he's alone in his Wolfington pile-on, glances up and over. His eyes lock on the girl, and he whistles. "Who's the Disney Princess smokeshow?"

I scowl, already annoyed.

This girl's got no damn business being here. In our town. In our bar. Especially when she could get hurt.

Still, I can't help but stare, my eyes drawn to her long tan legs, the pink pout of a rosebud mouth, the gentle curve of her hip. Plain and simple, she's fucking stunning.

She practically skips by our table. That's when I catch a whiff of her perfume. Christ, is that how she smells? Like strawberries? And how small is she? If I held her in my arms, she'd what? Barely come up to my shoulder?

Jesus. Regroup Charlie.

Even Davis, gentleman that he is, manages an exorcist head spin. I grip the table. It's all I can do not to adjust the position of his head on his neck.

What the fuck is the matter with me? I need to get laid, because I'm turning into some horny, territorial teenager all over again.

Now the girl's at the bar, trying to get Beef's attention. He barks at her, fixing her with a look as mean as a rattlesnake, but she holds her ground, her pink mouth moving. Her hands flutter as she raises the sign. What's she doing here? Clearly, in need of a job, but why the hell is she in Resurrection?

As she tries to push her way through the bar, following Beef, she keeps getting manhandled by the rowdy crowd. I try to avert my eyes, try not to see the wince flitter across her face, the way she rubs at her chest, the flush of her cheeks.

Scared. Now, she's scared.

Cowboy code says help her out.

Help her out and then get her gone.

"Fuck."

Beating Davis, I shove my chair back. Hard.

Someone has to rescue this doe-eyed Disney Princess before the entire bar eats her alive.

4

Ruby

THE MINUTE I SMELL THE STALE BEER AND HEAR the country music, I know I'm in heaven.

Resurrection, Montana.

The name alone conjures images of tough-as-nails cowboys getting gunned down in the streets, while silk-gartered saloon girls in the balcony hope for a wild night.

Judging by the look of this bar, it's not too far divorced from the past. Bikers clad in leather vests, girls with tattoos at the jukebox. Rugged and dusty and exactly the type of experience I want to have.

I chose Resurrection because of the name. I'm sure the original founders wanted it to instill gloom and terror in the heart of the residents, but to me, it's hopeful. Like flowers, things die but still live on. Main Street charmed me with its little boutiques and historical buildings and Wild West vibes. And the mountains. They're the most jagged piece of serenity I've ever seen.

Exploring can't come soon enough. I can't wait to make this town mine, even for a brief time.

But that's tomorrow.

Tomorrow, I intend to find a doctor and refill my prescription and find a place to live. Tonight is for a job.

Once again, I try to get the bartender's attention. He opens beers and mixes Jack and Coke with a surly attitude.

"Excuse me, sir?" Standing on tiptoes to see better, I wave the cardboard sign. "Mr . . . uh—"

"Beef." His vocal cords sound like someone grated them.

"Beef. Of course." I inhale. "I have this sign here that says you're hiring, and I was wondering if . . ." Beef's moving down the long line of the bar, leaving me in his dust.

Jerk. I tap a toe, considering my options.

I am not on this earth to have doors slammed in my face.

I am here to open all the doors.

Even if it is in some rowdy honky-tonk in the middle of Montana.

As I push my way down toward Beef, getting elbowed in the stomach and ribs, I catch my reflection in an old chipped mirror hanging behind the bar.

I wince.

My strawberry-blond hair is a mess. On the drive from Denver to Montana, I had the windows down, giving me a snarled air dry. I wear little makeup, and while I'm fully clothed, even I can admit the bright yellow sundress isn't quite right for the Carhartt-and-flannel vibe of the bar.

I'm about to the middle of the bar when a cowboy in a bolo tie shoves his chair back, pinning me in place.

"Excuse me," I say, speaking up to make myself heard. I push at the back of the chair to free myself. "I just need to—"

"You need to go," a deep, rugged voice rumbles.

Flustered, I look up to see a man the size of a mountain looming over me. His brow is furrowed, his dark bearded jaw clenched.

I shove at the chair with a frustrated sigh. "Well, I would if I could get by—"

Before I can say another word, the guy's strong-arming the chair forward, growling, "I'm moving your ass, Burt," before he sends the owner of the chair lurching across the table full of beers, giving me the space to get unstuck.

"Thank you," I say, sneaking past him to flatten myself against the wall papered with stickers. "I'm Ruby Bloom."

"Charlie. Montgomery." He says the words hesitantly, like they pain him.

"Nice to meet you." I smile, but judging by the arctic chill coming off him, the feeling is not mutual.

He takes a step closer.

I press a palm over my chest, willing my jaw not to drop.

Handsome. The word pounds its way into my heart.

The man standing in front of me, arms crossed, legs braced, is a bonified cowboy. The boots and big, bold western belt buckle give it away. He's well over six feet. Chiseled jaw. Trim beard. Piercing cornflower blue eyes. Mile-wide shoulders. He wears a black T-shirt that hugs his muscled chest and popped biceps. His mussed dark brown hair, curled at the nape of his neck, suggests he had a hat on at a previous time.

He frowns down at me, like this is the one emotion they taught in cowboy school. "Listen," he growls. His tan forearms, corded with muscle, flex. "Maybe you're lost, but

I don't think you know what kind of trouble you're in for being in this bar."

"Oh, I very much do," I reply with a bright smile. "I'm in Nowhere." I hold up a finger as his mouth snaps open. "And I—"

"Need to go," he barks in a hard tone.

"I am going. I'm going forth and conquering." I make a move toward the bar, but he steps in front of me and blocks my path.

I draw myself up, hoping to look imposing next to his towering form. "Listen, Cowboy. I'm not leaving here until I talk to Beef about this . . ." In my periphery, I notice a deep hole in the black wall. My eyes widening, I lean in and run a finger over the groove. My gaze flicks back to Charlie. "Is this from a bullet?" I gasp. "A real bullet hole?"

He stares at me, his expression a cross between disdain and amusement.

Beef is now hollering at a guy wearing a trucker hat and an "Armadillo by Morning" T-shirt who is arguing with a man dressed entirely in camo. Trucker Hat Guy looks eerily like Charlie. They have the same deep blue eyes, the same broad chest, the same square jaw. The only difference is Trucker Hat guy is grinning while Charlie is scowling.

Charlie groans, his eyes on the same scene I'm watching. It's funny. Two grown men, peacocking, arguing about horses while the entire bar minds their own business. I smile. Already, I like this town.

Keeping to myself should be easy.

Trucker Hat Guy punches his finger in Camo Guy's chest and shouts, "You stole my horse, you Tweedledum motherfucker!"

Charlie swears.

His blue eyes drop to my face. Without warning, he steps closer. One big hand lands on the small of my back. His earthy scent surrounds me and I feel dizzy. My head falls back on my shoulders as I gape up at him.

That's when I feel him. His hard body presses against me, every muscle tense like he's gearing up for something.

Oh, wait.

He is.

"What's happening?" I manage to remember how to breathe.

"There's gonna be a fight."

"What?" I gasp, both delighted and horrified. "Like a bar fight? Like fists flying and bottles smashing?"

He shoots me an irritated look. "Down."

"What?"

"Ruby. Down."

He remembered my name is my one idiotic thought before his hand closes on mine and I'm jerked down to the ground right as a chair sails across the room and smashes into the wall.

I let out a scream and clap my hands to my ears. "What do we do?" I yell.

It's the first time I've ever seen this man, but I trust him with my life.

"Crawl," he orders. "To the door."

Charlie makes it look easy, so I follow his lead. Together, on hands and knees, we shimmy through peanuts and splash through puddles of beer. I should be terrified, but I'm not. Adrenaline flows through my veins.

Above us, I can hear fists flying, the hard crunch of bone on flesh. Cheers. And jeers. Curses.

"I'm crawling through beer!" I shout, overjoyed at the riotous turn the night has taken.

I yelp as someone kicks me in the shin, and I escape a near miss with a boot crushing the top of my hand. But I can't stop laughing. I can't stop smiling. It all seems so surreal and I'm right in the middle of it.

But we can't get out. The crowd is thick and jostling and we're stuck.

Charlie hisses, "Fuck it."

I look over at him, a question on the tip of my tongue, but I never get to ask it.

We're not on the ground anymore. Suddenly, I'm in his arms, pressed tight against his broad chest—hard, hot muscle—and he's rushing us out of the bar. I feel his muscles constrict, the pump of his heart as he holds me close. Both sensations send an electrical current rushing through me. His closeness has my head floating, a dizzy feeling I want to hang on to.

I like it.

It's dangerous.

The door slams open, and then Charlie's setting me on my feet in the dark parking lot.

I try to ignore the pang in my chest at being separated from him.

We both look at each other.

"Wow." I tuck disheveled hair behind my ears. My legs are shaky, my heartbeat a kick drum in my chest. "My hero."

I mean it. He's like my knight in dusty cowboy boots.

Annoyance flickers across his face. "You were takin' too long."

"Something tells me you do this every Friday night."

I blush. "Fighting, I mean, not sweeping up strange girls in your arms."

He gives a brisk nod. "You're not wrong."

"I've never been in a bar fight before."

"Yeah, well, you shouldn't be," he grumps.

I shrug and smile. "It was fun. All the blood, the broken bones, the spilled beer."

He steps closer and his nearness warms my stomach. "You're kidding me, right?"

I open my mouth to tell him I'm very much not kidding, but I gasp.

I feel it.

A flutter.

Shit. Not here. Not now.

Not when I just bested a bar fight and am talking to a handsome, albeit grumpy, cowboy.

The signs are easy to spot. Black spots in my vision. The heavy beating of my heart echoing in my ears.

"Ruby?" Charlie's frowning.

"I just—" Breaking away to catch my breath, I close my eyes. I bear down and breathe out strongly through my mouth. A maneuver my doctor taught me to shock my heart back into a normal rhythm.

Slow, I urge my heart. *Stay calm. Slow.*

In seconds, the heavy beat of my heart slows. The spots clear, the head rush fades.

"Hey." A warm, broad hand slides down my arm to cup my elbow. "You okay?"

Blinking, I straighten up and brace a palm on the front of Charlie's hard chest to steady myself.

If I thought it wasn't possible for his entire body to tense anymore, I was wrong.

"I'm fine," I assure him, hoping the lie will stick. "Stomach cramp."

He regards me warily, brows furrowed tight with concern. After a second, he asks, "This bar doesn't scare you?"

He looks like he hates himself for making small talk, but the hardness along the length of his jaw has me riveted.

"Only thing that scares me is not having a job," I say brightly. "Think Beef'll hire me?"

Charlie stares at me a long beat before he shakes his head. "If Beef knows what's good for him, he won't."

I arch a brow, unsure what to make of his answer. "You plan to break his legs or something?"

His eyes narrow. "I might."

His response has my heart beating faster.

Charlie crosses his arms, causing his biceps to bulge. "Where are you staying tonight?"

"The Yodeler."

"Not there." He makes a face like he's stepped in dog shit. "Go next door to the Butterworth. Tell 'em I sent you."

"Care to tell me why?"

"Roaches."

"What if I like roaches?"

Charlie pauses his scowling to blink at my reply, but not before allowing his eyes to linger on my lips, causing a storm of goose bumps to break out over my arms.

He opens his mouth to say something when there's the unmistakable sound of glass breaking. We look over to see a boot fly through Nowhere's stained-glass window.

Charlie lets out a deep breath. Hooks a thumb back toward the bar. "I better get back in there. Help my brothers."

Ah. So that explains the doppelgängers.

"Sure." I lift a hand, but I'm sorry to see him go. "Thanks for the assist, Charlie Montgomery."

He takes a few steps towards the bar, stops, and turns.

"Listen," he says, pinning his eyes to mine. A muscle flexes in his strong bearded jaw. "This isn't the town for you, darlin'. I respect you tried . . .but leave. Go somewhere else. Anywhere but here."

Without another word, he stalks off, while I stand here watching his broad-shouldered form disappear into Nowhere, a warm gooey feeling settling in my stomach.

While I'm cozy in a plush bed at the historic hotel Charlie suggested, I count my heartbeats. They're fast, but not overly so. Outside, a toenail moon glows in the dark sky. The scent of pine floats through the cracked window as I think of the cowboy.

His broody but handsome face. Those piercing blue eyes and tan forearms corded with veins and muscle. Dark hair that kicks up in a cute cowlick in the back. The solidness of his broad chest tensed against me as he rushed me for the door. The way his eyes dipped to my lips and lingered there.

Charlie's words ring in my head.

Leave.

Never.

I have a good feeling about this town.

Resurrection, Montana, here I am.

5

Charlie

*L*EAVE. GO SOMEWHERE ELSE. ANYWHERE BUT *here.*

It was a prick move, saying those words to that girl last night. Even now, in the morning's stillness, they're rattling around in my head as I stride down Main Street.

I don't know why I said them. I don't know why I cared. If she stays or goes, it's no skin off my back.

Which is a fucking bullshit lie and I know it.

I care because she got a reaction out of me. When I held her in my arms, the feel of her small frame and silky skin was like a shock of adrenaline to my bloodstream. My blood ignited with fire. When I set her on her feet, my cock could've punched through drywall. I wanted more, and I had to fight the urge to pull her into my arms and keep her there.

I wanted to protect her.

It pisses me off.

I cared and I can't. The only people who get my worry are my brothers and my little sister. Not some bright-eyed, fresh-faced girl who looks like sunshine and smells like strawberries.

Leave. Go somewhere else.

Damn it. I was an asshole.

I'm also an idiot.

There was something about her. Something infuriatingly adorable. Sure, she looked like she climbed out of a fairy tale, but it wasn't just that. It was what happened last night. The entire world was falling apart around us, and she was smiling.

Fucking smiling. Like she had the best night of her life dodging fists and sliding through beer.

Too many red flags. Too much drama. With any luck, she left this morning.

Ruby Bloom. What the hell kind of name is that, anyway?

A motorcycle roars up Main Street, breaking the silence of the sunny June morning. I lift a hand to Rufus, leader of the Choir Boys motorcycle club, and watch him head to the Legion.

Already the town's bustling. Shopkeepers are outside setting up A-frame signs and sweeping the front stoops of boutiques and coffee shops. Summer in Resurrection means our tight-knit mountain community of 6,000 increases tenfold during the peak tourist season.

The sooner I can get back to the ranch, the better.

Still, I like this walk. This view.

Dense pine forest and the sun-drenched Rocky Mountains frame Resurrection, a former Wild West mining town that is snugly situated in a box canyon. In the distance is Crybaby Falls, the switchbacks that lead up to Glacier National Park.

I duck around the corner, stride up to the Bear Creek Clinic, and enter through the sliding glass doors. The elevator takes me to the second floor, where I enter a narrow hallway that connects the community hospital to the cancer center.

I step up to the front desk. "Hey, Kara."

"Charlie." She snaps a bubble. "Stede's back in his chair. He's ready for you."

"Thanks."

I walk down the hallway and enter the room.

Stede lifts a gnarled hand when he sees me.

The space is sterile and minimalist. There's a couch, a muted TV showing an old episode of *Bonanza*, and framed scenes of nature with cheery words of positivity printed beneath them. In other words, depressing as fuck.

"Hey, kid," Stede says, setting the book in his lap aside.

"Hey, old timer." I pull a chair around and sit in front of him. By now, like Stede, I'm used to the machines and the needles. "How you doin'?"

"Kicking ass, kid. You goddamn blind?" Stede drawls in his deep rumble, gesturing at the needle lodged in his arm.

I chuckle. "Nice to see you too, asshole."

Even stage two lung cancer can't keep Stede McGraw down. His thick silver hair is gone, but he still has his signature horseshoe mustache. Coming from a long line of prospectors and cowboys, Stede's ancestors founded Resurrection, and he looks the part.

The man's a legend in our small community. A retired pro bull rider who made millions working as a stuntman and livestock wrangler—he has pull, influence and the biggest ranch in Resurrection. He's been like a surrogate father to me and my brothers ever since we blew into town, guiding us and putting in good words with the locals so they didn't eat us alive. A man I admire and respect. A man who gave me a new start.

Ten years ago, I stumbled into the Nowhere bar and took a seat beside the man. When I told him I wanted some land to get lost on, he asked me only one question: "You from California, boy?"

"No, sir," I replied, five whiskeys deep by then.

Satisfied by my answer, he sold me the land.

It was a handshake deal. I used my rodeo prize winnings and cashed in on my trust fund to get enough money for a down payment. Buying the ranch means I didn't just run and piss away my future. I did something with it. The land I own is mine and nothing can take it from me. Even if the light at the end of the tunnel is still hard to see.

Stede stares me down, his gaze eagle-sharp. "We got to talk, kid. And talk now."

I sigh and scrub my hand down my beard. "Listen, if it's about the video—"

"I don't give two fucks about social media."

That makes two of us.

Although Davis might be right about putting some thought into it.

Advertising was one thing we never did. Social media was a pain in my ass, so I steered clear of it and relied on word of mouth. Slowly, after five years' operating as a working ranch, Runaway Ranch is showing small but consistent profits.

But it won't be for long if we don't get ourselves out of this mess.

No one wants to go to a ranch where they get yelled at.

I think of my little brother Grady and how he has a

following thanks to his social media account. Sure, we all gave him shit about it when he first started, but now he's opening for Cole Swindell so . . .

It grates at me. The fucking perverse hypocrisy of it all. Guests come to the ranch to get away, and us invading their solitude so we can put it on social media just to make a dime, to survive? It's horseshit.

Stede's expression turns grave. "Now I don't want to bring you more trouble, son, but unfortunately, that's what I'm here to do. We got some developers making the rounds again."

I roll my eyes. Every few years, some L.A. firm sends their suits to Resurrection. They make offers and try to buy up the land, but we all tell them to get fucked. No way in hell is anyone putting a Sweet Green on Main Street.

"Isn't just any slick-haired developer," Stede continues. "It's Declan Valiante."

I grunt. "That guy running for governor?"

I vaguely remember seeing aggressive campaign ads around town and on television. Some influential land developer with money who moved to Montana from L.A. and thinks he knows what the fuck we need.

A curt nod. "One and the same." Steed strokes his long mustache. "He's been sending people around Resurrection."

That gets my attention. "What kind of people?"

Stede holds my gaze. "Mean people, Charlie. People who make your life a living hell." He shifts, stretching out his legs. "DVL Equities isn't above playing dirty. Declan sends fellas from Montana. Men who put the west in this western. They come talk to you, make a deal, but if you refuse, they fuck you up. Find out what you owe, what problems you're having, and make it their business. Maybe they talk to your bank. Maybe they harass you. Maybe you take a trip downriver. Either way, it's some fucking under-handed shit."

"Should I be worried?"

"That's what I'm trying to find out. When I work my connections, I'll let you know." Stede winces as he reclines back in the chair. I lean forward and help him drag the blanket up his legs. "Now I'm not telling you this so you cave. I'm telling you this so you can take it personal, part-ner. So you can be prepared."

"How prepared?"

He thinks about it. "I reckon you can't go wrong with a shotgun and good security."

"Fuck." I run a palm over my jaw, trying to tamp down the pit in my stomach.

This is going to be a mess.

Once again, I wonder what I've gotten my brothers into. If the video affects the ranch, if we can't pay our loan, if the developers catch wind of our trouble . . . I don't have a plan out of this mess. It feels like everything is crumbling around me. And if we lost the ranch . . .

The rock in my throat turns to a boulder.

"Get out of here, kid," Stede says with a grin as a nurse approaches. "You don't want to see this."

I shove out of my chair and shake his hand. "Appreciate the advice, Stede."

"Don't forget, we got Family next week," he calls after me in his booming voice. "Get the boys together and we'll figure out how to fix this."

I swear under my breath and head for the elevator. The last thing I want to do is sit around a campfire with my brothers and tell them we're fucked. They shouldn't have to worry about me anymore. I got them into this mess, and it's my goddamn job to fix it.

Fuck. What else can go wrong?

I get my answer pretty damn quick when I step off the elevator and slam into a willowy wall of sunshine.

"Oh my god, I'm so sorry."

I glance down at the bright chirp of a voice.

On the lobby floor, Ruby's scrambling for her purse that got dropped in our collision. Unable to stop it, my eyes drift over her body. Long, tan legs. Rosebud lips. Shapely thighs. Supple ass barely covered by another damn sundress. Lavender this time.

She looks up and gasps. Her blue eyes go wide as she takes me in before she turns her attention back to her belongings.

Having her on her hands and knees in front of me is doing things to my sanity. Not to mention my libido.

I drop beside her. My gaze lingers on her things. The cell phone screen lighting up with five missed calls. The orange pill bottle toppled on the shiny tile.

The sharp bark of a question leaves my lips before I can stop it. "What are you doin' here?"

"I'm—" Her pink mouth opens and closes. "I have anemia," she blurts, snatching the pill bottle up before I can get a good look at it. It's the first time I've seen her look flustered.

I frown as we stand. "Is it bad?"

She tucks a long lock of rose-gold hair behind her ear. "It's fine. Not like it's your business." She slings her purse over her shoulder. "What are you doing here?"

I grit my teeth, annoyed by her comment. She's right. It isn't my business, so why the fuck am I bothered by it?

"Visiting a friend," I tell her. "He has cancer."

"Oh." Chewing on her lower lip, she locks her eyes to mine. "I'm so sorry, Charlie." The way she says it—with genuine sincerity—has a strange ache settling in my chest.

I open my mouth, but she cuts me off.

"See you around, Cowboy," she says, giving me a sweet smile and damn if it doesn't twist me up inside. She takes a step to the door, pauses, then turns and looks at me over her shoulder. "I'm staying in Resurrection, by the way."

Then she's gone, floating out the door into the bright sunshine, and I stand here like an idiot, watching the hem of her sundress flip up with the breeze.

Goddamn it.

After a long second, an internal war consuming me, I storm out after her.

6

Ruby

I'M A LIAR.

I'm not anemic, but I panicked, and it was the first thought that came to my mind. The only way to explain that little orange bottle spinning across the tile.

A great way to kick off this relationship, even if it only consists of glares and grunts so far.

But what was I supposed to tell Charlie? The truth? That my heart is planning to give out somewhere down the line? That I'm running away because I've never lived my life?

The truth is since the day I was born, I've been told I was most likely destined to follow in the genetically macabre footsteps of my mother and my aunt, who both passed away at age twenty-eight. My aunt had a massive heart attack. My mother died in her sleep. The doctors said her heart just gave out.

I refuse to understand that. How do you stop something beautiful from beating? How does the very organ which gives you life decide your time is up?

I have a heart condition called supraventricular tachy-cardia. SVT for short. While a normal person's heart rate is 60 to 100 beats per minute, mine varies between 150 to 220 beats a minute. My erratic heartbeat wreaks havoc on my heart's upper chambers, but I control it the best I can. A daily medication is all I need to slow it down. But if I'm really unlucky, stress makes it worse, as does excitement or overworking or being overtired. My cardiologist warned me not to drink alcohol, caffeine, or do high adrenaline sports because *what-if* . . .

It's the *what-ifs* that have ruled my life.

But not here. Not in Resurrection.

I *could* tell Charlie the truth, but I don't owe him that explanation. We're strangers. He's not planning to worry about me. Doesn't even want to know me. So, I'd like to exist in this town without a past. Just be a person without all the doom and gloom attached. It feels nice to escape that part of my life, if only for a few months.

Even if my old life still has skin in the game.

I went to the clinic this morning to transfer my information, get three months of medication refills and discuss my condition with a doctor. Now I'm beyond starving and excited to see Resurrection in the morning's bright sunshine.

I need a big breakfast and a map.

But I have a surly cowboy stomping after me. I can practically feel the street shake under his boots.

"Where are you going?" Charlie's deep voice rumbles behind me, sending a vibration through my core.

"I'm on a hunt."

When there's a grunt, I lift my gaze to see Charlie keeping pace beside me. Even in profile, he's handsome.

Bearded jaw so sharp it could cut glass. Eyes so blue they look like gemstones. "You could ask *for what* instead of grunt."

After a beat, there's a gruff, "For what?"

I smile. "I'm going to find the best cinnamon roll in the world and eat it." I stop in front of The Bean Goes On, a coffee shop. "And then I'm going to explore town."

Charlie props a massive hand on the doorframe, barring my entrance. "You won't find your cinnamon roll in there. Their coffee tastes like gasoline."

My eyes dart toward the door, hoping the front counter worker hasn't heard. Even if it is bad, they don't need the reminder. I prop my hands on my hips. "Where then?"

He looks resigned, but jerks his bearded chin. I follow his gaze three blocks down. On a wedge-shaped corner is a brick building with a bright green awning that reads The Corner Store.

Inhaling a breath, I walk toward the building. Hard bootsteps pound behind me.

"I thought you were leaving," Charlie mutters.

"You thought wrong." I rove my eyes around Main Street, smothering a smile. Patina-colored plaques identify the historic landmarks like an Opera House and a city hall. I'm surrounded by antique stores, ritzy boutiques, and souvenir shops. They have a salon called the House of Hair. I count five saloons and a steakhouse.

It's just a town, but Resurrection with its American frontier vibes and alpine scent, has breathed life back into my soul.

I look up at Charlie, who glowers above me. "No flower shop?"

"What?" He frowns at the question before dragging a hand down his beard. "No."

"Oh." I flash him a smile and shake off my disappointment. "Well, since you're here, you can give me the tour."

"You don't give up, do you?" he asks gruffly.

"Not really, no."

"Fine," he says with an irate acquiescence. He nods across the street at a building with a spiral staircase that rises to a balcony. "That's the brothel."

I sneak a curious look at Charlie. "Really?"

"Used to be, at least. Operated until the 1970s, if you can believe that. Now it's a museum."

My jaw falls open. I can almost see Resurrection's fevered history. Bootleggers wreaking havoc on livers and wallets. Painted ladies waving men up from the balcony.

We continue our trek to The Corner Store, walking in sync. Every so often our arms brush, his muscles flexing, and warmth curls in my stomach. Charlie grudgingly points out various bits of history along the way. The alley where Billy Bones was shot down in 1886 after stealing a chicken. The four bear skulls guarding the town square, the place of thirteen recorded executions in Resurrection.

We're nearly at our destination when a fawn-colored pit bull trudges out of the alleyway and blocks our path. Slobber drips from its lips, and I edge close to Charlie and grip his bicep. He stiffens.

"Charlie. Does that pit bull have a Newport in its mouth?" I ask. Then I do a double take. "Oh my god, he does."

The edges of Charlie's lips curl in the faintest smile. "That's Hungry Hank. He lives on the streets." An affectionate chuckle rumbles out of him. "He's a bastard, aren't you, boy?"

Worry churns in my stomach. "Hungry?" Stepping away from Charlie, I reach into the purse slung around my shoulder, searching for a granola bar in the jumbled mess of pill bottles and paperwork. "Poor thing."

Once I find the snack, I tear off a corner, and hold it out. "Here you go, pup."

The dog lunges.

Charlie lunges too. "Jesus, Ruby, don't." Worry laces his dark eyes as he snatches my hand, turning it over in his big palm like he's looking for blood. All he gets is dog slobber. His gaze meets mine. "Did you just . . .feed him?"

I smile brightly, watching as Hungry Hank devours the granola bar, wrapper and all. "He was hungry."

My heart skips several beats as Charlie wipes my hand high and hard on his T-shirt, giving me a sneak peek of hard, chiseled stomach and ridged abs. "He's a monster."

"That's what you think," I tell him as Hungry Hank waddles away.

I break away from Charlie and we finish walking the short distance to The Corner Store.

Inside, it's the most whimsical sight I've ever seen. The Corner Store is like some cowboy bodega with bright orange walls and aging newspaper clippings from the 1980s.

Rolling papers at the cash register. A bait and tackle counter in the back. Ammo on a bookshelf. Well-stocked shelves with dry goods and coolers with an array of beverages.

"The basement doubles as a moonshine still," Charlie says. "But you didn't hear that from me. C'mon."

I smile and follow him back to a small dining area set in

front of a deli counter. The scent of fresh bread and slow-cooked pastrami has my stomach grumbling.

"Wyatt isn't here," Charlie shouts when there's a clattering from the kitchen. "Just me, Fallon."

A girl with long thick hair the color of caramel storms out of the back room. She looks familiar but I can't place her. She wears a tattered apron and a frown to rival Charlie's. In her right hand, she holds a butcher knife that she promptly sets aside. She tosses me and Charlie a curious look but says nothing.

"Biggest cinnamon roll you got," Charlie says as we claim a table in the center of the room.

Fallon disappears.

I fold my hands together and lean in. "Thanks for the tour, Charlie Montgomery. You almost sound like a local."

He cuts me a quick glance. "What makes you think I'm not?"

"You have an accent." It's faint, but I locked on his voice as soon as I heard it. A slow southern drawl as sticky as molasses.

"I'm from Georgia," he offers. "Little town called Wildheart."

"I'm from Indiana. Big-little town called Carmel. Thanks for the recommendation on the hotel, by the way. It was lovely, but I can't stay there for more than one night. Especially if I'm staying in town. It's too expensive."

He sighs, and I wonder if broody is his normal expression. "You shouldn't stay at the Yodeler."

"Well, I am. I'm going to eat my cinnamon roll, and then I'm going to go back to Nowhere and get a job."

"That's your plan?"

"It's the best I have," I say, going for honesty.

After last night, Nowhere seems like a place I want to both conquer and avoid.

My phone buzzes in my purse. Damn Max. He's been on my case to come home ever since I told him I landed in a new town.

Nope. Not happening.

Charlie's brows rise. "You gonna get that?"

In answer, I silence my phone and eye the glowering man in front of me. "So, Cowboy," I say smiling big. "What do you do?"

He shifts like he's uncomfortable. "Own a ranch out of town," he says. Almost as an afterthought, he adds, "A ranch that's hanging on by its last goddamn string. You?"

"Social media manager in a past life," I say brightly.

"Great, you're one of them," he mutters, rubbing his brow with two big fingers.

"One of them? Like an alien or cyborg?" I tilt my head. "Charlie, are you okay?"

"I'm fine."

"Are you sure?"

His face darkens, a snarl of warning on the tip of his lips. "Ruby . . ."

"It's just . . . you have this vein right here . . ." My fingers dance up to my temple.

With a hitch of breath, his jaw tics, and annoyance clouds his expression.

Luckily, Fallon saves me from a future throttling by setting a massive cinnamon roll slathered in frosting in front of me. "Here you go," she says drolly. "Your daily caloric intake in just one meal."

Unfazed, I pull the plate toward me. "On that note, bottoms up."

Fallon glances down at Charlie. "You go see Stede?"

Charlie nods. "Yeah. This morning. We got it figured out."

"Good."

Then Fallon's gone without another word.

"She was at the bar last night," I say, remembering she was banging on the jukebox and swearing like a sailor. "She looks sad," I tell Charlie, twirling my mother's bracelet around and around on my wrist.

"Yeah. Well . . ." He spears a massive hand through his dark hair. "She's got a lot on her plate. Like everyone." When I'm silent, he exhales before continuing. "That's Stede's youngest daughter, Fallon. They own this place. She works here when she's not on the rodeo circuit."

I wrinkle my nose, putting the pieces together. The sadness in Fallon's eyes. Their conversation. "Stede—the man you were visiting at the hospital?"

"That's right. He sold me the ranch." I note the fondness in Charlie's voice. Even this tough cowboy has a sweet side.

"The ranch that's in trouble?" I love this insight into Resurrection. Immediately, I want to make this town, this cowboy—these people—my friends. I want to fit in, even for a little bit.

"It's a pain in my ass. Everything's a pain in my ass right now, and I gotta figure out some solutions fucking fast."

"I'm good at solutions. Sometimes people need help. Maybe *you* need help?"

His expression is reluctant, but there's another part of him that looks like he wants to combust and spill everything. "Fine," he says flatly. "We're getting skewered on social media because of one goddamn video and our bookings are dropping fast. We got employees to pay and animals to take care of. It's gonna be the death of me if we can't do that."

I flinch at the pain in his words. At the turmoil etched on his rugged face. Honor. Loyalty. They mean something to this man. I respect that. A hell of a lot.

Charlie shoves at the table. "I don't even know why I'm telling all you this." He leans forward and picks up my fork. "Eat," he says, handing it to me.

But I ignore the massive cinnamon roll, turning his words around in my head, searching for solutions. If I have something that can help another person, then I want to help them.

"How do you advertise?"

"We don't."

"So, word of mouth?"

He looks down at his hands and makes a fist. "Over the years, yeah."

"What do the comments on your Instagram say?" I press. When he's silent, my jaw drops. "You don't have social media?" I jab the fork at him. "That's your first mistake. It's not the end all be all, but I think it could help you, Charlie. A lot."

"That's what got us into this mess." He rolls his eyes. "Your precious social media."

I give him a stern look. "Look, I know social media makes you itch. You're a cowboy. You like horses, not hashtags. I get it, but . . ." A smile spreads slowly across my face. "It is mine."

He frowns, regarding me with suspicion. "What are you talking about?"

"I could do it," I pipe up. "I could launch your account."

"Don't need your pity," he says, folding his arms across his broad chest, the corded muscle in his tan forearms tensing.

"Oh, I think you do." I set my fork down, an eagerness unfurling inside of me. "But it's not pity. I don't want to wade through beer every night at Nowhere. I'd rather help you out. Please."

A muscle twitches in his jaw.

"Think of it as a favor," I say with a smile. "You saved me from a bar fight, I'll save your ranch."

Still that stubborn jaw pulses.

"I have experience. Connections at my tourism agency. I can pull all the strings. Besides, it'll just be for three months."

Interest flickers in his eyes. "What happens in three months?"

"I go to California."

He snorts.

"You don't like California?"

"Last place I ever want to be."

I ignore his disdain and give a bouncy shrug. "Can't knock it until you've tried it."

His eyes lock on mine before dipping to my lips. "Eat," he orders.

I pick up my fork and dig into the gooey mountain of dough and sugar. The taste of vanilla bean and cinnamon goodness is heavenly.

"Do you want some?" I ask Charlie.

He scoffs like deliciousness is beneath him. "No."

After licking a dollop of frosting from the tines, I set my fork down. "So, do we have a deal?"

He blinks. "A deal?"

"I help you with your social media, you pay me," I barter. "A perfectly professional business transaction. If you don't like it, you don't have to use it. You can delete the account in three months."

I watch him consider it, the muscle jerking in his bearded jaw.

He needs this.

And I need him.

He stares at me hard for a long beat. "Fine. We'll get your shit and you can stay at the ranch."

It's my turn to blink. "The ranch?"

"You're not staying at the Yodeler. I know you love roaches, but . . ." He hitches his broad shoulders in a shrug. "The job comes with free lodging."

I narrow my eyes at him. "Did you just make that up?"

Leaning in, Charlie pins his dark gaze to mine, his expression so fierce my heart slams into my chest. "It's not safe at the Yodeler. I don't want you there."

The intensity in his voice lights my core on fire.

"Because of the fistfights?" I ask breathlessly. "Cardboard sheets? Bloodstained mattress?"

A glimmer of a smile tugs at his lips. So faint, I almost miss it.

But it's there, and it's beautiful.

"Something like that." Charlie picks up my fork and hands it to me again. "Eat. Then we'll go."

7

Ruby

THE JOLT OF CHARLIE'S JET-BLACK CHEVY over the winding dirt road is the bounciest roller coaster ride I've ever been on. I practically vibrate beside him. I like the truck like I like the man. Rugged and rough, but deep down, solid and dependable.

In the truck's bed sits my suitcase and backpack. It's a thirty-minute drive to the ranch, and Charlie, not wanting me to get lost on the back roads, offered to drive and then send someone back into town to get my car.

The timeline of the last twenty-four hours feels like a surreal fever dream. Dodging fists and beer cans at a dive bar, now I'm stuck in a truck with a grumpy, albeit sexy cowboy, trading my wares for lodging and employment.

Just for the summer, though. I'll help this angry technology-challenged cowboy, save a ranch, see some horses, then go to California.

I follow Charlie's lead and stay silent. It seems like he exhausted his talking quota earlier in The Corner Store by telling me about the video making the rounds on social media. Still, my eyes flick to his handsome profile. What's he thinking about? Regretting his offer to hire and board me? He even fed me. I was fast with my wallet after breakfast, but he tossed down a twenty, including a generous tip for Fallon.

I gasp as we pass over a small creek and steel gates rise from the earth. The name RUNAWAY RANCH is branded at the top and bookended by horseshoes. I lean forward, held back by my seatbelt. My eyes can't take everything in fast enough. In the distance, is a spread of beauty. Vaulted mountain ridges frame the entire ranch. A gorgeous log home with wraparound windows sits smack in the field of emerald-green grass.

"That's the lodge," Charlie says as we pass through the gates. He lifts a hand to a guy leading a horse across the pasture. "We use it for check-in and a chow hall. My brother Davis lives on the third level." He glances over at me. "So he can play Rambo if things get out of control. Wyatt's in an Airstream because he isn't here half the time, but really, it's just because he can't clean worth a damn. And Ford's in an apartment above his garage."

"Your brothers?" I ask to clarify.

"Yeah. We're close, but *that* close, we'd kill each other."

I settle back in my seat. "I have a brother." Charlie looks over as my phone buzzes again. "Max." I ignore the call. "He's the one currently blowing up my phone."

"Big brothers," he says, seeming to unclench, and I smile.

"How many people can you host?" I ask, snapping into professional mode. I'm here to do a job, so I might as well work now.

"We keep it small. About forty." Charlie follows the

paved road, then veers left. Close to the lodge, maybe a hundred yards away, is a cluster of small cabins. They sit near a river, rocking chairs on each porch.

"Is that me?" I ask, pointing. They're so cute and cozy, like something out of Daniel Boone.

"No." He turns the wheel, his blue eyes falling on mine. "Those are the cowboy cabins. I'll take you up to the cottages. They're closer to the main house."

"The main house?" I bite my lip, my heart beating fast. "Is that where—?"

"I live," he says in a hard voice. "You need Wi-Fi. We have it up here. The cabins don't."

I sink my teeth into my lower lip. "Oh. Right."

Charlie turns the wheel. "We also have chalets back in the mountains. For movie stars," he says, sounding disgusted. "They come up to film a movie and want privacy. I think if you're here you should—"

"Stick it out with the rest of you."

"Yeah." His eyes flick to mine. "That's right." A rare smile graces his rugged face as the truck rattles up the never-ending road. "That's the main house where I live," Charlie says as we pass by a large two-story cabin with a balcony and a wraparound front porch nestled back against a grove of trees. "And that's your cottage."

"Oh," I breathe, pressing a hand to my heart. "Oh, wow."

The small cottage looks like something out of a fairy tale. While it keeps its rustic Montana charm, it has latticed wood eaves, a front porch, and a small rock drive leading up to the door.

Charlie unbuckles his seatbelt and I meet him outside.

For a long second, I take in the secluded beauty of the ranch. A light breeze plays with the ends of my hair. The crisp air smells of pine and aspen, mixed with the lingering scent of hay. Summer sunshine floats through the umbrella of trees stretching toward the sky. Far off, the flowing waters of a creek bubble.

I tilt my head with a soft smile. "It's so beautiful, Charlie."

"It is," he says stiffly. "I bought it sight unseen, but it was the best decision I ever made." He moves to the bed of his truck and picks up my bags. "Let's get you inside."

What kind of person buys a ranch sight unseen? Probably the kind of person who takes off on a whim and travels across the country.

I desperately want his story, but I don't want to push. Still, I'm intrigued. There's worry in his deep blue eyes. A stoic mystery I want to figure out.

I follow Charlie's broad-shouldered form and wait as he pulls out a ring of keys. He picks through, searching for the one he needs. "We have these cleaned every week, so it should be good to go. But if it isn't, you can call Tina at the front desk and she'll send down whatever you need."

"I'm sure it'll be—" I gasp as he swings the door open. "Perfect." I clasp my hands to my heart and bounce inside.

The modern cottage has maintained all the charm of a historic mountain cottage. A rock-wall fireplace frames the front room. A colorful rug covers a square section of the wood floor. Wood-hewn furniture. Record player with a selection of country albums sits on a small table. On the back wall is a kitchenette with a burner.

Charlie drops my bags. I can feel his eyes on me as I rush around the room.

My entire body is feverish with joy.

Mine.

This cottage, this dreamy cottage, is mine for three wonderful months.

I've never had my own place before.

It feels like power.

Like freedom.

I love, love, love it.

I gasp again.

In the bedroom is a plush bed with a mountain of pillows, a colorful quilt, and a clawfoot tub. A desk is pushed up against the sliding glass door that overlooks a babbling creek.

"Who decorated this?" I flush when I realize how it sounds. "No offense."

He chuckles. "I tried, but you're right. My sister hired someone for me."

I dip into the kitchen, peering through the window that overlooks Charlie's cabin.

Charlie shifts in his boots, crosses and uncrosses his arms. "You can cook here, but seeing as how we didn't stock up in town, all meals are served at the lodge. Guests can come and go." He nods my way. "There's a meal schedule on the fridge. Dinner's at seven."

"I love it, Charlie." I join him in the living room. "But you didn't have to do this. I would have been happy in a cabin."

He clears his throat. "I just thought it fit you."

Heat scalds my cheeks. I don't know what to make of it, but I'll take it.

"It's too much," I say. My lips pull high. "But I promise you, I'll make you a kick-ass social media account."

The corner of his mouth tugs up in an almost-smile. "It can't get any worse."

He holds my gaze, studying me with curiosity. Then, just as abruptly, his face hardens, his eyes fierce. "I . . .should go."

Charlie turns, smacking into the coat rack. With a growl, he steadies it and then steps onto the front porch. I go to the screen door and watch him stomp to his truck, drinking in the sight of his butt in those Wranglers. I offer a wave and a tentative smile as he drives away. My heart riots in my chest.

Looks like Charlie Montgomery's my new boss.

8

Charlie

THE SCREEN DOOR SWINGS OPEN THE SECOND I lift the coffeepot off the burner. I groan. It's too damn early for my brothers to come storming in here like cattle after the restless night's sleep I had.

I pour myself a cup of coffee, roughing a hand through my hair.

I blame Ruby.

I laid awake all night wondering about shit I had no business wondering about. Like that look of sheer joy on her face when she saw the cottage. I may as well have handed her a diamond necklace. Her feeding Hungry Hank like she wasn't afraid he'd chomp her goddamn hand off. That girl batting her lashes and strong-arming me into a summer job and me being the damn fool who said yes.

Hell, I had to.

There was no way I was letting her stay at the Yodeler.

"The barn better be on fire or someone better be injured," I snarl at the approaching clomp of boots. "Fatally."

"Hell, it's better than anyone being fatally wounded,"

Ford chortles, rounding the corner to steal my cup of coffee. After a long sip, he grimaces. "Christ, you make this like you're trying to give me a heart attack."

I snatch the cup back. "Make your own damn coffee, then."

Ford grins. "But I like insulting yours."

The door clatters again. I raise my eyes to the ceiling, wondering why I even bother. The main house where I live is the home base for all things Montgomery. Family traditions, poker nights, whiskey, and gossip. Good luck keeping anyone out.

Tearing the coffeepot off the burner, I refill my cup. I need the energy to deal with these idiots.

Ford raises a brow. "What's got you pissed?"

Before I can tell him to mind his own fucking business, Wyatt's voice rings out down the hallway. "Looks like we got ourselves a couple of nieces, assholes!"

At the news, I blow out a breath, trying to calm the hell down and focus on something good for once. "Everything okay with Emmy Lou?" I ask as Wyatt and Davis round the corner, shit-eating grins on their faces.

"Everything's great." Davis tosses me his phone. "See for yourself."

"Hell, I'm sending 'em a pony," Wyatt announces, staring at his own phone.

I read my little sister's text.

> **Meet Daisy and Cora, your new nieces and goddaughters. We're tired but happy. Call y'all later. Love you boys. EL.**

Beneath her text is a photo of snugly swaddled babies, one in pink, the other in yellow. Rosy-cheeked and cherubic. New Montgomerys. Instantly, my heart feels a thousand pounds lighter. Thank fucking Christ, everything's okay.

I give Davis back his phone. "Pretty damn cute. Identical?"

Ford shakes his head. "Nah. Taking after me and Davis already."

Davis leans on the live edge counter top. His eyes scan the cold scrambled eggs and leftover pastries from yesterday's breakfast before settling on me. "Now that we got the sweet shit out of the way, you wanna tell us what Stede had to say?"

Wyatt collapses onto a bar stool. "I'm more interested in Charlie giving away free lodging." He lifts a suggestive brow. "Taking in strays?"

I scrub a hand down my face. I'm not in the mood for Wyatt's bullshit. "If you'll shut the fuck up for one second, I'll tell you."

I cross my arms and rehash with my brothers the conversation with Stede about the threat of land developers.

"What do you think they'll do?" Wyatt asks when I'm finished.

"They'll be nice when they come to offer to take the ranch off our hands. When we tell them to go fuck themselves, that's when they'll start threatening us," Ford guesses.

"We'll be ready if they come." Davis's face is grim. "New security system's going up on the north side of the ranch. Eyes on the road."

"Got a time frame?" I ask, setting my now-drained cup on the counter.

"Next week sometime."

At the coffee pot, Ford says, "And the girl? What's Fairy Tale doing here? She didn't get enough action at Nowhere?"

Sighing, I rub a hand over my jaw. "She thinks she can help us out with our . . . issue. Start a social media account.

Give us some good PR or whatever." I look around at my brothers. "I hired her for the summer."

Wyatt, looking like he took a long whiff of dogshit, rolls his neck around on his shoulders. His haggard groan fills the kitchen and I roll my eyes. The only one more dramatic than our mama is Wyatt. Even Emmy Lou's got her head on straighter than this kid.

My brothers stare at me with doubtful expressions.

"Look, I don't want her here anymore than you do, but we gotta try something."

"If you don't want her here, then why she's in a cottage and not a cabin?" Wyatt asks with a sly smirk.

"What?" I snap. "Yeah, I'm gonna put her down by the river. You know those fuckers flood if we get two inches of rain."

Davis thinks about it. "It's a good idea, Charlie. We had three more cancellations this morning."

"Shit."

Maybe it wasn't the worst idea hiring Ruby. If we can co-exist for three months, get the ranch back on track to recoup some money and guests, then it won't be a complete loss.

"As long as she doesn't get in the way." Wyatt tears himself off the barstool and paces to the counter. "If she tries to fancy us up, I'm putting my foot down." Still grumbling, he dips down by the built-in desk and bangs underneath the cabinet. His voice comes muffled, annoyed. "She'll probably have us singing songs around the goddamn campfire by the end of the week."

"No one's singing," Ford barks.

"No one wants you to fucking sing." I pinch my brow.

So much for a relaxing morning. "Shut the fuck up, Wy. And what the hell are you doing down there?"

We all freeze when there's a light tapping on the screen door.

Heads swivel as a barefoot Ruby appears in the kitchen. A laptop's tucked under her arm.

Fuck me. Another sundress.

"Excuse me." Her pretty face is a beam of sunshine and hesitation. "I'm sorry to interrupt—"

"No interruption, honey." Ford lifts his coffee cup. "What can we help you with?"

I shoot Ford a warning look. If he didn't call every woman in town *honey*, my fist would be in his face.

"Hi. I'm Ruby," she chirps, before taking a step into the kitchen. As she tucks a long strand of hair behind her ear, her gaze locks on mine. "Charlie, I'm not getting Wi-Fi down at the cottage. It worked fine a second ago, but now there's no signal."

I frown.

You're welcome, Wyatt mouths to me before heading Ruby's way. "Hey, Ruby. I'm Wyatt, the handsome one." He shakes her hand, and I groan inwardly when I see the router cable sticking out of his back pocket.

"Nice to meet you," she says with a full-wattage grin. "All of you."

Ford gives her one of his charming grins. "I'm Ford and this is Davis, and what can we get you to drink? Water, beer, coffee? Have a seat."

"No, no, and yes, please." She pulls out a stool at the island and sets her laptop in front of her. "With cream, if you have it."

I cross my arms. "We don't."

Ford shoves me out of the way to set a steaming cup of coffee in front of Ruby.

"How's the ranch treating you?" Davis asks.

"Oh, it's beautiful. The fresh air's like knockout gas. I slept so well last night." Again, her eyes lock on mine. "I watched that video you told me about, Charlie."

The way she says my name, the way she stares at me like there's no one else in the room, does something to my stomach. Something I don't like one goddamn bit.

"And?" I ask.

"And it's bullshit."

Davis chuckles at the swear coming off her lips. It seems unnatural coming from her pouty pink mouth. Girl couldn't be more adorable if she were made of kittens. Christ.

Ruby's brow wrinkles in consternation. She looks so damn pretty, it's almost unfair. "That lady . . . it was almost like she wanted to cause trouble."

Ford looks over at me and Davis with a triumphant smile on his smug face. "See? She gets it."

"Amen," Wyatt drawls.

Ruby opens her laptop. "I also got started on your Instagram account."

I raise my brow. "That was fast."

She flashes a grin, takes a small sip of coffee like she's savoring it. "No time to waste, right? In fact, I thought we could get started today."

"We?"

I already don't like where this is going.

"Well, yes," she says, her bright smile growing. "I can do the whole setup on my own, but I'd like to see the ranch. So I can get a real sense of how it operates."

"Like research?" Wyatt's leaning in, so close he could

smell her damn neck. If she turned her face, they'd be inches apart.

I glare at him. We're a close family, but that doesn't mean I won't run my little brother's head into a fucking wall if he crosses a line.

"Exactly. It won't be so bad," Ruby reassures, no doubt seeing us all wilt. "I already snagged the username, and I'll spend a few weeks creating the content I need for the channel before I ramp up. I just have a few questions. Like how many acres is it? And how many employees? And the obvious—why is it called Runaway Ranch?"

She chirps on, her voice like a melody as she rattles off questions, oblivious to the silence that's fallen, but I'm not.

Tension as thick as fog rolls in.

I don't miss the concerned look Ford trades with Davis. I try to ignore how damn hard my jaw is clenching, how my fists have balled up, and my stomach's in a goddamn knot.

I grunt and shove back from the counter. I don't want to talk about Maggie. Diving into the specifics of how the ranch got its name isn't high on my list of priorities today. Neither is giving Ruby a personal tour of the property.

"I got morning chores to get to," I say roughly, dropping my coffee cup into the sink. "So, I'm afraid I can't help you right now."

"I could go with you," she offers, looking at me hopefully over the top of her laptop. Her eyes are wide and eager. "I can help with chores."

Silence.

Ruby bites her lip. "If you're busy, maybe someone else can give me a tour?" She glances around the kitchen, flashing all of us an encouraging smile.

The sound of her voice—cheery and relentless—has

irritation washing over me. She won't back down, and the thought of someone else showing her around the ranch raises my hackles.

That's when I realize what my fucking problem is.

There's something hypnotic about her sitting there with her bold blue eyes and cherry-red lips. In my kitchen, at my counter, drinking a cup of coffee like it's another normal morning on the ranch. She's a pleasant person to be around and I haven't had that in a damn long time.

She's pretty. Too pretty.

It scares the fuck out of me.

"Can't." Davis is already moving to the door. "Ford and I are taking a group up on the ridge for a cattle drive."

"I can't either," Wyatt says, slamming a Diet Coke and grabbing a pastry. His sweet tooth knows no bounds. "I'm training Fallon in the pasture today."

"Y'all gonna kill each other," Ford points out.

Wyatt laughs. "I keep hoping she falls off a bull, but I'm not gonna get that lucky." He wiggles his eyebrows at Ruby. "You get bored with Charlie, come see the show."

"Get outta here," I growl.

"See y'all around," Ford says, flipping a wave, and in return, I flip him off.

I watch as my brothers exit the house, their laughter carrying through the screen door.

Assholes.

Ruby slides off the barstool, the hem of her pink sundress riding up to expose long tan legs and a flash of a curvy ass. Her big blue eyes land on me, expectant. Her pretty face all business. "Should we get to it? Chores?"

Three months, I remind myself. Three goddamn months.

9

Ruby

"**H**OW MANY TRACTORS DO YOU HAVE? AND how many acres? And what about your employees?"

"Two tractors, and 17,000 acres." Sweat streams down his brow as Charlie looks at me under the brim of his dusty cowboy hat. A hard scowl creases his handsome face. "Do you really need to know all this?"

"I do. It's my job," I remind him. "Employees?"

He tugs a cluster of weeds from the side of a shed. My stomach squeezes as I note the rippling muscles in his sculpted back. "We have a twenty-six-person crew. They live on the ranch from April to September."

Without waiting for me, he starts across the gravel road toward the barn. I blow out a frustrated breath and chase after him.

He's a man of few words. I'll give him that.

I've trudged along with him for the last several hours asking him questions while he works. Watching while he chopped firewood and fixed the tractor in the shop.

Listening while he chatted up one of the hired hands about taking a new group fishing down at Elk River.

So far I'm impressed with Charlie Montgomery. Runaway Ranch is a well-oiled machine with a solid backbone behind it. The staff seem happy and the guests are having fun. In my opinion, the video was bad, but not bad enough to warrant the negative response. The woman almost acted as if she wanted to cause a scene. There was no reason for Ford to continually get ridiculed in her comments.

"What about activities?" I huff, trying to catch up with Charlie.

"What about 'em?" he shouts back.

I hide a smile at the ice in his tone as he stalks toward the barn.

That Charlie Montgomery looks like he'd rather have a fatal disease than me following him around only increases my desire to wear this man down.

I'm going to make him smile if it kills me.

All I need is a week to familiarize myself with the ranch, then I can work my magic in solitude. Me and Charlie Montgomery never have to see each other again. Even if the thought sends an ache deep into my belly.

I puff out a breath and hustle up to the man who left me in the dust. "Just do your thing," I say, slightly winded. "Don't let me slow you down."

"You already are," he grumbles.

The corner of my mouth turns up. I'm used to people scoffing at social media. I saw the doubt on their faces earlier this morning. The smug *yeah, right* glances that passed between the brothers. They don't think I can do it.

I can't wait for the chance to prove them wrong.

"What's that?" I point at a large red building that sits kitty-corner from the barn. The sign out front reads *Warrior Heart Home*.

"That's Davis's," Charlie says. "He rehabs military working dogs. Works with them until they're healthy, then either re-homes them, or we let them live out their days here."

"Really?" I make a note on my phone. "That's cool, Charlie."

He lifts his hat, dragging a big hand through his disheveled hair. "When we have a group of kids on the ranch, we bring them here. Teach them how to always be kind to animals."

My heart stutters at the sentiment.

It's beautiful. I wonder if he knows that.

I pause and snap a photo of the habitat, gathering photos for the Instagram feed. When I look up, Charlie's disappearing through the double Dutch doors that lead into the barn.

I chew on my lower lip and then hurry in after him.

Soft nickers greet me.

"Oh, my goodness," I breathe.

The massive barn could double as a second home. The stained and painted interior has stalls lining both sides of the barn. On the far side, there's a large hay storage room and a small kitchen with a cot and a bar. But it's not the size of the room that catches my breath. It's the three horses poking their noses over the stall doors, their dark eyes wet with curiosity.

Without looking up, Charlie hefts a bale of hay up into the loft and says, "Since I know you'll ask: Black one is Ghost. The chestnut is Big Red. Paint is Wesson. We got fifteen riding horses total. Colton has the rest out on a ride."

"Can I pet one?"

He straightens and shrugs those broad shoulders. "They're all kittens. Take your pick."

"I've never been on a horse," I say, walking closer to them. My to-do checklist rearranges. I mentally add *Ride a horse*. Ride it into the sunset, and pretend I'm a cowgirl, wild and free.

This time, Charlie looks interested. "Really?"

"Nope." I move around the stalls, scoping out Wesson. The pony's brown tail flicks away flies. "Never been on a motorcycle, surfed a wave, danced in a bar, or done drugs. Boring, I know."

Charlie grunts, tackling a second bale of hay.

I doubt he even heard me.

A rush of sadness, followed by a sensation of regret, burrows down deep in my belly. It stays there, the memory latching on like a leech.

The closest I've ever had to some excitement in my life was when I took ballet. When I was seven, barre and plié were my life. I'd practice for hours. I had a teacher I loved, who screamed *voila* every time I managed to pirouette. When I lifted myself on tiptoes, I felt like I could reach anything. It was the happiest I had ever been. Two months later, I was in the hospital, diagnosed with SVT. Despite the doctors' assurance that I'd be fine as long as I took breaks, my dad never let me go back.

I felt like I had lost my entire life that day, even though I was still alive.

My hand palms Wesson's cheek. Smiling, I relish the feel of her velvet fur on my skin. The soft puff of air from her nostrils. She's the best balm for making me focus on what's in front of me—my life.

Heavy steps sound across the floor, and I glance over my shoulder. Charlie's lugging a large bag of feed like it's a pillow. I watch his massive forearms flex as he heaves it into a small room.

"What's in there?" I ask.

"Tack room," he says. "We keep everything to outfit a horse. Saddles. Blankets. Medicine."

I give Wesson a last look and go to Charlie. "I can help."

He lifts the brim of his dusty Stetson hat. "You?"

A lip curl of distaste or consideration I can't tell.

I prop my hands on my hips, daring him to argue with me. "Yes, me."

For a long moment, he stares hard. Then he jerks his bearded chin. "Okay. Get the hose and fill up each of the water troughs."

For an hour, we work together in silence. While Charlie opens a grooming kit and gives each horse a good brushing, I spread new bedding down and refill water. It's gratifying work. Work my brother and my father would never in a million years let me do.

Even though I'm not asking questions, I'm learning. Charlie takes pride in his ranch. He does the work himself. He's respected. He's kind to the animals.

It very much makes me want to save it.

I'm wiping my sweaty brow when a flicker of motion catches my eye. Curious, I drift to the open Dutch doors and step outside. Across from the barn is a large, fenced pasture where two horses are locked in a kind of dance. The riders look like tornados, dust and dirt kicked up behind them.

Charlie's deep voice rumbles behind me. "C'mon,"

he says, handing me a bottle of water and motioning me forward.

I smile. It seems my silence has been rewarded.

We step into the sunshine and head to the pasture. The sound of hooves thunder across the grass, the vibrations making their way into my core. As we get closer, I note it's Wyatt and Fallon.

This time, I chance a question. "What're they doing?"

"Training." A half-grin cracks Charlie's rugged face. "Fallon's the reining barrel racing champ. She takes lessons from Wyatt when she doesn't want to kill him." He points. "See? She's supposed to be listening to him, but she's cutting him off."

Happy whinnies come from the horses. I stare at their massive muscles rippling in the bright summer sun. Flashes of rust and chestnut swirl through the churning dust.

"Don't forget, cowgirl, I can still beat you by a country mile," Wyatt calls out.

"Ha," Fallon scoffs, as they race past us. Her laugh is like a knife, sharp and cutting.

"She's gonna get good enough and whup his ass." Charlie chuckles and moves to the fence. "Damn," he says under his breath. "That girl can fly."

I chance a quick glance his way. His knuckles are bone white as he grips the fence, but pride lights up his expression.

My stomach sinks. I don't like the way he looks at her or the way I feel. Like I've lost something before I even had it. Not like I would win him. Nothing about Charlie Montgomery, especially his eternal scowl and angry grunts, has me thinking I even stand a fighting chance.

"You and Fallon?" I fight to keep the question casual.

He blinks. And then he laughs. A bright gorgeous laugh that has my heart racing. "Christ no. She's like a little sister. To some of us," he mutters.

I climb up on the fence to get a better view. "Do you train your guests?"

"We do. We have afternoon sessions where Wyatt offers instruction. But not like this. We don't want to kill anybody," he says wryly.

"You're just open for the summer, then?"

"Yeah." He moves closer, standing tall beside me. "June through Labor Day. In the fall, when we close for the season, Wyatt runs rodeo clinics here on the ranch for any cowboy dumb enough to take his lessons."

My gaze flies back to the riders. "Is it dangerous? The rodeo?"

His mouth thins. "It is. Wyatt's had broken ribs, broken wrists. Once, he got caught in the mouth with a hoof and had his front teeth knocked out."

I wince at the image. "Sounds like you know rodeos."

A tight nod. "I used to compete. A long time ago."

My mind overheats picturing Charlie on the back of a horse. A true cowboy. Solid and strong. With his dark hair, rugged features, and muscles corded like taut wire, the man looks like he was made from the dust and the grit of the rodeo. I wonder why he stopped.

My gaze goes back to the pasture. "Seems like a shame," I hedge. "To give it up."

Silence.

Fallon rushes by us, her tattoos lit up in the sun, her long caramel braid whipping the wind, and her face—

My jaw drops.

Holy shit.

Her face. It looks like she's given in to ecstasy and everything holy.

I want to look like that. I want to feel like that. I press a hand to my heart, wishing it could witness this.

What I yearn for.

The words pop out of my mouth before I can stop them. "I'd love to do that," I say breathlessly.

Charlie goes tense beside me, telling me I've said the wrong thing. The chill coming off him is like an arctic freeze. Instantly, his face darkens. "No, Ruby, you goddamn wouldn't."

Then he's turning away from me and storming back to the barn.

My weary eyes blink back hot, frustrated tears. His abrupt cold shoulder, his sharp tongue hurts.

Stings, in fact.

I can't win with this cowboy.

Well, screw Charlie Montgomery. I'm here to work. And that's what I'll do. With or without him.

I look up and down the pasture. Fallon and Wyatt bickering on their horses. The small shed with rainwater barrels out front. Dusty pickup trucks squeezed into a small lot on a narrow side road.

That's when a loud snort gets my attention. I turn my gaze to find a round horse pen, maybe forty diameters across and framed by steel bars, near the pasture. A storm of a horse, ebony with a white diamond marking on its brow, prances back and forth. It looks restless and angry, the way I feel right about now.

I cross to the pen and climb the rails, leaning forward to get a better look. "Hey there," I say before clicking my tongue like I saw Charlie do earlier.

With a harsh flare of its nostrils, the horse stomps out of my way.

Annoyed that this is one more being that doesn't like me, I inhale a determined breath.

I won't give up on it.

Heart racing, I stretch my hand out toward the horse. I climb higher on the rail, pushing up on my tiptoes. A mistake. Because I lean too far forward. I lose my balance.

And then I fall.

10

Charlie

I RUN.

For Ruby's fucking life.

She's sitting in the round pen where Wyatt keeps the "demon horses." Wild horses he rescued from bad situations that still need to be broken.

The horse could trample her.

That single thought has me racing to Ruby like it's ripping out my fucking soul.

She stares, unsure why I'm running at her like a damn idiot. And then she waves at me.

Fucking waves.

I don't have time to be angry. I have to get her out of there.

The horse thrashes around, and the bars clang as it ricochets off and around. When the horse's hooves barely miss crushing the top of her hand, Ruby realizes pretty damn quick why she shouldn't be in that pen.

Bright blue eyes wide with panic, Ruby crab crawls backwards. By feeling blindly and gripping the bars, she pulls herself to standing. She's trying to climb up, but the flailing horse whipping up dust and grass is making it hard for her to get a good grip.

In my periphery, I see Wyatt racing his horse to the pen. Fallon follows close behind. Ruby flinches, fear snapping in her eyes like a downed wire. Her rose-gold hair catches the sun as she presses her small frame against the bars.

And that's when I see her.

Maggie.

Maggie, in the alleyway, smiling that smug smile she wore like a badge, waiting to compete in her last barrel race of the season. Only minutes before she could compete, her horse got spooked and somersaulted backward on top of her. I fell to my knees in that arena and screamed. I didn't stop until my father took me to the hospital, where we waited to hear that Maggie was gone. I wanted to kill that horse, blast its brains out with a shotgun because it had stolen Maggie away from me.

I couldn't protect her. My one damn job in life and I couldn't do it.

I couldn't save her.

I couldn't.

And then the memory—the nightmare—clears.

Time speeds up.

Sound returns and I'm at the pen.

Heart hammering against my rib cage, I grab the middle bar and slide myself beneath the lower rung. I roll across the ground, then rocket up to stand beside Ruby.

She reaches for me, her face pale. "Charlie—"

I rush in front of her, putting my body between her and the thrashing horse. "Go," I order roughly. Her petite frame trembles against mine as her hand snakes up over my shoulder, sending a raging fire down my spine.

Adrenaline competes with attraction, but only one wins out.

I keep my gaze locked on the horse because if I see her face, I'll lose it. "Get up on the bars, Ruby, and climb. Now!"

She doesn't argue, thank fuck.

She scrambles up, and Wyatt's there, his fingers digging into the flesh of her ass to get a good grip and pull her out. And hell, we're going to have a talk about that later, but right now, I have to get *my* ass out of here in one piece.

"Charlie, hurry up, man!" Wyatt shouts.

I grab the lower rung and swing myself under right as the horse's hooves come down.

"Fucking close," Wyatt says, breathing heavily.

Too close.

I get to my feet and stare at Ruby.

She must see the look in my eyes because she takes a step backward.

Now I'm livid.

Wyatt clamps a hand on my shoulder, reining me in. "Dude. Chill. It's not the same."

"It is the same," I snap, then whip my head to Ruby.

"I'm sorry. I'm so sorry, Charlie," she breathes out, blinking back tears. Her hand, pressed to her heart, shakes. "I didn't know."

"You didn't know because you don't work here," I shout. "Because it's dangerous, and you pulled a dumb stunt that could have gotten yourself killed."

She flinches.

"Shut up, Charlie." Fallon gives me a *keep talking and I*

will kill you look. "She feels bad enough without you barking at her like an asshole."

"You shut up," I tell her, not in the mood to deal with Fallon McGraw's lecture.

Wyatt bristles, anger in his eyes. "Hey now—"

"You too." I turn my hard gaze back to Ruby. She looks so damn pretty—so innocent—with the strap of her dress loose over her bare shoulder and a dusting of dirt over her face. Anger and worry curdle in me again. "What the hell were you thinking? What were you even doing up there—"

She steps up to me, blue eyes flashing. "I wasn't thinking because I know nothing about this ranch because you won't talk to me, you big asshole." She pokes a finger into my chest and I'm effectively silenced. "I may be a pushover, and I may say yes more times than not, but I will not be yelled at by some rude cowboy who can't even act like an acceptable human being. And if I can remind you, yelling is how you got yourself into this mess in the first place."

"She's gotcha there," Wyatt mutters.

Fallon and I both round on him. "Shut. Up."

Looking back at Ruby, I clear my throat, but the apology sticks. Sweat runs down my back. My chest heaves, the air trapped in my lungs. Fuck. Her searing glare is like a red-hot poker on my tongue. Before I can get anything out, she beats me to the punch.

"If you don't want my help. Fine. Fix it yourself." Without another word, she turns on her heel and storms off.

I stand there blinking, feeling like shit for yelling at her, for acting like a maniac. Seeing Ruby in that pen fucked with my head.

Her earlier words pushed me over the edge. *I'd love to do that.*

All I wanted to do was grab her shoulders and shake some sense into her. Tell her she's fine the way she is. Safe. Beautiful. Quirky. She doesn't need to ride a horse. She doesn't need to be wild.

Wild gets you killed.

That thought has a hard sort of agony calcifying in my chest.

"You know you're going after her," Wyatt drawls, coming to stand beside me.

We both watch as Ruby hurries up the road to the cottage. She's fast, already halfway back by now.

I inhale deep to calm my racing heart. Letting her run off doesn't sit right with me. "Yeah." I run a hand through my hair. My Stetson's on the ground next to the barn. "Any advice?"

Wyatt shrugs. "Be yourself, man."

"That's what they say when you start kindergarten."

"Who says you're not?"

Scowling, I take a step forward, then pause. On the ground, buried in the dirt, is a small circle of silver. I pick it up and brush it off. Ruby's bracelet. I noticed her playing with it at The Corner Store. Blue opals on each end make it look like it holds the orbs of the universe.

I slide the bracelet in my back pocket and storm across the ranch, realizing Ruby's right.

Everything about today—it's my own damn fault. I was too busy being pissed off to teach her about the ranch. Christ, I told her every horse was as gentle as a kitten. She offered to help with chores and I shit all over that. That, in and of itself, is impressive. Half the guests on the ranch have to be sweet-talked to pick up a fucking shovel.

If I had taken the time to show her, if I weren't so clouded by my past, she wouldn't have been in this mess.

My stomach twists.

Shit. What if she's hurt?

I was too busy screaming at her to even check and see if she was okay.

Feeling like I'm approaching the firing squad, I inhale a breath when I reach her cottage and hammer on the door.

The door whips open. My gaze travels down.

Ruby stands there, rose-gold hair slung over one slender shoulder, one hand on the doorknob like she's readying herself to fling it closed.

"What do you want?" Stunning, angry blue eyes stare up at me. "Come to yell at me some more?"

"No, I . . ." My eyes can't help but catch the inside of the cottage. On the kitchenette counter is a small vase of wildflowers, along with small packets of tea and a Runaway Ranch mug purchased from the gift shop. She's set the kitchen table up as a workstation, and country music plays softly from the radio. From my vantage point, I can see her bedroom and the open suitcase resting on the bed.

She's settled in. Made this place a temporary home.

And now she's going to leave.

But go where? And stay with who?

A brick settles in my stomach.

Ruby sends me a withering glare. "If you're looking for something to say, it's called an apology, Charlie. Do you own a dictionary? Look it up."

A smile tugs at my lips. Seeing the sweetheart turn to a spitfire is goddamn adorable.

Squaring her shoulders, she says, "I'm good at my job, and if you don't want me here, I'll go. But I'm not leaving Resurrection. I'll sling beers at Nowhere and you can stay the hell away if it's so unsafe. But I won't stay here and get yelled at or scolded or—"

"Look, you're right," I growl.

She's silent, but her blue eyes still flash fire.

I lower my voice and hold out my hands. "I yelled because this is a ranch and that's what we do when there's trouble. It was a close call, and it scared me. But I overreacted. I shouldn't have yelled. I won't do it again."

"Oh." Her eyes widen. "Wow." And then she smiles, so bright it nearly takes me down. It's a smile I don't deserve, but damn, I eat it up. "I wasn't expecting that."

"I wasn't expecting you to fall into a horse pen today, but it looks like that's where we're at."

"Charlie." She laughs and tilts her head like she's examining me. "You made a joke."

I grunt. "Yeah, well, I have my moments."

Her eyes soften. "You should smile more. Because when you do, you look—" She breaks off in a wince. Her hand flutters up to press against her chest.

"You okay?" When I get no response, I duck my head to meet her eyes. "Ruby?"

In answer, her legs buckle.

I shoot a hand out and catch her around the waist, pulling her against me. In my arms, she's small, barely reaching the middle of my chest.

Her head falls back on a gasp. "I'm fine."

Bullshit. It's the second time she's done this since I met her.

Keeping her against my chest, I move her to the couch,

where we both sit down. I brace her up against my shoulder, not trusting her to sit on her own. I run my gaze over her.

Fuck but her face is pale.

"You okay?" A knot moves up and down in my throat. "You didn't get hurt out there, did you?"

My own fault if she did.

"No." She gives a faint headshake. "I didn't get hurt." Cheeks stamped pink, her eyes flutter shut. "I need to sit for a second. I'll be okay."

I stiffen when she lays her head on my shoulder.

"Can I do this?" she asks.

I wrap my arm around her, tucking her in close. "Yeah, you can."

Tiny and warm, she curls up against me. Her knees rest on my thigh and a little sigh pops out of her mouth. Jesus Christ, I'm getting a contact high from the feel of her. Needing a distraction, I let my eyes rove, taking in her delicate features. The soft pump of her pulse in her creamy white throat. Her dark lashes. Her bee-stung lips. She's sexy. Beautiful.

Too beautiful for the ranch.

Too dangerous for me.

Once again, my eyes land on the vase of wildflowers. "You like flowers?" I ask.

As stupid as the question is, it's something to distract us. Because right now, the only one talking is the erection trying to punch through the front of my fucking jeans.

She hums. "I do. My father owns a flower shop back in Carmel. I started a social media account for his company. Bloom's Blooms."

I chuckle. "What's your favorite flower?"

"Sunflowers," she says into my shoulder, and I feel her mouth curve as she smiles.

"Why sunflowers?" I could listen to the lively melody of Ruby's voice for days.

"They're perennials." At my grunt, she elaborates. "They're sturdy and happy and you couldn't kill them if you tried. Every spring, when the conditions are right, the soil soft, the sun bright, they grow back to live again. Come hell or high water, they survive. That's what I like about them."

I decide I like them too. Because at this moment, anything that's Ruby's favorite is automatically mine.

An easy silence blankets the room.

"How do I look when I smile?" I ask, my mind moving to her earlier statement.

"Hmm." She laughs. "Less surly."

Then, with a soft sigh, Ruby uncurls from my side. I resist the urge to pull her back to me and keep her close.

As she sits up, I pay close attention. She seems fine, thank God.

"Thanks for the use of your shoulder," she says, smoothing the hem of her dress.

"Anytime. Here." Adjusting myself, I pull the bracelet out of my back pocket. "I found this in the pen."

She gasps and stares at the bracelet, looking like I've rescued her favorite puppy from the pound. "Thank you. I didn't even realize it was gone." She takes it from me and slips it on her delicate wrist. "It was my mother's."

Was.

Here and now, I decide I want the story behind the bracelet. The story behind Ruby Bloom. It means nothing—it can't—but if we're working together for the next three months, I might as well make the best of it.

"Stay," I tell her.

Her shoulders slump. "Charlie . . ."

"I won't yell."

"I don't know." Her pretty brow furrows. "I'm good at my job, but to do it right, I have to see how the ranch runs. I can't do that if you won't let me."

Her stern words put me in my place, and I nod. "I understand. You're right. I'll let you do your job." I stare down at her. "I don't want you to go, Ruby."

When I say the words, I realize I mean them. I want to keep this sweet, happy girl on my ranch. Close to me.

Some of the wariness leaves her expression. "And you'll answer my questions?"

"I'll answer your questions. Tomorrow, I'll show you the ranch. The right way."

I offer a handshake and when she slips her small hand into mine, an electric sizzle races through my veins. This girl's a drug and she doesn't even know it.

11

Ruby

CHARLIE AND I GET STARTED AT THE CRACK OF dawn. We have breakfast in the lodge, a delicious cowboy feast of eggs, skillet potatoes, and biscuits and gravy. I'm so full I can barely walk. Charlie spends the next three hours introducing me to his staff. I meet Tina, the guest services manager, Silas, the executive chef, and various ranch hands. I make plans with all of them to sit down one-on-one and get their story later this summer.

I follow Charlie around the ranch, trying not to bombard him with questions while keeping a respectful distance. When I do ask questions, he answers me dutifully like he's trying to atone for yesterday's blow-up.

I take notes and log everything I learn away for future reference. The game plan in my mind is simple . . .

Flip the story.

Embrace the bad press.

Come get yelled at by cowboys.

Very, very, sexy cowboys.

The sun is high in the sky by the time Charlie and I get started on the hike up Meadow Mountain. He's promised me the best view around, one that captures the essence of Runaway Ranch.

"It's two miles up, two miles down." He spears me with a look. "Can you do it?"

I can.

As long as we don't go fast, and I'm on my medication, I can exercise. Yesterday's slip was because of adrenaline and stress. A calm hike up a beautiful mountain—I'll be fine.

He's staring at me, still waiting for an answer, but that typical look of annoyance he's worn since I met him isn't there. In its place is patience.

I smile up at Charlie. "Can we go slow?"

Those blue eyes stay locked on my face as he gives a curt nod. "I can do that."

In silence, we trek side by side, the low elevation of the ranch giving way to jagged mountains and towering evergreens that seem to stretch up to the blue sky above. I adjust my sunglasses, courtesy of my gas station friend back in Winslow, and inhale a deep breath of fresh air, taking in the stunning Montana view.

But soon, my eyes stray to the man in front of me.

He's lost in thought, walking with purpose. His boots crunch rock like he's ready to take on the mountain and win.

His white T-shirt molds to his biceps and broad chest, the muscles in his back rippling as he walks. Beneath the cowboy hat, his full lips wear a frown through his close-cropped beard. Despite the sun burning brightly overhead, goosebumps break out over my arms. His beauty overwhelms all my senses. He smells of sweat and hay and black coffee and man.

I've traveled half across the world and found the best view in the world.

And it's a cowboy named Charlie Montgomery.

Afraid I'll get caught staring, my eyes dip toward the ground. I stop and gasp.

Charlie startles at the sound and puts his hand out as I sink to the ground. "Ruby?"

"Look," I breathe, pointing at a cluster of purple flowers spread across the trail. "They're wild violets."

He gives me a look. "You're a strange girl." His eyes flicker over me—my lips, my legs—and his expression resets. "Stay that way," he says, then steps over the patch of flowers and resumes hiking.

I smile and straighten up. Coming from Charlie, it's the best compliment I've ever received.

We continue with the hike, falling into an easy silence for the long trek up. Fifteen minutes in, I realize Charlie's switched places with me. He's moved me to the inside wall of the mountain and he's taken the cliff edge.

Heat blooms in my core. It's a move both protective and caring and has my mind drifting back to yesterday.

I liked the side of Charlie Montgomery that came to apologize as much as I like the gruff cowboy who yelled at me out there in the pasture. Some might call it an overreaction, but I'm not sure. It told me he cared; it told me he worried, maybe more than he was trying to let on.

Yesterday, when he took me in his arms and held me on the couch, I could feel it. My heart. Beating fast. But not because of my arrythmia. Because of Charlie. He was kind and sweet, talking about flowers to distract me from what happened with my almost-flutter. Even if he didn't know about it.

The icky feeling of guilt creeps across my skin. I hate lying to him about my condition, but I don't want Charlie thinking I'm fragile like everyone else has in my life. It's not an option.

I want to be normal, even if all I am is temporary.

I can't let Charlie in. I can't tell him the truth.

It wouldn't be safe.

For either of us.

"Let's stop here." Charlie's tall, broad body walks to a lookout point, moving with a smooth confidence that tells me he knows and loves the land.

Taking a second to clock my heartbeat, I breathe slow and steady.

Charlie extends a finger out at a waterfall diagonal from us. "That's Crybaby Falls."

"Why is it called that?"

He looks grim. "As the story goes, a wagon train came up here. Camped out at the falls. Two days in, they were hit by a huge storm. The ridge flooded, and the water swept one wagon over the edge of the falls. It was full of children."

I gasp, stunned by its grandness, by the raging water cascading down the craggy rocks.

His gaze falls to my face. "People claim you can hear the babies crying at night."

"It's so Wild West," I breathe, horrified. Stepping forward, I snap a photo of the falls from my phone and then check it on my camera.

"You think that's going to save the ranch?" There's doubt in his deep voice, but also desperation.

"I do."

"I hope you're right. We had two more cancellations today."

"Really?" I frown and shake my head. "Well, don't worry. Right now, the wrong people know you, not the right ones." I smile. "Besides, life would be pretty damn boring without haters and doubters. We have to show them the light."

He chuckles. "How are you always so positive?"

"I always look on the bright side. I have to. In my family, I have to be positive."

"That's the reason you're here? Family?" His question comes out stiff, like he doesn't care, but beneath the surface, there's a lingering curiosity.

I give a one-shoulder shrug. "I guess it's just a midlife crisis type thing."

Charlie laughs, and my pulse trips at the sight. His laughter transforms his entire body, loosening his broad shoulders, crinkling the corners of his eyes. He's still rugged, only more at peace.

"If you're middle aged, darlin', I'm a fucking grandpa."

Darlin'. The endearment consumes me like a forest fire.

I hesitate, then, since we're semi-baring souls, I ask, "Why's it called Runaway Ranch?"

Charlie shakes his head, his handsome face darkening. "We're talking about you."

I frown. It's the second time he's avoided answering that question.

"Why are you here?" he asks, turning toward me.

Now it's my turn to avoid a question. Talking about why I'm traveling across the country feels like letting all the bad stuff back in. And I want to keep my slate clean in this wonderful little town.

"I'm here to have fun. To sow—"

"Wild oats?" His voice is gruff, irritated, but it makes me shiver. The intensity of his blue-eyed gaze burns a hole straight through me. "But why? People don't leave unless they're . . ." He stops himself before he can say the rest. But I can fill in the blanks.

Running away.

"How about this?" I announce. "I'll tell you why I'm here, when you tell me why it's named Runaway Ranch."

He scowls and I smirk. Bluff called. I feel better because now I'm not lying, only withholding. Just like he is. It's fair.

We trudge up the side of the cliff, and Charlie takes his place beside me on the outer edge. I kick at a rock and watch a hawk sail across the clear blue sky. A broad hand lands on my arm, and I look over, gratefully taking the bottle of ice-cold water that Charlie passes me.

"Up ahead," his rough voice rumbles. "The last lookout point."

It's sticky, and it's hot, but we keep climbing. The wide road soon spits us out on a narrow trail that edges right along a cliff. The path is too narrow to accommodate both of us, so Charlie takes a slow lope behind me.

"Is this your plan, Cowboy? Get me on a mountain and push me off?" I ask playfully, daring a glance over my shoulder.

He chuckles, but stays silent, keeping his gaze locked on me like he's tracking every step I take.

Finally, we make it to a narrow part of the mountain that juts over the ranch.

"Oh my god, Charlie." I look up at him with wide eyes, then back at the stunning view.

"Beautiful, isn't it?"

"Yes." I can't look away from the panoramic view of Runaway Ranch, the glittering falls, the town of Resurrection. I edge away from Charlie's tall, broad-shouldered frame and closer to the point.

Runaway Ranch is the most breathtaking place I've ever been.

The realest thing I've ever seen.

Holding my breath, I lean forward, wanting a better view. My heart hammers in solidarity with my recklessness.

I want to see more.

I want to see everything.

I inch forward and gasp when a red-tailed hawk flies in front of my face. My body becomes airborne as I'm picked up and then set back on my feet.

"Jesus." Charlie tucks me against his muscled chest, his handsome face as dark as a storm cloud.

I twist in his arms and lift my sunglasses, blinking up at him. He's still holding on to me, hand fisted in the waistband of my jeans. "What's wrong?"

Expression twisted in annoyance, he roughs his free hand over his beard. "You have got to stop doing that, Ruby."

"What?"

"Gasping." A crease forms between his eyebrows. His hand pulls me tighter to him. I glance down and see his fingers are white-knuckled, gripping the curve of my hip. "I thought you were fucking falling."

I want to tell him falling is the least of my worries,

to get used to my gasps of awe, but the fear in his heated gaze has me dropping the battle.

"Okay," I agree. When I settle in beside him, I hear his breathing steady. "I'll look from here." I glance up at him. "You can let me go now, Cowboy."

His throat works and the air between us rises several degrees. My pulse quickens at the mix of stern anger and reluctant concern on his face.

Finally, he drops his big hand from my waist and crosses his arms. Some of the tension leaves his expression.

With that, a comfortable silence falls between us as Charlie and I stand here admiring the scenery, the view our only witness.

"This is Runaway Ranch," Charlie says, pride in his deep voice. "What it's all about."

I see what he's trying to show me. People. Beauty. Wild wilderness.

Everything he cares about is on this land below us.

"Tell me why," I say, and put an earnest hand on his arm. "Tell me why you love it, Charlie."

He looks down at me, a muscle popping in his jaw, and our gazes pin. Those cornflower blue eyes flame.

At first, I think I've hit a nerve, I'll be met with another grunt or cold shoulder, but Charlie's deep voice rumbles out like a spool of velvet unfurling over me. "It ain't for everybody," he begins. "Loving the earth. But when something's made for you, you know it. You feel it." He inhales deeply and stares out over the land. His brow, his mouth soften. "Now, I don't love the land because it's mine, because you can never own that type of wild beauty. I love it because it's alive. Because it can't be tamed. You feel it in the air. In the sun that comes up over the meadow. When I rise, I rise with the land. And when my working day is over, I turn in. The land speaks to you, says you got something to live for. It keeps you going even when you think about giving up. To believe in the land means you believe in yourself. Means you do one worthy thing with the time you have left in this world."

My throat closes up for a second.

The man, his words, are magnetic.

It gives you purpose. Life.

"I love that, Charlie," I tell him, bringing my hands to my thundering heart. "I love your ranch. And we're gonna save it."

As I turn back to the view, our arms brush against each other, and my body heats.

Charlie looks down like he's felt it too. The shift in the air. Electricity.

The apple of his throat works over unsaid words.

I tilt my face up toward him. He's in the sun, his handsome face darkened by shadow, but I still see him. There's pride in his expression. But there's also something else too. Fear. Some kind of sadness there.

A sadness I used to have before I made up my mind.

A sadness I associate with loss.

I've seen it on my father's face.

His gruff voice breaks the silence. "You're getting burned," he says, and drops his cowboy hat on my head.

In this moment, I feel branded.

My heart stalls in my chest.

Can a heart overheat?

Can a heartbeat be wired for one man?

I think these are questions I better learn to answer pretty damn fast.

"What was your sunflower?" Max asks. His cat, Pepper, meows over the line.

"I went on a hike today."

Barefoot, I pad across the cool hardwood. After the hike, Charlie dropped me at the cottage. Now it's time to get to work. I need to put together a social media calendar and call Molly, my connection at the luxury tourism agency. By leveraging her influencers, she can increase the ranch's exposure. Maybe send some on a tour, which would be amazing.

Understanding why Charlie loves the ranch, seeing its beauty, has me wanting to fight even harder for it. I feel a personal stake in helping Charlie Montgomery and his brothers save this land that means so much to them.

"Rubes. A hike?"

The scolding snap in Max's voice has me rolling my eyes. "I can hike, idiot. I went slow and steady and only barely fell off a mountain."

He doesn't laugh. "Any flutters?"

"No," I lie, and refuse to feel guilty. Yesterday's episode barely counts. No loss of consciousness, no heart rate over 180. Even today's hike left me only slightly winded.

I'm fine. Perfectly fine.

"You feeling okay?"

I sigh and walk out of the house to stand on the small porch. The sun's rays bend, shades of pink and purple sweeping across the field. A group of laughing guests trek across the gravel road, fishing poles in hand.

"I'm great, Max. Let's not talk about me. Let's talk about the mountains I've seen. The horses I've petted. They feel like velvet, you know."

"You sound happy," he admits grudgingly.

"I am happy."

Really happy, I think when I spy Charlie through the large front window of his cabin.

"As long as you're safe, I won't worry."

"Good. How's Dad?"

"If you picked up the phone, you'd know."

"I know," I whisper, guilt flooding me. As much as I miss my father, miss our nightly routine of buttered saltines, homemade chicken noodle soup and reality TV, miss my garden full of foxglove and lavender, I absolutely cannot talk to him. The grief in his voice will bring me home. Texts are all I can do right now.

And even that hurts.

"We miss you, Rubes." Max's voice crackles over the line. "Get whatever it is out of your system, then come home."

My gaze returns to Charlie.

Something tells me getting this cowboy out of my system might not be so easy.

12

Charlie

ELEVEN.

That's how many times Ruby gasped on our hike today. Sweet, awe-filled exhalations that had my cock jerking to attention and my heart in my throat.

Even her gasps are adorable.

Like an idiot, I counted every little bright blast of joy from her pretty pink mouth. I thank fuck my brothers aren't around to haze my pathetic ass. Especially Davis.

Against all my good judgment, I enjoyed today. Showing the ranch to an outsider never gets old. And Ruby—the way she understood it, the look on her face as she took it all in—was pure wonder. I drank it up.

Especially our conversation. Opening up about the ranch. She pulled something out of me. Something raw and real. How she does it, I don't know. All I know is I can't get around the fact that I'm attracted to her. She's drop-dead gorgeous. Her carefree nature radiates. Every time she smiles at me, I have to glance around to make sure I'm the lucky son of a bitch who deserves it. And when she wears those sundresses . . .

It's all I can do not to haul her against me and kiss her senseless.

Bad idea.

I started over after Maggie and this is where I've landed. The ranch life, my daily routine—it's straightforward, rigid, and mine. Work from sunrise to sundown. The bar on Friday nights. Family on Sundays.

Distractions can't happen. Especially beautiful ones.

The end of summer can't come soon enough.

Frustrated, I trudge across the kitchen, covering up the leftovers Chef dropped by for us. Dusk has fallen, the sun muted as it dips in the sky, and when I look up to the window, my eyes find her.

Ruby's on the front porch of her cottage wearing a long T-shirt that shows off her slight curves, the soft swell of her breasts. Her bare legs are lean and long. Her hair is a tangled mess of wild waves that tells me she just got out of the shower.

Fuck.

It feels too damn intimate seeing her this way. I can't think straight. She's on the phone, her mouth moving, her pretty face amused. Who's she on the phone with? Boyfriend? Christ, what if she's still working? I don't know which thought I hate more.

Don't care.

Can't care.

I shouldn't care. But I do. Even after a week on the ranch, Ruby's as mysterious as she is an open book. A girl who shines like the sun and smiles at strangers and gasps at flowers and could charm even the Wolfington brothers without even trying.

That girl's got secrets I should stay far away from.

Her refusal to tell me why she's here was a good move. I'll give her that. But I recognize a runner. Hell, I've been one.

Don't let it be a man.

The thought has rage sparking through my veins. My fists clench at my side.

If someone fucking hurt her . . .

Just seeing her on that cliff edge today set off a primitive protectiveness inside of me. It wasn't enough pulling her back to my side. I had to hold on to her.

My chest tightens, and I glance up again at Ruby through the window.

If I told her my truth, I'd get hers.

But the truth about Runaway Ranch gets into why I left, which brings up Maggie.

Which tears open an old wound that's barely healed.

It's hard to explain that I had to run to keep myself sane. I'm not proud of it. Hell, I'm not proud of much I did after her death. I put my family through hell. Leaving my hometown. Giving up the rodeo.

I did it all.

And I never looked back.

The truth is ugly. And I sure as fuck don't want to relive it.

I cover the potatoes, then the macaroni and cheese, and stack the containers on top of each other. I walk to the fridge, open it, and glance back at Ruby.

Is she eating? I haven't seen her leave the ranch or go to the lodge. She's here to work, but she doesn't have to hole herself up in that cottage. Though the idea of her heading out on her own in Resurrection has me bristling. Does she have enough money for food?

Her laugh carries, a sparkling lilt that has my heart clenching. I grab a beer from the fridge and head out to my front porch.

Across the way, Ruby lowers the phone. She lifts her hand and smiles, the bright glow in her eyes catching me off guard.

She's gorgeous beyond words.

I take a step toward her.

The words *come over and have dinner* are on the tip of my tongue, but before I can make a move, the crunch of gravel freezes me.

A long black Cadillac drives up the winding road to my place.

Instantly, alarm prickles.

Nothing good arrives at your doorstep at night. Especially in Resurrection. Although the town is safe, backwoods shit goes on. There's been murders, kidnappings, and drug deals in the past. A year ago, a body was found down by the train tracks. Meth deal gone wrong. Or maybe right.

I meet Ruby's eyes across the twenty feet that separate our front yards. Jerking my chin, I send her a silent order to go inside. Now.

Thank Christ she does.

I make sure she's back in the cottage, the door locked behind her, then turn my attention to the two men striding toward my porch steps. One glance tells me they're the developers Stede warned me about. The suits give them away. So do the dipshit smiles on their faces.

"You lost?" I ask gruffly, setting my beer bottle on the arm of the Adirondack chair.

"Not lost," Suit Number One says. "Name's Malcom Moreau, and this here is Neal Trevino. We're from DVL Equities. Wanted to talk to you about your piece of land."

Malcolm's a tall guy with jet-black hair, glasses, and a round face. Neal is stockier, with a shaved head and tattoos peeking out of his suit sleeves. Brain and muscle, I bet.

Ignoring the business card, I cross my arms against my chest. I meet Malcolm's gaze with a cool stare. "Not sure what there is to talk about."

"Heard you were having money problems."

"Heard wrong," I growl.

"You sure about that?" Malcolm looks skeptical, a sneer on his lips. "Thought I saw some empty cabins down by the river. Wouldn't be on account of that video, would it?"

My fists clench, aching to punch a hole through this slimy asshole's face.

Goddamn that video.

With a smooth flourish, Malcolm hands over a business card. "Mr. Valiante put together a number he thinks you can work with."

I snort at the lowball offer. "The ranch is worth twice that," I tell them roughly. "And you fucking know it."

Neal steps in, lifting his meaty hands. "Help us, help you, Mr. Montgomery. As I'm sure you know, this is a desirable piece of property. Fifty miles from Glacier. Direct access to Bozeman via the pass. Let us take it off your hands before the bank does." He makes a face. "Cowboys like you have had a good run, but sometimes you need the smooth hand of a businessman to really make the land what it's worth."

"Let me guess . . ." I look at Malcolm. "You're the listener. The quiet one who comes up with the game." I look back at Neal. "And you're the fucker who's about to get his neck ripped off."

Neal smiles. "Mr. Montgomery—"

I take a step forward, making them take a step back. "You think you're gonna build a gas station, a strip mall on my land? Take your offer and shove it up your ass."

A muscle jerks in Neal's jaw. "DVL can make life difficult for you, Mr. Montgomery, or we can make it easy. The choice is yours."

"It's a real nice piece of land," Malcom adds. "But I imagine there are a lot of bad things that can happen on a ranch. Bones break. Maybe a fire. Maybe a horse gets sick. But I suppose that just comes with the territory, doesn't it?"

Fury boils inside of me. "Where I grew up, you threaten someone, you don't walk away in one piece," I growl.

He holds his hands up in mock fear. "No threat. We fight for the land we want."

"So do I." This town is mine. It saved me after Maggie, and I'll be damned if I let developers take it over.

My knuckles crack as I make a fist. My daddy raised me and my brothers to never throw the first punch, but we better throw the last. "Get the fuck off my property and don't come back. You hear me?"

"We hear you, Mr. Montgomery." Malcolm's eyes sweep over the ranch, then back to me. "Others might not."

It takes every ounce of my cool not to grab the guy by the throat and launch him across the field.

"Go," I snap. "Now."

I watch them get back in their car and head down the drive.

Others might not.

What the fuck does that mean? The idea of trouble coming to the ranch makes my stomach churn. How I didn't slam a fist into that asshole's smug face is beyond me.

When I turn to go back inside, I catch a flicker of movement.

Ruby.

She's watching from her bedroom window, her baby blue eyes wide and alert, her lips parted in a question.

A question I can't answer.

I give her a stern nod to stay put and head inside. But I still feel the heat of Ruby's gaze on me even after I drop into bed, the bright glow of her sunshine smile following me down into a restless sleep.

13

Charlie

"Y**OU'RE LATE.**" D**AVIS FROWNS AT** W**YATT** as he drops his lean frame into a chair in front of the fire pit.

I tip my beer. "Nice of you to join us."

Wyatt grins at Stede. "Brought you candy, old man," he says and dumps a shit ton of Hershey bars in Stede's lap.

Best way to get Stede off the cigarettes—give him candy.

"Take a load off, kid." Stede hands Wyatt a beer.

Ford and I exchange an eye roll. It's just like Wyatt to come strolling in late, turn on the charm, and be forgiven.

When Wyatt's settled, he looks all of us over. "Got into somethin' tonight."

"What kind of somethin'?" Ford asks.

"Prank of the century," he drawls.

Davis sighs.

I sip my beer and watch the fire dance in the firepit. "Gotta tell us now."

We're gathered on the front lawn of Stede's log cabin for Family, our monthly get together with the man who's become like a surrogate father to all of us. Now, after a dinner of T-bone steaks and baked potatoes, we sit around the firepit. With no fire restrictions in place this year, we're taking advantage any time we can.

Wyatt rubs his hands together. "Rigged up some balloons full of milk. Hooked those babies up in the Wolfingtons' barn. Won't know what hit 'em."

A round of chuckles erupt from everyone except Davis.

Solemn-faced, Davis shakes his head. "One day . . . it'll go too far, Wy."

I glance at Davis. He has that same hard-ass look on his face he wore when he caught me and Wyatt sneaking beers down to the river when we were kids. We were too young, we knew better, and he effectively threatened to tan our hides.

"Davis is right," Stede says. "Their daddy is in prison for shooting someone over a fender bender. Apple don't fall far from the tree. I wouldn't mess with what you can't control."

"End it," Davis orders Wyatt. "Now."

Their glares clash.

"Fine, fuck," Wyatt says.

Despite his grumble of agreement, I doubt Wyatt will fall in line. My younger brother gives a big middle finger to anyone who tells him what to do, especially Davis.

The crash of the screen door sounds from behind us. Fallon comes storming our way, causing Wyatt to straighten up in his chair.

Nodding at Stede, she says, "I'm off, Daddy. Got a shift."

Stede takes his daughter's hand, keeping her by his side. Looks at all of us. "Girl works too much." Guilt stains the old man's voice. Guilt because with Stede sick, Fallon's the one taking the brunt of The Corner Store during her time off from the rodeo.

Fallon shoulders her bag and shrugs. "Someone has to do it."

Ford kicks his boot up on his knee. "Dakota can't help?"

A snort comes from Fallon. "No. My big sister's too busy these days to even think about coming home." She dips to kiss Stede's cheek. "Love you, Daddy."

She slaps the back of Wyatt's head as she passes by, sashaying her way to the circle of trucks in the gravel driveway.

Ford lifts his brows. "She's pissed off."

Wyatt tucks his hands under his armpits. "Don't look at me."

Stede sighs. "We haven't told Dakota about the cancer."

Davis winces. "Jesus, Stede."

Stede puts a gnarled hand out. "I don't want to worry her. And I don't want her to come home either. She finally got her bakery off the ground. Can't keep interfering in her life. We all got a lot on our plate."

"Speaking of plates . . ." Ford looks my way. "You wanna tell us about the visit DVL paid you last week?"

All three of my brother's gazes lock on me.

Between taking a group for a day-long Yellowstone horseback ride and outfitting the horses, it's the first time I've been in the same place with my brothers.

I lean forward and rest my elbows on my knees. "Valiante sent his cronies. They offered to buy the ranch, and I told 'em to go fuck themselves. They left."

Wyatt lifts a disbelieving brow. "That simple?"

"Nah." I scrub a hand over my face. "I don't think so. They made some threats. Horses dying. Fires. Shit like that."

Davis and Ford swear in unison.

"I did some digging with my contact," Stede tells us. "DVL plays dirty. Resurrection is just another town on their list to destroy."

I grind my teeth. "I won't sell the ranch, Stede."

"You don't need them showing up at your place again, kid."

Wyatt's languid drawl cuts the silence. "What if we did sell it?"

I take a moment to process the weight of what my younger brother just said. Ford and Davis scowl at the question, but I see what Wyatt's trying to do.

He's giving me an out. Giving all of us an out.

My chest tightens at the thought.

What if I sold?

Last week, I was so sure of my answer. Sell? Fucking never. It's our ranch. It's my life. We'd let the town down if we sold. A strip mall, a casino, or worse, a Wal-Mart eating up the rugged Montana mountainside makes me sick to my stomach.

But what if my brothers want out? What if this summer goes to shit and we're forced to sell? We're already in the red and without a successful season, it's unlikely we'll be around to see next year.

I don't like being backed into a corner. I got everyone into this mess, and it's my responsibility to get them out.

I've never felt so goddamn helpless or pissed off.

"Charlie?" Ford begins in his soft southern drawl. "What are you thinking?"

I stare into the fire, my grip on the beer bottle tightening. "Not sure yet."

"When nothing goes right, go left," Stede says, his face crinkling in a wise grin. "You're working on a solution, son."

"That's the hope."

Ford's cell phone lights up and he shows me the screen. The first single square on our Instagram account is a photo of the Runaway Ranch gate entry sign backdropped against brilliant, indigo sky. The caption reads *Welcome to Runaway Ranch*.

Current follower count: 150.

An image of Ruby earlier this week pops into my mind. She had been all over the ranch interviewing our staff and hired hands. I caught her at the lobby bar on her laptop clicking away a storm, her pretty face intent and focused.

She's determined, something I appreciate. Out on the ridge, I believed her when she said she'd save the ranch. But as I sit here with my brothers and Stede McGraw, I'm not so sure.

"This gonna save us, C?" Ford looks doubtful.

I close my eyes, not in the mood for my older brother's criticism. "Hell, if I know."

What I know is if we can't pay back our loan, we default. Our small knit community is out of a job.

The thought cuts right through my heart. Gives me more stress than I can damn near take.

I drain the last of my beer. A mistake. The liquid settles heavy in my belly. "I'm headed out. I'll catch y'all on another day."

"See ya, man." Wyatt gives me a nod, his eyes asking me if I'm okay.

"Enjoy the fire. Last cool night before it gets hot." I clap his shoulder as I pass him and head for my truck.

Silver moonlight shines through the evergreens lining the two-lane country roads as I drive back to the ranch.

The cool night air sweeps away my worries from Stede's place, saving them for another time.

It's late, nearing eleven, when I pull up the long drive to my cabin. I slow for a figure crossing the road.

Illuminated in the glow of the headlights is Ruby. She's barefoot, in a white tank top and cut-off blue jean shorts that show off her long legs. Balanced on her hip is a mesh laundry bag we give to guests.

I frown.

What the fuck is she doing out here?

The ranch is safe, but still. I don't want her walking around by herself this late at night.

I pull my truck up beside Ruby. In the moonlight, she looks even more beautiful. "Working on the night shift?"

Seeing me, she comes to the driver's side window. "I haven't done laundry since I got here," she says, flashing a dazzling smile. Then she laughs and backs away from the window. "So, you might want to keep your distance."

I chuckle. Ruby could be covered in cow shit and I'd still do a double-take.

"Come up to the house and do it," I tell her. "I don't want you walkin' out here by yourself."

She hesitates and glances down at her laundry. "Are you sure? I don't want to put you out."

"I'm sure," I promise.

I park the truck at the house and hop out. When Ruby reaches my side, I take the laundry bag. She follows me up the porch and into the cabin. Her bare feet slap the hardwood floors and after I flip on a light, I realize what a goddamn bad move I've just made.

My breath hitches. She's stunning. Moonlight, harsh kitchen light, bar neon, Ruby Bloom blooms. She's tied her rose-gold hair back in a little white ribbon, and for some reason, it's the sexiest thing I've ever seen.

"Follow me," I tell her, clearing my throat. "It's down the hall."

I show her the laundry room, where the detergent and dryer sheets are located, and hustle out of there. She doesn't need me hovering while she sorts her clothes. And I don't need to see more of her underwear.

Purple panties.

Pink with polka dots.

I tear a hand through my hair, the thought going straight to my dick.

This was a fucking terrible idea.

I retreat to the kitchen and snag a beer from the fridge. On second thought, I grab another one and head to the living room, situated just off the kitchen.

I set the beers on the driftwood coffee table and drop down on the large leather sofa.

When she finally returns, Ruby perches opposite me on one of the two leather recliners. Her slender form leans forward, the scoop neck of her tank top dipping low to display full, creamy breasts. "I only have one load. It shouldn't take long, so you can do your own thing. You don't have to babysit me."

"It's no problem. Brought you a beer if you want it."

Her lower lip pulls between her teeth, hesitation on her face. Then she reaches for it and takes a tiny sip. "Thanks."

"You don't drink?" I ask.

"Not very much," she admits, tucking a lock of hair behind her ear. Her blue-eyed gaze bounces around the room, taking in the furnishings. Framed rodeo prints of cowboys in varying positions of being flung line the walls.

Rustic rugs protect the hardwood floors. Charcoal-gray beams lift the ceiling to sky-high levels. She stares a beat at the dramatic stone wall fireplace with deer antlers over the mantle. "I like your cabin. It's cozy."

I chuckle. "You wouldn't say that when you get all my brothers together. It's more of a madhouse."

She giggles, and my chest clenches. That laugh. It's enough to push my self-control to the limit.

"I finished the June calendar." Tucking her legs beneath her, she settles back against the recliner. Her short shorts ride up and expose the curve of her supple ass.

I lift my beer. "Saw the first post."

Her mouth curves. "Unimpressive, I know. For now."

"I hope it works, Ruby. I really do, because right now you're our Hail Mary."

She considers this. "I hope so, too. I think it will. I sent my employer your information. They're a luxury travel planner. They're reaching out to their partners." She tilts her head. "I also messaged some rodeo stars that Wyatt's rode with. Cade Elliott and Nash Mason. They said they'd help."

I nod, impressed by Ruby's tenacity. I realize I haven't given her or her job enough credit. "Big names."

"Well, we need big guns." Her pretty face softens, and she studies me. "I'm not going to let them trash you, Charlie. It's your ranch and we'll save it."

Right now, her determined words are the light I need. Scrubbing a hand down my beard, I lean in. "How do you do it?"

"Do what?"

"This. So positive. So happy." I let out a breath, the weight of the last week stacking on my shoulders. "You seem so damn sure that everything will work out. If I had half of what you did, I'd actually have some hope for once in my life."

A shadow passes across her face. "I just . . . I try not to worry about the future. I know it's easier said than done, but I try to live in the now. I'm thankful for the day I have because you never know how long it'll last." For a brief second, her eyes cloud, then she smiles. "I think of my sunflower."

"Your what?"

"Sunflower and thorn. It's a game my brother and I've played since we were little. Your sunflower for the day is something happy that happened, like fireball happy. Thorn is your typical not-so-great shitty thing." Eyes lighting up, she stands and moves to sit on the coffee table in front of me. Our knees touch, just a soft graze, but sparks flare in my gut. "Here. You do it."

"Ruby—"

"C'mon," she coaxes. "Try it." Then my hand is in hers and she's settling it on her warm thigh. "Tell me your sunflower for today."

I grunt. "Didn't have one."

She frowns, her nose wrinkling with the motion, and damn if she doesn't look cute. "Charlie, everyone has a sunflower."

"Not today." *Not for a damn long time.*

Ruby sits straighter, determined to pull something out of me. "Your thorn then?"

I want to refuse, to push, to growl, but the way she's staring me down with those big blue eyes, I lose the battle.

Something tells me I always will with this woman.

"It's not just the video threatening the ranch," I say, and Ruby raises her brows. "We got some big-time developers on our asses. That car you saw last week—those folks offered to buy the ranch. I said no, and they got pissy about it. But . . . sometimes I think I should have said yes."

"Why?"

"Because of my brothers." I glance down at her hand, the past sliding beneath my skin. "Sometimes I think they'd be better off elsewhere. They all followed me out to Montana. Gave up everything to help my ass out. Ford was in the major leagues. Davis in the military."

Ruby squeezes my hand. "Why'd they follow you?"

I tip the lip of my beer toward her. "Why you runnin'?"

She juts her chin, defiant. "Who says I'm running?"

"I do. Why?"

"Why's it called Runaway Ranch?"

Fine. Point taken. Her refusal to tell me why she's here is bothering me more than I want to admit. Still. It's her right.

I exhale. "This isn't what my brothers signed up for and they're stuck because of me."

"You love the ranch," she says.

"I do. But I love my brothers more. Sometimes what I'm doin' to 'em . . . if I sold the ranch, everyone could get back to their own lives."

Ruby's eyes get big at my reveal. "Have you told them that?"

It takes me a second before I can look at her. "No," I say grimly. "I don't want them to worry about me. They've done enough."

Fuck.

I feel gutted. It's the first time I've admitted out loud how damn guilty I feel. This wide-eyed girl keeps side-swiping my heart and blowing all my expectations out of the water. She listens like she cares. Like she understands.

"Oh, Charlie," Ruby breathes. She squeezes my hand

for the second time and I tighten my grip on her so she can't go anywhere. "You should tell them."

"Yeah." I give her a nod. "Maybe."

For a moment, the only sound in the house is the rhythmic spin of the washing machine.

"What about you?" I ask, clearing my throat. "What was your sunflower?"

She thinks about it. "You know what? This actually. Tonight," she decides and hits me with a blazing smile. "I like talking with you, Cowboy. When you don't yell."

Damn. Speared in the heart.

I'm not used to this. Having someone around to talk to. After a long day spent on the ranch, I usually have a beer, do some paperwork, and hit the hay. I don't spend the night talking to a beautiful woman. Ruby's taking my logic, my good common sense, my routine, and smashing it to fucking smithereens.

"I promised," I rasp, leaning forward. "I won't yell, Ruby. Not at you. Never again."

Before I can stop myself, I run my palm up her hand to encircle her delicate wrist. My rough fingers graze her soft skin, skimming the pulse that beats there, and it's like a tether between us snaps taut.

Ruby lets out a small whimper and my cock jumps in my pants.

We sit staring too long, her hand still in mine. My lungs burn. I can feel the heat of her heartbeat pulsing against my fingertips.

Ruby watches me through heavy-lidded eyes. "Charlie," she whispers.

My gaze drops to her full red lips. Unable to help myself, I tuck a lock of rose-gold hair behind her ear. Then I slide my hand over the high arch of her cheekbone. Her long lashes flutter with surprise. Lust flames in those pretty baby blue eyes. Instead of pulling away, Ruby tilts her head, letting me cradle her face in my palm.

Fuck it.

I lean in, ready to crush her mouth against mine, when a violent rattling noise comes from the hall.

I tense and freeze.

Ruby jerks back, her cheeks flushed pink. "The laundry. I need to get the laundry."

Adorably frazzled, she hops up and disappears fast down the hall. The swing of her hips, the curve of that ass, causes my body to react in ways I didn't know existed.

Shit.

A muscle jumps in my jaw. I war with myself, head versus heart versus cock.

Wanting this is wrong. But I do.

I want her.

I want to be inside of her, kissing those pouty red lips. I want to scrape my beard all over that pretty pink skin and rub it raw. I want to fuck her senseless and have her fucking own me.

Then, every ounce of control snaps, and I shove up off the couch and follow her down the hall.

14

Ruby

I TRANSFER MY LOAD TO THE DRYER AND HIT START.

I stare at the timer. Thirty minutes.

It's a cruel joke from the universe to see if I'll last the next half hour with Charlie Montgomery.

I've been curious about this brooding cowboy more than I'd like to admit. The way he wakes at three thirty in the morning and doesn't return home until the sun is down. The reason for the grumpy scowl on his face. How his ranch got its name.

But standing in his house at midnight sharing strange truths isn't the way to get answers.

Breathing hard, I press a palm to my chest. My heart pumps like a freight train.

I'll stay in the laundry room until my clothes are done. Then I'll leave.

I look for a window to shimmy out of. No such luck.

Bad idea, this is a bad idea.

I know my own head. My heart.

Yes, I want sex, but sex with Charlie Montgomery

skirts dangerous territory. Even the simple act of holding a conversation was a turn on. A spark ignited in me as his calloused thumb swept over my pulse. So intense, so intimate, I feel weak.

A rush of heat warms my core. I can't imagine this cowboy in bed. And I can't imagine myself with him.

Even if I want nothing more.

"Ruby."

The deep rumble causes me to gasp. I spin around to find Charlie standing in the doorway of the laundry room.

Suddenly I feel so very dizzy.

"You scared me," I manage to say.

"I'm sorry," he grits out.

He looks like a raging cowboy—muscled and chest heaving, hands fisted at his side.

"I'm almost done," I breathe. "Then I'll get out of your hair."

Suddenly, Charlie isn't blocking my exit, but right in front of me, hauling me to his broad chest. His lips crash against mine. Our kiss is desperate and hungry. His big hands frame my face as our tongues tangle, and I moan into his mouth, losing myself in his passion.

I wind my arms around his neck, and with a groan, he hooks his large hands under my thighs and lifts me in his arms. I wrap my legs around his waist and shove my hands through his dark hair.

In response, he growls into my mouth and pulls me tighter against him, our tongues battling for a win.

Lightheaded with desire, I whimper into his mouth. God, even a kiss from Charlie is so much better than the sex I had on graduation night.

It's like I've finally let out a scream that's been building in my lungs for the past twenty-six years.

And then the worst thing happens. He stops.

Jerking back like he's been burned, Charlie slams into the washer, causing a hollow clanging sound to echo around us. But still, he holds onto me.

"This can't be anything," he grits out, his cornflower blue eyes wild and glassy with lust.

"It won't be."

My to-do list is a siren song inside my head. Logic out the window. All I want is good sex. It might as well be with Charlie Montgomery. He's just a man. Just a cowboy.

"I'm leaving in a few months," I gasp against his lips. "And you have a ranch to run."

This isn't real.

All it is, is the right now.

I kiss his lips again before trailing down to nip at the pulse in his throat. He moans, and I drop my hand, cupping his massive erection through the front of his jeans. He's so big and solid, and I desperately want him inside of me.

A tortured growl shakes out of him. "What do you want, Ruby?"

His hard jaw is set. In his eyes, I see he's waiting for me to give consent.

I shiver. "You, Charlie. I want you. One night."

His Adam's apple bobs. "One night?"

"One time."

His eyes darken, then flare, like every ounce of control inside of him has snapped. And then his mouth is on mine, and he's carrying me down the hall and up the stairs. I nip at his throat, his bottom lip, the lobe of his ear. Tug on his belt, the waist of his jeans. I want every part of him beneath my hands.

I've never been so happy in my life. I would hand this man my heart and soul right here and now if he gives me what I need.

I need to be touched.

I need *him*.

In seconds, we're in his room and Charlie's setting me on my feet. We come together like magnets. Shed our clothes like we're on fire. I tug at his belt greedily, and soon his jeans are gone and I'm in my bra and panties. A painful-looking erection strains against the thin fabric of his black briefs.

"Jesus," Charlie says hoarsely, a shudder rolling through his broad shoulders. He devours my body with his dark eyes. "Ruby, you could kill a man with a body like that."

I flush, strangely not self-conscious about the way he's staring at me. "Never seen a woman before, Cowboy?" I tease.

"I've never seen you, Ruby," he rasps. "You're goddamn beautiful." Hardworking hands grip my waist. "I don't have a chance with you around, do I? You're gonna ruin me."

I give him a flirty little smile. "You afraid of me, Cowboy?"

His handsome face sobers. "Deathly."

He backs me up toward the bed, his mouth on my throat, trailing my collarbone.

I put a hand on his shoulder, and Charlie freezes. "What's wrong? Do you want me to stop?" No anger in his eyes, just a simple question. And because he's a good man, he'd stop if that's what I wanted.

"No. I just . . ." I lick my lips, thinking of my doctor's advice. "I need to go slow."

Worry stains his drawl. "Are you a—"

"No," I rush out, not wanting to scare him off. "I haven't had a lot of experience." Heat creeps across my cheeks. "I've never had a . . .well, you know."

His gaze turns almost feral. Like it's a challenge, and he's glad for it.

"Ruby." His voice is rough as his hands tighten on my waist. "Baby, you have no idea what I'm gonna do to you."

Baby. The term of endearment has me going weak-kneed.

"I'll go slow," Charlie says as he sets me on the edge of the bed. He leans in, sweeping a kiss across my mouth. "I'll give you whatever you want. You're in control."

"Me?" I whisper against his lips. It's a stunning notion. Control. That this man is letting me take the reins and lead, never treating me like I'm weak or too fragile to handle.

Instead of nerves, all I have is exhilaration.

"Yes, *you*," he growls. "You have me."

I close my eyes at his words, not even trying to pretend I don't like the way the statement sounds in his mouth.

You have me.

Charlie drops to his knees in front of me. I grab the hem of his T-shirt and tear it off.

"Oh," I whisper, coming back to my senses. I press a hand to my heart. My pulse pounds in my ears.

His body is spectacular. Charlie's a chiseled mountain of a cowboy, lean and muscular from years of ranch work, from years of roping horses. The dark dusting of hair on his ridged chest and over his tan forearms steals my breath. Everything about him screams real man.

I lean in and slide my hands over the hard, cut angles of his body, the rippling flex of his shoulders. A muscle tenses in his jaw, his expression warring between flat out torture and amusement as I continue to stroke my hands over his body.

I haven't touched a man like this, but with Charlie, it's instinctual. My hands and lips know where to go.

Like we're matched.

"You're beautiful, Charlie."

Whipped by my words, lust flashes in his piercing blue eyes as he pulls me close.

I moan as his big hands—rough, rugged—slide up my legs, squeezing my thighs so hard I hope they leave bruises.

It's automatic the way my body responds. I lie back on the bed's soft brown blanket, and Charlie traces a finger around the lacy edge of my panties.

That's when I realize what he's doing.

I jerk back and prop myself up on my elbows. "You don't have to."

He watches me closely. "I want to." He leans in, his brow wickedly arched. "I've wanted a taste of you ever since you got here, darlin'."

My mouth pops open in surprise. All I can do is nod.

"I'm gonna make this good for you, Ruby." Without missing a beat, he tugs my hips closer to the edge of the bed, and I lie back down. "So goddamn good I'm gonna ruin you for every man who comes after me."

No one. No one but you will ever do this to me.

Charlie hooks a finger through the strap of my underwear and drags them off. "Fuck me," he rumbles, running a finger through my damp slit. "You're soaked, baby."

I whimper. My arousal lit up like kerosene.

"I have to taste you, Ruby." Hot breath fans over the inside of my thighs. My heart palpitates. "Legs open, baby."

I tremble as his hands split my knees.

When his mouth meets my sex, my hips buck. The sensation is wondrous. I moan as Charlie seals his warm lips to my clit. He sucks slow and fast, hard and soft.

"Ohhh," I cry out. Instinct takes over, and my back arches. "Charlie." My fingers claw at his hair and he makes a throaty rumble of approval. "Charlie, *please*."

He pauses long enough to say, "Scream for me, baby," and then locks his mouth to me again. Long, lavishing strokes, then teasing flicks, stimulate my clit.

It's too much; it's not enough.

The build-up of pressure, of friction is like a fever dream.

"Oh my god," I cry out, gripping the blanket, relishing the coarse feel of his beard scraping against the inside of my thighs. "Charlie, don't stop. *Don't.*"

He doesn't. Gold dances in front of my eyes as my body bucks, but Charlie pins an arm across my hips and brings me back to the bed. He won't let me dislodge him. He's *here*, and that thought sends me over the edge. My thighs tremor, and every muscle in my core tightens. And then, blast off. I come for the first time.

My scream is long and loud, and I let myself feel it.

I own it.

I buck against his mouth and an unholy sound rips out of him. Smug. Satisfied.

My eyes roll back and my entire body practically levitates off the bed. Long trails of wetness stream from my sex to trail down my thighs. My breath shakes out in a tremble and my heartbeat tremors, but steadies.

Long breaths, I take long breaths.

"You okay, Ruby?" Charlie rasps and I realize he's up on his knees, watching me. His bare chest heaves and his beard is damp. Because of me.

I smile. I love it.

I sit up. "Better than." My body feels limp and empty in the best way.

He chuckles. "Don't know if that counted as slow."

I frame his face with my hands. "More," I say, kissing his mouth softly. "I want more."

"More, huh?"

With a pleased grin, he hooks a tan forearm around my waist. His body is massive, strong like an oak. And I'm his willow.

Eyes locked on mine he says, "I've wanted to do this all night."

Then, reaching up, he pulls the white ribbon out of my hair, letting it flutter to the floor. My hair tumbles over my shoulders, and Charlie makes a low growl of satisfaction. I watch him, heavy-lidded, as he removes my bra. When my breasts spill out, his eyes darken and he dips low, taking the creamy peak of my breast into his mouth. "Fuck." He moans around the bead of my nipple. "Baby, you taste so fucking good."

"Oh," I breathe, my head spinning. "Charlie . . . Charlie."

He shakes against me. "I know," he husks, his beard scraping over my breast as he gently bites my nipple.

Tensing, I cry out at the sensation. Charlie fists my hair, jerking me back to look into my eyes, then with a growl he slams his mouth to mine.

I kiss him deeply. Desperately. Charlie holds me close,

like he wants all of me. He drags me back on the bed, and I revel in his possessive touch.

I gasp as he shrugs out of his briefs. The only word that comes to mind is *huge*. I close my eyes to ward off the worries that he won't fit.

Charlie grins, reading my mind. He touches my chin, bringing my gaze to his. "Don't worry, darlin'. I'll make sure you're ready to take all of me."

I flush beside him, appreciation dawning. He's going to give me what I want, while making sure I'm okay. I trust this man. With all of me. With my body. My heart.

Just like that, every worry falls out of my head. Reaching down, I take his thick cock in my hand and stroke. It's the most natural thing, having my hands all over Charlie.

"Ruby, you're gonna have me goin' off too damn fast," he pants. The handsome lines of his face look tormented, like he's wrestling for control of a darkness that's been in him for too long.

I bite my lip to keep from grinning. "Then fuck me, Cowboy. I need you inside me."

His eyes flash.

I shiver at the boldness of my words.

I'm doing this.

Sex. Good sex.

Charlie's massive body hovers over mine. Somewhere in my daze, he finds a condom and slips it on. Reckless need builds in me. I gulp air, desperate for him to fill me up inside.

The corners of his bearded lips rise. "Lift your hips, baby, and hang on."

He takes his time sinking into me, bearing down

against my body. My thighs tremble as I slowly suck him in. The sensation is so intense, so overpowering, all I can do is *feel*.

"That's right, darlin'. Fuck, but that pretty pussy grips my cock so goddamn good." Charlie's eyes close and he groans low. "Just a little bit more."

My heartbeat quickens as he sinks another inch into me. My vision blurs. It's too much. It's perfect. I feel powerful. I'm on fire. And all I need is Charlie.

"Harder," I demand as he rears back to pull out. "Deeper."

Heat blazes in those cornflower blue eyes. "Beg for my cock, darlin'. Take it like a good girl."

"Yes," I gasp, letting my thighs fall open wider as I buck against the massive man on top of me. I slide my hands down his back and grip his ass with my nails. "Yes."

And then, a guttural growl on his lips, he surges forward, burying himself the rest of the way into me. My heat sucks him in, every muscle in my body burns as I rock against him slow and steady.

A moan erupts from my mouth. Heaven.

He's heaven. Hot, hard, and thick.

"Fuck," Charlie says on a haggard groan as he tucks me against him and thrusts. His eyes are wild, his jaw locked as his fingers dig their way into my hips, gripping harder. "Look what a good girl you are. Taking all of me."

Every inch of him spreads my legs further and further apart. I mewl, wanting more. "Charlie, please. More."

"Easy, baby," he whispers. "Slow."

I nip his shoulder. "Slow."

"So tight," he mutters through gritted teeth. "You're so goddamn tight. You're perfect, Ruby. Fucking perfect."

"Charlie," I breathe, the compliment sinking into me like sunlight.

He buries himself in me. He isn't gentle, but he goes slow like I've asked. Deep rhythmic thrusts that have me coming unglued. His muscles ripple as he hovers over me. My entire body vibrates with the weight of him.

I relish it all.

Someone being rough with me. For years, I was so careful. Now, out in the wilds of Montana, all I want to do is be fucked hard and ravished by a cowboy.

He's giving me all I ever wanted and everything I didn't know I needed.

I spread my legs wider, and he sinks in deeper.

"Good girl," he breathes against my neck. His praise spreads through me like wildfire, has me bucking my hips and arching my back in ways I never knew I could move.

Has me feeling things I never knew I could feel.

His jaw is tight as he pumps into me, his gaze locked on mine. I sink my nails into the hard muscle of his back and circle my hips in a way that is uncontrollable, primal.

Warmth spreads through me, a golden bloom of bliss.

Another orgasm.

I tense, my hips thrusting as Charlie hammers into me.

This orgasm's electric, shooting through me so powerful and *fast*, I gasp.

I scream out and grip the wire frame of his headboard as my body trembles from head to toe. "*Charlie*! Oh god."

His grunt is guttural, triumphant, as his large body jerks. His eyes snap shut as he grits out my name. "Ruby," Charlie growls into my neck, his voice breaking with tormented agony. "*Ruby. Ruby.*"

With a heaving sigh, Charlie collapses onto my chest.

But he doesn't move. He stays buried inside of me, pressing soft kisses to my neck. In that moment, our hearts sync. His pulse is steady and strong and I want to tattoo it onto my bones in memory of this moment.

After a few minutes, he rolls off me, sweeping a kiss to my temple.

My breath slows as I lie in the cool sheets, palm pressed over my heart. Its beat is erratic, but it's nowhere near flutter status.

Charlie has me, easily.

Forever altered the electrical charge of my heart.

I smile in the darkened room. For once, my body allowed me to do what I wanted to do.

What a glorious notion.

The bed shifts as Charlie sits up and tosses the condom in the trash beside the bed. "You okay?" he asks.

The concern in his voice makes my chest ache.

I cup his strong jaw. "It was perfect."

His eyes flick to my hand and the minimalist tattoo on the inside of my ring finger. "What's this?"

"A heartbeat," I say, hesitating. "I got it in Charleston. It's a reminder to live while I can."

He adjusts us in the sheets before kissing the inside of my finger, where my tattoo lives. "Been everywhere," he observes.

"I have." I rest my head on his hard chest. "But this is my most favorite place I've been, Charlie."

It's the wrong thing to say. His handsome face sobers.

"One night, Ruby," he says on an exhale.

"I know." I sit up, running my gaze over his bedroom. Suede pillows, terracotta comforter, traditional cattle-branded symbols framed above the bed. There's a balcony that looks out over the front yard. It's cozy and rustic and makes me want to stay in his bed. Still, I say, "I should go."

His Adam's apple bobs. "That's probably a good idea."

Charlie's words sting, but he's right.

One night.

And now it's over. No matter how much I wish things could be different, they can't.

I need to stay away, so no one gets hurt.

He reaches for his jeans. "Walk you out."

"You don't have to—"

"Won't argue about that, Ruby," he says, giving me a stern look.

Slipping out of bed, I dress quickly. Once I gather my laundry, Charlie walks me back to my cottage.

Just like that, no strings attached.

But I can already hear that greedy little voice in my mind whispering *more*.

Because once with Charlie Montgomery is never enough.

15

Charlie

EVEN THE SANCTUARY OF THE BULLSHIT BOX and the stack of bills in front of me can't keep my mind off the one person plaguing me for the last week.

Ruby.

I want her. So fucking bad.

Which pisses me off.

That girl was like a ray of sunlight making me come alive. Her laugh, her sweet kiss, hell, even her adorable ramble of curious questions. If she's not giving them to me, I don't want anyone else to have them.

Ever since our night together, when I was the asshole who kicked her out, I've thought about her more times than I can count. Which means I've stayed away from her. Pure fucking torture. But it's the smart thing to do.

We're both here to do our jobs.

I need to put my focus on the ranch and not on the girl skipping past my cabin every goddamn morning.

Shifting in my chair, I ignore the sound of my brothers'

boisterous laughter as they crowd into the Bullshit Box. Gritting my teeth, I shuffle through payroll and vendor purchase orders. Only it's fucking pointless. Every thought is of her.

My eyes fall to Ruby's white ribbon tied around my wrist. I meant to give it back to her, but there's something in me that knows it's mine.

It felt right with Ruby that night.

That one night and *only* that one night.

No more.

Even though I know once wasn't enough.

Even though I fucking crave her. Those pert breasts. That tiny waist. Her long rose-gold hair. But it's not just the sex I crave. I crave *her*. I miss talking to her. The conversation we had at my place was like a shot of calm for the soul. When I woke up the next morning, I realized I still wanted her. I wanted that sun-drenched creature in my sheets. I wanted to go back for round two, to fuck her until we were both limp and panting, and then bring her coffee in bed.

Hell, she was just as eager for it as I was.

The thought has my dick jerking in my pants. My goal that night was to make it the best she ever had. To feel her come undone around me and send her off with the memory of my cock inside of her.

Christ, who am I kidding? *I'm* the one who's come undone.

She's not out of my system.

Not by a country fucking mile.

My gaze lifts from the desk to linger on the window. Every ounce of self-control disappears as I search for Ruby, for a flash of sundress, for that strawberry blonde hair.

I grunt. Fucking unfair is what it is.

Because now I have to walk around this damn ranch acting like I haven't seen her naked. Like I haven't tasted that perfect pussy of hers, had her perfect body spread out on my bed just for me.

Because that's what Ruby is.

A perfect fucking angel.

How I'll ever be able to stay the hell away from her, God only knows.

"Charlie, you listening?" Davis's even rumble tears me from my thoughts.

"What?" I tear my gaze from the window, trying hard not to let on I'm looking for Ruby. My brothers stare at me with various degrees of amusement on their faces.

"I said I got the security system up and running," Davis says.

I grunt. "Good."

Wyatt looks at me with suspicion. "What's that?"

"What?"

He swirls a finger. "On your ugly face."

Ford wiggles his brows. "Wy, I think it's a goddamn smile."

Davis pauses the new security monitors to watch the harassment. "I think you're right," he says, sounding only a little irritated we've interrupted his spiel. His eyes drop to the ribbon tied around my wrist, but he keeps his mouth shut.

Unlike Wyatt.

A smirk spreads across my brother's face. "I'll be damned. You got laid."

I ignore him. Any fool who talks about the woman they had in their bed doesn't deserve them.

But Wyatt doesn't take the hint.

"Was it Ruby?" he demands.

"If you gotta know . . . Fallon." I flash him a smug look and settle back in my chair.

His smile drops off the face of the earth. "Asshole."

Davis snaps his fingers, getting us back on topic. "We're up to twenty posts now." He pulls our Instagram page up on the computer. "Five hundred followers."

I stare at the screen. Social media's Greek to me, but if it works, it works.

Ford runs a hand through his shaggy dark blond hair. "Not bad."

I shrug. Once again, my eyes scan the window for a familiar sundress. "Getting somewhere."

"Morning, boys."

We all look up to see Tina in the doorway.

"Hey, Tina," Ford drawls. "Come for a kiss?"

Davis shoots him a glare. "Let's fix this mess before you get us hit with another lawsuit."

Tina chuckles. "A kiss can wait. This can't." She sweeps her chocolate curls away from her face and looks my way. "Charlie, we have a call about a group for next year. Are we taking reservations that far in advance?"

Davis straightens. "How big?"

"For two weeks," Tina says, leaning against the doorway. Happiness dances in her eyes. "The entire ranch is booked."

Excitement crackles around the room. While we always have guests, we're never to capacity. Truth is, we've been running the ranch more like a hobby than a business.

Davis blows out a breath and looks at me. "That's good."

"That's great," I agree.

With a hoot, Wyatt rips out of his chair. "Fuck yes!"

He glances at Colton, who's loping around the corner. "You hear that kid! Forty guests already booked for next year."

"Cool, man." Colton flashes two thumbs up and a bright smile.

"Lock 'em in, Tina," Davis orders.

"Yes, boss," she says, and disappears with Colton.

"Damn," I marvel, rubbing my jaw. It's working. Whatever Ruby's doing, she's doing it right.

Pride flares through me. This girl's saving our asses, all by herself.

I shove up from the desk.

Ford spins around in his chair. "Where you going?"

"To find Ruby."

I'm at her place faster than I knew I could walk. Heart thrumming in my chest, I rap my knuckle on the screen door. When there's nothing but silence, I open the door a crack and step inside.

"Ruby?"

More silence.

My eyes drift. On the table is her laptop, a small note-pad beside it. But what catches and holds my attention is a journal on the coffee table, opened to a lined-page. From my vantage point, I can see it reads:

Ruby Bloom's To-Do List (so do it!):

1. ~~Get a tattoo.~~
2. ~~Have sex. Good sex.~~
3. Stay up all night and see the sunrise.
4. See a California sunset.
5. Swim in the Pacific.
6. Go dancing.
7. Ride a horse.

Is that what she's doing? Traveling across the country to finish a bucket list? I chuckle, something warm and hard hitting me in the chest. Only she would do that. This sweet, wild girl who has me thinking about her more than I should.

As I take a second look, I'm pleased good sex has been crossed off the list, but my mood sours when I stare at the rest of it. Ruby on a horse—hell no. And picturing Ruby dancing or watching a California sunset with anyone other than me pisses me the fuck off.

Then I swear, realizing I'm acting like a possessive bastard.

I exit her cottage, feeling like an asshole for invading her privacy, and rake a hand through my hair. I'm getting antsy. I don't like not knowing where she is.

Truth is, no matter how much it scares me, I can't stay away from her.

I don't want to.

Playing with the ribbon wound around my wrist, I scan the ranch for blue eyes and a sundress. Then I start walking.

I know where to find her.

She's in the barn.

It's the fifth time this week I've caught her sneaking out of her cottage to make her way down the east trail path.

Ruby stands at the middle stall, speaking in soft gentle tones to a young Appaloosa foal. She's on tiptoes, her long hair swishing across the middle of her back, looking so much like a down-home country girl that I bring a hand to my chest to rub at the ache in my heart. The dress she's wearing could be made of glass. I can see every curve, every gorgeous piece of Ruby Bloom.

Damn.

Goddamn.

I cross my arms and clear my throat. "Another man stealing your heart?"

At my voice, she startles, then half-turns. Her face brightens the moment she sees me. "What's it to you, Cowboy?"

Cowboy. I like it.

Fucking love it.

I eye the pony, nuzzling his way back to her out-stretched hand, and lift a brow. Lucky it's a horse and not a man.

I can't even fight the grin on my face. "I went looking for you." At her raised eyebrow, I go on. "Got a group of forty booked for next year. Ranch is filling up. Got some followers too."

Joy leaps into her eyes. "Good. My partners put the word out. I'm so glad, Charlie. It'll only get better. You'll see."

Her sincere yearning to help us, her kind words kick me in the balls. I've never met anyone like Ruby. Someone so . . . so good.

Golden.

Self-control fucked, I cross the space between us. "How many you have in there?" I ask, slipping her hand into mine. I run my thumb over the delicate skin on the underside of her wrist.

She stares at me. "How many what?"

"Hearts." She jerks her wrist away, but I lean in, my

gaze locking with her gorgeous blue eyes. "Because you, darlin', have got more life in you than a field of wildflowers."

Her lips curve upward. "Sweet talk will get you nowhere, Cowboy."

"No sweet talk. We got some important things to address."

"Oh?" she says, studying me with curious eyes.

"You've been staying away," I say, backing her up against the stall door and pinning her in place. My voice comes out thick, strained.

"We both have." She meets my stare with steely defiance. "This is a job. That's all."

Fuck, but I hate how much it stings.

"It is, but—"

She puts a palm on my chest. "No buts, remember? We agreed." Her gaze drifts down, her long lashes black against her cheek. "One time." She says it easily like it hasn't just set off a lightning strike inside of me.

"That's bullshit." I say it before I can stop myself.

Her blue eyes widen. "Charlie—"

"We'll come back to that." I run my hands down her shoulders, over all that smooth skin, and hold her close. "Now we're gonna have a talk about your open-door policy."

Ruby's cheeks pink up. "It's the country."

"It's Resurrection." Skimming a hand over her delicate jaw, I tilt her chin up so she meets my eyes. "You lock it, you hear me? It's not up for debate."

Her luscious lips part. "I will."

"Good." I drop my hands to her waist, needing to come clean. She expects honesty from me and she'll always get that. "I won't lie, Ruby. I went into your cottage looking for you. I saw your list."

Fear flashes in her eyes. "And?"

"Mighty long list of to-dos."

"So. I'll get them done."

"Maybe I can help."

"Help me? How?"

"You're helping us, and I'll help you finish up that list." Her attention flicks to the pony. "No horses," I say, clenching my jaw. The thought of her on a horse has me losing my mind. "And no California sunset. But everything else I can do."

Her brow arches. "You've got big ambitions, Cowboy. Don't you have a ranch to run?"

The thought comes automatically—fuck the ranch.

I run a thumb over her full bottom lip. Hands-off isn't happening. Not anymore. "Whatever you want this summer, Ruby, I'll give it to you."

Her wary gaze drops to the ribbon tied around my wrist. "Just the summer?"

"Just the summer." This ends when the season does.

"Are you sure?" A teasing smile toys at her lips, but not before I catch a hint of sadness in her blue eyes. And damn, do I want to understand it. "The last thing I want to do is make you fall in love with me."

I chuckle, despite the clench in my chest, her words ringing in my head. "Never gonna happen, darlin'."

Interest dances across her face. "And why is that?"

"I don't fall in love."

Not anymore.

"Lucky me," she says and bows back against the stall door as if to rope me in even more.

And goddamn does she. Like a moth to the flame, I follow.

I can't stop myself from grabbing her up in my arms and holding her to me. Ruby rides her small hands up my chest. A sexy little gasp pops out of her mouth and my dick clenches.

I lower my mouth to hers. "Say yes. Say yes and I'll help you with every damn thing on your list."

I need to hear her say it. I can't handle the possibility that I've had her in my bed for the last time.

"Yes," she whispers on a breathy sigh. "Yes, Charlie. You. I want you."

Thank fuck.

"The summer," I say.

"The summer," she agrees.

And then she smiles. It breaks every hard shadow inside of me.

Her light.

Framing her face with my hands, I put my lips on hers and inhale. She tastes of sunshine and flowers. I want to breathe her in deep and keep her there.

This girl's gold. I can't stay away.

Ruby moans into my mouth and I kiss her deeper. Harder. I slide my hands into her silky hair, grip her by the neck and keep her there. Against my lips.

The summer. This only lasts for the summer.

Her tongue slips over mine, but before I can slide a hand down and part her slender legs, the pony's long velvet nose nudges her shoulder, breaking our connection.

Ruby laughs, light and musical, a delicate sound that has my cock turning to concrete.

I eye the pony with a wry grin. "Thanks a lot."

"He's jealous," Ruby says, her eyes glassy and heavy lidded.

"I don't blame him," I tell her, and then I'm drawing her back into that kiss. I crush her against me, desperate for this girl who's wrecking me from the inside out.

Her heartbeat mingles with mine where our bodies join, and for the first time in a long time, I feel sunshine in the darkest parts of me.

16

Ruby

I TILT MY PHONE AND LOOK AT THE PHOTO ON THE screen. Colton, who looks more like a floppy-haired surfer than a young hired-hand, leans up against the barn, boots kicked out like a country singer.

"That's perfect," I chirp, glancing up. "But how about one more?"

"Sure thing, Miss Ruby." Colton adjusts his flashy belt buckle and scuffs his heels in the dirt. The soft nickers of the horses make up our background noise.

Today's job duties include snapping photos of each employee to profile for Runaway Ranch's Instagram feed. I plan to build up a solid cache of photos and social media posts to give to Charlie for when I'm gone.

I wipe my brow and scan the ranch. On this Saturday, the ranch is bustling with new groups arriving and others leaving. The blazing sun sits high in the sky, and even the cool breeze can't stop the sweat rolling down my brow. I wave at Wyatt, returning from an early-morning ride. This morning, he and a handful of guests headed out to get acquainted with the horses and wranglers.

The ranch seems busier than when I first got here, but maybe that's wishful thinking.

I flush when I glimpse Charlie exiting the lodge, the two-way radio in his hand.

At the very sight of him, my heart is a riotous pump. Maddening.

Compelled to catch him in his element, I raise the camera and snap a photo. I smile at his stoic expression, then bite my lip at the slow pulse of warmth in my core.

He's so damn handsome.

And for the past two weeks, he's been mine.

I hold my breath, waiting for him to look my way, but he disappears into the Bullshit Box.

Damn my disappointment.

Damn my heart.

It's a slow burn, this game we've been playing. We meet at night, on lunch breaks, or whenever we can sneak away. Giving our hearts a distraction to sink into. Barely able to keep our hands, our lips off each other, Ever since Charlie offered to help me with my to-do list, *good sex* is the only item we've crossed off.

Over and over again.

I never spend the night. That's too dangerous. Because the once-in-a-lifetime feelings Charlie Montgomery gives me make my heart beat faster than SVT ever could.

We're temporary. But it doesn't detract from what we're doing.

Sex. In his plush bed, in that gorgeous room. His muscular arms wrapped around me, his calloused hands dragging their way up my spine, over my curves.

Sex. Good sex.

Still, I know myself, and I know my heart. If I keep doing this, I'll fall for him.

If I haven't already.

I get hopeful when I see Charlie, thinking he might actually care. I love when he half-smiles at me like it takes everything out of him. His intense, broody gaze when we catch each other around the farm. But most of all, I love how he's been slow and sweet with me. This rugged cowboy has the gentlest hands in existence.

I close my eyes. I should call it off.

My end goal is California. Living my life to the fullest. Not giving up my heart.

Even if it feels so damn good.

Jumping into bed with Charlie Montgomery is just one check off my bucket list.

And when it's over, I disappear. There is no need to tell him about my heart. No need to pretend this is anything more than a summer fling.

"You do all of this for the internet, huh?" Colton's cheerful voice snaps me from my daze. "Run all those accounts?"

"I do. It's my job." I wipe my screen off, sticky from humidity. "The goal is to keep doing this until we get the ranch booming." I smile and raise the camera. "Strike a pose."

He gives me an adorable *aw-shucks* grin, fingers through his belt loops, in a classic cowboy pose. "Perfect," I chirp, snapping the camera. "Got it."

"And how long is that?"

Examining the photo, I murmur, "How long is what?"

"How long you sticking around for?"

I give him a small smile. "August. By then this place should be hopping."

I have confidence this will work. I have to. I love this ranch, and I see how much Charlie loves it. After a month here, I have a good handle on the inner workings of Runaway Ranch and its people.

Davis, who is always in that red brick building training his dogs, barking his commands, keeping them to heel, but also giving them a shelter when they'd have none.

Ford, knocking baseballs into the pasture with any kid who dares to take him on, can fix anything on the ranch, whether it's a tractor or a truck.

And Wyatt's never without a cowboy to train, running his workshops in the evenings. His sharp shouts of instruction carrying across the pasture.

It all feels like mine. For the summer, at least.

As Colton adjusts his position, a shiny glint catches my attention. His silver and gold belt buckle shines in the sun.

"I like your buckle," I say. "It's bright."

Colton laughs and pulls a can of Skoal from his back pocket. "Graduation present."

"Thanks for the pictures," I tell him. "You're free."

"See ya, Miss Ruby," Colton calls over his shoulder as he lopes off.

I wave over the next cowboy, waiting for his glamour shots. Sam Hopkins, the cattle foreman, stomps my way. Disdain fogs his leathery face as he grudgingly settles next to the barn. I smother a smile. By now I'm used to people hating on social media. Don't get me wrong, it has its negatives, but if it can bring people together and help small businesses, well, that's the kind of goal I love.

"You need me to pose, sweet thing?" he drawls. His gaze skates over my legs, stopping at my breasts.

"Just a smile, thanks."

Angling my camera, I back up to get a clear shot.

Too far.

The backs of my legs hit the round galvanized steel water tank the horses use for their water. Tottering, I half-turn, bracing a hand on the tank's sun-warmed side to steady myself.

That's when my gaze lands on something white.

Something in the water.

Logs.

Not logs.

My eyes widen. My heartbeat races in my chest.

Bones.

17

Charlie

TEARING MY GAZE FROM THE WINDOW OF THE Bullshit Box, I drop my ass in the chair and slam the desk drawer. Bills need paying and schedules need to be assigned, but all I can do is sit and glower.

I rub the back of my neck, annoyed that I'm annoyed. Minutes earlier, I saw Ruby with Colton, snapping photos for our social media account. The vibrant sound of her laughter ringing out across the field was like a dagger in the chest.

The awareness that she's laughing for somebody else, that she's sixty feet away and I'm not touching her, has me feral. Colton's hanging on her every word. And who can blame the kid? She's too beautiful and the entire ranch knows it.

Hell, she's got the entire ranch wrapped around her finger. With her sweet nature and bright smile, everyone wants to be her best friend. They practically trip over their damn boots to talk to her.

What is it about this girl? She has me wanting to smile

at her and punch someone for smiling at her at the same time.

I don't have the right to be pissed off. We're doing what we're doing for the summer and the summer only. I've made it clear to her I don't want more.

Even if I can't get enough of her.

Every night we fuck, I'm shattering. Having her perfect tits in my face, her hair swirling around me like a halo, clouds every ounce of resolve I've been holding onto. All my doubts, all my fears, disintegrate.

I can't tell if she's a real person or an angel.

And it fucking terrifies me.

I sigh when I come to a bill marked past due. When I see the vendor's name, I frown. Field and Farm, a local farmer Silas sources produce from.

I glance over at Davis. He's at the dartboard with Wyatt, engaged in an epic battle to see who has to take a group up to Crybaby Falls.

"Since when is F and F collecting early?" I growl. In the years we've been working with them, they've always waited for payment until the end of the season.

Wearing an identical frown, Davis grabs the bill and examines it. His expression fades to worry. "You think this is DVL putting pressure on small businesses to collect? Forcing us to fall behind on payments?"

I lean back in my chair and pinch the bridge of my nose. "Fuck," I mutter, closing my eyes for a brief second.

Wyatt walks closer. "I can pull some money out of my rodeo fund—"

"No." The last thing my little brother is doing is bailing my ass out. I have faith in Ruby. In what she's doing.

I'm opening my mouth to say just that when the sound of shouting drifts through the open door.

"Shit," I say, already out the door and running. I hear the scrape of chairs and know my brothers are right behind me.

My heart stops when I see Ruby with her hand slapped across her mouth, her expression petrified. She's backing away from the water tank where a crowd has gathered. Sam wraps an arm around her waist and pulls her away, but she stumbles and falls to her knees on the grass.

I can't get there fucking fast enough.

And then I'm hitting my knees beside her, pulling her against my chest. "Ruby, baby, what is it? What's wrong?"

"Charlie . . ." Her eyes shutter, and she melts against me, her hands clamping down on my shoulders for dear life. She's pale, the beat of her heart haywire. "In the water . . ."

She doesn't need to finish her sentence. When I glance over, Ford's lifting a leg bone out of the water tank.

Guests gasp and cover their mouths.

Fuck.

Leave it to Ford to turn on the charm, holding up a hand to calm the rabble of the crowd. "It's fake, folks," he drawls to the gawkers. "It's all okay, just a prank." As if to prove his point, he tosses away the bone like it's nothing but a beer can.

"Goddamnit," I snarl, wrapping my arms tighter around Ruby.

The last thing we need is gossip going around that we have bodies popping up on our ranch. Not to mention, Ruby's fucking terrified.

Ruby.

Sensing her panic, I tuck her against my chest to shield her from the sight of the bones. Her small body trembles in my arms. Instinct has me sweeping my lips across her temple. "I got you, baby. You're okay."

"Charlie," she whispers, and every hard corner of my soul softens.

Fuck that I've called her baby in front of half the ranch. Fuck that I feel my oldest brother's intent gaze on us. All that matters is Ruby.

"Go on up to the bar, everyone," Ford says, nodding at the lodge. "Get free beers for your troubles."

Guests cheer and drift away, chuckling at the appearance of a Halloween skeleton.

When they're gone, Ford looks at me. "Wolfingtons?"

"Assholes," Wyatt hisses.

Davis looks pissed. "Y'all gotta stop this shit," he barks at Wyatt, shoving up his sleeves to fish out the remains of the skeleton.

Even I agree with Davis. This prank war bullshit is out of hand.

I help Ruby stand. "You okay?" I ask.

She nods, lower lip trembling. "I'm okay. It just scared me, is all."

Bullshit. She's shaking and her face is as white as a sheet.

"You're not okay." I reach for her, not caring we have the entire ranch's eyes on us.

The step she takes away from me does something to my heart's electrical wiring. I hate it.

"I have to get back to work," she whispers, her hand hovering over her heart.

"Ruby—"

"I have to go, Charlie."

With that, she turns so fast she almost slips, then she hurries across the dirt lane and up the road.

Sam comes up beside me and licks his lips. "She's a pretty little thing."

A streak of protectiveness consumes me. It's easy for people to take advantage of Ruby because she's kind. She's too damn innocent to see the way Sam's leering at her. I don't like his body language, angled toward her like he plans to follow her.

"You into her, C?" Sam's eyes drift to the soft shake of Ruby's ass as she floats away from us.

"Yes," I admit through gritted teeth. I want to grab Sam by the throat and throw him in front of the fucking tractor.

"Shame. I'd have her walking bowlegged in a week."

My head snaps to him. I ball my fists, trying to keep my rage on simmer. "Talk about her like that again, and I'll break your fuckin' jaw. Got me?"

He gulps. "Yes, boss."

I watch Sam slink off, making sure he's going in the opposite direction of Ruby, before I make a move toward her cottage. As I head after her, my arm's snagged by my brother.

"What?" I snap, annoyed.

"Charlie," Davis says in a grim voice. "These bones are real."

That sobers us all.

I stare at the pile of bones, gleaming white in the sun. "Christ."

With the toe of his boot, Ford nudges what looks like a femur. "Where'd they even get a skeleton?"

"Dickheads," Wyatt swears. "I'm gonna—"

"No. No more." Davis levels a stern finger at Wyatt, the lines of annoyance around his mouth deepening. "Knock it off with the Wolfingtons."

I clap Wyatt's shoulder. "It's not the hill to die on."

Wyatt nods, but he doesn't look happy.

I know my younger brother well enough to know it's not over. I'll have to talk to him later, without Davis around. I don't have time to referee that fight. Wyatt will bitch and Davis will lay down the law and everyone will yell and it's not the time or place.

"She okay?" Ford asks, his brown eyes following Ruby up the path.

"I don't know," I say, rubbing my jaw. I need to go to Ruby, but my oldest brother's eyes on me stop me.

"We focus on the ranch," Davis orders. "Fixing things."

Hands fisting at my side, I nod and put Ruby out of my head.

The ranch is my priority. That and nothing else.

18

Ruby

I smile as I read the comments on the Runaway Ranch Instagram page, hearting them as I scroll through. Today's most recent post is a photo of Meadow Mountain, lit up by a stunning sunrise. The simple caption reads *Mornings on the ranch.*

How do I get dropped off and stay there forever?

Can't beat that view!

Visiting soon! Cannot wait.

This is what I've wanted for Runaway Ranch ever since I got here.

Love.

Sending myself a mental high five, I stretch out in my seat at the kitchen table. A cool breeze passes through the screen door. This town could convince me to stay here. The warm drench of sunshine. Crisp alpine scent. The rush of wild.

A ping on my phone signals a new comment.

I pull it up and read.

Many people won't wake up this morning at all, but I'm glad you're able to enjoy your mornings on your stolen land.

I shake my head at the nasty comment. Trolls. They come for anything good and happy.

My eyes drift to the user handle. *Lassomamav76.*

I recognize that name.

On a whim, I click on the Instagram handle, which leads me to a private account. The avatar image is a blonde woman sitting on a horse. Adorned in expensive looking western wear, she lifts a hand to the camera. I download the photo and save it to my desktop.

Next, in a new tab, I open up the TikTok website and find the video of Ford barking at the city woman.

Bingo.

The woman in the TikTok video is the same person behind the user handle trolling Runaway Ranch. Their avatars and names match.

Alarms go off inside of me, so I switch tabs and comb through previous Runaway Ranch posts. *Lassomamav76* has commented on every one of them.

Runaway Ranch is a scam.

Real cowboys don't work there.

How often do you screw over your guests?

Guess you're not letting people know about the dead bodies on your ranch, huh?

My jaw drops. How does she know about that? It's the last comment that sets a puzzle piece turning inside of me.

Squaring my shoulders, I sit back in my chair and contemplate what to do. Right as I'm about to dive into more research, my attention's diverted by the hard stomp of boots.

Smiling, I shut my laptop and cross the kitchen floor to the tall, broad-shouldered man on my front porch.

"Door's still not locked," Charlie says. His gruff growl of a voice warms my stomach. But it's what's in his arms that has sunshine—bright, brilliant—splitting my chest open.

Sunflowers.

He brought me flowers. The mere thought makes me dizzy.

I push open my door, smothering a smile at the sight of this brawny rancher cradling two delicate pots of sunflowers that have his biceps bulging.

"Flowers?" I arch a brow.

Charlie shifts on his feet, his expression chagrined, almost boyish. "Apology flowers."

"For what?"

He sets the pots on the porch and straightens up, the muscles in his tan forearms rippling. "For my idiot brother almost scaring you to death yesterday."

I flash him a wan smile. If only he knew the truth of that statement.

Seeing the bones shocked my heart into haywire status. The stress of it all had me fumbling. I had to get out of there before I fell over. I couldn't chance Charlie seeing that happen to me.

Removing his cowboy hat, Charlie runs a big hand through his unruly dark hair. "I promise Wyatt's not really an idiot. He just acts like one." His eyes crinkle when he smiles. It makes him look soft and strong at the same time.

I glance down at the bright yellow pots with sunflowers planted haphazardly in the soil. My father would have a fit at the messy planting job, but I love the way it looks. Love that this man took the time to do this for me.

I swallow, my heart melting into a gooey mess. "They're beautiful. Thank you."

"I should've come by yesterday and made sure you were okay." Regret creases his face. "We just . . .had some shit to take care of for the ranch."

"Those rival brothers?" Worry for Charlie hits me like lightning. "Is everything okay?"

"Yeah." A muscle flexes in his jaw. "We'll get it handled."

I nod at the pots. "You look good with flowers, Cowboy." Stepping onto the porch, I sink down beside his sweet gift. Gently, I swipe a reverent finger over the delicate flower petals. "Think you need them all over the ranch." I gasp, a thought hitting me. I look up at him. "Maybe you need a garden."

Amusement flickers in his eyes. "A garden, huh?"

"Oh, I think very much a garden. Set back against your cabin. In the mornings, when you have coffee, they'll be your best view."

He grunts. "Think I got a pretty damn good view already." His gaze falls to my lips and my face grows hot.

"Hydrangeas," I blurt. "Larkspur. I think they'd grow in this weather." I brighten. "I could show you how to garden."

He chuckles. "I'll add it to my to-do list." Then he sinks beside me, watching as I dip my hand in the soil. "Did I do okay?" he asks, tilting the front brim of his cowboy hat as he sets it back on his head.

Though his voice is gruff, the question is earnest and has my heart palpitating.

"Better than," I tell him, and his eyes turn soft and heated.

I glance back at the flowers. I miss my garden, but my heart, my soul is rooted in this Montana dirt.

I run a finger along one of the blooms, examining them close. A gorgeous bicolor mix of cream, dusty rose, and ruby red. I gasp as realization dawns. "These are Ruby Eclipse." I smile at him. "You found my name in a flower."

He studies me, clearing his throat. "Meant to be."

"Yeah," I whisper. "Must be."

When I go to stand, Charlie reaches down and takes my hand, helping me up.

I bite my lip and look up at him with heavy-lidded eyes. "I should get back to work."

"Take a break. You're off the clock."

I prop a hand on my hip. "Says who."

"Your boss."

"Is that what you are?"

"Gotta keep my employees happy."

I am happy.

Too happy.

"It's Saturday," Charlie says, squeezing my hand. And that's when I realize he's still holding it. He hasn't let go.

He glances at my computer on the table. "Shouldn't be working, anyway," he says, voice low and rough.

I eye his sweat-stained shirt and dusty Stetson. "What about you?"

"I was thinkin' we could go out."

I tilt my head. "And do what?"

"Spend the day with me?"

"And do what?" I ask again, breathless.

For me, this is it. Bliss. Spending the day with Charlie Montgomery. I'm too excited to worry about every moment after this that could be the end. I just want today.

I just want him.

Reaching out, Charlie sweeps my hair off my shoulder and sweeps his fingers across the curve of my throat, over my pulse. The primal action has my composure spiraling. "Thinkin' we could knock two of those items off your to-do list."

Now that Charlie knows about my to-do list, I've tacked it to my fridge. Every morning I see it. It's like some proud badge of honor I can't wait to cross off. Even if I'm not being honest with him, it feels nice to have someone in it with me.

I bite my lip, hopeful. "Ride a horse?"

That smile on his handsome face dips. "No. Not ride a horse, Ruby."

"Then what do you have in mind?"

"We go out and do some dancing. Watch the sunrise."

My heart somersaults in my chest. It sounds perfect.

It sounds disastrous.

"Thought we didn't do that stuff."

He grunts in disagreement. "We're having fun. That's all."

"I don't know, Charlie . . ." His hands drift, sliding over my waist to palm the curve of my back. "What if I'm an awful dancer?" I whisper.

His lips lift in a breathtaking smile that has me forgetting we're just for the summer. Has me forgetting this is a bad idea.

"You won't be. Not with me around." He tilts his head toward his pickup truck parked in the drive. "C'mon. Let's go."

Flashing a bright smile, I let him draw me into his chest.

It's the best kind of feeling. That I'm wanted.

"Taking off in the middle of the workday?" I palm his bearded cheek. "You surprise me more and more each day, Cowboy."

His steel-blue eyes blaze. "Ruby Bloom, I could say the same thing about you." He kisses the tip of my nose. "Let's go live it up."

19

Charlie

"I LIKE THIS BAR," RUBY SAYS, HER EAGER EYES glowing as she drops onto a stool at the high-top table.

I settle beside her. "Better than Nowhere?"

She gives a mock gasp before a teasing smile appears on her pretty face. "I don't know. Will there be another handsome cowboy carrying me out of here tonight?"

Something sharp stabs me in the chest at the thought of Ruby in another man's arms. "If you want to start another bar fight, sure."

She props her chin in her palm and smiles. "Maybe I will, Cowboy."

When she calls me "cowboy," it's like throwing an accelerant on my heart.

After a full day of showing Ruby around Resurrection—with a better attitude than I had the first time—I've taken her to the Neon Grizzly on Main Street. Though the bar is loud, it's honky-tonk-lite, catering to a mix of tourists and locals. Muted TVs play country music videos, while servers wearing mechanic aprons fight their way through the crowd. It's safer here. No fistfights.

What isn't safe is what I've just done. Without meaning to, I've taken Ruby on a goddamn date.

All I could think about earlier today was seeing her. Helping her with her to-do list. Apologizing for scaring the shit out of her. Plus, I won't lie. It feels great to take a break from the ranch, even for a night. I needed a day out, and she was the perfect person to distract me.

Only she's not a distraction. She's Ruby. The girl who twists me up inside every time I glimpse her gorgeous face.

It's been a long time since I haven't let the ranch fill my days with work from sunup to sundown. I'm busy, but these days, I'm never too busy for Ruby.

My stomach clenches as my eyes settle on her delicate profile. Her rose-gold hair's wild around her. The purple strap of her sundress has slipped off her shoulder. She's crossed her legs, causing the hem of her sundress to ride high, exposing the smooth underside of her thigh.

I scrub a hand over my beard, glancing down at my dirty blue-jean shirt and muddy boots. Damn if I don't feel like a peasant sitting next to a princess. "I should have cleaned up," I grumble.

"No," she squeaks and then bites her lip. "I like you better like this."

"How's that?"

"Dirty." A pink flush stains her cheeks. Damn, she looks cute.

The waitress appears, flapping an impatient hand. "Drinks?"

"You pick," I tell Ruby. "It's your night."

She gasps. "How is that fair? You finally took a day off in what? A millennium?"

I smile at the truth of her words. "Something like that."

"My night, huh?" Uncertainty fogs her face as her eyes scan the chalkboard menu. "How about . . . a whisky pickleback shot and two beers."

The waitress disappears.

I drum my hands on the table. "Now you're speaking my language."

"What? Rough and rowdy? Or grumpy and glowering?"

I laugh. Caught off guard by the sound, Ruby and I both jump.

Jesus. When was the last time I laughed like that?

"See . . ." she says, her small hand fanning out to cup my jaw. "You can laugh."

I roll my eyes, fight my ever-widening smile. "Yeah, well, don't get used to it."

"Oh, I am very used to it, Cowboy. No take backs. You must now smile at me at least two percent of the time."

Well aware the whole damn town has its eyes on us, I grunt. It's instinctual, the way I reach for her, the way I need her. I pull her stool closer, wanting her next to me so I can inhale her strawberry scent and bask in her sunshine glow. I can't keep my hands off her. I'd fight the world for just her smile. There's something about Ruby that calms the strife and the bullshit inside of me.

She's different from what I'm used to. From what I thought I wanted or needed. I try not to compare women to Maggie. Especially not Ruby. They are completely different species. Maggie was like a storm cloud, and Ruby's a gentle breeze. But the one thing they have in common is their hearts.

I might be made of gravel, but Ruby—she's made of gold.

Ruby spears me with her big blue eyes. "I've never been in a bar before. Not like this."

Screws tighten in my chest. The more she talks, the more it sounds like she's lived in a tower her entire life. It doesn't sit right with me. But before I can ask, she leans in and whispers, conspiratorially, "So, what do we do?"

I chuckle. "We drink. We people watch. And then we dance." I point at the band, which is just one guy in suspenders and a top hat, setting up his guitar and an amp. "That's Marvin. He swears aliens abduct his cows every Tuesday, but he can play a mean cover of 'All Along the Watchtower,' so we refrain from tarring and feathering him in the square."

Giggling, she claps her hands together in delight. Right on time, the drinks arrive. "Like I said, I love this bar."

"Yeah, well, just wait for him to bust out his Irish jig." I lift my shot. "Cheers, baby."

"Cheers."

Ruby takes the shot. I hide a smile at the way her eyes fly open. "Wow," she breathes. "That's strong."

"Hey, check it out." I point at a muted TV and Ruby's eyes follow. On screen, Grady, wheeling a guitar, stars in his first music video. "That's my little brother."

She flashes me a grin. "Another brother?"

I take a swig of my beer. "Yup."

"Big family," she muses, tapping a nail on the table.

"Getting bigger by the second." I pull out my phone and show her the photo of my nieces. "My baby sister just had twins. Cora and Daisy."

"Oh, Charlie," Ruby says, her eyes lighting up as she swipes through the photos. "They're beautiful."

Pride swells in my chest. "They are. Need to make it down to Nashville one of these days."

Ruby's gaze flicks to my face, assessing. "You like kids?"

"Yeah." I clear my throat, the admission like a switchblade in my gut. "I do. I love kids."

As one of six, I want the mess and chaos that comes with a big family. Whatever the world threw my way, I had my siblings. No dull moments, lots of laughter, love. Family rests at the core of who I am as a man. It's everything that's important, that matters in this world.

When I glance over, I see Ruby's lost in thought, her light dimmed.

I don't like it. Reaching over, I smooth a hand down her bare arm, wanting to make her happy. "You all right?"

"I'm fine," she says on an exhale. She takes a sip of her beer and shrugs a slender shoulder. "Just . . .taking it all in."

So that's what I do too.

From my seat, I can see the entire bar. Couples two-step across the dancefloor, and there's a group of cowboys playing darts. Tina, off tonight, sits with her husband at the bar. An unfamiliar group of city kids, wearing backward baseball hats and polos, pound shots at a horseshoe booth.

That's when I see Wyatt and a woman with a mass of blue-black curls, her lips red as a crime scene.

He's at a corner table cozying up to Sheena Wolfington, My brother nods at me, but returns his attention to Sheena, wrapping an arm around her and pulling her close.

Sheena, a stylist at the House of Hair, has tried to work her way through us since we came to town. But we've all been smart enough to leave her alone.

Until now.

What the hell is Wyatt doing?

Sheena's trouble. Stilettoed, murderous, cold-blooded trouble.

I swear when I spy Fallon. She floats through the room like a shark, eyes narrowed, her slender body tense as a rod.

"Fuck," I mutter.

Talk about the triangle of doom.

"Charlie?" Ruby's soft voice calls me back. "What is it?"

"Nothin'," I say, not wanting her to worry over Wyatt's bullshit.

The faint strum of guitar strings catches my attention. Marvin's butchering an old Alan Jackson song.

Fuck this. Fuck worrying about Wyatt. Fuck work.

Time to get this girl in my arms.

I slip Ruby's hand into mine. "You wanna dance?" I ask, lifting a brow. "Check off that to-do list?"

I'm rewarded with a smile brighter than a hundred suns. "Yeah. I'd love to." Her adorable nose scrunches. "I just don't know how—"

"I got you."

Before she can slide off her stool, I pick her up by the waist and set her next to me, my hand on the small of her back. She gasps when I whirl her into a spin.

Montgomery men aren't shy about knowing their way around a dance floor. It's what we were raised on—country music, two-stepping, and honky-tonks. Dancing gets your boot in doors, gets beautiful women in your arms, and right now, I'm a happy man.

"Scoot your boots, baby," I drawl, locking my hand to hers.

Ruby laughs and hangs onto me. She's light in my arms

as I bring her into an easy two-step that she soon gets the hang of.

One song turns to two turns to three.

We cut our own private square on the dance floor, burning it up like wildfire. Tightening my hold on her, I keep her close, careful to keep her away from other idiots on the dance floor. Some asshole knocking into Ruby isn't happening.

"Charlie," she breathes, her smiling growing. "You're going to spin me out of my shoes."

I grin down at her.

The hem of her sundress flares up, and in that moment, I know God invented dance floors just so he could watch Ruby twirl in a skirt.

"That's how you know you're doing it right," I murmur against her lips.

I hold her tight to my chest, pushing her into my body, wanting all of her against me. She giggles as I give her a twirl and rest a palm on her ass. Taking her hand again, I spin her out. When she comes back into me, I dip her low, tipping her head back until her hair meets the floor. Her lithe frame snaps back up, and all I can do is marvel. She's gorgeous as hell, with her messy hair and flushed cheeks, all carefree and wild and blooming.

But then Ruby's pulling away, her eyes wide and fearful. "Oh," she gasps. "I need to stop, Charlie."

Before I can grasp what's happening, she tears out of my arms and grabs our table, rocking our second round of drinks. Beer sloshes over the sides of the glasses.

I don't think. I just move.

I'm by her side instantly.

"Ruby?" I glance down, scanning her for injuries. "Darlin', you okay?"

With a flinch, she doubles over. Her eyes fall shut, her knuckles white as they clench the tabletop. "I'm fine. I got dizzy for a second."

"You're not fine," I say gruffly, unsettled by her pale face. Her breathing's shallow, and she looks like she's going to faint.

A feeling I haven't felt in years rises within me. Care. *Fuck. I care about her.*

I wrap an arm around her waist, glancing around for the back door. "We're going. Right now."

"No!" She straightens up and I brace her against me. "No way. We're not leaving." Her laugh is shaky. "I don't do this a lot. Drink. Dance. I just need to catch my breath."

"Don't argue with me."

"I'm not. I'm convincing you."

"Are you sure?" I study her, dangerously close to tossing her over my shoulder and hauling her out of the bar. She can argue with me all she wants back at my place.

"It's my night, Cowboy." Stubbornness flashes in her big blue eyes, and some of my worry ebbs. "I'm having fun. I don't want to leave." She slides a hand up my chest and my entire body locks at her calming touch. "Please, Charlie, let's—"

A hard crack cuts off her words. Instinct has me stepping in front of her, shielding her with my body.

The bar falls silent.

That's when I see Fallon's palm tear away from Wyatt's face. His left cheek flames bright red as they glare at each other. Then, Fallon mouths something that looks like *fuck you* and storms out the back door.

I frown, noticing the way Wyatt half-rises to go after her, but Sheena tugs him back down beside her.

"Jesus," I growl.

This will be all over Resurrection. In a town this small, gossip spreads like wildfire.

"What's happening?" Ruby whispers. She grips my shoulder, standing on tiptoes to see better.

Dragging a hand down my face, I turn to her. "I take back what I said about Wyatt. He is an idiot."

"I should talk to her." Ruby gives my arm a squeeze before looping her purse around her chest and rushing to follow Fallon outside.

I shoot my dumbass brother a glare as Sheena coos over him.

I'm pissed. Really fucking pissed. Wyatt's gone too far with Fallon. Whatever he's doing, my brother needs to learn not to fuck with a good woman's heart.

I glance at the back door where Ruby disappeared and wonder if I should take my own damn advice.

I wonder if it's already too late.

20

Ruby

I TAKE A DEEP BREATH AND APPROACH FALLON. SHE'S standing next to the dumpster in the alley, smoking. Up close, she looks pissed off and violent. A small silver scar runs down her jaw, her caramel and chestnut hair falls to the middle of her back. The cut-off shorts she wears show her colorful rodeo tattoos that extend up her hips, accentuating her lean, muscular thighs.

Though we've had run-ins, I'm not sure if she'll be receptive to me lending an ear. Truth is, I admire Fallon. Envy her. Her tattoos and her horses and her freedom. She's unsheltered and fierce and doesn't have a ticking time bomb in her chest.

Fallon ashes her smoke when she sees me. "Shit. Don't tell my dad."

I smile. "Secret's safe with me."

She hums and takes a long drag on the cigarette. Smoke curls in the air between us.

"I'm sorry," I say, thinking of that woman in the booth, stroking her blood-red fingernails down Wyatt's arm. If it were Charlie, I'd pick up my shot glass and hurl it at his head. "About Wyatt."

Fallon offers a one-shoulder shrug. The blazing anger in her eyes is the only telltale sign she's hurt. "There is no Wyatt," she drawls with a vigorous shake of her head. "He is an absolute clown shoe I plan to stay far, far away from."

Not speaking, we stare into the darkened alleyway. Stars sparkle in the inky night sky. There's enough moonlight to see the graffitied brick walls and beer cans trashed on the ground. The scent of pine and summer hangs in the air. A cool breeze dries the sweat on my brow and I inhale deep, breathing it in.

I'm glad for the break after what happened back in the bar, courtesy of the shots and the fast dancing. I press a hand to my still-thundering heart, willing it to return to a normal heartbeat. One that won't have me passing out on the dance floor.

The thought is like a taser to my emotions, bringing me down. Tonight is an awful reminder about the truth of my situation. My condition.

I close my eyes.

I'm lying to Charlie.

My heart isn't fine, will never be fine.

Charlie wants kids. Something I can never give him because of my heart.

I shake my head, angry at myself for even entertaining the thought. It doesn't matter. We're not there and never will be.

In eight weeks, I'm leaving.

A crunch of rock and dirt sounds as Fallon tosses her cigarette on the ground and grinds the ember out with her boot. "So. How goes the dance floor with Charlie Montgomery? You two looked good out there."

"It's fun. Summer fun," I amend, not sure why I'm trying to clarify it. Maybe because denial's easier when you say it out loud. When you allow other people to hear it and give it life.

She considers this, her hazel eyes flittering. "Do you like it here? In Resurrection?"

"I do. I love it."

"But not enough to stay?"

I hesitate, debating on saying more, saying everything. "No. I can't."

"You're lucky," she says, longing seeping into her husky voice. "You can leave whenever you want."

But I don't want to leave.

This town feels like mine. I feel like I belong. The air's different here. My heart's different here, like it pumps harder for the sheer reason of being on Runaway Ranch.

I thought I could do this. I thought it'd be easy. Make some money. Help some ranchers. Have good sex with the grumpy cowboy and then fly the coop.

No strings.

And yet . . .

Charlie still wears my ribbon on his wrist.

What does that mean?

Nothing.

It has to mean absolutely nothing.

"What's it like?" I ask Fallon. "To ride?"

Her hard eyes soften. For a few seconds, she's quiet. When she speaks up, her expression is ethereal, dreamy. "It makes me crazy, but it makes me live." Passion laces her voice. "I would *die* for it. I would die if I could never do it again." Arching a brow, her gaze lands on me. "I'm well aware those two things are mutually exclusive."

A shiver runs over me. I feel the same way.

"You've never ridden a horse?"

"No. Charlie won't let me." I take a step forward, looking up at the darkened brothel bathed in moonlight. Knowing a good photo op for Runaway Ranch's Instagram account when I see it, I take out my phone and switch it into night-mode. I look at Fallon. "They're his horses, you know. I can't just steal one."

Fallon smirks. "Well, technically, you could . . ."

Just talking about Charlie makes my heart squeeze. A smile tips my lips as I think back to the growling man I first met at Nowhere. A cowboy I pegged as cold and unsmiling. But I was wrong. There's been so many small moments where his tender actions have chiseled away at the man I assumed I knew. Charlie bringing me flowers, taking me dancing, wearing my ribbons around his wrist . . .and the sex. The sex isn't just good—it's spectacular.

Heart changing.

Charlie's hard shell is a shield to keep out the things that hurt him.

I'm doing the same thing. By not telling Charlie about my heart, I'm keeping him at arm's length.

"He's got his reasons," Fallon says, and I wonder at the hesitation that crosses her face. "Charlie's a good guy. I've known him ten years now, and he's . . .intense, yeah. But I've also never seen him with that look in his eye."

It doesn't matter how he looks at me, I want to tell her. Even so, my heart hammers and I can't help but ask, "And what look is that?"

Fallon smiles. "Like you own every single atom in his body."

At her words, my breath catches in my throat.

"Oh," I manage weakly and raise my phone to take pictures of the brothel, trying to chase away the desperate feeling swelling inside of me.

Before I can snap a photo, laughter rings out above us. I freeze, my eyes darting to Fallon, who shrugs. Footsteps clang on the wrought-iron patina balcony of the brothel. A man and woman come into view through the slats. They're hard to make out, but the woman has long auburn hair and a husky laugh. The man's tall with silver hair and a thin, fox-like face.

There's a rustle of fabric, the jingle of a belt, the drop of pants. Like a snake, the belt curls through the slats, the gleaming belt buckle catching the moonlight. And then the woman's sinking to her knees and opening her mouth.

"Holy shit," Fallon says. "Peep show time."

"I thought it was a museum," I whisper, tilting my head all the way back to look up. Moans cut the cool night air.

Fallon's face is rapt. "Looks like it still operates after-hours."

Curiosity has me positioning myself to see better. "Do you know who they are?"

"No." She squints. "Can't see." Her sharp elbow digs into my side and I smother a yelp with my hand. "Get a photo. We can zoom in."

I stare at her in open admiration. "Why?"

"Because I'm fucking curious, that's why." She gives me a push forward. "You fuck on open balconies in my town, you don't deserve privacy."

She has a good point.

"C'mon, Ruby," she says and grins at me. "Live a little."

Keyword: live.

Adrenaline and excitement have me angling the camera at the mysterious couple.

And then I do it.

I snap a photo.

Snickering, Fallon grabs me and drags me back into the shadows. "Wild little rebel," she hisses, pride resonating in her voice.

I stare at Fallon's arm looped through mine, her tight grip, her beautifully long fingers adorned with turquoise rings. And I have never felt such a rush of friendship, of cahoots, of safety in my life.

Movement comes from above us, the scrape of the belt as it's retrieved, and then the laughter and voices disappear as the door slams shut.

Silence strings through the alleyway.

I zoom in on the photo as Fallon stares over my shoulder. "You know him?" I ask.

"Nope." She seems disappointed. "Well, it's been a trip." Fallon takes a step into the alleyway. "Baring souls. Catching strangers in clandestine affairs. We should do it more often." She gives a one-shouldered shrug. In the shadows and the moonlight, she looks like some wraithlike cowgirl ready to wreak vengeance. "I'm headed home. Go back to your man, Ruby."

"He's not my man," I insist, even though her words send a curl of warmth through me.

Her grin's a flash of amusement. "Whatever you say."

I watch her stroll off into the night. Then I laugh and shake my head.

I think we're both liars.

Still musing on Fallon's words, I walk down the gloomy hallway to the mouth of the bar.

When I turn the corner, a boy steps into my space, barring me from entering the dance floor. He wears a pink polo and a backward cap and is as out of place in this honky-tonk as I was in Nowhere. With a raised brow, he gives me a head-to-toe sweep that makes me feel slimy.

"Excuse me." I try to push past him. By now, there's a large crowd on the sawdust dance floor. Charlie must be caught up somewhere in the mass of people.

He forces me back into the hallway and puts his hands on my waist. "We're dancing tonight." His voice is slurred with alcohol.

I draw up my shoulders and stand taller, hoping to look intimidating. "I don't want to dance. Not with you."

He lets out a short laugh. "First time? Don't worry. I'll take care of you, pretty girl."

My throat bobs, fear prickling my spine. I'd take nasty comments on Instagram any day, instead of the nasty boy leering in front of me.

He crowds my space and my heart speeds up. I don't like it. He's not Charlie. He's not my Cowboy.

"Let go of me." I give him a shove, but he blocks me in again.

"You heard her. Step the fuck away. Now."

Charlie's rough voice has my heart bottoming out.

Polo snorts. "Fuck you, dude—"

Before he can say more, a massive hand's darting out and grabbing the guy by the back of the neck to yank him away from me. Polo's tossed into the wall like he's nothing more than a bag of trash.

"You okay?" Charlie asks, taking his place beside me, but his eyes stay fixed on Polo. Charlie's fists are clenched, his muscled body locked and loaded.

It's obvious if I weren't here, Charlie would pummel Polo right now.

"Yeah," I breathe, frozen by the man in front of me. Drawn to his dangerousness.

"Fuck you, bro."

Not taking the hint or the death rays emanating from Charlie's eyes, Polo takes a step forward, but Charlie props a hand on his chest.

"Bad idea," he snarls.

Polo's eyes land on the ribbon on Charlie's wrist. My ribbon. "What's this big guy? Feeling pretty tonight?"

The second he tugs on the end of the ribbon to untie it from Charlie's wrist, Charlie grabs his arm. Twists.

Ice skitters down my spine at the way Charlie's eyes turn feral.

"Ow, fuck, man!" Beads of sweat stream down Polo's face. "I was just playing."

Face tight, dangerous, Charlie growls, "Touch that, touch her, I'll rip your arm off your fucking body."

The air sharpens with fear and Polo tries to take a step back.

But Charlie holds tight. Steps forward. "I'll say this one time. When a woman says no, she means no. Do I make myself clear?"

Polo gulps air. "Yes, sir."

"Get the fuck out of here," Charlie snaps. With a grunt, he shoves Polo out of the hall and onto the dance floor.

Then he whistles, and the crowd comes alive. Locals pull Polo toward the exit, pouring beer on him as they send him out on his ass.

"You planning to fight over me, Cowboy?" I ask, slowly sidling toward him, drawn by some magnetic sensation.

I hate how badly I want to be back in his arms. Charlie looks so handsome. In his faded blue jeans, soft denim shirt shoved up to the elbows, worn boots, and shiny brass belt buckle, he's the epitome of a man. Everything about him, I crave. A real cowboy who loves the earth and his animals and works with his hands.

Already, I want him.

"Damn right I will." He advances, his dark eyes swirling with protectiveness and lust. He hauls me to his chest, his rough, cut muscles tightening as he tips my chin to meet his searing gaze. "Seein' someone else touch you, Ruby, drives me fucking crazy."

In one swift movement, my lips are on his. I moan, running my fingers through his dark hair. The kiss turns urgent, desperate, and every inch of my skin heats. I feel the familiar quickening of my pulse, reveling in it. Only Charlie can do this to me.

I whimper when we break apart, grabbing the front of his shirt.

His intense gaze is still pinned on my face. Then, a sexy half-grin tips his lips. "What can I say, darlin'? Tourists."

I smile up at him. "Easy, Cowboy. That was me four weeks ago."

"Not anymore," he says. "Haven't you heard? You're a local, Ruby." Tipping my chin up, he sweeps the pad of his thumb across my bottom lip. "At least to me."

I flush and arch a brow. "That's not what you said the night we met."

"I was wrong," he says, and this honest admission, the gruff softness, has my heart beating wildly. "C'mon." He places a protective hand on my waist, monitoring my footing, safely guiding me back into the bar. *I'll always protect you*, his touch tells me. *I'll always have you.* "Dance floor missed you."

I missed you.

"You okay?" he asks as he pulls me into a slow dance. Marvin sings a slowed-down melancholy version of Nitty Gritty Dirt Band's "Fishing in the Dark."

I look up at him with heavy eyes. "Better now."

"Fallon okay?"

"She went home. But I think she's okay. How's Wyatt?"

"Don't worry about Wyatt."

My gaze flicks to the ribbon on his wrist. "How long you plan to wear that ribbon, Cowboy?"

"As long as you want me to."

"Oh," I breathe softly.

My heart races. Fire licks the air between us.

His raw statement turns my legs to jelly, has my heart skipping every beat in the medical book.

I don't know what his response means, I just know it feels like too much.

Too big.

Like it could break both of our hearts.

I lay my head on his chest and listen to his heartbeat. It's so beautiful. So healthy.

I inhale strongly. He doesn't smell like rich cologne. He smells like a hardworking man, like a cowboy, like dirt and sunshine and life.

Out here on this dance floor, we don't feel so temporary. He holds me close, like I belong to him.

Worse, I don't know if I want temporary anymore. I said I'd leave my head in charge, but it's my reckless heart taking over.

Charlie's making it easy to fall. I hope he doesn't know that.

I hope he doesn't follow me down.

When the song stops, so does Charlie. His eyes meet mine. "What's next?"

I drink in his handsome face, the hard line of his set jaw. "More drinks, more dancing, more *you*."

Charlie swallows, and then he smiles. It's the biggest, brightest one I've seen yet from him, and my entire body melts. "You got it, baby."

He leans in and kisses me, and I can't stop kissing him back.

And then I'm not thinking about how not to fall in love because I'm throwing my arms around his neck and jumping into his arms.

Live every moment with Charlie Montgomery.

Live like it's my last.

21

Charlie

"I THINK I'M BUZZED," RUBY GASPS. WIDE-EYED delight shines on her pretty face as she wobbles on her bare feet.

Crossing my bedroom floor, I grin and pull her against me. "Baby, I think you're drunk." Wiggly and giggly, she's the cutest lightweight I've ever seen.

"What're we doing now?" she asks.

"Sunrise, remember?"

Three shots, two beers later, several spins around the dance floor, we closed the Neon Grizzly down and came back to my place.

"But that's not for hours." She stands on tiptoes, slides a hand up my chest, nips at my throat. My resolve weakens, and my cock swells in my jeans.

I brought her back to my place because I didn't want her to be alone and drunk. I didn't bring her back to get laid.

"What until then?" she breathes. The heat from her core radiates off her in waves.

I frame her face and frown down at her. "You had some drinks. If you're not okay with this . . ."

She bats long lashes at me and giggles, a melodic lilt that has my arousal spiking. "I may be buzzed, but I am very, very okay with this."

"You sure?" I warn roughly. "I don't want you doing anything you're not up for."

"Cowboy, stop talking and kiss me," she says, right before crushing her mouth to mine.

Every ounce of blood in my brain, every protest, drains down into my cock.

I pull back. "That dress needs to come off."

She pretends to pout, her smoky-shadowed eyes fluttering. "You don't like my dresses?"

"I love 'em, baby." I give her a grin. I like this side of Ruby. Playful, flirty, sweet. Every side of her I see, she keeps getting better and better. "I just love 'em better on my floor."

"Cowboy laying down the law." A hint of a smile plays on her lips. She shimmies, lifting the hem of her dress to flash a peek of creamy white thigh. Purple panties. The apex of her sex.

My cock flexes at the teasing tone in her voice. Any willpower I had to go slow flies out the window. I don't want to wait. I press her back up against the wall and grab her ass.

"Fuck, baby," I growl, burying my face in her neck as I drag off her panties.

Her back arches, and her breasts plump against the heart-shaped bodice of her dress. She whines and tears at my shirt, running her small hands over my body. Greedy. I goddamn love it.

I yank her sweet pussy against my thigh. She grinds against it, soaking through my jeans, and I fucking lose it.

With a growl, I tug the front of her delicate dress down, exposing her bare breasts and perky pink nipples. With both hands at her waist, I lean low, sucking in the creamy white swell of her breast, letting my tongue tease her nipples, whipping them to hard peaks.

A delirious cry escapes Ruby. She shudders and tilts her head back, her eyes fluttering, lips parted.

Arousal glistens on the inside of her thighs. I run my palm through the slick moisture, then dip my fingers inside of her. Teasing. Toying.

She lets out a low moan, her nails digging into the meat of my shoulder. "Charlie . . ."

She's tight, wet, hot.

Mine.

No one's ever going to have another chance with this girl. Never. Seeing her tonight with another man damn near ruined me. I had to restrain myself from killing the guy, because if I go to prison, not only can I not run my ranch, it means I can't fuck Ruby. And that'd be a goddamn shame.

With that thought, I slide my hands up her body, taking her dress with me, stripping her bare.

I cup her supple ass and lift her up. She hooks her legs around my waist I capture her mouth, inhaling every kiss, every ounce of air she blesses me with.

I want more of her.

I need to taste her.

Because this girl's my favorite fucking flavor.

Setting her on her feet, I lean in. "Stay," I order.

"Yes," she breathes.

"Good girl."

Her bedroom eyes have me on my knees so fast I get whiplash.

I spread her legs, then, hands gripping her waist, pin her back against the wall. I lick the inside of her thighs, lapping the slick trails of arousal like a lovesick puppy dog. Because it's true, I'm a fucking famished man.

I push her legs farther apart, eating her sweet pussy out so deep heaven could be on the other side.

Ruby slumps against the wall, body shuddering, thighs trembling around my ears, her eyes squeezed shut in ecstasy. Her pussy flexes against my mouth and I let out some strangled sound.

Christ, she tastes like strawberries. How is this fucking possible? Once again confirming my suspicions she's a literal angel.

Pulling back, I trail a finger in her damp folds and she sucks in a breath. I put my lips to her clit and suck.

She gasps. "Charlie . . . I can't . . . I . . ."

I growl, loving the sensation of her tugging at my hair. Changing it up, I lick the bead of her clit, press my mouth hard against it, and rotate my tongue. Any way I can devour this slick, sexy pussy, any way I can keep my girl satisfied is my end goal in life. I take her ass in my hands and jerk her forward, riding her on top of my tongue.

"Oh god. Yes. Yes." Ruby's lower body lurches, her thighs tremor uncontrollably and then she screams. Her orgasm moves over her like a wave and I can feel her flesh swell and plump.

With a soft mewl, her eyes glaze over and she goes limp, sliding down the wall with buckled knees.

I stand and gather her close. When I pull her against my chest, I freeze.

"Jesus." I laugh without humor and place a hand over the channel of her breast. "Your heart's racing." It feels unnatural, overly fast.

Her head falls back as she looks up at me. She inhales a shaky breath, her eyes going momentarily sad. "Because of you, Charlie." She lays her hand over mine and keeps it against her heart. "You see what you do to me?"

"What I do to you?" I growl. "Baby, you got me on my goddamn knees just for a taste of you."

She smiles.

I kiss her mouth, her tongue diving deep inside of mine. When I pull back, her face is flushed. She sways in my arms and I hook an arm around her waist to keep her steady.

"Fuck, baby, you good?" I rasp the question, winded.

Not done.

She looks at me and grins. Then she says the most beautiful word in the English language. "More."

I lift her, she's featherlight in my arms, and set her on the edge of the bed.

"Shit," I swear, searching the nightstand drawer. My balls are heavier than lead. "I'm out of condoms."

"I'm clean. I'm on birth control. I've barely been with anyone except you," she whispers. Her eyes meet mine, not a trace of doubt on her face. "I trust you, Charlie."

Trust.

It sends a fireball up inside of my chest, has my cock surging.

Fucking Ruby bare. Taking care of her. Giving her what she wants.

Jesus, I don't stand a fucking chance.

I'm on the bed fast, growling with approval, grabbing her to me. "I'm clean too."

"I need you, Charlie," she whimpers. Her body arches toward me, pushing those sweet breasts against my chest. "Tonight, fuck me fast."

"Are you sure?" I ask, looking her in the eye.

I've always gone slow like she's asked. But with her permission, I can't wait to ride that perfect pussy hard and fast.

"So damn sure."

My pants are off. I pin her body to the bed.

At the rough contact, she gasps.

"Fuck," I moan as I slip into her slick pussy. She's so wet she draws me inside without a fight. "I'm gonna make you fucking shake, baby. Spread those legs."

She does, and I burrow deeper. "Christ," I growl through gritted teeth. "Every inch of me fits you perfectly. Perfection, baby."

Whimpering, she spreads her legs and arches her back, her fingers twisting in the sheets. A slow, innocent smile spreads across her face. "I love it. I love it, Charlie."

I'm ruined.

Absolutely wrecked.

"Faster," she whines, writhing like some magical creature, beautiful and reckless. "Faster."

"You sure?"

"Yes, *yes*."

This time, I pump ruthlessly, ramming my hips, driving my cock into her slick, hot channel. Hard thrusts that have her body tensing. The way she sucks me in, the way she pulses around me and keeps me there has me losing my mind.

I need to go deeper.

She gasps, her small body trembling beneath me. "Oh. *Ohhhh*," she pants, her breath turning erratic.

"Fuck, you break me, Ruby," I grunt, thrusting deeper than ever, my balls so goddamn heavy as my peak grows closer.

I never want to let her go. Never felt anything like this before. She's small and warm and perfect, stripping me of my control so easily I can't even fight it. The way she fits me, Jesus, I'm a desperate goddamn man.

Blood pounding in my temples, I glue my mouth to hers and I pump hard. I pump fast. Our heartbeats thunder.

"Fuck, baby, I'm gonna come," I gruff into the nape of her neck. The bedsprings squeak wildly. Our bodies connect with unleashed fury. Every slam of my body against hers drives her tiny form several inches up the mattress.

"Charlie," Ruby pants, digging her nails into my back. Her eyes lose focus, sweat beads her brow. Then she trembles, bucking violently, as her orgasm crashes over her. Her melodic voice is a chant on high.

"Oh my god. Oh my god, Charlie . . . *Charlie* . . . yes—"

I snap.

With one last thrust, I drive my cock hard into her. Her walls clench around me, keeping me there, and the second I feel Ruby's slender arm on my back, feel her going limp beneath me, it pushes me past my breaking point. I come as fast as quicksilver, bellowing my release.

Panting, I collapse on top of her, burying my face against her neck, breathing in the strawberry scent of her skin. "You fucking wrecked me, baby."

Silence.

My frame locks. Fuck. If I was too rough with her, I'll never forgive myself. Kissing her bare shoulder, I push up.

Ruby lies there, eyes closed, lips parted. Hair spread out like a blanket of gold.

"Ruby, you okay?" I rasp, but her body remains limp on the bed, unmoving.

Panic twists in my chest like a knife.

"Baby, you need to open your eyes," I order roughly, pulling her into my arms and cradling her head in my palm.

She doesn't respond.

I can't think. Can't breathe.

The world around me tilts and blurs, but before I can lose my mind, a whimper slips from her mouth. When her blue eyes flutter open, my chest caves in with relief.

"Hi," she whispers.

Sweeping my finger under her chin, I make her look at me, checking her eyes. Glassy, but they're alert. "You passed out." It's a statement, not a question, because that's what happened.

"I got dizzy," she admits, her voice groggy. "I drank too much. I shouldn't have."

Guilt sideswipes me. I should have paid better attention.

"Come here, baby," I whisper, gathering her tiny frame against my chest.

Bouncing back and forth between panic and worry, I climb off the bed and reposition Ruby back on it, setting her down gently into the pillows.

"I just need a second." She gives me a weak smile, rubbing a slow circle on her chest. My stomach churns at her ghost-white pallor. "You wore me out."

"Stay here." Kissing her temple gently, I take off to grab a towel from the bathroom.

"You don't have to do that," Ruby says when I return and wipe the mess off her legs.

I toss the towel in the hamper and sit beside her. "Yeah, I do." I keep my eyes on her face. "You scared the hell outta me."

"I'm okay, Charlie," she assures me. With a small smile, she slides off the edge of the bed to collect her dress. Her movements are slow, unsteady.

"Where are you going?" I snag her hand. Soft. Warm. My heart clenches.

"Back to my cottage."

"Not tonight."

Shaking her head, she sighs, and my gaze latches onto the way she holds my bedframe as if to stay steady. "Charlie. We don't do this."

"Yeah, well, we do tonight. Sunrise, remember?"

Her lips flatten. A universal gesture that tells me she's planning to argue with me.

I sigh, frustrated.

I don't like it. I don't like the fact she's leaving in the middle of the night. And I don't like the fact she drank so much she passed out in my arms. Worse, I don't like the fact that I'm close to getting on my knees to beg her to stay.

She looks exhausted and fragile, and I want her to sleep. I want to keep her here and know she's safe and okay and not fucking worry about her.

I want to protect her.

I sweep a thumb over the inside of her wrist. "Stay. I want you to."

Her eyes go dreamy. "Okay."

I don't give her a chance to reconsider. Grasping her wrist, I tug her back toward me and sweep her into my arms. A little gasp slips from her lips. I settle her in bed and climb in beside her. It feels too intimate, her spending the night, but I don't give a shit. I've wanted this—craved this—since she left the first night and every night after.

Consider this my battle of wills broken.

Consider the rest of the summer fucked. This woman has a stranglehold on me, on my cock, my head and my heart. There's no one like her.

With a little sigh, Ruby snuggles against me, placing her head between my collar and chest. I wrap her naked body in my arms. Her heart's pounding like she's run a marathon double time.

"Sunflower." The happy whisper pops out of her mouth.

"What's that?" I ask.

"This was my sunflower, today. You."

"Mine too," I admit. The rock in my throat makes it hard to get any more out.

Her glazed eyes find mine. "Really?"

"Really." I kiss her temple. "Ruby?"

"Hmm."

"What's your middle name?"

"Jane. It was my mother's."

"What happened to her?"

She sighs, drowsy. "She died when I was a baby." Her voice is soft, almost slurred.

"How?"

"Health condition."

I glance down at her pale face. When she offers nothing further, we lie in silence, leaving me to stew. What does that mean? Health condition? What kind of health condition? It eats at me and I don't know why.

Because she's stubborn.

Because I care too damn much.

I trace a circle on her arm. "Why are you here, Ruby?"

"Runaway Ranch, Cowboy," she breathes. "Then we'll talk."

She's good, I'll give her that.

It pisses me off.

It scares the ever-loving shit out of me.

Maybe because I find myself wanting to tell her about Runaway Ranch. Maybe because that means I learn more about Ruby. This sweet, gorgeous girl who blows up my heart like an atom bomb.

Or maybe it's because this is the first time I've had a woman spend the night since Maggie. With Ruby in my arms, I don't feel so hollowed out. I don't feel so broken.

I'm in too deep. I'm drowning, but the thought of grabbing a life preserver isn't happening.

Ruby's dreamy voice breaks the silence. Like she's read my mind, she says, "You might not have been prepared for me, Charlie Montgomery, but I've been ready for you."

Her sweet words have me by the throat.

I gather her closer to me. "Sleep, darlin.'"

"We'll miss the sunrise," she murmurs. I feel her yawn and I smile.

"I'll wake you up," I lie. I already know I'm following her down into whatever restless sleep awaits.

Her breathing slows, steadies. I lie beside her, my hand over her thundering heart.

Hard truth is, I can't stay away from Ruby.

Even worse, I don't want to.

22

Charlie

I WAKE WITH A SMALL, WARM BODY NESTLED AGAINST my side.

Ruby.

I turn my face to the balcony, wincing at the bright blast of morning.

A groan tears from my chest.

I'm a man who never sleeps past seven. But this morning, the sun is at an angle I haven't seen in a decade. At least not in my bedroom. Which means I've slept in. Something I never do. In the years since Maggie's been gone, not once have I slept through the night.

My sleep last night—dreamless. Fucking perfect.

I blame the girl in my bed.

A soft sigh sounds from the sheets and Ruby wiggles closer, snaking an arm around my torso. I can feel the soft orbs of her breasts plump against my back and instantly, I'm hard as nails.

Carefully, I roll to face her.

She sleeps with one hand pressed against her chest,

the sheet tangled around her naked body. Her thick rose-gold hair is wild and swirled up around me. A constellation of freckles is scattered across the apples of her cheeks and the bridge of her nose.

I lie here, watching her, waiting for regret to wash over me, for that telltale hollow ache in my chest, but there's nothing. Just Ruby, soft and safe, beside me.

Hands down, last night was the best night I've had in a long damn time.

Unable to help myself, I caress her cheek, and she wakes.

Her long lashes flutter open. Sleepy blue eyes stare back at me. "Hi," she says.

"Mornin'." After a brief second of hesitation, I sweep a kiss to her brow. "How are you feeling?"

After Ruby fainted and her reluctance to stay over, I spent a good hour lying awake next to her, making sure she was okay. She scared the fuck out of me last night. Had ratcheted up the unease in my veins, that slow snap of fear that threatened to choke me.

"I feel great," she says, stretching in the sheets, making a squeak of joy. Then she gasps and sits up. The sheet falls away, giving me a glimpse of her beautiful body. "Charlie, we missed the sunrise."

"Guess that means we'll just have to try again."

A happy glow lights up her face, like I've promised her the moon, and I'm hit with the strange sensation to make her look like that all the time.

A door slams downstairs. The smell of coffee.

"Shit." I shove up in bed and shrug on a pair of jeans. I need to take my own advice and start locking my door. Not like it matters to my brothers. Chimney, underground tunnel, parachute, one way or another, they'd find their way in.

"I need to go deal with my brothers," I tell her.

Ruby sits up, her bare legs drawn up to her chest. With messy hair and flushed cheeks, she looks like a wild forest nymph.

It hits me sudden and sharp.

I want to keep her.

Biting her plump bottom lip, she pulls the sheet up around her. "I should go."

The words are on the tip of my tongue to tell her to stay, ask what she has planned for her day, but I clamp my mouth shut.

It's better this way.

We have lines, we keep them.

Even if after last night, it feels like we redrew every line between us.

I exhale, turning away from her to get my bearings, to find my fucking mind before I lose it.

Sex, good sex.

That's all it is.

I can't go down this road.

Easy to throw caution to the wind last night, but in the bright light of morning, it's dangerous.

I stiffen when Ruby's small hand runs up the curve of my back, her touch like a flame.

"Charlie?" she asks, worry in her voice.

I give a nod and look at her. "Take your time. Use the shower if you want. Make yourself at home."

"Okay." She tucks a lock of hair behind her ear and stretches out her arms.

I allow myself one last eyeful of her pert breasts, then

I shrug on a T-shirt and hustle downstairs. Davis is in the kitchen pouring coffee while Keena noses her way around the room for fresh scents. There's a brown paper bag on the counter from Zeke's Hardware telling me he's been into town.

"Mornin'." I reach into the cupboard for a mug, keeping myself angled toward the cabinets, hoping it hides the fact I'm still sporting wood.

Davis lifts his mug in greeting. The dog tags around his neck catch the sunlight through the window. "Took care of the horses for you."

I pour myself a cup of coffee, trying to fight off the guilt in my chest. "Thanks." My mind should be on the chores I've ignored, instead they're on the girl in my bed.

A smile tugs at the edges of Davis's lips. "Heard you went dancing last night."

"Heard right," I say coolly and take a long sip of coffee. The Resurrection gossip hotline took less than twenty-four hours.

Davis clears his throat. "Playin' hooky looks good on you, C."

I grunt.

Glancing down the hall to the stairs, my brother says, "You got your girl here?"

My girl.

"Yeah. I do." I grit the words out, trying to ignore the way they light up my chest.

Good things don't last. Ruby isn't an exception.

Deciding to let it go, thank fuck, Davis rests his elbows on the island. "Need to talk to you. We got problems."

"With the ranch?" I ask, smearing a hand down my beard.

"No, with Wyatt."

"Saw him last night at the Grizz."

"With Sheena Wolfington?"

"Yeah. Why?" I feel a headache coming on.

"You hear what he did?" When I shake my head, Davis continues. "I saw her in town today. Hair's chopped to her chin. Word's going around town Wyatt's responsible. Sheena says she took him back to her place and when she woke up, he was gone and so was her hair."

The coffee scalds the back of my throat and sears my lungs. I sputter, choke. "The fuck?"

Anger flashes in Davis's eyes. "That's what I'd like to know."

"That ain't Wyatt," I insist fiercely.

Davis considers this. "You think?"

"I know."

I'd stake my life on it. Wyatt's as reckless as the day is long, but him laying hands on a woman like that isn't happening. "Wyatt wouldn't take Sheena to a public place where half the damn town was, if that was his plan."

A muscle jerks in Davis's jaw. "He's on his way over. We'll get to the bottom of it."

I open my mouth to tell him to take it easy on Wyatt, but the sound of soft footsteps stop me.

"Hi," Ruby squeaks, moving fast past me and Davis. Her cheeks are unnaturally pink. "Sorry. I'm just gonna go . . ."

She's fast, but I'm faster.

"Hey." I stop her at the front door, snagging her wrist before she can slink away. For some reason, I don't want her leaving thinking the wrong thing. I pin my eyes on her. "I had fun last night."

A shy smile pulls at her lips. "I had the best time, Charlie." She hesitates, her eyes flicking to Davis, who stands there grinning like a smug son-of-a-bitch, then stands on tiptoes to press a soft kiss to my cheek. "See you later, Cowboy."

I can't help it. I tug her back toward me. "Tonight?"

I don't want to miss a day with her.

Her brilliant blue eyes widen, and she smiles. "Yeah. Okay." Her flirty little grin's enough to have me wanting to toss her over my shoulder and take her back upstairs.

She gives a wave as she goes. I watch her sashay out the door, sundress clinging to her tight little ass like cellophane.

"She's good for you," Davis says when I return to the island.

I know what he means. She's the first woman I've been with where I'm not looking for a ghost.

I toss Keena a bone from the Folger's can. "She's good for a summer."

Davis gives me a *yeah right* look, because he knows I'm a goddamn liar.

Good for a summer.

The words settle in my stomach like a brick. It feels wrong to put Ruby in a box like that. Like she's just another girl.

The door eeks open and Wyatt enters the house, looking like the cat that ate the canary. Just as I'm ready to ask if he needs a fucking neck adjustment because of the way he's staring after Ruby, he turns to me. "How was the date?"

"Wasn't a date," I insist.

Wyatt smirks. "So, you're saying Fairy Tale's gonna fuck you, not date you?"

"Shut up," I snarl. If Wyatt wants me as backup with Davis, he better quit talking while he's ahead.

"I think Charlie is saying it's complicated." Davis crosses his arms, his biceps bulging. "And we're not here to talk about Charlie and this girl he's supposedly not serious about. Even if he is gonna let her go at the end of the summer and end up regretting it for the rest of his life." I roll my eyes, hating my big brother right now. "We're here to talk about you."

"Man." Wyatt exhales and drops his lean frame onto a stool at the island. "What'd I do now?"

Frowning, I search my younger brother's face for guilt, but there's nothing to give him away.

"Sheena Wolfington," Davis announces, in full-on interrogator mode now.

"What about Sheena Wolfington?"

Davis tucks his hands in his pockets, his expression poker-faced. "She was in town this morning telling everyone about how you chopped off that head of hair of hers."

Honest surprise crosses Wyatt's face, and I know he didn't do it.

"What?" Wyatt straightens and looks at me, his eyes wide with shock. "No. I wouldn't fuck her and I definitely wouldn't cut her fucking hair."

"Then why were you out with her?" Davis demands.

Now, Wyatt looks guilty.

"I wasn't trying to get in her pants, I was trying to ..." Embarrassment stains his expression. "I was trying to figure out where the Wolfingtons stashed that colt." The last of the sentence rolls out of his mouth in a drawl of a mumble.

I groan.

"Jesus a horse?" A vein pops in Davis's temple. The universal signal his patience is hanging on by a thread.

Nostrils flaring, Wyatt rips off the stool with a clatter, causing Keena to launch into a series of frenzied barks. I dig my thumb into the throbbing spot between my eyebrows. "It was my horse," he snaps back. "Dad gave me that thoroughbred. I fucking trained that horse. It was mine, and those assholes stole it."

"Calm down," I growl. "Both of you."

Still staring daggers at Davis, Wyatt tears a hand through his hair, twists it. "I thought one last prank. I'd find the horse and take it back. But she wouldn't tell me where it was, and I left."

Davis considers this. "And that's all it was?"

Wyatt presses the heels of his palms in his eyes. His voice comes out pained, muffled. "Why're you fucking breaking my balls, man? I told you I didn't do it." On a sigh, Wyatt lifts his face. Weariness burns bright in his eyes. "You know that isn't me, Davis. Messing with a girl like that . . .never. I didn't touch Sheena. In bed. Or her goddamn hair."

"I believe him," I tell Davis.

Wyatt gives me a look of thanks.

"I believe him too," Davis finally says. "But the town won't." He looks at me, then back at our younger brother. "It's bad. It's still bad, Wy."

Davis is right. It's gone too far now. Even if Wyatt didn't do it, the Wolfingtons think he did it.

Wyatt swallows, chagrined. "What kind of bad?"

Davis looks grim. "The kind that means we better watch our fucking backs."

Worry has me turning my gaze to the large front

window. Has me whipping my eyes to Ruby as she tends to the sunflowers on the front porch of her cottage. The need to go to her, to call her back into my arms, a raging beast inside of me.

And as the clear blue Montana sky stretches out over the ranch, I hope like hell my brother isn't right.

23

Ruby

JULY SCREAMS ITS WAY INTO RESURRECTION WITH celebratory fireworks over Main Street. The Montgomerys host a fourth of July BBQ at the ranch, and it's packed.

Thanks to me.

Runaway Ranch is up to five thousand followers on Instagram. A video I posted of a shirtless Wyatt roping a bronc went viral. A famous bull rider named Jed Jones stopped by for a photo op. The ranch is booked through the end of the season with a thirty-person influencer group Molly put together. There's been no more comments from the *Lassomamav76* account, which means I've held off on telling Charlie about it. He doesn't need more stress in his life.

Still, that doesn't mean I will let it drop. Maybe it's simply she's a scorned guest. Maybe she has a grudge to pick. But why the hell would this woman waste her time giving these cowboys grief? Both Charlie and Davis have reached out to her via social media, offering her a free stay and a chance to make it up to her, but their messages have gone unanswered.

It's a mystery I want to figure out, something that feels important, but I don't know why.

I don't know a lot of things.

Like what I'm doing with Charlie.

Where we'll end up should be obvious. A goodbye at the end of summer. One last kiss before I leave for California. No matter if I want more. No matter that every day I spend at the ranch consists of him and him alone. Every thought, every kiss, is him.

Heaven.

Charlie and I have been using the sunrise as an excuse for me to stay over the last two weeks. Endlessly talking late into the night, then falling asleep, Charlie's strong arm anchoring me to his side. As for the sunrise, we still haven't seen it yet.

We're too busy in bed.

Sex, good sex.

Too good of sex, in fact.

Charlie's need for me has my heart both stuttering and stopping.

I've never felt so alive.

After swallowing down my medication and grabbing a pair of gardening gloves and my phone, I exit my cottage for the front porch.

Between Charlie wearing me out in bed, and my job, I've been a neglectful plant mama. I kneel beside a gigantic bag of potting soil. It's time to replant these beautiful blooms Charlie brought me. They're outgrowing their space and need a refresh.

My hand sinks into the soft soil. The familiar, silky

sensation is as calming as one of Charlie's hugs. I can't help checking the sun in the sky. The lower it gets, the more my heart bounces in anticipation of seeing Charlie.

A bright pop from my phone has me smiling.

I prop it up against the pot and accept the FaceTime call from Max.

"Hi!" I sing cheerfully.

Max's blue eyes narrow. "You're in a good mood."

"I'm always in a good mood," I tell my scowling brother. "I'm planting flowers. Sunflowers." I wave the phone at the bright plants and reposition it. "Charlie brought them for me."

"That's nice of him." My brother sounds suspicious.

"It was." I scoop up dark soil and layer it in the pot. "The ranch is something else, Max. It's beautiful here. If you haven't seen a Montana sky, then you're not living."

"Better than the city?"

"Oh, yes," I agree. "Better than the city."

Much better.

"This farm. Where's it at?"

I snort. "Ranch. And nice try."

At the rumble of an engine, my eyes dart to the road. Coming up the ridge in his pickup truck is Charlie.

My heart rate speeds up, watching as Charlie drives across the ranch. His dusty cowboy hat casts shadows across his strong jaw, the ends of his dark brown hair curling at his nape. One muscled arm hangs out the window of his truck. Face contemplative or scowling, he always looks like he's searching for something out on his ranch. What that is, I don't know.

We've left our secrets in the dust.

"Is that him?" Max's voice crackles. "Are you looking at him?"

I tear my gaze away from Charlie.

I stick my tongue out at Max. "If you must know, yes."

"What's he like?"

"Oh," I breathe. How can I accurately describe the living dream that is Charlie Montgomery? "He's quiet. A cowboy. He's got blue eyes and a dark beard and he's got me doing things I've never done before. And he . . ." I trail off, a furious flush heating my cheeks when I realize I've been rambling.

Max chuckles. "Sounds like quite a cowboy." He narrows his gaze, his smile fading. "He's your boss, right?"

"He is," I say slowly, uncertain where he's going with this.

"Does he know?"

"Know what?"

"Ruby."

"Why are you so involved in my love life?"

"Is that what it is. Love?" There's a bite in my brother's voice.

I flinch. Max may be a thousand miles away, but he'll always be my overprotective big brother who beat the shit out of Kyle Hoke in third grade for calling me Frankenheart. The last thing I need is Max thinking I'm in love.

Love.

I sit back on my heels, tucking a lock of stray hair behind my ears. "No . . . it's . . ."

Once again, my gaze finds Charlie, his truck disappearing over the ridge. I don't know what I'm doing with him. We're blurring lines all over the place and I like it. I love spending all my days and every moment with him. Because when I'm in his bed, his strong arm wrapped around me as he kisses his way down my body, I don't feel so lonely.

I feel free.

If I thought I had any willpower when it comes to a man in jeans, boots, and a cowboy hat, I'm sorely mistaken.

Strike that.

This man.

Are we going too far or is it just far enough?

"So, he doesn't know about your SVT." A statement, not a question.

I turn my attention back to Max. "I haven't told anyone," I admit.

"Rubes. Don't you think someone should know?" Max's voice is a growl of frustration. "You're alone out there on a ranch in the middle of nowhere. What if something happens?"

Shards of glass line my stomach. Max's words have me flashing back to the night after the Neon Grizzly.

We shut the bar down, went wild.

Too wild.

Before I passed out in front of Charlie, I felt it coming, a rush of adrenaline from my orgasm, and then my heart crashed. It was a bad combination—sex, dancing, alcohol—and it backfired.

I can't risk that again. Can't risk Charlie asking questions.

Since that night, slow and steady is the way to go.

"Nothing's happened," I lie, pushing a big hunk of hair out of my eyes. "I still have Zooms with Doctor Lee. I'm taking my medication. I'm okay, Max."

"What about him? This Charlie guy, this cowboy, does he feel the same way you do?"

I sit back on my heels, letting the gardening gloves slide from my hands. This isn't the conversation I want to have with my brother.

Resurrection is my escape, but clearly, I can't run far enough away from my brother's worry.

"Even if you tell him, you'll get hurt. He'll get hurt. You'll both get hurt."

I glare at the screen, ignoring the ache in my heart. "We aren't anything. Besides, he's not in it. I promise you, when I leave, he won't even miss me."

"Ruby." Max sighs. He looks up and waves as the bell chimes. His smile is sad. "Everyone who knows you misses you."

I swallow.

"You can't stay there forever," he reminds me.

"I wasn't planning to."

Liar. The whisper in my head coils around me, has me trying to pretend I haven't been imagining myself living in Resurrection. Having a garden, getting a house, meeting my neighbors, running a flower shop downtown. This town is like a soul revival, and I'll never be the same. I don't have that restless feeling I had back in Indiana, in any of the cities I've stopped at on this road.

Here, with Charlie, it feels like home.

Deliriously so.

Maybe it's my fault.

Maybe I have this misplaced daydream I've had all my life. Positivity. Happiness. Gratitude. Even in the face of death, I'm content to play an idealist, where Max and my father are realists. Alarmists.

Fear doesn't solve anything, and the longer I'm in Resurrection, the more I realize something deep in my heart.

Without fear, you have freedom. Fearlessness. No restraints. Every doubt I've carried my whole life, I've left in the dust here in this wild Montana earth. I've grabbed onto my life with both hands.

Because of Charlie.

And I don't want to give it up.

"There's a study." Max's strained voice has me freezing and my sunny mood comes crashing down like a crumbling wall. "At Stanford University. For SVT. It's new, but it could be something good, Rubes."

I know all about studies. Clinical trials waiting to see what works. Pills to calm the heart. Surgeries to stop syncope. More monitors and more hospitals and more doctors. No, thank you.

"It starts next month."

"I still have two months here, Max."

"It might be too late, Rubes."

His words are like a slap in the face. Hot tears hit my eyes.

All I hear is *Don't, Ruby. Don't hope. Don't dare. Don't live. Don't love.*

I meet Max's gaze on the screen and manage a dry laugh. "Too late, huh? For me or the study?

"Damn it," Max hisses, his face contrite. "I didn't mean it like that." He inhales a hard breath. "Tell me. What's been your sunflower today?"

I sigh and reach for the phone. He's trying to apologize, to change the subject, but I don't have the energy for it. "I don't want to do this, Max."

Suddenly, I hate this game.
I hate my heart.
"Ruby—"
With shaking hands, I end the call.
Maybe Max is right.
Maybe I'm in too deep.
I'm an asshole for lying to Charlie.
I should leave.
A tear slips down my face.
Maybe it doesn't matter anymore.
Maybe all I am is a thorn.

24

Charlie

RUBY'S A GODDAMN BEAUTIFUL SIGHT.

I slow my stride, pausing in the doorway of the stables to take in her tiny, willowy frame. She's at the new pony's stall, a cremello colt that's just arrived. Her delicate hands smooth over his cheek, his creamy mane, his pink nose. What I wouldn't give to be a horse right now.

My boots crunch the dirt. "Second time this week," I tell Ruby. "This who you're sneaking around on me with?"

Still petting the horse, she says, "I love him. He's such a sweet boy. What's his name?"

"Doesn't have one. Namin' them is bad luck. Means we keep 'em."

Ever so slightly, her body tenses. "You're not keeping him?"

"He's going to a buyer in Deer Lodge next month."

"Oh."

"Fastest way to get that colt broke is to go out there and break it."

She nods and leans her head down to touch her forehead to the pony's. "Guess we're both taking off soon, huh?"

Her words cause my stomach to drop.

When she turns around, it damn near bottoms out.

I've never seen beautiful look so sad.

"Hey," I say, closing the space between us. The sight of her sad face is like a gut punch. Her blue eyes, always filled with joy and sunshine, are dim. "What's wrong?" I glare around the ranch. "Someone say something to you?"

"No. Nothing's wrong."

A lie. The red rims around her eyes tell a different story.

"Bullshit."

Her lower lip trembles and I don't like it. Not one damn bit. I want to track the motherfucker down who stole the sunshine from her face and beat him to a pulp.

I sweep my finger under her chin, lifting her gaze to mine. "Baby, out with it."

"I don't know," she whispers, a single tear trailing down her cheek. "I had a bad day."

I run my hands down her shoulders. "That's why you're here? You had a thorn day?"

A little gasp pops out of her mouth. "You remembered." The faintest smile tugs at her lips.

I can't forget. I've had thorns every damn day of my life, but this summer, my sunflower has been Ruby.

"I did. I had a thorn day. And I love the horses," she says with a reverence that twists my stomach. "They calm me." She casts her eyes down. "I just needed somewhere to go."

Fuck but I hate that she didn't come to me. That she's

trying to solve our problems at the ranch but won't let anyone solve hers.

I wait for her to elaborate, but she doesn't. Suddenly, I'm pissed as hell. I don't like where we are. Some sort of tentative in-between. We're not together, but I sure as fuck don't want to be strangers.

Not anymore.

I'm losing it. Losing my edge, that casual indifference I've tried so hard to keep ever since she set foot in my town.

I used to think her a distraction on the ranch, but not anymore.

She's more than a distraction.

More than joy.

She's become my person to seek out. The one I want to see every morning when I wake up. I like telling her about my day, asking about hers, sleeping beside her at night and earning that dreamless, fucking fantastic night of sleep.

She's my everything.

It feels wrong not knowing more about her.

"Horses calm me too," I say, rubbing her arm. She smiles, despite the sad look on her face. Whatever's bothering her, it's my business to get to the bottom of it.

"They do?"

"Yeah. Whenever shit went wrong when I was a kid, I just lit out of my house and saddled up," I tell her. "Spent the day at the creek and when I'd get back home, I'd be in good shape. There's nothing as free as bein' on a horse."

"Free," she whispers. Then she clears her stormy eyes and blinks up at me. "Was it like that in the rodeo?"

"It was." I force the words out. "I started out helping my dad break colts when I was seven years old. Competed in rough stock in high school before I tried out for the big leagues." At the question in her eyes, I add, "Bareback riding."

"Ah."

Memories surface. Me and Wyatt comparing injuries after the Last Chance Stampede in Helena. I had a busted collarbone; he had a torn tendon in his shoulder. We were beat up, bruised and fucked up, and we had never been prouder.

Competing in rodeos with my brother was like a breath of fresh air. That feeling I could spur anything down, of being tossed on your ass in the dirt. Adrenaline, plain and simple. It was a thrashing that lasted eight seconds, and I loved every second of it.

Her lips curve upward. "You win any medals, Cowboy?"

I chuckle. "Prize money, baby." I kiss her lips. "Loads and loads of prize money."

She half-turns, blue eyes scanning the stalls. "Which one's yours?"

Taking her hand in mine, I move down the row, stopping in front of a massive black stallion.

"This one. Arrow." I palm his cool nose. "My dad got all of us horses for our tenth birthdays. Tradition."

"He's a beauty," she breathes.

"He's a bastard." I chuckle, swiping Arrow's silky tuft of hair away from his face. His dark eyes aren't amused at the affection. "The amount of times he's tossed me on my ass are legendary."

Ruby laughs in delight as she stands on tiptoes to scruff his mane. Arrow nickers, leaning into her touch, snuffling her palm, and picking up her scent. I watch, amused. Of course, he treats Ruby like a literal princess, but acts like an absolute dick to everyone else.

As I watch her croon to Arrow, I see the sad yearning in her eyes. She wants to ride.

That's when it hits me—with or without me—she'll ride.

One day. Somewhere.

When I'm not around to catch her.

A cold sweat erupts on the back of my neck.

I clench my fist, heart racing. The thought is almost too much.

She's not Maggie. She's okay.

I take a breath. "You wanna go for a ride?"

She turns, her gorgeous blue eyes rounded in surprise. "Really?" Her joyous grin is a lightning strike to my heart.

Then and there, I know the lengths I'd go to make her happy are infinite.

"Really." I cup her face in my hands. "I'll go slow."

She nods, like she's following my train of thought. "For me?"

No, for me. If we go anything faster than a trot, I'll lose my damn mind.

"I'll take you out to the creek. We'll ride double." I'm not brave enough to let her ride alone.

She lets out a little squeal and throws herself into my arms.

Instead of listening to every excuse why we can't be anything other than sex, instead of fooling myself one more goddamn second, I do something I've been wanting to do all day.

I pull her tight against my chest and kiss her.

In, I think.

I'm in it with this woman and I don't want out.

25

Ruby

AFTER PULLING A BAREBACK PAD AND SADDLE out of the tack room, Charlie readies Arrow for our ride. "Hey, boy, you ready to roll?" he rumbles, patting Arrow's muscled chest.

The smile on my face is uncontained. Seeing this sexy cowboy being kind to his animals is like dopamine injected straight into my veins.

"How about you?" he asks, turning to me. "You ready?"

I smile and approach the horse. No nerves, just excitement.

"All my life," I breathe.

After a second of hesitation, Charlie lifts me onto Arrow's back. He does it carefully, delicately, like he's afraid I'll break. I throw my leg over the saddle and grab the reins for dear life. Charlie looks up at me, his handsome face serious.

I can tell he's running down a memory in his mind. I remember the way he reacted when I fell into the pen. The way he watched Fallon jump those rails.

My heart vibrates in my chest. He's worried about me.

I lock my eyes on his. "I'll be okay, Charlie," I say, because it looks like he needs the assurance.

"I won't let you fall, Ruby," he growls, his jaw locked tight.

I smile brightly. "I know you won't."

His eyes flash, and he gives me a quarter smile that goes straight to my heart.

Arrow shifts on his feet, and I squeal as my center of gravity is rocked. I lean down, wrapping my arms around Arrow's long neck. "What do I do?"

He gives a low, short laugh. "Hold on. I'm comin' up."

With a well-practiced ease, Charlie jumps up to sit bareback behind me. He wraps an anchoring arm around my waist and pulls me tight against him. In one hand, he gathers up the reins, clicks his tongue, then Arrow trots down the road.

I cry out in delight. We're not going fast, but to me, this feeling is everything.

It's freedom. It's flying.

Living.

"Oh my god!" I grip Charlie's tense forearm when Arrow snorts. "I can't believe it. I'm riding." I glance back at him, catching a glimpse of his stern, chiseled profile. "What do we do now?"

He leans forward, his coarse beard tickling me. I feel the smile on his face as he presses his mouth against my cheek. His deep, masculine rumble of a voice sends sparks through my core. "We'll go slow until we get out of the ranch, then pick up the pace."

I wave at Tina, at Colton, and hold my breath as we exit the ranch to cross over the creek. Aspen trees quake delicately in the light breeze as we trot up the hill. Over the clearing, Charlie nods at Davis, who takes off his cowboy hat and stares with a dropped jaw.

Closing my eyes, I rest a hand over my heart.

Please behave.

"See how I'm holdin' the reins?" Charlie asks. "Loose, straight forearms. Keep 'em looped over your palm, like this. This lets you talk to the horse with just your wrists. Here, feel how I do it."

Logging his instruction away for later, I wrap my hands around his and squeeze. "This is amazing, Charlie."

In no time at all, we're far from the ranch. Charlie's body has relaxed, and he looks more at ease astride his horse than he does on foot.

"How did you get into horses?" I ask.

"I was raised on a horse farm. My parents retired last year, and my little sister runs the ranch now. My daddy always said if we could walk, we could work. And we did."

I giggle, picturing Charlie as a little farm boy, lugging feed buckets and chasing chickens. "Tough man."

"He was. But we had fun too. Played hard, worked hard." Charlie laughs, sending a rumble vibrating through me. "There's nothing like small towns. Running from the cops. Back roads boozing. Fishing in the middle of the night." He presses his body closer to mine. "Kissing pretty girls in stables."

I shift in the saddle, the spot between my legs pulsing at the hungry tone in his voice. I rest my head back against his broad chest, liking the protective way he keeps me anchored close to his body. All my senses are full of him. I want to kiss him, grip his hair, and run my tongue over his chest. But if I do that, our ride's over and I very much want it to continue.

Glancing down, I run a finger across a large scar on his tan forearm. It's gnarly, but I love it. "What's this from? Barbed wire? Bar fight?"

"No. Wyatt." He steers Arrow down a sloped ravine. Off in the distance, the sound of water. "We were rough-housing in the barn when we were kids and he shoved me off a rafter and into a pile of hay. Nicked myself on a pitchfork that was buried in the hay." He chuckles. "It was a damn close call. He begged me not to tell our dad. Did my chores for a week."

"Are you closest to Wyatt?"

"We're all close, but yeah, I am. With six of us, they always split us into pairs. Emmy Lou and Grady were the babies. The twins always had each other, and the good graces of our parents." A grin tips his lips, brotherly affection staining his voice. "Wyatt and I were the lone wolves who got into mischief and wreaked havoc on the farm when we could." Charlie's big hand drops to my thigh. He gives it a squeeze. "He's my best friend. The first one to follow me to the ranch when I left Wildheart."

"Oh," I say, looking up at his bold blue eyes. A strange sadness lives there, but also a calm I haven't seen before. "Well, I love your crazy brothers."

"Crazy brothers," he echoes, his gaze dancing over the meadow. "Big gift, bigger pain in the ass."

At the mention of brothers, my brother's words from earlier infiltrate my mind.

You'll get hurt. He'll get hurt. You'll both get hurt.

I swallow hard. It's pointless telling Charlie about my SVT now. I'm leaving. He has the ranch to focus on and

I have my life. All I see is a headache when I just want to enjoy what I need right now.

Which is Charlie.

I like him. More than I want to admit.

"You want to kick up the speed?" Charlie's gravelly voice sideswipes my thoughts.

I smile. "Let's do it."

With a smooth *heeyah*, Charlie digs in his heels, and Arrow launches into a lively trot. I giggle as the momentum sends me rebounding into Charlie's chest. Thick muscles ripple beneath me as we bounce across the bright green field, over rock and hard earth. The body of the horse moves like Charlie's trusted friend, and as we ride, Charlie points out sights on the ranch I have never seen. A field where a herd of cattle graze. A trout pond. A small cabin nestled back in the woods.

Thirty minutes later, I hear rushing water.

When we reach the creek, Charlie dismounts and helps me down. I slip off my shoes and sit on the creek's edge, running my hand over a bright patch of Asters while Charlie lets Arrow drink. Today, he looks like a modern cowboy in jeans, a white T-shirt, and a baseball cap. The carefree look on his face is a rare sight.

I wish I knew what took that away from him.

Charlie turns to me. "So, what else is on your bucket list?" He makes his way back to the bank, wiping water on the thighs of his dusty jeans before settling beside me on the blanket we've spread out. "Rob a bank? Jump out of a plane?"

You. Just you.

The thought has me flushing and I duck my head, bumping my shoulder to his. "Still need to see a sunrise."

"We will. At least you can check riding a horse off your list." His chuckle is like whiskey and velvet. "Which reminds me. You never told me what your thorn was today."

Damn him. He's being too sweet. I'll cave.

"Ever done something you shouldn't? Like a bad deed, but you don't regret it?" An expression I can't make out filters across his face. When he says nothing, I tuck my hands between my thighs and exhale. "Because I have. I might have done something bad to someone I care about." My eyes fall to the rocky bank where a patch of glacier lilies grow. Guilt wells inside me, my stomach tightening. "I lied to them. And if they ever found out, I don't know if they'd forgive me."

"They'll forgive you." Reaching out, his fingers fiddle with a lock of my hair before tucking it behind my ear. "You don't have a bad bone in your body, Ruby."

I look past him to the creek. My tears are on the verge of unleashing. "What about a bad heart?" I whisper.

I'm close. The words are threatening to burst out of my chest. *I'm lying to you. I'm sick. And in two years, I'll probably die.*

Get it out, get it over. But it crosses a line, because we're not together. We're not anything. And we can't be.

Even if a tiny voice inside my heart whispers to me that it could be possible.

That I could have a choice.

He shakes his head. "No bad heart."

I note he hasn't answered my question about bad deeds. This man's a lockbox.

But I think I have him beat.

"Not you," he says, and as he watches me, lust laces his dark blue eyes. "You're a sunflower."

My cheeks heat, his words filtering through me like sunlight. "Sunflower, huh?"

"Sunflower. That's what you are." Turning, he pulls me onto his lap so I straddle him, his big fingers tangling in my hair. "Resilient. Beautiful. My sweet sunflower." A ragged breath shakes out of him like he's in disbelief. "You got me living, Ruby, and I haven't done that in a long time."

My heart can't stop slamming into my chest. "Living is good."

"It is."

"You're my sunflower." His heated gaze skates over my face. "This day, and every day you've been on the ranch, you've been my sunflower."

"Oh." My eyes grow to saucers.

It's too much. He's too perfect.

Thank god, I'm leaving.

Then, looping a broad arm around my waist, Charlie hauls me against him and kisses me. My tongue runs over his, and a growl catches in his throat, his big hands framing my face. He takes my air, my senses, and I drink him in.

I've wondered all my life where I'll be when my heart pumps its last beat. If I am here, in Charlie's arms, it would be more than enough.

It would be everything.

Because this sweet cowboy of mine owns my whole heart and soul.

With a groan, Charlie pulls away from our kiss. "Lessons," he says in a tight voice, and I slide a hand up the stone wall of his chest. "If you want to ride the rest of the summer, I'll teach you."

"You will?"

"I will," he grates, one rough hand of his cupping my

cheek. "But you gotta go slow and listen to me." His Adam's apple bobs, worry creeping into his expression. "I mean it, Ruby. You get hurt up there . . ."

"I'll go slow. I promise." His offer means so much to me because I know it's hard for him. "I'll listen. I won't get hurt. You'll be around to protect me."

A muscle in his jaw jumps. "I won't let anything happen to you, Sunflower."

The nickname, the intensity, the protectiveness in his voice sends goosebumps whispering across my skin.

I fan my fingers out across his beard. "You're going to send me off to California a cowgirl." I say it in a teasing way, but it sends a storm cloud rolling across his face. His grip on me tightens.

"What about you?" I ask.

"What about me?"

"You never told me your bad deed."

"I'll tell you later." Piercing blue eyes scan the horizon, and he nods at the black clouds in the sky. "We should get back."

I nod, but don't move.

As I take in the creek's beauty and the mountains in the distance, I realize it's the ideal spot for a photo. The perfect place to make Runaway Ranch's followers want this lifestyle.

My eyes land on Charlie, an electric shiver zipping through me as he gives me one of his reluctant crooked grins.

Make them love a cowboy.

I smile, touching my fingertips to my racing heart.

And I feel it, really feel it, what this man is doing to me.

"Hold on. Can we take a photo?" I ask, my lashes heavy. "For the feed."

Charlie nods slowly, looking boyish and shy suddenly. "You tell me, darlin'. What do we do?"

"Kiss me," I breathe, my heart ballooning in my chest. "You be the cowboy. And I'll be the girl who rides off into the sunset."

His eyes turn molten.

Then his muscular arms sweep around me, crushing me to his chest. I wiggle on his lap, freeing my arm to lift the camera up high. Our eyes lock and then Charlie kisses me, fusing his lips to mine. Heat charges between us, and I lean into his tight grasp.

I snap our photo.

And right here on the banks of the creek, I fall in love with Charlie Montgomery.

26

Charlie

AFTER A LONG DAY SPENT PICKING UP BAGS OF feed and waiting to get a saddle repaired in town, I head back to the ranch. An old country song plays on the radio as I steer my old truck down the winding backroads. I glance at the buckskin cowboy hat with a blue ribbon tied around the crown in the passenger seat. A gift for Ruby. That girl needs a damn hat. While I love the freckles that pop on the bridge of her nose when she gets a little sun, her getting burned isn't an option.

I check the time and punch the gas. It's later than I'd like, nearing six o'clock. I had hoped to finish up some chores on the ranch, but now, all I want to do is get Ruby in my arms.

Ever since our ride to the creek last week, she's become a seamless part of my daily routine.

Mornings, she joins me for coffee in my kitchen. We talk about our day, then we get in some time in with the horses. Afterward, we each break to go about our days. Then, we come together at night.

I don't know what I was thinking, offering to help that girl ride. Watching her wide-eyed wonder and listening to her squeals of laughter around the horses has a permanent lump lodged in my throat. Riding puts a smile on her face and I want to bust my ass to keep it there.

Or maybe, selfishly, I want to keep her here.

Even if it terrifies me seeing her up on a horse.

But it's what she needs, and if I'm honest about it, it's what I need. Ever since Maggie, it takes everything I have to watch a woman on a horse.

But with Ruby, I don't see Maggie. Because Ruby is not Maggie.

She's the one girl I never saw coming. And I'm realizing she's the best thing that's ever happened to me.

I like her beautiful soul. Her gorgeous face. Her sexy little gasps that have me going hard every time I hear that sharp intake of air. Her wide-eyed sweetness. I want to give her every damn sunrise in the sky.

Hell, I'd take her to California if she asked.

Christ. Is that how far gone I am?

Yes. With Ruby, the answer is always yes.

Slowing at a stoplight, I check my phone. As if on autopilot, my fingers pull up our Instagram page. More often than not, I catch myself scrolling through the feed when she isn't around. Because goddamn, do I miss her.

The photo she snapped of us is up to three thousand likes. Comments vary.

Y'all did that 100 percent.

You two are beautiful together.

Where are the mountains?

How can I find a cowboy?

But fuck the comments and fuck social media. The

only thing I'm focused on is Ruby's smiling face. I must have stared at it fifty times in the last week.

She looks drop-dead gorgeous in the photo, luminous like the sun, hair blowing in the breeze, pressed into me like she belongs there.

And hell, I look like a happy man.

The thought is like a kick to the sternum, uprooting everything I know. But I can't ignore it anymore.

It's more than good sex.

Christ, I gave her a nickname.

She's my sunflower, causing chaos ever since she came into my life. Chaos I can't do without.

I tear through the bright green blaze of the traffic light, taking a left to hit the road to the ranch.

There's no denying it. She wrapped me around her finger with a single kiss. Every day, she lights up my life with a smile. A fucking smile. How she does it, I don't know. All I know is I want it around me. Because when I'm done busting up ranch work, all I can think about is rushing back to her.

And the closer we get to each other, I wonder if I've been fooling myself all this time. Letting fear rule this entire summer. The fear of caring for anyone else, of losing anyone else ...

Of starting over.

Do I want to do it?

Yeah. I fucking do.

As I approach the entrance to the ranch, I ease off the gas. Ford's truck sits at the end of the creek near the road. I spot my older brother in the ditch, tugging out rotted fence posts. Bypassing the turnoff, I pull over and hop out. Ford grunts a hello, his face shaded under his baseball cap.

Without talking, I pick up a hammer. Despite the back-breaking labor, Ford cussing the sun, we finish removing the posts in just twenty minutes.

I wipe my brow. "Wasn't Wyatt supposed to do this?"

A nod. "Wyatt's MIA. Haven't seen him all day. I might knock him in the mouth. Or the head. I haven't decided yet." He jerks his chin down the line of the creek. "Some idiot clogged up the creek bed with beer cans, so that's next on my list."

"You call him?" I ask, already picking up my phone and dialing Wyatt.

"Twice."

It rings and rings, finally switching over to voicemail.

"He could be out of range," I say. Sporadic bursts without cell service are typical on the ranch. If he's out of reach, there's no way to get ahold of him until he moves in closer.

"I'll head back," I tell Ford, trying to shake off my worry. "See if he's there."

On the short drive back to the cabin, my mind stays on Wyatt. I don't like it. He dicks around, sure, but it's not like him to shirk his responsibilities. When we were kids, he was always up with the sun to help me with the horses and our chores.

When I pull into the gravel drive of my house, I spy Ruby making her way back from the lodge. Her dress hem flares out as she floats toward her cottage with a bag of apples in her hand.

Instantly, at the gorgeous sight of her, all thoughts of the ranch, of Wyatt, evaporate.

I throw the truck into park, grab her hat, hop out, and meet her between my cabin and her cottage.

She brightens and bounces over to me.

"Hey, Cowboy," she drawls, lifting the bag of apples in greeting. "Chef gave me some extra apples from the baking contest." She leans in, her blue eyes sparkling. "I still think you need a garden."

I chuckle and shake my head. She's practically the queen of my ranch.

Fuck. I like that. A whole damn lot.

The thought hits me like a bullet.

She belongs here.

She belongs with *me*.

Setting the bag of apples down, Ruby nods at the hat clenched in my hand, her red lips parting. "What's that?"

"Got you somethin' in town." I drop it on her head and suppress a grin. It makes her look like a tiny, sassy cowgirl. "You gonna ride right, you gotta dress right."

She gasps. "Oh, Charlie," she says, clasping a hand to her heart, joy a charm on her pretty face. She looks up at the brim, then her gaze meets mine. Tears glitter in her eyes. "Thank you. I love it so much." The breathless appreciation in her voice lands like an arrow to my heart.

Adjusting the hat, she gives me finger guns, then twirls. The hem of her sundress flutters in the breeze and something hard lodges itself in my throat.

"Well," she says, propping her hands on her hips. "How do I look?"

Like you're mine.

"Perfect," I rasp out. "Cowgirl looks good on you."

She does a slight one-shouldered shrug and flashes a flirty smile. "Well, see you."

Oh, hell no.

I snag her wrist before she can turn away. "Hey, where you goin'?"

Her eyes widen with that stunning, earnest innocence I'm used to. "Back to work. I'm slammed, Charlie. Your website needs more copy. Not to mention, I have to finish the calendar before the end of the—"

I kiss her to make her stop talking. No more about her leaving. I can't handle it.

With my hands on her waist, I sweep my tongue over hers, pressing her tiny form against my chest. She clutches my neck and whimpers into my mouth. My cock aches for her. Our hearts thunder as I consume this woman who has me on the verge of insanity on a daily basis.

Right now, right here, is how I want to stay.

With her.

"Come over," I tell her when we pull away. I slip a hand into her silky tresses and cup the back of her neck. Need has me by the throat. "Stay the night."

She laughs, looks at me like I'm crazy. "I've already been staying over."

"Stay the weekend."

I don't want her leaving.

She shakes her head, peering up at me beneath long lashes. "Charlie . . ."

"Pack a bag," I order. "Don't argue with me."

"When?"

"Now." I thread my fingers through hers, stopping her from pulling away. "Dinner. Whiskey."

Surprise crosses her face. "You're cooking?"

"Damn right." I chuckle. "Not sure what you'll get, but I'll wrangle something."

"Okay." Her eyes glimmer in the setting sun. "I have to photoshop some photos for the August posts. Give me an hour."

I grab her around the waist. "Twenty minutes."

She giggles, throwing her head back, a musical sound that jerks my cock to attention.

"Soon, Sunflower," I growl, dipping my head to nuzzle her neck. I inhale her strawberry scent. "I can't get you out of my head. I've been without you for less than twenty-four hours and I'm mad. You drive me fucking wild, Ruby."

I've laid all my cards on the table and I couldn't care less.

She props a hand on my chest to push me away, her face flushed, triumphant. "Don't you worry, Cowboy. I kinda have a thing for you, too."

My gaze dips to her plump lips, and I slip a finger under the strap of her sundress. "Baby, I'm already counting the hours."

Eyes turning dreamy, she kisses me again, grabs the bag of apples, then extricates herself from my grip. "See ya soon."

Heart thundering, I watch her as she skips up the steps to her cottage and disappears.

Then it's my turn. I pound up the porch steps to the cabin, my mind already on tonight.

Already on my girl.

"Out," I growl as soon as I hear the screen door slam.

I glance at the clock on the wall. Any hope of a night alone with Ruby dashed. I need to move to the goddamn moon. Burn off my fingerprints, pack a U-Haul and get my ass living on a mountainside, far, far out of reach. Because the last thing I need is my idiot big brothers chiming in on what Ruby and I have going.

Ford and Davis swagger inside with shit-eating grins on their faces and scour the mess I've made of the kitchen.

"Really clocking right out at the end of your shift, huh?" Ford lifts a brow.

I glare. "Had better things to do."

"That better thing . . . she comin' over or . . ."

"She's coming over for dinner," I snap. "So y'all gotta get the fuck out."

I set the one bottle of dusty wine I have in the fridge on the counter. Frowning, I jerk open the freezer, studying the contents. "We still got those steaks from last month?"

Davis crosses his arms and drops onto a stool. He looks every bit the smug bastard. "She still the good-for-a-summer girl?"

I freeze, painfully aware of my words from weeks ago.

I'm a fucking bastard. If Ruby heard me talking like that . . .

It would hurt her. And that would break my goddamn heart.

The words don't sit right with me. Not anymore. She's more than a summer fling. She's Ruby. She's sunshine scorching the darkest pieces of me, a glow filling the cracks in my heart. Cracks I tried to fill with alcohol, with the ranch, with silence and anger. It feels like I've had a hangover for ten long years and I'm just getting sober.

"No," I admit. "She's more than that."

Davis looks surprised, and for once in his life, he doesn't have a know-it-all comeback.

"Sunk. Like a goddamn ship." Ford hoots, pounding the countertop.

I stare, trying to glower when all I want to do is grin like a sorry son of a bitch.

"Head over boots, brother. Head over boots. You put her name on 'em yet?" Ford asks, opening a bottle of whiskey and pouring out shots.

Head over boots. It's what our father always said. When you find the right woman, you fall head over boots, then you write her name on the outsole, a mark she's yours.

I grunt. "No."

"You rode on a horse, Charlie." Davis studies me for a beat. "For fun."

"I don't know what I'm doing with her," I say, swallowing the whiskey, letting the sting of the liquid loosen my tongue. "All I know is I like her. A whole hell of a lot."

Davis threads a hand through his dark hair, his face sober. "I haven't heard you talk like this since . . . well, in a long time."

"Since Maggie," Ford says. He gives me a sorry shrug, exchanges a look with Davis. "We've all been all thinking it."

I inhale Ford's words, Maggie's name, and when I let the breath out, it doesn't hurt so much.

"Smile looks good on you, brother." Davis clears his throat. "Keep it there."

I glance out the window at Ruby's cottage. "I intend to."

The radio on Davis's hip crackles and Sam's cigarette-riddled voice croaks out, "Hey, y'all seen Wyatt?"

Davis lifts the radio to his mouth. "No. Why?"

"We found Pepita over on the ridge. She's got a real bad limp. No sign of your brother."

Dread fills my stomach. Ford's attention shifts from the whiskey bottle to me, his lean form tensing.

Davis's jaw clenches. "She okay?"

"We're takin' her to the stables to check her over. Reckon she is, though. We'll let you know. Over."

"Thanks, Sam. Over." Davis ends the call and swears.

The rare emotion from my level-headed brother sends alarm racing down my spine. Wyatt treats his horse like gold. There's no way he'd let her run off hurt and not go after her.

"Where the fuck's our brother?" Ford demands, worry blazing bright in his eyes.

The sentence lands like a wrecking ball and sends me flashing back to Wyatt getting bucked off a horse and knocked unconscious for two days. The whole family planted roots at the hospital. Our brother was hurt. That meant we weren't okay. It also meant he could count on us to be there, to look out for him.

Always.

My hackles rise. "I don't like this." I pick up my phone and dial Wyatt's number, but there's no answer.

"Round up the staff. Start looking for him." Davis shoves himself off the stool, his expression grim. "I'll get Keena and see if she can sniff him out."

The back door bursts open just as I'm grabbing my keys.

"Y'all got an ice pack?" Wyatt drawls, limping into the kitchen. He looks pale and tired. Blood's smeared across his temple. He wears a baseball cap pulled down low, but I can see the beginnings of a black eye.

The room erupts into pandemonium.

Thundering across the floor, Davis strong-arms Wyatt toward a chair at the kitchen table. "Sit."

Wyatt does, wincing as if the very motion is painful, and I want to hunt down whoever hurt him and turn their face into ground beef.

"Who the fuck do I need to kill?" Ford demands, prowling behind Wyatt's chair.

Davis removes Wyatt's baseball cap and tilts his head back to examine his pupils.

"Start talkin', Wy," I warn, slapping an ice pack into his hand, a glass of whiskey in the other.

My brother meets my gaze. "I was headed to help Ford with the creek when someone ran me off the road." He hisses a breath as Davis peels back his hair, blood spilling faster now from the shallow cut. "I fell off Pepita and knocked myself out. I think they kicked me around when I was out, because my ribs hurt something fierce. When I woke up, I hiked my busted ass back here." He exhales, trying to keep a cocky grin on his face, but the clench of his jaw tells me he's in pain.

Blood pounds in my head as I stare at my little brother. Wyatt's sitting there bleeding and I feel so goddamn helpless.

Ford swears and his head whips to me. "The Wolfingtons are dead—they're fucking roadkill."

I nod, rage simmering in my veins.

Wyatt can get knocked around on horses all he wants. Break ribs, get concussions, but someone fucks with my little brother, with my family, all bets are off.

"Keep it together," Davis orders. "We won't solve anything if you two go off half-cocked."

"Fuck that, Davis, and fuck you," Ford snaps. He yells so loud the whiskey glasses rattle. "They've gone too far this time."

"I'm with Ford." Stomping toward the door, I yank it open and scan the ranch. Outside, big black storm clouds threaten to unleash. "Go out there and snap some fucking necks."

If the Wolfingtons are stupid enough to come onto our property and attack our brother, they better watch their backs.

Davis draws himself up, eyes flashing, pissed at being out voted, ready to knock our skulls together, but Wyatt waves a hand, silencing all of us. "I don't think it was them," he says with a wince. "That's givin' 'em too much credit. They couldn't find their dicks with a lasso." He huffs a laugh, then groans, pressing a hand to his ribs.

I whip around, my boots grinding to a halt. "Then who the fuck was it?"

27

Ruby

I CAN'T CONCENTRATE ON WORKING WITH CHARLIE'S offer hanging over me.

Pack a bag. Come over tonight.

Charlie and I—we're not keeping our distance. Every boundary, every agreement we've made since I arrived at Runaway Ranch is dust in the Montana sky. I only have a month left and the thought of leaving hurts.

This ranch is good for me. For my heart.

I push my laptop away, deciding to give up on editing the photos and finish them later. From the corner of my eye, I catch a glimpse of my bucket list on the fridge. A bright smile spreads across my face. I've crossed off more to-dos here than anywhere else. All thanks to Charlie.

He makes me feel like I can do anything.

He makes me see how my entire life could be different.

My smile fades when my gaze lands on the cowboy hat in the middle of the kitchen table. It's beautiful and fits me perfectly. I love it, but it's a gift. It's too intimate.

Permanent.

The cowboy hat changes things. For the better, I don't know.

Even though I'm already in love with him, Charlie absolutely cannot fall in love with me.

He isn't.

I squeeze my eyes shut, feeling the shaky beat of my trembling heart.

He won't.

All I am to him is a fling. Good sex. *Great* sex. He's not emotionally invested. He's made it clear we are summer bound.

Saying no to him and staying at home tonight would be the smart thing to do.

But I can't stay away from him. I'm obsessed with Charlie Montgomery, this rough around-the-edges cowboy. The days are ticking down and I'll have to leave soon, but until then, for just one summer, I very much want to be his girl.

Because I won't beg anyone to love me and I won't shame myself for wanting good love.

This is how it has to be.

For so long, I've held my heart hostage. No more.

I check my phone, and a squeak pops out of my mouth when I see the time.

I'm late.

Hurrying into the bedroom, I open my smaller suitcase and drop in a few nice pieces of clothing I haven't worn yet. In the bathroom, I pack a small bag with my medication and toiletries. I take a second to touch up my makeup and apply light pink lip gloss, dabbing it onto my cheeks for added effect.

My phone pings.

I scowl when I see the ranch's Instagram account has a comment from *Lassomamav76*.

Sick of these boring, blah pictures.

I shake my head vigorously, irritation weaving through me.

Who are you?

I don't wait. I head straight for my computer.

On impulse, I drag *Lassomamav76's* downloaded avatar into my photo editing software. I work quickly, changing the pixel dimensions to enlarge the image. There has to be something I can find out about this woman.

There.

I see it.

I lean in to my computer, stomach churning.

Her belt buckle.

It's shiny, studded with turquoise, two crossed shotguns in the middle of the scalloped rectangle. Etched below them are the words *Be Victorious. Be Valiant. Be Vicious.*

That's when something clicks on in my head.

I've seen that phrase before. But where?

I have to tell Charlie.

Moving faster, I hop up from the kitchen table and rush into the bathroom. I zip up my toiletries bag. Through the small bathroom window, I catch a glimpse of Charlie's cabin. Thunder rumbles across the sky. Sun and shadow cross paths, casting strange umbras over the ranch.

That's when I hear my front door open.

I freeze.

That's when I hear it lock.

Unease prickles at the back of my spine as I leave the bathroom.

"Charlie?" I breathe, stepping into my bedroom doorway to peer into the living room.

I gasp.

A man stands in the entryway, wearing a black mask. He's tall but hunched over like he's trying not to be noticed.

Don't hurt me, I want to say, but I can't form the words.

We lock eyes for a long second, then he shuffles forward, almost hesitating.

And then—we both move at once.

I jerk backward, trying to slam the bedroom door to lock it and buy me time, but he's in the room before I can get it closed.

He advances, rushing the space between us. In a panic, I scramble onto the bed and try to unlatch the window. If I can crawl through, I can make it to Charlie's. I'm sliding the window open when he grabs me by the ankle and pulls me off the bed. I kick back and struggle, rolling around on the ground in a desperate attempt to free myself. Finally, my foot connects with his knee and he swears, lets me loose.

I'm up.

I try to run past him, hoping to make it to the front door, but he catches me by the left wrist.

"Fuck you," I say and take a swing at him.

Add this to my bucket list. Fistfights.

I punch him in the eye, my knuckles connecting hard, and he swears.

I let out a blood-curdling scream.

"*Charlie!*" I inhale again. "Charlie, help—"

A hand slaps across my mouth. My scream smothered. I struggle to break free, trying to pull away as his arm hooks around my stomach. The man pins me back against him. My bare feet drag the ground. I fight against him but he's strong.

"Leave before someone gets hurt," he says in my ear. "Before it's too late." His voice isn't mean or angry like I expected. Instead, it's gentle, hesitant.

Adrenaline spikes, causing my heart to race. Its beat is shaky, and my head spins, dizziness spreading through me. I've never heard a heartbeat get this loud. It pounds in my head. I can feel the soft spot on my throat pulsing.

"No," I whimper, my mouth muffled by the man's palm. "Please," I beg. "Please, stop . . ."

It's too much, too much for my heart.

The room sways left and right as my vision warps into a sparkly tunnel slowly being eaten up by blackness. I can't speak, I can't scream. There's a ringing in my ears that I know all too well. My head lolls as I fight to stay conscious. A soft *uhnnn* parts my lips. I go limp against the man holding me, unable to fight the unconsciousness creeping over me like a black lake.

"Fuck." The voice is shaky. Afraid. "Miss Ruby?"

Miss Ruby.

"Charlie," I gasp.

My breath stalls. My heart stops.

Then I faint away into darkness.

"Ruby!"

Blackness ebbs. My eyelids fight to open. That's when I realize I'm on the floor of my cottage.

Cradled in the arms of a cowboy.

Charlie's ragged voice breaks through my

semi-consciousness. "Ruby. Ruby, baby, talk to me. Open your eyes, Sunflower," he begs. "Let me see those pretty baby blues."

The world swims. My head lolls against a hard chest, and a moan splits my lips. I hear a sharp intake of breath.

My entire body comes alive hearing Charlie's voice, like a flower in desperate need of the sun. When I open my eyes, I see Charlie's worried face staring down at me.

"Thank fucking God," he rasps.

A curse, a prayer, a combination of the two.

"My heart," I croak.

My trembling hand moves to my throat, and Charlie's hand follows. His cool palm cups the curve of my throat, where my pulse pumps at a frenetic rhythm.

I try to focus on him, but I can't. Drifting between consciousness and unconsciousness, my eyes roll back, my wrist sags to the ground.

"Eyes on me." Charlie's demand is urgent, desperate. "Keep 'em open, you hear me?" His frantic hands race over my body as he positions me on his lap.

Despite being hot and sweaty, I shake like it's winter. My chest heaves. "Yes," I whisper, locking my eyes to his handsome face. "Yes."

"Who did this?" Body bent over mine, Charlie tucks me tighter in his arms. His clenched jaw looks like it's on the verge of snapping in half. "Who hurt you?"

"I—I don't know," I whisper, my head lolling across his forearm. "I don't . . ." I stumble over the words, the memory of what happened. A typical response to one of my flutters. My brain's washed out. I feel so weak and all I want to do is sleep.

I close my eyes, letting my body and the memories return to me.

"Ruby?" Charlie's panicked voice calls me back.

I shake my head as an icy wave of nausea washes over me. "There was a man in my cottage." A whimper escapes me at the rapid images hammering my mind. Rough hands on my mouth, that soft snarl in my ear. "He attacked me."

"Christ," Charlie grits out, a strangled sound erupting in his throat. The rage in his eyes makes me go weak. "I'm going to kill whoever did this to you."

My pulse quickens. "He told me to leave before it was too late. Before someone gets hurt."

A growl rips out of him as he pulls me deeper into his arms.

"Must've gone out the bedroom window," a muffled voice says.

More muffled voices float. Boots stomp.

When I realize there are other people in the cottage, I struggle to sit up in Charlie's arms. My eyes widen at the sight of the smashed door.

With shaking fingers, I palm his bearded cheek. Breathless, I ask, "Did you do that?"

He laughs, but his face is tight. "Baby, I was gettin' to you, one way or another."

"Jesus," a drawl says. "Someone ransacked the shit out of the place."

Davis and Ford storm around in the living room. Two towering ranchers never looked so murderous.

Ford glances down at me, compassion in his brown eyes. "Fairy Tale okay?"

"Fairy Tale?" I wonder.

"No," Charlie growls. "She isn't."

"Oh no," I whimper, finally making sense of Ford's words as I take in my surroundings. Hot tears flood my eyes. My poor cottage is trashed. I glance at my shattered laptop. The broken flower pots and dark soil stamped across the rug. My to-do list crumpled in a corner. And—

"My hat," I whisper, crestfallen. My beautiful cowboy hat from Charlie lies trampled on the floor, the crown smashed like a flower.

Scalding tears spill out of my eyes, streaming into the corner of my mouth. "My cottage."

A big thumb tracks its way across my cheek. "Shhh. It's okay. Don't cry, baby."

With tender care, Charlie lifts me up. His expression is hard now as he looks at his brothers. His eyes breathe fire. "The same person who attacked Wyatt attacked Ruby."

"What?" I lift my head, worried. "Wyatt's hurt?"

Davis shoots a glance in Ford's direction, then smiles kindly at me. "He'll be okay. He's at Charlie's gettin' checked over by our staff doctor."

Charlie's anger flickers, but seeing my gaze on him, he stamps it down. "And that's where you're going," he says gruffly.

"No." I shake my head, wanting to avoid any run-ins with a doctor. Reminders of my health unwelcome at the moment. Not when I've got my cowboy.

I loop my arms around his neck, ignoring the urge to break down. "I'm okay, Charlie."

"I'm not okay, Ruby." Pain crosses his face, and he tips his forehead to mine. A ragged exhale tears from his chest. "Finding you like this, holding you limp in my arms . . .I'm not okay. I'm not."

He sweeps soft kisses on my lips, my temple, my cheek.

Holding my head on his chest, he runs a hand through my hair. "I'm so sorry," he tells me. The broken rawness in his voice makes me ache. "I'm so, so sorry."

My pulse races, the enormity of tonight sinking in.

My heart.

My health.

My life.

My safe space violated.

A cry wrenches itself from lungs. I twist my body in Charlie's arms, burying my face against his shoulder and weep.

He says something in a low rumble to his brothers, and I let him hold me, relishing the strength of his body.

"You're safe. I have you, Ruby." Charlie's voice is a ragged promise that breathes murder and tenderness all at once. He carries me out of the cottage and heads to his cabin as raindrops fall from the sky. "I have you, and I'm not letting go."

28

Charlie

THE HARDWOOD FLOORS CREAK BENEATH MY boots as I pace a hole in the hallway, my fury on a rolling simmer. Thunder rumbles outside and I glance at the open doorway of my bedroom. Ruby's laid out on the bed talking in low tones to Curt, the staff medic we keep on site. As if sensing my eyes on her, she turns her head to meet my gaze. Heavy lidded eyes look back at me, her rose-gold hair spread out on the pillows, and she graces me with a small smile.

Something protective and primal snaps inside of me.

War. This is fucking war.

On instinct, my hand balls into a fist and I lift it, aching to take a swing. I want to plow my fist into someone's face over and over again.

"You wanna punch something, wait for the Wolfingtons," Ford says as he and Davis come to the top of the stairs.

I release my breath, loosen my fist. "I'm going to kill them."

"Easy, man." Ford claps me on the shoulder. "Don't lose your head."

"It's already fucking gone," I grit out, tearing a hand through my hair.

The Wolfingtons don't know what they've done. No one touches Ruby.

The image of finding her crumpled on the ground is seared in my brain. Slipping her limp body into my arms, not knowing whether she was alive or dead, pulled me apart. An undeniable reminder that I could lose her. The relief I felt feeling a pulse. The rage I felt knowing some-one had hurt her.

She needed me and I wasn't there.

Once again, always a minute too late, a heartbeat away from my girl.

Wyatt comes limping down the hallway. "When we fightin'?"

"Shut up and rest," I bark, giving him a worried once over. He's got a minor concussion, but damn if that can stop the kid.

Eyes glassy, Wyatt leans on the wall. "Damn. I get kicked around and I still don't get any respect."

"C'mon," Ford says with a wide grin. He steers our lit-tle brother away. "I'll tell you a bedtime story about how much of a pain in the ass you are."

Davis watches them lope down the hall, then turns to me. "We wait," he says in a low voice, his face all busi-ness now.

Even though he's cool-headed and responsible, Davis is the one to worry about when trouble touches our fam-ily. I see blood in his eyes.

"We give it a few days. Let Wyatt heal. We go when

they least expect us, so we get the jump on them. We'll weed the Wolfingtons out first. If it's not them, it's DVL."

I nod.

"Charlie," he says, a tightness in his voice that has me frowning. "I checked out the security footage. With the new cameras installed . . ." He sighs. "Ruby's cottage was just out of reach."

I close my eyes and try not to throw up. "You've got to be fucking kidding me."

"I know." Guilt stains his voice. "I'll fix it."

I'm about to tell him it's too late to fix it, Ruby's hurt, my heart is on fucking fire, when Curt exits the bedroom.

"How is she?" I demand.

"She's fine," Curt says, his words immediately bringing relief to my troubled mind. "Her heartbeat's irregular, but all she needs is rest. Make sure she eats something and takes it easy for a couple of days."

I run a hand through my hair, keep it there.

Davis gives me a look tinged with amusement and sympathy. "Let her rest, Charlie. She'll be okay. Don't worry."

"She's staying here," I tell him, already headed for Ruby. The thought of not being near her has me unhinged. I won't be able to relax until I see her.

Inside the bedroom, the lights are dim, the door to the balcony open slightly to allow a draft of cool air. Ruby's propped up on pillows, eyes closed, looking small and fragile in one of my T-shirts.

My insides turn cold. That old familiar feeling I've lived with the last ten years slices through me like a blade.

Fear. Helplessness.

She's battered and bruised. Had the living hell scared

out of her. She was attacked. Threatened. Assaulted under my watch.

And it's all my fault.

Why wasn't I there? Why didn't I protect her?

At the sound of my bootsteps, Ruby opens her eyes. "Charlie?" Her voice is barely above a whisper.

"I'm here, darlin.'" I approach the bed to sit beside her. "How are you doin'?"

"Better." Her long dark lashes bat against her pale cheeks. "Now that I have my Cowboy."

The soft tease in her tone settles me, and I give her a quick once over. Her blue eyes are focused, but she looks worn out and all I want to do is put her to sleep.

I pick up her hand, running my finger over the silky smoothness of the inside of her wrist. She has bruises on her knuckles that I recognize from my barfight days.

"Hit the guy, didn't you?"

"Yeah." She smiles wanly. "Tried out my uppercut."

I kiss her bruised knuckles. "Good girl."

Pride sideswipes me.

She might be a fairy tale, but she's also strong. Mighty. A fighter.

The reminder that someone tried to hurt her, meant to do God knows what to her, has my insides turning to ice. I couldn't live with myself if something happened to her.

A rocky exhale tears from the inside of my chest. "Ruby."

"It's okay, Cowboy," she says, but her voice tremors.

"*Ruby.*"

With a little whimper, she closes her eyes, and then our chests collide as I crush her tight in my arms. I need to touch her. I need to hold her and know she's safe. The feel of her heartbeat hammering against mine is enough to put me in the grave. Goddamn this woman. This fucking bright force of an incredible woman that someone tried to take away from me.

Ruby being hurt would end me. I know it with every breath in my body.

"I screamed," she whispers, arms looped around my neck. She trembles against my chest. "I screamed, and you came for me."

"I'll always come for you. Never doubt that." I kiss her temple, inhale her strawberry scent, and finally my mind comes back down to earth, my rage steadying knowing that she's okay.

"Thank you." Her silvery exhalation of gratefulness carves me up inside.

"Don't thank me." I pull back to look her in the eyes. "Not for that."

She shakes her head. "Charlie . . ."

"What is it?" I ask gruffly, tucking strands of hair behind her ear. "What's wrong?"

Tears spill down her cheeks, the sight of them shattering my heart for the second time tonight. "I didn't lock my door." Her bottom lip trembles. "That's how he got in."

Fury snakes through my veins. "That's not your fault. Someone hurtin' you is never your fault." I nudge her chin up with a stern finger. "You hear me?" I say firmly, wanting her to understand.

She blinks back tears and nods quickly, absorbing the words.

Hating to let her go, but wanting her to rest, I lie her back against the pillows. "Do you remember anything else about what happened?"

"I don't think so. Not yet. My head . . ." She winces. "It's still fuzzy."

There's more to ask her, but her dazed expression stops me. She's been through enough tonight. Questions can wait. All she needs to know is that I'll fix this. That she'll never be hurt again.

Ruby sighs and stretches out in the big bed, looking soft and small. "Is Wyatt okay?" she asks.

She was just attacked, and she's worrying about Wyatt. Goddamn.

This girl breaks my heart in the best way.

"Wyatt's fine." I cover her with the blanket and take her hand. "I want you staying here, Ruby."

Her eyes are two huge saucers. "Charlie, I don't think—"

"Baby, it's not a request," I growl, and she silences. "You're staying. End of story. I want you safe. I want you with me. Until we find out who's behind this, you're not leaving my sight. No arguments," I say, reaching out to cup her cheek. She sighs—a fact that I take as a good sign she's giving in—and nuzzles her lips into my palm. "Not about this. Not when you were hurt."

"Okay," she breathes.

Slowly, she sinks back into the pillows. With relief, I note my hand's still in hers. It disintegrates something inside of me. Every closed off wall I've bricked myself into over the years crumbles.

The trust she gives me. I'm honored. Humbled.

"I want you to get some rest," I say, my fingers tightening around hers. "But first, I want to tell you something. Last week, you asked if I've ever done something bad. A bad deed I don't regret."

I blow out a breath. Why I feel compelled to tell her, I'm not sure. Maybe because I want her to know that tonight has been my goddamn kryptonite. Maybe it's because I need somewhere to lay my rage and guilt. Maybe because I've realized how much anything happening to Ruby would end me.

Seeing her hurt, seeing what I could lose—

It turns me into a fucking desperate man.

Only instead of wanting to run away from that, it has me wanting to hold tighter to her.

"There was this guy," I begin, my voice a low rasp. "Back in my hometown. He was a close family friend. We grew up together. Played football. Last summer, when I went home, I found out he had hurt my sister."

Memories of last summer come rushing back.

Emmy Lou and bruises on her wrist.

Red dirt earth and headlights.

Slayton on his knees, hands raised in front of his face.

The gun in my hand.

Ruby stays silent, lying frozen and wide-eyed.

"So I hurt him."

I scrub a hand down my beard, letting that same restless, raging feeling from last summer overtake me. "I didn't know about it for a long damn time."

Shame still eats me alive that my little sister and little brother were the ones dealing with it. I was the big brother. I was supposed to keep them safe. It's a gutting feeling I know Ford and Davis share.

"It was midnight. I drove him out on this long dirt road in the middle of nowhere. I beat the shit out of him. I made him tell me what he did to my sister. I busted open my knuckles. I broke his ribs, his face. I did anything to make that piece of shit feel pain."

I ball a fist, clearing the hoarseness from my throat. "And then I pulled out a gun."

I dare a glance at Ruby. If I'm scaring her, I can't tell. She sits still, her face pale, but placid.

"I had him there. In the dirt, the headlights, and he looked so fucking pathetic, crying his bullshit tears." A muscle in my jaw jerks. "I felt nothing. I wanted to kill him so fucking bad. I put the muzzle against his forehead. Put my finger on the trigger."

Lower lip trembling, she asks, "Did you kill him?"

"No. I thought of my brothers. My sister. If I killed him, no one would win." I press Ruby's hand to my heart. It's pounding against my ribs. "I drove Slayton to his parents' house and I made him tell them what he had done to my sister. And I promised that motherfucker, if he came back home again, he was a dead man."

The longest silence falls.

And then Ruby tilts her head and asks, "Why are you telling me this, Charlie?"

I look her in the eyes. "I'm telling you this because I will always keep you safe. I will always protect you."

She gives me a sad smile. "You can't protect me from everything."

"I can. And I will."

If it's a lie, I don't believe it.

I believe in her, in myself.

I lean in, cupping a hand to her cheek. "No one puts their hands on you, Ruby. Do you understand me? No one touches my girl."

A little smile curls her lips. "I'm your girl, Cowboy?" Her voice is dreamy, tired.

"You are." The words wrench from my chest. "You're my girl." I sweep the hair from her eyes, urging her to sleep. "And I will never let anything happen to you."

"Never?"

"Never."

Ruby makes a sleepy hum of affirmation, long lashes fluttering closed. I keep her small hand in mine. Her pulse beats in my palm. I hold it against me, the very beat of it precious.

I can't deny it anymore.

Brain, body, heart, soul—this woman's got me roped.

29

Ruby

Y OU'RE MY GIRL.

Three days later, and Charlie's words still spin in my head like a record on repeat.

You're my girl.

His tender words consumed every ounce of my soul. There's a new energy between us, a fierceness in Charlie's expression every time he looks at me.

Maybe because we're wrapped up in each other.

Maybe because we've burned all the boundaries between us.

Maybe because I've all but moved into Charlie's cabin.

He won't leave my side. The flutter that night took everything out of me. My mind, my heart; it drained me. But Charlie was there, helping me shower, keeping me steady when I stood. It gave me a glimpse of how it could be if he knew about my SVT. Tender and strong and protective. But I can't do that to him. I won't be his burden.

I rub my chest and track the familiar beat of my heart. For the first time in my life, I'm truly scared.

What that night did to my heart is bad. It took me two days to get my bearings. I've never been like that before. What it means for my health—I don't want to know.

What I know is that my clothes are in a drawer in Charlie's room. My toiletries are next to his. Every night, I sleep in his strong arms, safe in his hold.

The closer we get, the more I ache that I'm lying to him.

Even though my brain is telling me this will end, someone will get hurt, my heart is all in.

I'm in love.

Something I've always wanted.

Something that makes my heart race.

Something that is my everything.

And that everything is Charlie Montgomery.

My cowboy.

I think I know what my father meant when he said loving someone means you eventually get hurt. Just because you know what's coming, doesn't make it sting any less.

It'll hurt when I leave.

What if I stayed, though? The thought creeps out of my hopeful heart. I scowl, feeling my cheeks flush with warmth. It's just silly lovesick dreams. Hope and nothing more. Sure, Charlie said I'm his girl, but it's for the summer, right? It has to be. There's no forever with me.

Crossing the kitchen floor, I sit at the kitchen table. Through the big window, I watch guests and hired hands stroll back and forth. Ominous black storm clouds elbow the sunlight out of the sky.

My gaze zeros in on one person in particular.

Colton.

He's loping across the lawn, a two-way radio in his

hand, his cowboy hat tugged down low on his face. I track his steps as he heads toward the barn.

Miss Ruby?

I shiver at the memory. His warm breath in my ear as I slowly lost consciousness.

It was him that night. I know it.

Now I have to prove it.

Intuition tells me my first stop is the belt buckle.

Because I've seen it before and now, I remember where.

I open my laptop, the new one Charlie had overnighted for me, and give a quick glance around the kitchen.

Charlie's left me alone for a couple of hours, but it's nearing noon, which means I have about ten minutes before he gets back and starts fussing. I love it when his broody face watches my every move, like he'll put me back in bed if I try to lift anything heavier than a feather. It warms my heart.

I go to *Lassomamav76's* TikTok account page and pull up the video of her and Ford. I watch it play through once, then, on my second viewing, I stab the pause button. She's wearing the same belt buckle in her Instagram avatar.

Be Victorious. Be Valiant. Be Vicious.

I pull out my phone. I locate the image I took of Colton and zoom in.

"Oh my god," I murmur shakily, my gaze locked on the photo.

The belt buckles match. The slogans, the turquoise, the crossed rifles. Stunned, I shut my laptop, then push up out of my seat, sirens going off in my mind.

Eyes watering, I walk to the window, folding my arms around myself. My heart pumps hard and I take slow breaths. I can't get worked up. My heart needs me calm.

Even if it's the last thing I feel.

It's not an angry guest with a grudge. It's sabotage. Colton wanted to hurt the ranch. He attacked me and Wyatt. But why? And how are he and this woman connected?

My stomach caves in on itself as I'm hit with a sinking feeling that I've made this worse for Charlie and his brothers. Me being here only caused trouble. Because the ranch isn't failing, it's thriving, and I'm the one responsible for it.

What if the danger isn't over? What if it's just beginning?

"Ruby."

Charlie slides his hands over my shoulders, and I'm so startled I jump. So lost in thought I didn't hear him come on.

I smile, trying to rope my hammering heart back into my chest. Angling my face up, I meet his lips, already inbound for mine. He pulls me into his large body, crushing me against him.

"What's wrong?" His handsome face is a frown as he quickly picks up on my emotions. Damn it. He's getting too good at it. "Sunflower, you okay?"

I open my mouth to tell him about Colton, but something in his face stops me. Our conversation from the night of my attack rings in my head.

No one puts their hands on you, Ruby. Do you understand me? No one touches my girl.

His admission to nearly killing a man doesn't scare me. In fact, it makes me love him more. I understand why Charlie is who he is. Intense. Protective. Loyal and fierce. A man who would kill for the people he loves.

Which is why I can't tell him.

I need to get answers first.

Because the minute he hears Colton was the man who attacked me, he'll be out of this house so fast I won't be able to stop him. Colton will be a dead man, and we'll be without answers.

"I'm fine," I say, bouncing into him and cupping his bearded jaw. "Just tired."

He skims his thumb across my lower lip. "That's why you shouldn't be working."

My fingers curl into his T-shirt and I bring him closer for a hit of his scent. Hay. Horse. I bury my face in his chest. "Cowboy, you're fussing. What will the ranch think?"

"Don't give a fuck what the ranch thinks." He pulls back, cradling my face in his large hands to bring my gaze to his. "You are what matters, Ruby. *You.*"

"Charlie," I whisper as my heart trembles from need. From the weight of his words.

"Listen, baby," he murmurs, sliding a hand into my hair. "I gotta go out for a few hours."

I nod.

"I want you to stay in the house, Ruby." He says it forcefully, his brows furrowed deep as he stares down at me.

I let out a deep breath. I don't like the look in his eyes. "Where are you going?"

As if in answer, the front door swings open.

A minute later, Ford, Davis and Wyatt are in the kitchen.

Ford points the baseball bat he's carrying at Charlie. "Y'all ready to go hunt some wolves?"

I look at the bat, frown as hard as I can at Charlie. "What're you doing with that?"

Ford pretends to knock one out of the park. "Practice."

Davis shakes his head, rolling his eyes at his twin. "Leave the bat, Ford."

Ford heaves an exaggerated sigh and leans the bat up against the wall. "Ruins all my fun."

"That's my job, brother," Davis drawls.

"Don't worry, Ruby," Wyatt tells me, leaning his athletic frame on the kitchen island. His black eye's faded to a dull yellow. He wiggles his brows. "It's small-town legal."

Teeth gritted, Charlie turns to his brothers. "Let's finish this."

The dangerous tone of his voice sends a chill down my spine, and I wrap my hand around his bicep. "Charlie."

His face softens as he turns to look at me.

I bite my lip, eyeing the pack of angry cowboys ready to snap spines and break bones. "Don't kill anyone on my account."

A faint smile tugs at his bearded lips. Then he kisses me, once, twice. "Stay in the house, baby. And lock the door."

"I will," I lie. Adrenaline has my heart hammering.

He stares at me and I try to keep my face neutral so he can't read what I'm about to do.

I wait for them to leave, and when I hear the rumble of the pickup truck echoing across the ranch . . .

I pick up Ford's bat.

Runaway Ranch is alive and electric on this sunny Wednesday afternoon. The guests are happy. A cool breeze blows. Sam waves people into the lodge, a surly smile on his sun-weathered face.

Baseball bat in hand, I sweep the hair out of my eyes as I trek across the pasture to the barn.

Charlie may be going into town today to pound someone's face into hamburger, but I'm pounding pavement.

Curiosity and determination overtake rational thought. What would my father think? What would my brother say? Then I realize it doesn't matter.

It's not about them anymore. It's about me and the choices *I* choose to make.

I have to do this.

I want to know why Colton and this woman are fucking with Charlie's ranch. I have a personal stake in it.

Because by being here, I feel like I've made this all worse.

Colton's in the barn, adding new bedding to the stalls. The horses are gone, out on rides or being cleaned by a farmhand.

I slip inside, leaving the door open. Just in case.

Heart hammering, I grip the bat tight, and before I can chicken out, I say, "Colton, hi."

Colton's head snaps up. It's fleeting, but I see the shocked fear skitter across his boyish face. "Miss Ruby, hey. How goes it?"

My throat constricts.

What am I doing?

Colton could have meant to kill me that night, and here I am, up close and personal. But it's too late to back out now. Swallowing down my nerves, I take a step toward him and force a bright smile.

"You think I could get another photo for Instagram?" I chirp. "I need to pair a quote with a cowboy."

Straightening up, he fumbles with the pitchfork as if

it weighs more than him. He's angled his hat so the left side of his face is in shadow.

"I don't know." A nervous laugh squeaks out of him. "I'm sure you could get someone better. What about Sam? Hang on, I'll get him."

He starts for the door, but I stick the bat out, blocking his exit route. "Colton, wait."

He freezes, and I notice the clench of his fists. My stomach turns, but I force myself through my fear. I move closer, but keep watch on the open door, in case I need to run or get away. I take low and shallow breaths, hoping to calm my rapid heartbeat.

"Take off your hat," I tell him softly.

He manages a dry laugh. "What?"

I nudge his chest with the bat, willing my hands not to tremble. "Do it."

To his credit, he doesn't run. His hands move, and then he's dragging the Stetson off his head. His black eye shines.

"You did it," I breathe, more wondering than accusatory. My gaze falls to his belt buckle. "You attacked me."

All the wind goes out of him. "Fuck. Fuck. Fuck." He drops the hat, his face twisting into a grotesque mask of regret. "I didn't mean to hurt you. I just wanted to scare you. But then you fainted and wouldn't wake up." A sob racks his body. "I thought I had killed you."

Despite what he's done, sympathy wells inside of me.

"Why?" I ask, my mouth going dry. "Why would you do this?"

"Because." He swallows like the explanation's stuck. His eyes are wild, his mind elsewhere. Tearing his hands through his blond hair, he sinks into a squat. "I'm dead.

I'm fucking dead." His voice shakes with desperation. "This wasn't supposed to happen."

I crouch beside him and meet his terrified gaze. My pulse is deafening in my ears, but I force a deep breath. "What was supposed to happen?"

Colton's head drops and he covers his face with his hands. "Please don't ask me that," he pleads.

"That woman," I muse, remembering the matching belt buckles and putting two and two together. "The woman from the video that got Ford into trouble. She's your mother, isn't she?"

A strangled moan rips out of him. "Fuck, he's gonna kill me."

"I won't let Charlie hurt you," I say earnestly. "He might get a swing or two in, but he won't kill you."

I hope.

Charlie.

He's going to be so, so pissed at me.

"I'm not afraid of Charlie," Colton rasps, squeezing his eyes shut and taking deep gulping breaths. "I deserve it. I deserve whatever he gives me. If he kills me, I'd be better off for it."

I frown. "Then who are you afraid of?"

He shudders. "My father."

30

Charlie

WE SLAM INTO THE WOLFINGTONS' TRAILER so hard we leave the screen door hanging by a hinge. I'm on edge and ready to destroy whoever is fucking stupid enough to put their hands on Ruby. I haven't slept since she's been hurt.

Her attack sent me into a dark, deep tailspin, questioning why I couldn't protect her. My daily nightmare come to life. I've barely been able to entertain the what-ifs of what could have happened that night.

What if she was hurt? What if she was taken from me?

Never. I'll never allow anything to happen to her.

Lionel Wolfington's in the living room, sitting in his recliner, wearing only his underwear. The cigarette drops from his mouth as we come in blazing.

Clyde bolts for the kitchen.

"Aw, man, don't be rude." Whip-quick, ready to go immediate Old West on these morons, Wyatt grabs the back of Clyde's neck and slams him up against the wood-paneled wall. "You're leaving when we just got here."

I scan my eyes around the trailer where they grow their shitty shotgun weed. It reeks of piss and cigarette smoke. Beer cans litter the linoleum. There's a fridge in the living room.

Adrenaline hammering in my veins, I step in front of Lionel. Davis slides in next to me. Ford hangs back, arms crossed. Our typical MO ever since we were kids fighting in the cornfields.

"What the fuck, Charlie?" Lionel snarls, picking up the cigarette he dropped. "Don't you got enough problems on that ranch of yours?"

Clyde laughs, looks at Ford. "Talking about you, man."

Ford flips him the middle finger.

I kick the footrest of Lionel's recliner, snapping him into a sitting position. Adrenaline, rage hammer in my veins. Davis gives me a look to cool it, but I ignore him. This is Ruby we're talking about, our brother. Fuck letting this go.

"I got problems, now you got problems," I assure Lionel grimly. I lean in, resting my hands on the armrests, trying to keep a lid on my anger. "You wanna tell me where you were three nights ago when my brother got the shit kicked out of him and my girl was attacked?"

Lionel chuckles. "Someone got the jump on Wyatt's ass?" He settles back in the recliner, a smug look on his face. "Good for them."

Wyatt, still pinning Clyde to the wall, glares. "Man, fuck you. You ain't gonna be laughing when Charlie puts your ass through the window." Then he glares at Davis. "Told you. They're too stupid to get the jump on us."

"Man, is this an interrogation or what?" Clyde moans, his voice muffled from Wyatt's face plant against the wall.

"I've already been to the slammer this year. I can't have another delinquency on my record."

"Talk," I demand of Lionel. "Because you're this close to getting the beating of your life. Where were you?"

To my surprise, Lionel's face colors and he averts his gaze.

"Spill it," Davis orders. "Charlie isn't feeling so nice right now. His girl got hurt, and I'm half tempted to let him kick the shit out of you for answers."

A long silence, then . . .

"We were in Billings. At the craft show."

The edges of Wyatt's lips twitch. We all stare at Lionel as if he's just admitted to first-degree murder.

Ford makes a sound of disgust. "We're gonna believe him?"

"Why would he admit that?" Wyatt argues.

Lionel shifts in his recliner. "Why would we attack Wyatt? We got beef at the bar, nowhere else."

"Even with Sheena going around saying that bullshit about Wyatt?" Ford asks.

Lionel lets out a cackle of laughter. "Man, that is water under the bridge. We knew the next day that Wyatt didn't touch our crazy cousin."

Wyatt's confused eyes flick to mine.

"Then who the fuck cut her hair?" Davis asks impatiently.

"She did it herself."

"Christ," Ford says at the revelation.

Lionel ashes his cigarette on the carpet, twists in his chair to look at Wyatt. "You wouldn't fuck her, right? That's Sheena. When she doesn't get what she wants, she destroys." His face clouds. "She flushed our sea monkeys down the drain when we were kids because hers died and ours didn't." A shrug. "She thought she'd fuck you over. Make you squirm."

"How do you know that?" I snap.

"She fessed up."

Ford steps forward and stares at Lionel. "Why?"

"Fallon," Clyde says, and Wyatt looks as surprised as I've ever seen him. "She cornered Sheena at the House of Hair. Waved some shears around, shredded every chair in her shop, broke every mirror, and told her to tell the truth. Set things straight in Resurrection or else."

Lionel laughs. "I thought Sheena had fangs, but Fallon, that woman's as mean as a snake."

Wyatt, sucks in a breath, stiffens. "Watch your fucking mouth," he snarls, smashing Clyde into the wall like he's a ball of putty.

"So, nah, man," Lionel says with a smirk. "We may want to put Wyatt in a headlock more often than not, but we wouldn't hurt your girl."

"You better be telling me the truth." My hands ball into fists. "If I find out you're lying, I will put you in a fucking grave. Do you understand me?"

This time, real fear flickers in his eyes. Good. This motherfucker better get it through his head that I'd kill him, plain and simple.

Lionel, suddenly looking tired, runs a hand over his buzzed head. "Look, we got shit going around our ranch, too. Someone broke into our barn and let out all our livestock. It took us three days to round up our cows. I heard DVLs been creeping on the south side. Coming into town late at night. Wrecking shit." Lionel gives a dry laugh. The thin mustache on his upper lip twitches. "So, you better

lock up what you still wanna own, because these cowbo-
zos from the suburbs are shaking down anyone they can."

"Those bastards are trying to run us off our own damn
land," Ford says, anger shining in his eyes.

"It'll get worse," Clyde says, suddenly sounding like
the smartest guy in town.

An image of Ruby crumpled on the floor of her cottage
flashes in my mind, and a chill goes through me.

"They're right," Davis says. "I talked to Sheriff Richter
and other ranches in the area. Billy Mayson found rattle-
snakes in his barn. Vendors are collecting early because
DVLs putting the pressure on them."

"Truce then," I say, crossing my arms. My gaze pinballs
between Wyatt and Lionel. "Until we get this shit handled
with DVL, no more pranks."

"You're the last sons of bitches I'd expect to partner
with, but . . ." Lionel stamps his smoke in the ashtray, gives
me a nod. "Truce."

"We have the same goal," I say. "Protect our ranches,
our animals, our people."

"And tell us where our goddamn horse is—"

"Jesus Christ, Wyatt," Davis and Ford shout in unison.

I turn to my brothers. "C'mon. Let's get out of here." I
want to get back to Ruby, not stick around here and bullshit with these idiots.

With a flip of his middle finger, Wyatt snatches a beer
from the fridge by the door. "See ya, assholes."

Lionel's voice stops us at the door. "You wanna know
where the horse is? Fine, I'll tell you, so I don't have to kick
your ass every weekend at Nowhere." Wyatt snorts. Lionel
continues. "We took her. It was a joke. We meant to give
her back, but . . ." Something dark flickers in Lionel's eyes

and he looks down at his lap. "Our ma sold her, okay? We needed groceries that month and . . .well, we didn't know what else to do."

A stunned silence coats the room.

Wyatt clears his throat. "Well, fuck."

I look at Lionel, sitting there in his recliner, looking embarrassed as hell. And I get it. I don't like the guy, but I understand. Desperate people do desperate things, because when I look at Ruby, I feel the same way.

"Now get the hell outta here," Lionel snaps, suddenly looking like the asshole we've always known.

We climb back into the truck, Davis at the wheel, Ford and Wyatt in the backseat. "That was a bust," Ford drawls cheerfully.

"Tell me about it." Wyatt rolls down the window, lifts his beer in the air. "Least I got a party favor."

Davis shakes his head. "If it's not the Wolfingtons, it's DVL."

A muscle clenches in my jaw, and I inhale trying to keep my anger at bay. We should have seen this in the first place. The bones found on the ranch, the vendor shakedowns, the attack on Ruby and Wyatt. That was all DVL. They want to scare us away from the ranch, bully us into selling. Take over Resurrection for good.

Over my dead body.

As my brothers pick apart what just happened, my phone rings. I grab it up when I see Ruby's name on the screen.

"Charlie?" The tremble in her voice has me white-knuckling the phone.

"Ruby, you okay?"

"I'm fine. I just . . ." She exhales a breathy sigh. "Look. You can't kill anyone."

I growl, not liking where this is going. "Out with it, Sunflower."

"It's Colton. He's the one who attacked me."

Her revelation's like a shock of cold air in my lungs. Then, after I digest her words, I frown down at the phone.

"And how do you know that?" My right eye's beginning to tic.

She hesitates. "I asked him."

I inhale deep down into my lungs to force away the rising panic. "Baby, tell me you're not in the same room with the guy."

"Okay," she says in a small voice. "I won't."

"Ruby, get the fuck away from him," I growl. "We're on our way."

"Charlie—"

"Baby. Go. Now."

Davis rips the truck out of the gravel drive.

"We're in the barn," she chirps like it's nothing, like my heart isn't hanging on by its last thread, then ends the call.

"*Fuck.*" I tear a hand through my hair and look at Davis. "We got a problem."

31

Ruby

THE SQUEAL OF TIRES CUTS THROUGH THE silence of the summer air.

Colton makes a kind of squeak when he sees them coming. Four pissed off cowboys storm across the gravel drive toward the barn like some sort of take-charge Wild West swat team coming to lay down the law. Fists clenched, faces tight.

Colton's eyes flick to me, the color draining from his face. "He's gonna hit me, isn't he?"

I bite my lip and say nothing. Charlie's expression is a man rage bent and hell bound.

That's the least he's going to do.

Colton inhales a steeling breath, drawing his shoulders up. "Okay. Fuck. *Fuck.*" Fear ghosts his youthful face.

I feel bad for him. But then I remember my poor cottage and my crushed cowboy hat and my broken plants and my panicked heart and him trying to sabotage Runaway Ranch and the cowboy I love and I don't feel so sorry anymore.

I feel as pissed as Charlie looks.

"Move away from her. Now." My heart jumps at the fierceness in Charlie's voice.

In two larges strides, he's planting his muscled body in front of me.

"You get one minute," Davis calls out.

The rest of his brothers hang back, arms crossed, stances defensive.

Then Charlie takes the first swing.

I jump and clap my hand across my mouth.

Charlie's brick of a fist connects with Colton's jaw, sending the kid crashing against the door of the tack room. Colton doesn't even try to fight back. He stands there, stunned, plastered to the wall for support. Blood trickles from his nose, his eyes glassy with pain.

Before Charlie can get in a second punch, I step in front of him.

His eyes flash, but he drops his fist at my appearance. "Ruby. Don't make me put you over my shoulder."

Charlie's voice has dropped to an unearthly authoritative growl, and my stomach clenches. I hate that it turns me on.

"No." I cross my arms, drawing myself up tall. I press a hand against his rock-hard chest, pushing him back, ignoring the amused smiles Wyatt and Ford trade. "You can't hear what Colton has to say if you break his face."

Our gazes lock, war.

"She's got a point," Ford says mildly, swaggering inside. Seeing the baseball bat in the corner of the room, he gives me a nod of approval.

Charlie swipes the back of his hand over his brow like I'm making him sweat.

Maybe I am.

"Listen to him," I order, scanning the brothers. "All of you."

They need to know what I know.

"Let's get comfortable, asshole." Wyatt kicks out a feed bucket.

Ford grabs Colton's arm and slams him down on the makeshift seat. The Montgomerys surround him, looking like executioners.

Colton's eyes lift desperately to me like he doesn't know where to start.

"Don't look at her," Charlie growls through his clenched jaw. The icy mask of rage he wears has me going still. "She won't help you. Look at me and tell me what you did."

All at once, adrenaline leaves me. My breath is a shaky hitch and right before my legs can turn to jelly, Charlie wraps an arm around me, steadying me against him.

"Go on," I tell Colton. "Tell them what you told me."

Colton swipes at his busted lip. "The woman in the video of Ford . . . she's my mom."

Ford jerks back with an expression of shock.

"And my father . . ." Colton gulps. "He's Declan Valiante." His whisper lands like a grenade.

"Holy shit," Wyatt breathes.

Wide-eyed, the brothers share stunned glances. Charlie squeezes me against him tight, like he'll never let me loose, like it's all he can do to control his fury.

I know the feeling. It was sabotage, coming from inside the house. The most prominent developer in Montana, a man running for office, sent goons—his own son—to sabotage small-town ranches.

Sighing, Colton continues. "We thought if I got a job

here, if my mom posted that video, we could sabotage the ranch from the inside. If it got bad press, it'd force you to fall behind in payments. And you'd either default or sell to DVL."

"Underbid by about two million bucks, bud," Ford says.

"That was the plan." Colton swallows. "Get it for cheap. Get all the land in Resurrection for cheap."

Davis scoffs in disgust. "And let me guess. Strip our land. Call it progress."

Colton hangs his head. "Something like that."

Hearing it all over again has me clenching my fists, just like Charlie. My heart hammers in solidarity with this family.

"It wasn't personal," Colton whispers, eliciting a growl of warning from Davis. "I wanted to get out of this town. If I did what my dad wanted, spent one summer here, he'd pay for my college. I could go anywhere. I could get *out*." A helpless expression crosses his face as he looks pleadingly at Charlie. "I had to do it, man. I had to."

"You attacked Ruby. My brother. How do you justify that?" Charlie spits.

"I didn't attack Wyatt. Those were people my dad hired. As for Ruby . . . she's turning the ranch around. You don't need to sell now." Colton's gaze drops to the hay-covered floor. "My father wanted me to scare her away. I didn't mean to hurt her."

His statement has Charlie's fist flying out to grab a hunk of Colton's T-shirt. He yanks him off the bucket. "You did hurt her," he snarls, steel in his voice.

"I know." Colton hangs in Charlie's tight grip. "I'm sorry."

"Damn." Wyatt swears, looking like a leaner, boyish version of Charlie. "I liked you too, kid."

Ford shakes his head. "We trusted you, you little shit."

A tear tracks its way down Colton's cheek. "I know."

Davis, fists clenched, says, "I think you know what this means."

"I'm fired." Colton looks miserable.

Still fisting the front of Colton's T-shirt, Charlie leans in, his blue eyes searing and murderous. "You should be dead right now, but you're not because of her. So get your shit and get the fuck off my ranch. If I see you again—if you breathe in Ruby's direction—I'll hang you in the town square." Charlie releases him, shoving him in the direction of the door.

Colton turns toward me, and Ford puts a hand on his chest. "Don't even think about it."

Charlie levels a big finger at Colton. "Tell your father if he's got a problem, he can come back and talk to me."

We watch as Colton slinks off and then four sets of eyes land on me.

"Ruby, how in the hell you figure this out?" Davis sounds impressed.

"The belt buckles," I tell them, flushing. "Colton's matched the woman's Instagram avatar."

Ford's brow bunches. "What the hell's an avatar?"

I stifle a smile. "Her profile picture," I explain. "They had the same motto on the belt buckle. Like some weird dysfunctional family crest."

Wyatt cackles. "Check it out. Fairy Tale hunting down bad guys."

I blush, chance a glance at Charlie.

He doesn't look as amused as his brothers. Jaw tight,

fingers flexed at his side, face stormy. He looks downright terrifying.

"What do we do about the developers?" Wyatt asks.

"I'll talk to Sheriff Richter and the surrounding ranchers," Davis says. "Get everyone on the same page and let them know what's happening." Grooves deepen around his mouth. "I'll help anyone who needs it with security. If we can get some proof they're trespassing, we might have some recourse."

Charlie nods, his expression hard now. "Good idea."

Ford sighs, glancing out the barn doors. "Better make sure the kid gets off okay. Don't want him sticking around here longer than necessary."

"Y'all go on up to the house," Charlie grits out. "I wanna talk to Ruby. Alone."

As soon as his brothers disappear, Charlie turns his fury-filled gaze to me.

Goosebumps break out over my arms.

That look. A look I love. A look I've seen before. A thrill of anticipation rolls down my spine.

I'm in trouble.

32

Charlie

"**I**'M GOING TO YELL," I WARN RUBY WHEN MY brothers clear out of the barn.

She gasps playfully and backs up. "You promised." Her eyes are glittery, like she knows what's coming. Adorable, but I'm not swayed.

My gaze darkens. "Cashing in on that promise right now won't help you, darlin."

"I won't apologize for helping you," she says, stubbornly jutting her chin.

I advance, pushing her into one of the stalls. "You never should have tried to talk to him by yourself. You should have fucking waited for me." I cage her against the wall, pin her in, when all I want to do is get her body in my arms and protect her with everything I have.

Keep her safe from the entire world.

She pokes me in the chest. "You don't scare me, Cowboy."

"You do." I take her hand and kiss the pulse in her

palm. Its rapid beat has me on my knees. "*You* scared me, Ruby. What if you were hurt? What if—"

I can't even get my sentence out.

Goddamn this woman.

Beautiful, tiny chaos. That's what she's been ever since she set foot on the ranch. I've faced down bulls, broken bones, roped wild horses, and the only thing that terrifies the fuck out of me is this this five-foot-three fairy-tale slip of a girl.

I grip her waist. "No more detective, Ruby."

"I just wanted to help."

"Help? You almost helped me have a goddamn heart attack."

She pales.

"You end me, you know that?" I whisper, my hands sliding up to cradle her face.

Her stunning blue eyes flutter shut. "Forgive me, Cowboy."

"Baby, you could be a serial killer and I'd forgive you." I pull back and give her the fiercest glare I can manage. "Never do that again."

"I'm sorry, Charlie. I'm sorry." Lifting on tiptoes, she kisses the corner of my jaw. Small soft warm kisses that have my cock begging to be inside her. "I'm so sorry."

Fearless, that's what this girl is.

My chest tightens. A ragged breath shakes out of me. Stepping closer, I flatten her against the wall. Electricity crackles in the air between us. "You have no idea what you do to me."

Lust darkens her expression. "Show me, Charlie."

Her words are like the stinging slap of a rein, making me move. I haul her to my chest and kiss her until we're both without breath. Ruby moans and threads her hands through my hair. The delicate whimper she lets out turns my cock to a rod of steel. Starving for more, I kiss the pulse in her throat and drag my tongue down the column of her neck.

Every ounce of control deserts me. I'm obsessed with this woman. She's ruined me today. Single-handedly taken years off my life.

Adrenaline, worry, fear, has me tearing at her skirt. She gasps when I shove it roughly above the V of her thighs. I whirl her around and flip the hem of her sundress up around her waist, exposing her bare ass. The ripest peach I want to sink my teeth into.

I drop to my knees and gently bite the smooth flesh of her ass, branding her.

Mine.

She squeaks and then mewls breathlessly, "Oh, I like that. I like that, Charlie." Ruby glances over her shoulder at me, eyes heavy-lidded.

"On my knees for you, baby," I drawl. "You like *that?* 'Cause that's how you're always gonna have me."

She nods, her face glowing.

I slap her ass, not hard enough to hurt, but hard enough to make that gorgeous fucking mouth moan my name. And then I surge to my feet, yanking her back against my chest.

My mouth nips at her shoulder blade as I reach around and drop my hand, groaning when I find her swollen and soaked. My fingers slip inside her. She shudders. Tightening my grip, I pull her close, working her into a fever.

"You're so beautiful," I say with reverence, watching her face as I stroke my fingers over her clit. "So fucking perfect."

She whimpers and rests her cheek against the wall. Her red mouth pops in a pretty pout, her eyes rolling back in her head when I rotate my thumb.

"You keep this sweet pussy on lockdown, you hear me?" I rasp in her ear. "Me, and only me, baby. I'm the one who tastes it. Eats it. Fucks it."

"Yes, Charlie," she says on a broken sob. Her hips buckle as she comes, slapping the thighs of my jeans. "Yes. *Yes*."

I want all of her. I can't get enough of her. I have to be inside of her.

It's cruel taking my hand away from all that sweetness, but I do. I'm already unbuckling my jeans.

Fabric falls, bunches around my hips, and cold metal presses against warm flesh as sweat drips down my chest. My hands travel up her thighs, leaving trails of wetness. Every inch of her velvet skin, I drink in. I smooth a palm over her spine and she arcs into my touch. With a growl, I pull her back flush to my front. And then Ruby's opening her damp thighs for me, and I slip my throbbing cock inside of her. We're in sync so goddamn good as her tight walls clench around me and I give a hard thrust.

A little mewl spills from her lips.

Her back arches, a slow, delicate movement that has me groaning at the ceiling. Ruby's head falls back on my chest, giving me a million-dollar view of her gorgeous tits. Eyes closed, her slender arms reach for me, twining around my neck.

"Slow, baby," I grind out against her ear. My heart feels like it's going to split open. "Slow and steady for you."

Her breasts rise and fall. The neckline of her dress has slipped down, and two pink nipples peek out, nearly destroying me.

"Charlie," she begs, her voice sweet, tremulous. "*Ahhh, Charlie!*"

"Quiet, baby," I say, remembering we're in a barn where anyone could walk in on us. I glance around, hating the thought of someone barging in and seeing Ruby naked. Gently, I grip her neck and run my hand up her throat. Her pulse hammers in my fingertips. "Quiet, Sunflower."

She pants. Her breath warm against my palm, her body undulates with mine, her perfect ass making rhythmic circles against my groin as I drive into her over and over again.

Slow. Steady.

She's so wet. So tight.

I slide my thumb into her mouth and nearly come when she bites me sharp and hard with her teeth. She smiles, savoring the contact.

Fuck.

Heart pounding wildly, I pull her tighter against me, crushing her in my arms, and thrust.

"Look me in the eye when you come, baby. You hear me? I want your eyes on me. I want you to see how fucking bad you own me."

"Yes," she gasps, her slender body twisting against me, sweat pebbling in the channel between her breasts. Her eyes are locked on mine, that wild halo of hair swirling around us. "Yes, Cowboy."

This isn't sex. Not anymore.

My world is all Ruby.

Her sunshine smile, her sweet heat coming from her core, her gorgeous face.

With a ragged growl, I grip her hips and thrust.

Hard.

Deep.

The deepest I've ever been.

This time I can't stop Ruby's scream. Her high-pitched cry echoes in the barn and I lose it. A shiver rolls down my spine at the same time a growl wrenches from my lips, and I spill into her. Her orgasm follows, her pussy squeezing around me as I still pump away. The frantic urge to never stop with this woman, to never let go, is all-consuming.

"You listen to me, you hear? You fuckin' behave yourself. I can't have you hurt. I need you here." I rasp the words into the curve of her dewy throat, kissing her and pleading with her all at once.

Ruby shudders against me, still trembling from the force of her orgasm. I anchor her small body to mine, keeping us joined. Her arms slide down, her hands running through my beard, before she goes limp against me and I sweep her up in my arms.

Heaven.

If I never come back down, I'll be a happy man.

End of fucking story.

Ruby sighs as I gather her against my chest. We lie in the fresh bed of hay, a blanket spread beneath us so she doesn't get scratched up. I rake my gaze over her body. Gorgeous. Glowing. Her halo of rose-gold hair fanned around us. The inside of her thighs wet and sticky. The impression of my belt buckle's branded on the outside of her hip.

Branded.

A proud growl rumbles in my chest and rips out of me. Mine.

She's mine.

"So, how many girls have you had in the stables?" she asks with a melodic teasing lilt to her voice.

"None," I tell her roughly.

Back in the day, it had been a teenage Charlie's wet dream, but the only woman I've ever had in the stables is Ruby.

And I don't want anyone else.

She smiles and snuggles deeper into my chest like she can't bear to have any space between us. Hell, the feeling's mutual. As I glance down at her pretty profile, worry wraps around my throat like a noose.

I'm very fucking aware that the stubborn girl in my arms put herself in danger today. All to help us out. To protect the ranch. Hell, half of Resurrection will know who to look out for now, thanks to her.

I'm still pissed off about it. That kid was right under my nose the entire time. I never thought to dig into the woman who posted the video, just figured she was an angry, vengeful Karen. But Ruby, my girl, knew better.

Now, a fuse is lit. It's not war anymore, it's Armageddon. This ranch business is getting dangerous, and Ruby's mixed up in the middle of it. It fills me with a helplessness that makes me feel like I'm drowning.

Nothing will happen to her. I'll walk through the fires of hell before I let anyone hurt her.

"What scares you, Charlie?" Ruby's soft voice sweeps me from my dark thoughts.

I hug her hard. "Why do you ask?"

She curls her fingers in my chest hair, and clear blue eyes slide my way. "Because you're so strong and grumpy and serious, sometimes I can't tell."

Today. Today and every day you've been at this ranch they scare me.

"Losing people I love." I stroke a hand over her silky rose-gold tresses. "You?"

"Mine is not living." She yawns, her voice sleepy. "But I feel like I've lived a thousand lifetimes here at this ranch." Pushing up on her elbow, she stares at me with dazed bedroom eyes. "That's why I went to Colton today. For you. I promised you I'd help you."

"It was too much of a risk," I say gruffly.

If Colton had hurt her, there's not enough bail money in the world that would get me out of jail.

"I don't mind taking risks." She smiles brightly and another jagged piece of my heart resets. "The most risk I've ever taken is this summer here with you."

Her sweet innocence unravels me. I sit up beside her and press my hand to her breast, her heartbeat imprinting on my palm. "I've never met anyone like you," I tell her. "So full of life and light. You carry an entire heart in your soul, Ruby."

At my words, her eyes widen.

"You like my heartbeat?" she asks, a hopeful note in her tone.

Slipping her hand into mine, I bring her wrist to my mouth and kiss the pulse that beats there. It's fast. Almost shaky. "I love this beautiful beat of yours. It's the best damn thing I've ever heard."

It's like I've given her the moon.

Tears flood her beautiful baby blues. "Oh, Charlie,"

she says breathlessly, her swollen red mouth tilting to accept mine. I feel it then. The end of me. And I don't fucking care. I lose myself in her sweet sunshine kiss. Then her arms loop around my neck, and I'm pulling her back down beside me, covering her with the blanket.

Minutes pass, and we lie here, our heartbeats coming back down to normal.

"I could die," Ruby whispers fiercely, sounding strangely content. "I could die just like this."

"Hey." Frowning, I lean up to look at her. "Don't say that."

I feel like I'm about to be gutted.

The way she talks . . .

I can't stand it.

Before I can say anything, she stretches her arms up and out, exposing her bare breasts. I glance at the door, not wanting my brothers to come in and get an eyeful of the best view in the state of Montana.

"Why not? It's true." She nuzzles against me, kissing my throat and distracting me from my grim thoughts. "You're wonderful, Charlie."

Her sweetness, her vulnerability, has my jaw clenching. I tighten my arms around her, tucking her head under my chin.

The ache in my chest intensifies.

And I give in. Give into everything I've been denying this entire summer and face the fucking facts.

Ruby's it.

Inevitable.

My everything.

33

Charlie

"**T**HIS IS LIKE THE MOST PERFECTLY SHAPED apple," Ruby announces as I slam through the front door, wiping sweat from my brow. She sits at the kitchen island, barefoot, wearing a white sundress, laptop open in front of her.

I kiss her first, then toss the stack of bills nabbed from the Bullshit Box onto the countertop. As she bites into the red apple with a satisfied moan, I pour myself a cup of coffee and chuckle.

"Sunflower status?" I drawl, leaning back against the cupboards to watch her. I love how the tiniest things in life light her up.

"Oh, most definitely," she deadpans, licking juice off the corner of her wrist.

My gaze lands on her plump lips, and my cock jumps to life. "Are you trying to turn me on?"

She laughs, her bare feet swinging on the stool. "I'm trying to eat an apple, Cowboy." Never wanted to be an apple so bad in my life.

"Taste," she orders. She holds the apple out to me, a flirty smile on her face. "Taste how good it is, Charlie."

Arching an amused brow, I close the distance between us. "Rather taste you," I growl, running my palms over her smooth, bare thighs.

"Taste," she commands again, looking at me earnestly.

With a chuckle, I comply, willing my cock to play dead as I take a bite of the apple. Sweet. Crisp. It makes me think of Ruby and has my dick aching even more.

"Good?" she asks, looking at me from beneath long lashes.

"Good." I dip my head, drawing her closer. "But this is better."

And then my lips hit hers. Ruby's breasts crush against my chest as she winds her slender arms around my neck. I inhale, feeling closer to heaven every time I breathe her in. My blood simmers as need, fierce and desperate, threads its way into my veins.

When we finally tear away, we're both panting.

Face dazed, a sexy little gasp pops out of her mouth. "Better," she echoes, her eyes glassy.

I press a kiss to her brow. "You feeling okay today?" I ask, scanning her pretty face. She's pale and has dark circles under her eyes. The last few nights, I've woken up to find her downstairs, curled up on the couch in a blanket.

"Just fine," she says in a silvery little breath, but her attention drifts to the window. "How was your day?"

"Sprayed some weeds up on the north side of the ranch. Bastards are making our cattle sick." I pull the stack of bills toward me. "Now paperwork."

"You like paperwork or ranch work more?"

I bust out a laugh. These days, I'm getting used to them.

"Darlin' I'd rather haul manure any day of the week than deal with paperwork."

She leans in and sniffs my chest. "Well, you smell good to me." Her fingers curl into the neck of my T-shirt as she tugs me down for a kiss. "Maybe this is my sunflower of the day. Your shirt still warm from the sun."

I pull her into my arms to remind myself what a lucky man I am.

There's something about a long, hard day on the ranch and coming home to Ruby. The angel kiss she lays on me the second I walk in the door. Sharing a cold beer on the porch after the hard work's done. How much light, warmth, and energy she's brought into my life.

The doors and windows of the cabin are open, and a soft breeze blows in off the mountains. Her flower pots take up all the available real estate. Three small pots of violets on the counter, and two cascading ferns on top of the fridge. She put the sunflowers I gave her in the kitchen so they can eat up the sunlight from the front window. I've never seen my place so cheerful.

The last two weeks, we've fallen in to our own little groove.

I fucking love it.

There's no chance in hell she's moving back into her cottage. Even though we know DVL is behind the attack, and what they're doing, I'm not taking any chances. We've beefed up security, alerted our neighbors and the sheriff. If they come again, we're ready for them. And Ruby's safe with me. Her being here takes away the guilt over her getting hurt in the first place.

I'll never be able to do enough to protect her.

"How about you?" I nod at her open laptop. "What have you been up to?"

"Oh, I've been up to a lot." She stands, bouncing into me. With flourish, she slides a paper folder my way. "Here. More paperwork."

I band an arm around her waist. "What's this?"

"Your social media calendar planned out through the end of the year."

I flip through the calendar she's put together. It's impressive. No bullshit marketing blather. Ruby's telling our story in the most authentic way she can. Our local vendors. Our employees. That we're family, and this ranch means something.

Suddenly, there's a knot in my throat I can't unstick.

This intelligent woman worked her ass off to understand Runaway Ranch, and it shows. She gave a voice to our ranch, our employees, our town. She's not some stranger in another city on a computer blowing smoke. She's in the shit with us. I've never been more proud.

"This is a printout, but I'll send you a digital file for whoever you get to take it over," Ruby chirps, dragging me from my thoughts.

"Take it over?" The air's sucked out of me.

"When I leave, you'll need someone to post." She giggles. "I don't think it's going to be Wyatt." Her fingers fly over her keyboard. "Now I know you're a tech-challenged cowboy, but I made a Dropbox account and uploaded a ton of photos for you to use. I think you have enough for the next two years . . ."

She goes on, chattering in her sunny lilt, but the only phrase that makes sense is *she's leaving*.

A knife to the heart.

I want a drink, mind-numbing liquid to bring me back down to earth.

Summer ends in four weeks.

Another knife. Another realization.

How different my life will be without Ruby.

She fits here. Her creamer in my fridge. Her strawberry-scented shampoo in my bathroom. Her laughter in my kitchen. Her beautiful body in my bed.

She's the heartbeat of the ranch. *My* heartbeat. It's like my pulse kicked in the second I met her. I'm alive because of her.

And that's when I realize my mistake.

I've claimed her as mine, but not out loud.

Not in a way that means anything.

She's moving on soon. She'll find someone else, whisper another man's name at night. Her blue eyes will light up when she finally sees her California sunset, getting that last check off her to-do list without me around to make sure she's satisfied. She'll have babies with someone else, a family, a forever.

Another man will get her sunshine and her kind heart and her smiles and it sure as hell won't be me.

The thought nearly strangles me alive.

"Charlie? Are you okay?" Ruby's soft voice upturns my thoughts. A pretty frown creases her brow. "Do you not like the calendar?"

"The calendar's great." Wrapping my hands around her waist, I lift her onto the counter. Move between her legs so she can't get away. "Listen, baby . . ."

My mouth goes dry, words fail me.

And it's here, in my sunlit kitchen, Ruby's bright blue

eyes on mine, a sunshine smile on her face, that it hits me—I've never loved anyone so much in my entire life.

She giggles and tilts her head, almost in wonder. "Cowboy, you look nervous."

Stay. Ask her to stay. Tell her you love her. And never let her go.

If I don't tell her how I feel, she's gone. Never seeing her again, never holding her again at night, it's a bullet to the heart. No way will I let that happen.

Ruby's as much a piece of me as the land I live on.

I hang my head, a ragged breath shaking out of me. "Sunflower."

Playful smile falling from her face, she sobers. Her small hands palm my bearded cheek. "What? What is it?"

Say it. Tell her.

When I lift my face, we lock eyes, and it's like she's heard every word I've left unspoken.

She sucks in a breath, and her eyes get as big as saucers. She puts a palm out as if she can stop me. "Charlie."

My hands slide up her hips to grip her by the waist. Heart slamming against my ribs, I clear my throat. "Ruby, baby, I—"

The screen door clatters open.

Wyatt stomps inside, his faced flushed. Keena skitters beside him. "Charlie, we got cows flying, man!"

"What?" I bark over my shoulder before turning my gaze back to Ruby. She searches my eyes, her lips parted, an expression of confusion on her pretty face.

"Those cows from the meadow got over onto the ridge. One fell into the ravine."

"Fuck." This isn't what I need today.

I tear a hand through my hair, hating to leave it like this, but I won't keep a cow in pain. "I gotta go."

Her fingers tighten on mine. "I know."

"Charlie," Wyatt blasts, and I growl at him. "Say your goodbyes, kiss your girl, and let's go save some fucking cows."

I hustle out after my brother, leaving Ruby staring after me, feeling like I've missed my chance to say something important.

34

Ruby

MY PULSE FLUTTERS WILD AND RECKLESS IN my neck as I slide back onto the bar stool.

My brain whirls at Charlie's words, the strange look on his face . . .

Charlie had something to tell me. But what? It can't be what I think it was, can it?

No. We are temporary and he knows that.

Doesn't he?

But *what-if*?

What if he loves me?

Oh god.

There is no way I should want it, but I do.

I want my love returned, even if it is a bad idea.

A soft smile curls my lips when I think about how my life has changed with Charlie.

I love waking in the morning's twilight, Charlie holding me tightly to him. The first ride of the week with the wind in my hair, Charlie hustling alongside me to keep up, pride in his eyes. The way he leans in to kiss me when he gets home from the ranch, turning me into a molten puddle of need. And best of all, the way I go limp after a night of spectacular sex, Charlie whispering in my ear that I'm the most beautiful girl he's ever seen.

I've never felt this before. Dumb, dangerous hope.

With trembling fingers, I reach for my purse. I open my medication and dry-swallow a pill.

A ping sounds from my laptop. I set my medication on the counter.

I scowl at the email from Max with a link to the Stanford study. My big brother's been on my case for the last two weeks to enroll. I haven't told him anything that's happened on the ranch. He and my father know I'm safe. Anything more would cause them to worry.

> To: Ruby
> From: Max
>> Hey killer.
>> I'm sending a link to that study.
>> I know you don't want to hear it. And I know you're scowling that weak ass scowl right now, because you can never really be mad at anyone, but humor me and read it. It'd be a stop on your road trip. And your annoying family would come out and take care of you.
>> They're saying this new study is good. That it could change your life. So read it, Rubes.
>
> Max

But my life has already changed, I think.

Still, I click the link. Wrinkle my nose at the cold clinical trial speak. Ablation. Catheters. Hospital stay. Scrape your heart and hope for the best.

I don't know what my best is.

I don't know what I want anymore.

I should do the study. It's in California, and Max is right. It aligns perfectly with my to-do list.

Truth is, I've been moving slowly the last week. Ever since Colton attacked me in my cottage, my heart feels shaky. I've had heart rate spikes so strong they wake me up at night. I think I'm smart, escaping downstairs to let my heartbeat come back to normal, but Charlie always finds me and carries me back to bed.

It scares me.

For the first time since I've been on the road, my heart isn't cooperating.

I wring a dish towel in my hands.

Screw doubt. That's best left with my father and brother. I am healthy. And happy. My heart has never been better. Because of this summer.

Because of Charlie.

My eyes flutter shut. His sweet words from that day in the barn—*I love this beautiful beat of yours*—lit a fire inside of me. They shouldn't mean anything, but they mattered to me. So, so much. They gave me hope, like maybe he could understand my SVT if I told him. That he'd forgive me for keeping the truth from him about my health. Even if the whole idea is ludicrous.

We have a deal, though. Runaway Ranch for the truth about why I'm on the road.

And he hasn't ponied up, so why should I?

Sighing, I shut my laptop and slide off the stool. Still, I hate lying to him. The guilt that crashes over me is as frenzied as my heartbeat.

I scan the kitchen, deciding to tidy up. I set Charlie's mug in the copper bucket sink and shut off the coffeepot.

I put my creamer back in the fridge, throw away my apple. Mundane tasks that calm my heartbeat.

Although I miss my charming cottage, I love Charlie's log cabin. It has a personality as big and powerful as the man himself. Wood, log, and stone—the holy trinity of Big Sky country—keeps it true to its western roots.

My gaze lights on the calendar tacked to the fridge. Tomorrow's August. My deadline to leave looms.

Four weeks.

Should I leave Resurrection? It's a question very much in need of an answer.

If I don't go, what does that mean for me and Charlie? But does he even want me to stay?

It seemed like he might. The way his hands gripped my waist, scorching me through my dress. The strange look on his face. Haunted. Nervous.

My tough cowboy was nervous.

A huge smile overtakes my face. What if he feels the same way?

I love you.

I imagine him saying it in that deep southern drawl that's like a caress over my entire body.

Oh god, I've never wanted anything so bad in my life. Being loved back would feel beautiful. Not dangerous or dumb.

I chose this man, and maybe he's choosing me.

Maybe we could do this.

Grabbing up a stack of napkins, I laugh aloud in the middle of the kitchen. "What if?" I murmur, heart fluttering in agreement.

I open the junk drawer where takeout napkins and ketchup packets live and deposit the napkins. As I do, my thumb catches a piece of paper. Curious, I sweep away the junk to find a photo. I lift it to eye level.

A girl in blue jeans and a simple white tank top sits on the back of a champagne-colored horse. She's laughing, looking away from the camera, leather reins in her hand. Her long, fiery red hair flows behind her as she rides. She's beautiful, yet there's a fierceness in her eyes that catches my breath.

A throat being cleared has me jumping.

My head jerks up and I blanch. "I'm sorry," I say, dropping the photo on the counter. Ford stands at the island. He looks like a leaner version of Davis, except with shaggier hair and a relaxed grin. A rush of shame hits me that he caught me snooping. "I was cleaning up, and I—"

"You don't have to explain." A muscle jerks in his jaw as he nods at the photo. "That's Maggie."

"Maggie?"

I look back at the photo. It's been buried deep within the drawer, but not deep enough that it can't be found. The corners creased like it's been handled often. Recognition dawns. It resembles a worn-out photo of my mother that my father—

Oh god.

Oh my god.

A heart strangling thought hits me.

The worst thought.

The worst possibility.

I gasp.

In an instant, the pieces of the puzzle drop into place. The reason Charlie's so hesitant to speak about his past. The way he stares at me when I'm on Arrow, his eyes glued to every move I make when I ride. His deep frown, his protective nature, his gruff growl. It's all because he's a forever grieving cowboy who lives alone on his ranch and doesn't talk to anyone.

Pressure builds behind my eyes. I look up at Ford. "She died?" I whisper.

He nods again. "She did. Been gone ten years now." Hesitation crosses his face, then he says, "She and Charlie were engaged."

My eyes widen. My heart drops.

"I didn't know. He didn't tell me."

"I figured." Dragging a hand down his handsome face, Ford shakes his head. "Charlie, he's not so good with talking about his past."

"You don't have to explain." A tear rolls down my cheek. "He should be the one to tell me when he wants to."

After one last look at the photo, I gently put it back where I found it. It's important to respect Charlie's privacy like he's respected mine.

That's when Ford's brown eyes flick to the counter. To my pills.

The breath leaves my lungs, and every ounce of blood drains from my face.

For a long few seconds, silence.

I hurry across the room, grab them up and shove them back into my purse.

"Listen, Ruby," Ford says, as if carefully selecting his words. "I know y'all got some boundaries and my brother may be too stupid to say it, but he likes you. A lot. You're the reason he's out there saddling up with a smile today."

His statement doesn't make me feel better. It makes me feel worse.

"We got him back because of you." His jaw flexes,

and I'm horrified when his voice cracks. Like a million pieces of the past are shattering inside of him. "I'm asking you, honey, don't be his new heartbreak. We can't lose him again."

My heart hammers faster. A wave of guilt rocks me like a rogue wave.

"I understand," I whisper.

I wait until Ford leaves, and then I put my hands on the cool counter top. I try to breathe evenly, but I can't. My breath comes out in shaky bursts, wreaking havoc on my heartbeat.

Heartbreaker.

That's what I am.

The worst kind of person.

Because loud and clear, I heard what Ford was telling me.

He loves you. Don't fuck with his heart.

A strangled gasp escapes me, and I squeeze my eyes shut. Hot tears drip down my cheeks.

What I'm doing with Charlie is too dangerous. Reckless.

It was different when no one was saying the words. When we could pretend it was all temporary, all about good sex.

But now . . .

Charlie's loved and lost before. Had I known that, I never would have played this game. I thought I was using my heart to change my life. Turns out, I'm destroying one.

My heartbeats come to a halt. I sway where I stand, gripping the counter for support.

I can't do this to him. I can't hurt him. He's been

through loss before, and all I'm doing is leading him on because, in the end, my heart will give out like my mother's.

I won't put Charlie through that.

Not again.

A sob rips out of me, deep, like a part of my soul's being wrenched into ragged pieces.

I have to end it.

I have to end it all.

35

Charlie

"**A**RE YOU GOING INTO TOWN TODAY?" RUBY asks from her spot in the bed.

"Yeah." I sit on the corner chair and tug on my boots. Sunlight streams through the open doors of the balcony. "Ford and I are meeting up with Stede. Then we're driving to Deer Lodge to drop that colt off with a buyer from the livestock show."

"Oh." Her gaze drops to the comforter. "Tell him goodbye for me."

"You want to?" I hate myself for selling the cream-colored pony she loves, but it's been paid for. Hell, I want to keep it for her and let her name it whatever the fuck she wants.

She shakes her head. "No. It's too hard."

Scrubbing a hand over my beard, I yawn, wishing the coffee were already made.

Wishing I had another two hours in bed with Ruby.

When I arrived home yesterday from the ravine dirty as hell, I had the best greeting of my life. Ruby threw herself into my arms, kissing on me, and I barely got a word out before we fell into bed.

Once again, we missed the sunrise. And I never got to tell her I love her.

I'm ready, though. Ruby deserves it done in the right way, so that means figuring out how to say it today.

A date. Dancing. Flowers. No interruptions.

I look over at her. She's watching me with serious blue eyes, her lean legs pulled into her chest. Her hair's disheveled, long rose-gold strands framing her face, making her look more gorgeous than she has the right to be.

I shove out of the chair and sit beside her, running a hand down the slender curve of her shoulder. "Sunflower, you okay?"

She meets my gaze for a second, then turns her face toward the balcony, forehead furrowed. "I'm fine, Charlie. Don't worry about me."

I frown. The shadows under her eyes from last night are still there and her sunshine glow is missing. I don't like her being sad. It kills me.

"Hey." I kiss her sweet lips and pull her into my arms. "Tonight, we try for the sunrise."

Tears fill her eyes.

"Baby, what'd I say?" My thumb sweeps away the lone tear that escapes.

"Nothing." Inhaling a breath, she forces a shaky smile. "You'll be gone all day?"

I stroke a hand over her hair. "If Ford has his way, yeah."

Then I swear, seeing the time on the nightstand clock. I'm late. Standing, I collect my wallet and my keys and head toward the door. Ruby's voice stops me.

"Charlie?"

"What is it, darlin'?" I drawl.

"I'll miss you." Her smile is watery.

Grinning, I head back to the bed. "Take a day off," I tell her, running a finger over the curve of her flushed cheekbone. "I want you in bed when I get home."

Long lashes lowering, she draws a heart on the comforter. "Yeah. Maybe."

I give her one last kiss, then grab up my hat and go meet Ford.

We burn five hours in town. Dropping off Ruby's colt, loading up the truck with supplies, and bullshitting with Stede at the cancer center. Finally, around four in the afternoon, we hit the road back to the ranch.

Later than I liked.

The knot in my chest hasn't loosened since I left Ruby. I feel unsettled leaving her alone by herself, and all I want to do is get back to her. Our conversation has been rattling in my head throughout the day. I don't like what I saw on her face, even if it was hard as hell to read it.

Ford yawns from the passenger seat, searching for the baseball game on the radio.

"Look, I'm just saying if the White Sox didn't want drama, they should have traded Ham Jeffries. That fucker couldn't hit a fastball if I soft-served it."

I snort. Though Ford's retired from the major leagues, it doesn't stop him from interjecting his colorful commentary on all things baseball.

I scruff a hand through my hair. "What'd you think about Stede?"

Ford shrugs. "Think he's ornery as ever."

"He's on good meds. He'll outlive us."

"Speaking of meds—" Ford twists in his seat to stare at me. "What about Ruby? Has she told you about her thing?"

My eyes flick to him. "Her thing?"

Ford shoots me a *don't be an idiot* look. "Those pills she's taking. Don't tell you haven't seen them."

"She's anemic."

"That what she said?"

"That's what I believe."

"Then why she's hiding them?"

"She's not."

"Ever seen her take them? Seen the bottle?" he demands.

I frown. "What are you getting at?"

He makes a noise of frustration. "I didn't take you for a sucker, Charlie."

Frame locking, my knuckles go white on the wheel. I don't like what my brother's implying. I don't like the way my heart skips several hundred beats at the thought of something being wrong with Ruby.

"You trying to piss me off, Ford?" I snarl.

"I'm trying to protect you." The truck bounces as we pass over the Wolfingtons' rusty cattle guard. "What do you know about this girl?"

My glare is hard, unyielding. "I know enough."

I know she likes flowers and the way my hand fits into the small of her back. Her favorite color is lilac—not purple—and her middle name is Jane, and every morning she eats small bowls of oatmeal, and sings in the shower. She smells like sunshine and soil and it's my favorite fucking scent in the entire world. I know she gasps when she's happy and gasps when she's sad and I love them all.

I know she's mine.

I know she's the one.

Still, with Ford's doubtful gaze searing a hole through me, it's hard to make it make sense. Half of me wants to tell my cynical, love-averse brother to fuck right off, but the other half knows he's right.

I have no idea why she's here.

"She's takin' pills. She's got a bucket list." Ford arches a brow. "Bucket lists are end things, Charlie."

I almost swerve off the road.

"Ford. Don't make me pull over and punch you in the fucking face."

I haven't wanted to hit him this badly since he sprayed two full cans of Axe body spray into my tent when we were camping.

"New topic, then." He jabs his crooked index finger at me, the one he broke pitching the strikeout fastball that ended the World Series "You."

I curse under my breath. Ford and his big, fat mouth.

"What about me?"

"What are you doing with her? Because she's good for you. She's got spunk. She makes you smile. Hell, she makes all of us smile. I like the girl a lot. But you still haven't told her about Maggie and in four weeks, she's gone."

"Yeah. I fucking know," I grit out, voice ragged.

"Do you love her?" Ford looks worried.

"Yeah," I snap. My brother's pushing me and it's working. The lump in my throat expands. "I love her."

The words come easy.

I've known it since the night she floated into Nowhere in that yellow sundress.

That this woman was going to blow up my life.

Now she's everywhere. In my head, and my heart, and

under my skin. And I've been the damn idiot who fought it. Fought *her*. Punishing myself. Gun-shy of this incredible girl who showed me how alone I was until I met her.

Smirking, Ford crosses his arms and leans back in his seat. "Then what are you gonna do about it, asshole?"

I open my mouth to tell him I'm going to beat the everloving shit out of his smug ass when we get back to the ranch, and then tell Ruby I love her, but the buzzing of my phone breaks our hard stare down.

Glaring at Ford, I put it on speakerphone. "What?" I bark.

"Hey, uh, Charlie?" Wyatt's voice crackles. "You almost home?"

"Yeah, why?"

A long pause. Then—"I think Ruby's leaving."

I punch the gas.

"What?"

"She's cleaning out her cottage. Packing her car."

"Fuck," Ford says.

My stomach lurches. "Keep her there. Don't let her go," I rasp, my hands throttling the wheel.

Everything in my mind empties.

Ford's warnings. The boundaries I put up. Ruby's secrets. All I can think is *I'm too late*.

I've been so set on living in the past, I couldn't pull myself together to see the future I have right in front of me.

I increase my speed, the old truck fishtailing on the winding road.

I'm keeping this woman. Fuck letting her go.

And fuck me for not giving her what she deserves.

36

Ruby

THE SHRILL SCREECH OF TIRES CUT THE EVENING air and my head jerks up from the trunk.

Shit. Oh shit.

A furious cowboy stomps his way toward me. I've never seen a man move so fast in my entire life; sparks could shoot out of his boots. I slam my suitcase into the trunk and back away, eyes wide.

This isn't what I wanted. I wanted to get out clean. No cuts.

On the cabin porch, Wyatt watches with arms crossed. "If you're trying to get away, Fairy Tale, you gotta be faster than that," he calls out.

I shoot him a glare.

Because he's right. I should have moved faster, but I spent the day packing, saying goodbye to the horses, crying in Arrow's velvet coat and telling him how much I loved him and Charlie.

"Get outta here," Charlie shouts at his brothers.

Wyatt promptly heads to the pasture, and Ford gives

me a long look of concern before heading down to the lodge.

And then Charlie's in front of me, legs braced apart like he's ready to go into combat.

"You're leaving," Charlie grits out.

I stare up at his stiff posture, his jaw set in a tight line, and I've never seen a cowboy look so damn sexy. So pissed off.

My chin comes up in defiance. "Summer's almost over."

"Still got four weeks," he says in a low voice.

"It's close enough." I move for the trunk.

He mutters a few curses before he catches me by the arm, drawing me forward. "Not close enough, Ruby." His gaze searches my face. Heated. Angry. "You were gonna leave without saying goodbye."

The accusation stings.

"It's too hard to say goodbye." I drop my gaze to the ground. "Besides . . .I did what I came to do." I swallow hard. "The ranch is safe. It'll be fine. You won't even miss me."

Some sort of miserable noise shakes out of him. "Won't miss you? How can you think I wouldn't miss you? I miss you *now*." He runs a hand down my bare arm, fists the material of my dress. I can feel my traitorous body, my heart, aching to arc into his. "Every day I'm not by your side, I miss you. Every day you're not in my bed, every day I'm not kissing you, I fucking miss you, Ruby."

Each word is like a stake in the heart. Beautiful. Devastating.

"Charlie, don't do this."

Wrenching away from him, I try to close the trunk, but

his massive hand catches the lip before I can slam it shut. Reaching inside, he takes the bag and sets it on the ground.

I glare at him, then I swear, because I left my laptop in the cabin.

I punch a finger in his iron chest. "I'm leaving, Cowboy, and you can't stop me."

His eyes flash. "The hell I can't."

Ignoring him, I spin on my heel and stalk toward the cabin.

"Runaway Ranch."

The deep, rumbling voice behind me causes me to freeze in my tracks.

"Don't." I squeeze my eyes shut, trying to ward off his words. If he goes any further, I'll launch myself into his arms and never let go.

I hear the crunch of gravel before Charlie's broad-shouldered form stands in front of me. "You wanted to know." There's desperation in his tone, an urgency I've never heard before.

"Not anymore. It's too late."

He flinches like I've twisted a knife in his chest.

Heart racing, I rush up the front steps and into the cabin. I can't let him do this, especially now that I know about Maggie.

Too deep.

We are both in too deep.

Floorboards rattle as Charlie storms after me.

Inside, the air is thick with sunlight and mountain air. I grab my laptop off the kitchen table and hold it to my chest like a shield. "I don't want to know, Charlie."

He stands in the doorway, his hands fisting at his hips. There's a war playing out on his face, emotions attacking like a battle. "Fuck, but I'm tellin' you anyway." A steeling breath catches in his lungs, then he says, "It's called Runaway Ranch because I loved someone and she died."

"No. No." I shake my head, backing away from him. From his confession, from the awful look on his face, and especially from the frenzied beat of my heart. "Charlie, don't do th—"

"I loved her and she died and I lost my mind. I came here. I wanted to forget, so I ran away from everything and everyone." His throat works. "And you're the first thing in ten years I've wanted to run toward."

Oh god.

I'm shaking. I set my laptop back on the counter so I don't drop it.

Expression thunderous, Charlie stomps his way to me. Rough hands shoot out to grab my arms. "I asked you what you wanted after our first night together. And you said the summer."

"That's right. And we've done that." My eyes water, the back of my throat closing up. All this man has done for me—I'll never be able to repay him. "You gave me a beautiful summer, Charlie, and I'll take that memory with me forever."

His eyes don't—*won't*—leave my face. "Now it's my turn to tell you what I want."

"I don't care what you want."

Hurt scars his handsome face. "You're a liar."

I wiggle in his tight grip. "Let me go." My body buzzes, every breath in my lungs gone.

His eyes close briefly, his chest heaving. "I want *you*, Ruby."

"You don't want me," I whisper, bursting into tears.

Desperate, dizzy with disbelief. "Charlie, I'm bad news, okay? I'm temporary. We were supposed to be temporary."

"It's not temporary." He takes a shaky breath, his big chest heaving. "Not anymore. Not for me."

"Charlie . . ."

"I'm not the smartest man, darlin'," he says gruffly, curling his warm hands around my shoulders. "I'm a cowboy. But I know what I want. I know how to hold on to things. And I know a good thing when I see it. Like this ranch. Like you, Ruby. And I'd be a damn fool to let you go."

Lips trembling, I tilt my face up to meet his gaze. "And what am I if I stay?"

He meets my gaze. Steely, unflinching.

Certain.

"You're mine."

Mine.

The words make me wilt.

He's claimed me.

I let out a sob and would crumple to the ground if Charlie weren't here to catch me. He sweeps me into his strong arms, pulling me up to face him. Heat rolls off his body, curls through my core.

"I want you here, Ruby," he husks. "On the ranch with me. In my arms. In my bed and no one else's."

My body bends to him, as if it knows how badly it needs him. "You can't," I sob. "You can't fall in love with me."

He freezes, a strange look on his face.

Then he smiles, a beautiful smile that has my heart fluttering, and says, "Ruby, baby, I already am."

I gasp, sagging into his chest. "No. You don't love me."

He chuckles. "If you think I don't love you, then you need to get those beautiful eyes checked. Because you're all

I see. You're all I've seen since you walked into Nowhere and into my heart." He sweeps his hand under my chin. "I fucking love you, Sunflower, so deal with it."

Love, my heart whispers. I want it. I need it.

Even if it can't last.

Because I won't last.

Because I don't deserve him.

His grin fades into a serious expression. "I know it's fast. Tell me I'm outta my mind. Tell me you love me a year from now. But stay. I want you here. I need you here. I'm not letting you go. I've waited ten years for you and I'm not losing you now." His hand frames my face as he kisses me hard and desperately. "Let me love you, Ruby. Because I do."

At the injustice of it all, more tears fill my eyes and my heart pounds. How can he think I don't love him?

"You stupid cowboy!" I cry out. Charlie freezes and with trembling hands, I palm his stunned face. The dark beard I love scrapes over my fingertips. "You're so stupid. Of course, I love you. I love you with my entire heart, Charlie."

"Say it again." Voice breaking, his forehead drops to mine.

"I love you," I say on a sob. A hot tear slides down the side of my cheek. I feel like I'm dreaming, stuck on a cloud nine high I never want to come down from.

Relief blazes its way across Charlie's face. Joy too. His breath shakes out of him like he's been holding it in his entire life.

And then he laughs. The beautiful burst of sound has me finally giving in and launching myself into his arms. He catches me like I knew he would, lifting me up his body and crushing me to him. I loop my legs around his waist, and then his mouth is on mine.

Heated, frantic, consuming.

"Stay," he growls against my lips. "Stay and I'll give you everything." Those calloused hands cup my cheek and our gazes lock. Hold. Burn. "The ranch. Every sunrise. My heart. But that's a lie because you already have it. You own me, Sunflower."

Tears stream down my face. "You're gonna break my heart, Cowboy," I whisper, winding my arms around his neck. I hold on to him like the world is ending.

He grins. Handsome. Shattering. "Never, darlin'. You just worry about letting me love it."

A fresh wave of warmth crashes over me.

Love.

"Stay," he says, his lips skimming my throat.

"Yes," I whisper, overcome by how much I love this man. By how vulnerable he's made himself. He put all his cards on the table to make me believe. "I'll stay."

If something's going to break this wild, reckless heart of mine, it may as well be a cowboy.

My cowboy.

And then he's capturing my mouth again, holding me tight against his hard chest. Charlie's hands are in my hair, my heart is between his teeth, and he's walking us down the hall and up the stairs to the bedroom. Our racing heartbeats match beat for beat.

I've never been so happy.

I've never been so afraid.

37

Charlie

THUNDER RUMBLES. A DARK CLOUD COVERING sweeps over the mountains. Ruby sits at the patio table on the small balcony off the bedroom. She's wrapped in a sheet, her legs drawn up into her body, cheeks flushed, her dazzling blue eyes on me as I stride her way.

Hours ago, she was leaving.

Now, her *I love you* has decimated me. I'm a wreck of a man, but I wouldn't have it any other way.

"There are storms coming," she murmurs, her gaze on my bare chest.

"Every summer," I say. "They blow in off the mountains and last until the end of August."

Dropping the bottle of whiskey on the table, I glance over my shoulder at the rumpled sheets in the bed. The smell of sex lingers in the air. I drop a kiss to the top of Ruby's messy head of hair and she smiles so bright my chest locks up.

Everything that matters is here in front of me. My

sunflower girl, my saving grace, the sun in my sky when for so long all I could see were clouds.

But first I have to give her my story. I owe her that. Especially if she's staying.

I pull out a chair and sit across from her. "I want to tell you about Maggie."

She flinches. "You don't have to."

"Let me do this, Ruby," I say gruffly.

With a nod, she sits up straight. "Okay, Cowboy." Then she reaches over the table and touches my arm. Just like that, I'm calm. It's Ruby's magic. Her love brings on something so serene I can't describe it. All my doubts, all my nerves, swept away in a rush of love.

"We were childhood best friends. She was my high school sweetheart. I proposed when we graduated." I smear a hand down my face. It feels wrong to give the Cliffs Notes version of what Maggie and I were, but as I look at Ruby, I want it out so I can move on. Dwelling in the past is not an option anymore.

"It was the last competition of the season. She was a barrel racer." I blow out a slow breath, memories burning. "I was there when it happened. Her horse got spooked in the alley and fell on top of her. She was killed in front of my eyes."

Ruby gasps, a hand lifting to her mouth.

"That's why you looked like that." Her blue eyes glisten with unshed tears. "Why you didn't want me to ride. When I got too close to that horse. You yelled. You looked sad."

I should have known I couldn't hide everything from Ruby. My girl is smart.

She listens as I tell her how my life exploded with Maggie's death and how I didn't know how to get it back.

How I ended up at Runaway Ranch and how my brothers followed me.

"That's the long story." I reach over and take her hand, lacing my fingers through hers. "Short story is—I came to find you."

Ruby's silent for a long minute. "I'm so sorry, Charlie." She gives me a sad little smile. "To lose someone you love . . .it would be awful."

She stares at the horizon, then she sighs. "I found her photo." Guilt stains her voice as her pained gaze sweeps to mine. "She was beautiful."

I curse, hating that I left her alone to think God knows what. "I should have told you."

"No. That's your business." She casts her eyes down. "We all have secrets."

I can't hold it in anymore.

No more distance.

I stand and trade seats with her, pulling Ruby into my lap. I secure her in my arms and tuck her head against my shoulder. I'm still not over her almost getting away.

"You can talk about her, Charlie," she says, smiling up at me. "You don't have to hide her away. You don't have to run anymore."

Her hand is on my heart and my heart is in my throat. *This. This is why I love her.*

I realize that, all these years later, I'm still punishing myself, still paying penance for Maggie's death. For dragging my brothers out here.

It feels good, feels right, to share this with someone.

I'm a lifetime away from the man I was at the start of the summer. Taking Ruby up that mountain, growling at her, having no idea how much she'd change my heart.

How much she'd bring me back to life.

"Thank you," she whispers. "For telling me."

There's one more thing we need to get straight.

I rotate a fraction to look down at her. "You're running too," I tell her.

Sitting up, Ruby pulls her slender shoulders back. Her chin trembles, and fear settles in her eyes, rendering me breathless. "I am."

Her flinch sets my soul on fire. My hands fist. But I force myself to focus on Ruby. She's what's important.

After a long silence, she speaks. "You're right. I ran away." Her voice breaks, breaks me. She looks toward the balcony as if she's searching for the answer in the sky. "I—Charlie, I—I'm—"

I silence her confession with a kiss.

Fuck playing this game. The deal we made doesn't matter. I won't push Ruby into her truth. Whatever she has to tell me, it won't make me love her any less.

"When you're ready." My hand lifts to cup her cheek. My heart hammers in bone-deep fear. In rage. "Just tell me one thing."

"What?" she whispers, blinking back tears.

"Is it a man?" I brace myself for it, thinking of Emmy Lou, of places to hide the body, of a feral protection I'll never get over, not as long as she's on my ranch, in my arms. "Ruby, if someone hurt you—"

"No," she says breathlessly. Tears stream down her face as she shakes her head. "It's not a man, Charlie."

I growl my relief and hold her to my chest. "Tell me soon, Sunflower."

Nodding, she relaxes against me. "I will."

So much more to say. To plan. But all that can wait. This can't.

I kiss her.

My mouth devours her tongue, her puffy pink lips. Her body arches toward me, twisting in my arms, as she straddles me. Using her hips as handles, I yank her closer. Her heart beats against my chest—my soul—so fast I ache.

She moans into my mouth, her hands combing through my hair.

"Charlie," she says, her eyes glazed with desire. "I love you."

"Baby, I love you." I skim her cheek with my finger. I have to say it again to make it true. "And you're stayin'."

I have had everything I have ever wanted in my life, but nothing, fucking nothing, compares to having Ruby.

"I'm staying." She giggles, her eyes shiny with tears. Then, her light dims. "But . . .are you sure you want this? Whatever it is. Whatever we are."

I give her a stern look. "There's no messing with my mind, Ruby. I fell a good long way for you, darlin', and I'm not walking away now. Especially not from what's between us."

I swear to Christ her smile's powered by the sun.

"And what's that?" she asks, placing her small hand over my heart.

"All of me, all of you," I tell her. "Forever."

38

Ruby

"A guide?" CHARLIE LAUGHS AS I RUN A currycomb over Arrow's jet-black locks.

I stick my tongue out at him. "I could do it. Follow Ford around and learn the ropes. Take guests to the fishing pond."

"Baby, Ford would run circles around you."

"I want to help around the ranch, Charlie." Puffing a lock of hair from my face, I try to frown as fiercely as I can at him.

He raises a brow. His piercing blue eyes dance with laughter. "Help, huh?"

Smiling, I bounce across the grass and into his arms.

I love my silent and broody cowboy, but I love this happy one too.

I run my fingers down his dark beard. "Didn't you hear? I have to sing for my supper, Cowboy."

"Not on my ranch." A low growl rumbles from deep in his chest. "Not on *your* ranch."

I blush.

I love this man. With everything in me.

He gives me a lazy grin and leans in for a kiss. Until Arrow shoves his nose between us, earning a low growl of disgruntlement from Charlie. "Bastard," he says, giving his horse a gentle pat.

My heart flips over in my chest.

This man is in this tenfold. And so am I.

It's reckless.

It's devastating.

It's exactly what I want.

I'm in charge and I chose love. The ranch. Charlie.

Yet my heart wars with my conscience. I'm in the wrong. So wrong. I'm selfish getting into a relationship with Charlie. It's serious now. It's forever. If I die, if I get sick, it will destroy him.

I need to tell him.

Soon.

He gave me grace, and I have to give him the truth.

I had my chance last week after he told me about Maggie. He stopped me, but I should have pushed on. Instead, I chickened out.

Doctors' appointments, new medications down the line . . .I can't hide that forever. My sickness won't fade away.

I'm delaying it because I'm frightened.

If he sees me differently, or fragile, or sick . . .

If I lose him . . .

"If you could do anything for work, have any job in the world, what would it be?"

Charlie's velvet drawl pulls me from my thoughts.

"Open a flower shop."

He blinks. "In Resurrection?"

"Yes, in Resurrection." I give a little twirl, pick up the

currycomb again and attend to Arrow. The horse snorts his approval, pawing the ground triumphantly. "Bloom's Blooms. The second iteration." I wiggle an eyebrow. "Everyone needs flowers. Even grumpy cowboys."

He chuckles.

"I'd put it on Main Street, in one of those vacant spaces down by The Corner Store. White shutters. Wildflowers." I glance over at Charlie. His expression has gone from amused to thoughtful. "I bet I'd increase romance tenfold. Even Sheena Wolfington would find someone to love."

At the rumble of a truck, he glances over his shoulder, his brows hardening. He's been doing that all afternoon. Watching. On alert. Like he's expecting someone.

But it's only Sam sending off a group of guests in a van bound for the Billings airport.

"Everyone's leaving," I murmur, lifting my hand to wave at a little girl.

"Yeah," he tells me. "We'll get one last wave before they all clear out of here for good."

"End of summer?"

"End of summer."

"And then the party?"

Charlie arcs a wicked brow. "Baby, we always have our party."

I heard all about this big bash from Wyatt. Some honky-tonk celebration that closes down the ranch with beers and bonfires.

"I'm going to put together a video," I say, setting the currycomb on the fence post. "We can use it as marketing for next year."

He grunts, but he doesn't discount the idea, which has my heart doing slow somersaults in my chest. Though I know Charlie will forever be a technology-challenged cow-boy, he trusts me and it means so much.

I step over to the blanket draped over a fence post. Charlie follows me, his eyes tracking my motions. I lift the blanket up, and with a heft, toss it across Arrow's back.

"Is that right?"

"Almost." Charlie helps me adjust the blanket. "Now the saddle." His rugged face crinkles as the corner of his lips rise. "Slackin' on the job, Sunflower."

I mock gasp and kiss him before heading toward the saddle. We've been riding for a few weeks and he's been doing most of the work. But today, I've asked him to show me how to get a horse saddled for a ride.

When I bend to lift the saddle, my heart sputters. Like an engine that's revved up and then cuts off.

The world spins. Black spots dance in my vision. The sound vanishes from my ears. I sway and fall onto my hands and knees on the green grass.

"Whoa, whoa, hey." A strong arm bands around my waist. I hear the rough sweep of Charlie's voice in my ear. "Ruby? Baby?"

A whimper escapes my throat. The erratic thumping in my chest has panic crashing over me. I squeeze my eyes shut as my chest rises and falls in an uneven rhythm.

Charlie's hold tightens. "What is it? What's wrong?"

My heart. It stopped.

But I don't say that.

When I open my eyes, Charlie's face has worry all over it. "I'm bad at this," I whisper.

"Nah." He gives me a sweet grin. "Saddle's too heavy for you is all."

But it wasn't too heavy. It was my heart.

He helps me to standing, and I watch him saddle up Arrow. I don't miss his dark gaze on me. Wondering, worrying.

Biting my lip, I clutch my chest, willing my hands not to shake, willing my heart to keep pumping.

He's not stupid. He's going to figure it out. And if he does, before I come clean . . .

I follow Charlie's long-legged stomping stride back to Arrow, a sense of dread building in my chest.

But it's quickly replaced by a feeling of strength. My mother's words echo from somewhere in the cracks of my mind.

Honor your heart until you become it.

He'll be okay.

We'll be okay.

I inhale a breath.

Stepping close, I grip his massive forearm and hold tight to him like he can anchor me. Looking up into his eyes of blue, I say, "Charlie, I—"

A clanging noise shatters the calm silence of the ranch. Charlie and I both pull back a little from the loud, screeching metal noise.

A horse trailer sits in the gravel drive. Charlie says nothing, his intent gaze on my face.

Then Wyatt's hopping out of the cab of the truck with a loud whoop. He opens the back door of the trailer, and after a few tries with the lead rope, the beautiful butter-cream-colored colt I've loved since I got here backs out of it. The one Charlie took to a buyer in Deer Lodge.

My mouth falls open, and I turn to look at Charlie. He's grinning.

"Charlie . . . what?" I pause. "I thought he was gone."

"Not anymore. I called the buyers the day you said you were stayin'. I know how much you love him."

Tears fill my eyes. "Why? Why would you do this?"

He chuckles as if I've asked him the most obvious question in the world. "To make you happy."

He bridges the gap between us, staring down into my eyes. "He's yours, baby. If you want him."

"Of course, I want him. I just . . ." A kaleidoscope of joy bursts inside of me as I glance at the horse.

Mine.

This beautiful pony I've loved since the day I set foot on the ranch is *mine.*

What Charlie's done says so much. Permanence. Forever.

My cowboy would do anything for me.

Hot tears burn the backs of my eyes.

And then I'm jumping into his arms and kissing him with every breath in my body. Kissing him with a desperate need to sear his touch, his lips to my very soul. A rough growl leaves him as he hikes my legs around his waist, pinning me to him.

"Yes." I gasp, pulling back to cradle his handsome face. "Thank you. I love him. I love *you* so much, Charlie."

His throat works like he's not used to me saying the words. "All he needs is a name, darlin'."

"Winslow. His name is Winslow." I don't even have to think about it. My mind journeys back to that hot Arizona town, the site of my spin-the-bottle roulette, the day I made a choice and decided on my future, even if I didn't know it at the time.

The day I jumpstarted my heart.

39

Charlie

MY TRUCK BUMPS ALONG THE GRAVEL ROAD from the creek bed back to the lodge. I rove my eyes around my ranch, appreciating the beauty. The green pasture. Bright blue skies. Jagged peaks of Meadow Mountain. The long hot summer days are about to be drenched by summer storms. I spent most of the day adding gravel to places where rain creates big potholes and putting in automatic water tanks for our bull pens.

Every cell in my body screams to be at home with Ruby. Although she's most likely in the barn. I haven't been able to drag her away from Winslow. The look on her face when I gave her that colt—such awe and joy. I want to make her look like that every day for the rest of her life.

Because she's turned my entire world around.

She's the neon light I've been looking for.

I pull over on the side of the road, allowing the cattle to cross. Their deep lows fill the air. With the end of summer nearing, the cows are restless and want to move closer to the ranch.

In two weeks, Runaway Ranch will close for the season. The arrival of crisp air and shorter days brings new work. Checking winter forage inventory. Sending Wyatt's horses to auction. Fixing up the ranch for next year. Even when it's a hundred degrees, I can't help but plan for the fall.

I can't help but plan for Ruby. There's so much more I want with her.

Because she's staying. She's home. This is her ranch now and building our life starts here. Before long, I'll put a ring on her finger. Give her a garden. Finish her bucket list. Take her back to Wildheart and introduce her to my family. Have babies.

Fuck anyone who thinks it's fast. I've been living in slow motion for the last ten years.

She's shown me a million ways I could live my life, but all I want to do with it is worship her.

For all the directions she's pushed me this summer, I'm still aware she hasn't told me about her past. While I told her about Maggie, she looked up at me with an expression I had never seen before.

Dread.

My hands tighten on the wheel.

Either she's lying about something or I'm lying to myself. Have I been blind this entire fucking summer, and the answer has been right in front of me? Ford's words come back to haunt me. Is he right? Something's wrong with her? The mere suggestion has a knot forming in my gut.

Fuck but I don't want to push her. If something was wrong, she'd tell me, wouldn't she? She promised me no one hurt her, and I believe her.

Muscles tensing, I blow out a breath and pull back on the road.

She's given me the summer, she's given me my ranch back, but more than that, she's given me her trust. Her heart.

Messing with that isn't an option.

She'll tell me when she's ready.

Five minutes later, I'm parking the truck at the Bullshit Box. When I stomp inside, all my brothers are here.

"Hey, Charlie." Wyatt waves a hand. "Just in time for paperwork."

Davis and Ford look up from their poker game.

"We workin' or we dickin' around?" I drawl, dropping into my chair.

"Almost done kicking Davis's ass." Grinning, Ford flashes me his hand. Royal flush.

"We got everything set for the farewell dinner?"

Davis nods. "Talked to Silas. He's burying a pig and hoping like hell no one calls PETA."

I chuckle, scrubbing a hand over my face.

Looking around the Bullshit Box, I survey the scene. It's clean. Organized. The filing cabinet has actual labels. A stack of paid bills. The space heater is gone. Our new security system is linked up to multiple TVs showing various angles of the ranch. I watch Sam lead a group of kids to the Warrior Heart Home. On another screen, Tina greets a new group—the last group of the year—with cold bottles of PBR.

Pride fills me up inside.

Maybe we can do this and actually make money. Maybe next year we can start from a place that's not fucked.

That's the hope I've been looking for. Everything I need to move forward with my ranch.

It's the push in my gut, the resolution to grow some goddamn balls and tell my brothers the truth. Make the last ten years up to them.

"So, listen," I say, leaning forward in my chair and steepling my fingers under my chin. "I've been meaning to talk to y'all about something for a while now."

"Royal flush," Ford says with a smirk as he slaps down his cards.

Davis scowls. "Dick."

I roll my eyes. "It's about Runaway Ranch," I say, and everyone stops what they're doing. "We've been doin' okay for a few months now. Since—"

"Since Fairy Tale," Wyatt interjects.

I nod. "Since Ruby helped us out." Letting out a deep breath, I curl my fingers into a fist and squeeze, pressing on. "Y'all gave up everything to be here for me. And I want you to know I'm gonna be okay. The ranch is gonna be okay. So if y'all want out, go. Now's the time. Get on with your fucking lives."

Davis and Ford exchange a surprised glance. Wyatt's eyes have drifted to the window.

The knot in my chest loosens.

"Y'all had lives before this. I appreciate it—what you did coming here and putting me back together—but it's time," I grumble. "Y'all deserve to get out of Resurrection." I look around at my brothers, willing my throat not to close up. "Davis, you've been pissed since you got here. Wy, you can do the rodeo circuit full time if that's what you want. Break some more goddamn bones. Ford, I have no idea what the hell you'd do, but you can figure that the fuck out."

After a long stretch of silence, Davis studies me for a beat. Then he chuckles, says, "You're an asshole."

"Feeling's mutual," I assure him.

Ford gives a dubious grunt. "I can't play baseball now. Too damn old." He nods to me. "Besides, I wouldn't go anywhere if I could, Charlie. Fishing and riding every day, I got it made."

"I want to be here," Wyatt adds, and my gaze flickers to him. A muscle jerks in his jaw. He's hurt I haven't talked to him about this. "This is my town. We're fucking family, man. You're not getting rid of us now that you got yourself a girl."

I hear conviction in my brother's voice and relief fills me.

My brothers want to be here.

It's like the anchor of guilt in the pit of my stomach has finally been freed.

Goddamn, it's nice to be back.

"I've been pissed," Davis admits slowly, shaking his head. "But it's not because of you, C." He pauses, suddenly looking like he wishes he could walk back his statement. "But Wy's right and you're wrong. As usual."

Wyatt and Ford swing their heads in my direction and laugh.

"Oh, fuck y'all," I say, giving the room the finger, but there's no fight in it.

Ford leans across the table to ruffle my hair. "Yeah, yeah, we love you too, dick."

A rare grin twists Davis's lips. "We want to be here. And I'm sure as hell glad that girl of yours pulled your head out of your stubborn ass."

I snort.

"She staying?" Davis asks, still grinning.

"Yeah," I rasp. "She is."

"How long?"

"As long as I can have her," I say. "When you know, you know."

"Yeah." Giving an approving nod, Davis drops his eyes to my boots, where I've scrawled Ruby's name on the outsole. He looks up at me. "Don't let her go, you hear me?" Davis clears his throat and digs through the desk drawers, pretending to search for something I doubt is there.

Strange. Ford and I share a look. If Ford seems confused about his twin's statement, then I sure as hell am. There was something in Davis's voice, an undercurrent of rough resentment. Only not directed toward us. As close as we all are, a brick wall would open up more than Davis.

"So, what's next with y'all?" Wyatt drums his hands on the desk. "Take her home to Mama?"

I snort. "I take her home, we're gonna lay down some laws real fast."

No way in hell am I subjecting the sweetest girl in the world to Mama Belle's sharp-tongued antics.

Wyatt smiles. "I don't know what kind of spell that girl put you under, Charlie, but hell . . ." A muscle works in his jaw and throat. "It's nice to see you."

"Good to be seen," I reply gruffly.

Nothing's ever felt this right. Ruby. My brothers. My ranch.

"Shit," Davis growls, immediately punching the keyboard. His radio appears in his hands.

My head snaps up, whipping to the first security monitor. A long black Cadillac snakes its way up the gravel drive to my cabin.

A chill freezes my heart.

Ruby.

I shove out of my chair, my hands balling into fists. "Meet me at the house," I say and take off running.

By the time I make it to the cabin, Ruby's at the front door, hands propped on her hips, smiling politely at the black-suited man in front of her.

Me—I'm not that nice.

My hand balls into a fist.

"You're trespassing," I bark. Stomping up the porch steps, I step in front of the bastard and block Ruby with my body. "Get back in your car and drive."

The man isn't fazed. He stares at me with a cool expression. "In due time," he says. "I was just talking to your pretty friend here . . ." His eyes move from me to Ruby.

"Ruby," she chirps, and I make a mental note to tell her later she shouldn't be so nice to everyone. It's one thing I love about her—her innocent sweetness—but it also terrifies the fuck out of me.

"Ruby," the man repeats, his gaze zeroing in on her like a target.

Shoulders locking, I spin her away from him.

"Mr. Montgomery. It's about time we met." He extends a hand my way. "Declan Valiante."

A gasp pops out of Ruby.

Fuck. It is him. The man on all those campaign posters. I recognize the silver head of hair and his rigid, robotic face. Gold-flecked eyes like a reptile.

I refuse his handshake. "You have no business here."

"Oh, but I do." He adjusts the sleeve of his suit. "I understand you've met my wife. My son, Colton."

Ruby pales.

"I have," I tell him, edging closer to Ruby. "And they've done nothin' but cause trouble for our ranch." A chuckle shakes out of me. "Sending in the boss. Things must be bad for business."

Declan's face stays placid. "I'll admit I was wrong," he says. "I should have offered you what your land is worth. I should have tried other negotiation tactics. So, I've come to make amends. Your community is loyal. Your town is honest, which has me feeling . . . let's just say generous."

"Negotiations?" I take a step forward. Ruby slips her hand around my bicep, her touch calm and reassuring. "Don't you mean sabotage? I know what you tried to do."

"Call it what you will, but putting hands on my son wasn't a wise move, Mr. Montgomery."

I clench my teeth so hard my jaw aches. "I'll put hands on anyone who touches my family. Your son got off lucky in my book."

A long sigh, then the mask slips on Valiante's face. "I've been a nice man, Mr. Montgomery. I've sent someone to talk. I've offered money. I have pushed. But now . . ." Declan unbuttons his suit jacket, exposing a holstered gun on his waistband.

All I see is red.

Is this motherfucker really threatening me?

"Ruby," I say, pressing her back slowly. "Go into the house. Now."

She doesn't move.

I glance down at her. She's staring at Declan with narrowed eyes.

"Go, baby." I give her a pat on the ass, and she scowls, but lets me usher her inside. Relief courses through me.

I want her far away from this confrontation, because Declan's about two seconds from getting his head ripped off.

"This isn't up for discussion," I say gruffly. "We're not selling, so get off my property."

His lip curls. "You might want to rethink your decision. By refusing DVL, refusing me, you play with fire, Mr. Montgomery. I know people in Chicago who can make your life a living hell."

I snort as he buttons up his jacket. This piece of shit is all show. Never in a million years would he use his gun. He'll get someone else to do his dirty work.

That's when I see Declan's eyes on Ruby. The angle of his gaze, intense and scrutinizing, sets off an atom bomb inside of me.

No more calm. No more thinking. I act. I bare my teeth and advance, grabbing the collar of his shirt to shove him backward off the porch, putting Ruby out of his sight.

And then I hit him with the crushing blow of a car crash, pinning him up against the side of my cabin.

Declan makes some type of huffy protest, but I shut him up real fast when I tighten my grip.

"Don't look at her," I growl, and his panicked eyes flick to mine. "Look at me and hear what I'm telling you. I'll say it once. You think you know people? I *am* the people. Stay away from my land. Stay away from my family. You come on my property again and I won't call the cops. I'll take care of it right then and there. You think I have ten thousand acres just for cattle, you worthless piece of shit?"

With that, I leave the man sputtering in my gravel drive and storm inside, slamming the door behind me.

Seconds later, the sound of an engine.

Ruby's at the island, her eyes glued to her phone. She's trembling, her face pale, but her expression determined.

"Baby." I go to her, wrapping her up in my arms. "You okay?"

"He's a bad man, Charlie," she whispers against my chest. "He's the one who hurt Wyatt."

I grip her chin and force her gaze to mine. "What did he say to you?"

"He didn't say anything."

I exhale and hold her tight, drawing comfort from the feel of her body, soft and safe in my arms.

Through the window, I see Davis's cherry-red F-350 rumbling down the drive.

Fucking took them long enough.

"Charlie," Ruby says in a voice that sends shivers down my spine. She stands straight, looking up at me. Her phone's clasped to her heart. "I need to show you something."

The living room is bathed in light. Whiskey bottles crowd the coffee table. Ford and Wyatt are sprawled out on the couch. Outside, thunder rumbles.

Davis paces behind the couch, his eyes on Ruby's phone, on the photo of Declan Valiante.

Ruby stands shyly on the sidelines, back by the fireplace, until I murmur into her hair, "Sit down, Sunflower."

She shakes her head. "This is family stuff."

"You're part of our family," I tell her firmly, staring into her bright blue eyes. "Whether or not you like it."

A beam of a smile hits her lips.

Davis lifts his hand. "Charlie, you just saw this?"

I rub my jaw. "I did." I look at Ruby, her pretty face uncertain. "Tell 'em, baby."

Perching on the edge of the couch, Ruby spends the next ten minutes explaining the night she took the photo to all my brothers. She and Fallon in the back alley, watching the scene at the brothel, not knowing that the man in question was Declan Valiante.

I stand behind Ruby and cross my arms over my chest.

When she's done, she puffs a lock of hair out of her face. "I didn't know who he was," she says. "I just took it." Her nose wrinkles. "Blame Fallon."

"Fuck," Ford exhales, taking the phone from Davis.

The image is clear enough. It's gold.

Declan Valiante with a woman at the brothel, pants around his ankles. No denying his trademark shock of silver hair, or the belt buckle shining bright with his family crest.

The same belt buckle that ties him to his wife and son.

That ties them to their dirty summer deeds.

Ford passes the phone to Wyatt.

"Damn," Wyatt says. "Ruby went hard as fuck for real."

I grin.

That's my girl.

She flops back against the couch, curling her legs beneath her. "I don't want this to cause trouble."

"Nah." Davis tosses Ruby a smile. "It won't. You helped us out. A hell of a lot."

Wyatt grins, tilting his whiskey toward me. "We got ammunition now."

Ruby looks uneasy.

"Valiante say anything else when he was here?" Ford asks, his eyes on me.

"Typical bullshit," I grouse. "Said we were playing with fire. That he knows some folks in Chicago who could make our lives hell."

Wyatt scoffs.

My free hand balls into a fist. I rove a cool gaze around Ruby, my brothers. "They're not turning Resurrection into some cement city. This is our town and we protect it."

A blanket of seriousness falls over the room.

"They used social media to fuck with us. We use it when we need it," Davis's loud voice booms. A gavel of finality.

Ford shoots back his whiskey. "Campaign season."

"Damn straight," I agree.

Releasing the photo will blow up Valiante's entire world. It'll ruin his wife's business, his son's chances at college, destroy his career as a politician. With one hell of a fight on his hands, he'll have more important shit to deal with than targeting the ranches in Resurrection.

"Stede has that contact in Missoula at the paper," Wyatt reminds us. "We could give the photo to him. Let him put it on all that social media shit Ruby loves."

Ruby's teeth sink into her lower lip. "Is that smart? Should we do that?" She looks around the room, worried, then up at me.

I blow out a deep breath and put a reassuring hand on her shoulder, pulling her closer, needing the proximity to her.

She still seems concerned.

Davis, locking his eyes to mine, laughs and sighs at the same time. "They declared war first. We're just gonna end it."

Wyatt lifts his whiskey glass in a toast. "Cheers to social media."

Ford rubs at his temples. "Let's hope we get out of it in one fucking piece."

40

Ruby

DROPPED TAILGATES, BEER ON ICE, THE END OF summer. The shuttering of Runaway Ranch for the season.

Everything about the farewell campfire dinner is chaotic and magical and it's never been more perfect.

As Davis lifts a cooler, I duck under his arms and spin around to snap a photo of him in his element. I giggle when I examine it. He's scowling, his dog tags glinting in the descending sunlight. I don't think these Montgomery men could smile if their lives depended on it.

Lowering the phone, I study the rugged landscape and the ranch.

The Montgomery Brothers—they do Montana proud.

Every guest has a beer in their hand. Chef Silas digs a shovel in the earth, uncovering the pit-pig he buried yesterday. Music plays on the speakers from an ancient stereo. A small campfire burns proudly in the center of the field. Beyond us, the mountains stretch the sky, the sunset a vibrant lilac glow.

Ford, Davis and Charlie stand around like broad-shouldered bouncers waiting to rush in if there's trouble. There's an energy radiating off the Montgomerys. They're wired. Proud. They love this ranch so much it shines on every one of their faces.

Guests sit on long logs, laughing, eating their feast on paper plates. They snap selfies and chat with the ranch hands and staff. Soon, they'll go back to their lives, but I hope they take a piece of Runaway Ranch with them.

It's what I've done this summer.

I belong here.

It won't be easy to tell my brother and father I'm staying, but it won't be hard either.

My entire happiness, my heart, is here with Charlie.

Even though Runaway Ranch will be closed until next summer, I plan to continue with their social media posts. The more I can grow their account, the better. And by working with my travel agency to pre-book influencers and get the word out via social media, there's no doubt in my mind that next year, they'll open with a bang.

Next summer and every summer after.

And I'll be here.

Smiling, I glance up at the clear blue sky, the new cowboy hat Charlie bought me perched atop my head. With the wind at my back, the sunshine beats down my face. I close my eyes and inhale deeply.

At last, I feel complete.

This summer I learned there is so much I can do.

I've chosen the direction of my life. No one else.

I'm strong because of my heart, not in spite of it.

I have a cowboy who loves me.

I have friends and found another family.

Staying with Charlie, living in Resurrection, it's what I'm meant to do.

When I glance over, I catch Charlie watching me with pride in his eyes. He gives me a wink, and my stomach warms in the way it does whenever I see him.

With life.

With love.

Raucous laughter gets my attention, and I see a group of guests dancing in the pasture.

I back up to the edge of the tree line, wanting to get a group shot for the end of the year video I'm putting together. As soon as I snap my photo and lower the phone, my world spins.

"Oh no," I murmur. *A flutter.* Black dots pinprick my vision.

Wanting privacy, I move into the woods and press two fingers against my throat, monitoring the rapid pulse of my heartbeat. Between hauling firewood for the farewell dinner and running back and forth to the cabin for supplies, I've pushed myself too hard today.

"I'm sorry," I whisper, pressing a hand to my heart. "You're okay. You'll be okay."

I have to be.

A rustling in the woods startles me and I spin around.

Ten yards away, Fallon and Wyatt stand in the clearing, inches from each other. Their low voices sound heated.

I bite my lip. I'm a witness to something I'm not supposed to see, but unable to turn away.

With a soft growl, Wyatt plucks the cigarette from her mouth and grinds it out on the bark of a tree.

Fallon glares daggers at him, but Wyatt's hand reaches out to find hers. She tries to stubbornly pull away, refusing his touch at first, but then she gives up the fight. I watch as their index fingers loop around each other's like curled-up bits of vine. Wyatt tugs her close, saying something, but she refuses to budge. Then Wyatt drops her hand and heads toward his Airstream.

Breath held, I step back, pressing myself up against a tree.

Fallon glances around. The light from the forest dances over the silvery scar on her delicate jaw. Her narrowed hazel gaze takes in her surroundings, and after a second of hesitation, she follows Wyatt.

I smile.

When I exit the woods, another truck has joined the circle. An older man, clad in a cowboy hat, and sporting a long white mustache, stands talking to Charlie.

As I approach, the man glances my way, thumbs hooked in his belt loops. "This must be her."

"It is," Charlie says, sliding his arm over my shoulder. "This is my girl, Ruby."

My girl. My lips pull high because I see he's proud, anxious, even. It's in his eyes and in the space between us. Love.

Charlie continues with introductions. "Ruby, this is Stede. Fallon's father and the toughest old bastard in Resurrection."

Stede barks a laugh and shakes my hand with gusto. His long mustache reminds me of some wise western cowboy. "Nice to meet the heart of Charlie's ranch."

"Hi, Stede. Nice to meet you." I flush at the compliment, flash Charlie a playful smile. "That's a tremendous honor, though. Not sure, I've earned it since I'm not a local."

Stede's brows shoot up.

Charlie growls at me. "I get the point, Sunflower." His

expression turns serious as he looks back at Stede. "She's as much as a local as you and me."

Stede chuckles. "I take your word on that, son."

"Y'all can make small talk at the ridge," Ford barks, hustling back to us. In his hands, he carries a long lighter and a portable speaker.

Davis appears with a cooler. On top of it rests an axe and paper lanterns. "Let's get," he says, thundering to his old Chevy. "We got Family tonight."

I turn my cheek to look up at Charlie. "What's Family?"

Ford throws his arms around me and Charlie and sticks his grinning face between us. "Family is where we all get together and bitch about Charlie."

I giggle at the brotherly banter, smiling as Ford messes up Charlie's hair. Cackling, Ford ducks away before Charlie can snag his shirt and take a swing of his own.

Charlie scowls after his brother, but I can hear the smile in his voice. "It's the one day of the month we can't get out of. Even if hanging out with Wyatt's like pulling teeth."

Ford glances at the campfire. "Where is he, anyway?"

The tips of my ears go pink, thinking of the scene I saw in the woods.

"I think he went to the house for more beer," I lie, wanting to buy them time.

Commotion ensues as everyone packs and preps.

"We don't need to stick around here for the party?" I ask Charlie.

"No," he says. "Everything's handled. We got our time in. Now we let our guests enjoy and we go have our own party. It's Runaway Ranch tradition."

"I can't wait to see this," I say, bouncing into him. His eyes darken and he kisses my lips.

Ford grins. "Hell, yeah. When that summer sun starts sinkin', it's time to take it to the ridge."

"Whooo-whee," Wyatt hoots, suddenly appearing out of nowhere. "Looks like we got some rowdy friends ready to raise a ruckus tonight."

Charlie cocks a dark brow. "Where's the beer?" he asks.

Wyatt looks confused.

"It wasn't in the house?" I ask, giving Wyatt a look and hoping he picks up on the message I'm sending.

His attention flickers to me and he nods. "Sure wasn't, Ruby. Davis must have grabbed it."

Davis eyes his little brother shrewdly. "Shirt's on backward."

"New trend," Wyatt swaggers. But the tips of his ears, barely covered by his shaggy mop of hair, are bright pink.

Minutes later, Fallon appears, her expression unreadable. She goes to Stede's side and slips her arm through his.

Clocking that everyone is present and accounted for, Davis lifts a big hand and motions us all forward. "Let's go."

"You ready, Sunflower?" Charlie asks. And then he laces his fingers through mine and pulls me toward his truck.

My heart leaps.

I'm so fucking ready.

41

Charlie

WE GET UP TO MEADOW MOUNTAIN AND unpack everything. Coolers of beer. Paper lanterns. A small Bose speaker cranks out Sturgill Simpson while the campfire burns. Ford and Wyatt stand at the edge of the sandstone ledge, looking south across the vast canyon landscape as they light sky lanterns and let them loose into the air.

Ruby watches with wide eyes, her hands clasped to her chest. "Oh," she gasps, trailing the glowing lantern with her finger. "There it goes." She looks up at me. "What happens to it?"

I keep a protective hand on the small of her back, reminded of the last time I took her up here. Last thing I need is her getting too close to the edge.

"It'll float down there," I tell her, pointing below the cliffside. Runaway Ranch is microscopic, but we can see the smoke from the campfire. "It burns out in the air but stays lit long enough for the guests to see at the end of the night."

Her mouth drops.

She looks ethereal in the setting sun, her long rose-gold hair falling across her face. Montana may be majestic in her beauty, but so is Ruby.

"Make a wish," Ford drawls, lifting another lantern into the sky.

"Make a wish?" Ruby asks.

"Hopes. Dreams. Wishes." Hand dropping to her waist, I lean in and explain our annual tradition to Ruby. "For next season."

Ford kicks us off. "To the Braves winning."

Davis rolls his eyes. "He means the ranch, asshole."

"To next year," I grunt, giving Ford side-eye. "No more goddamn videos."

Fallon extends her arms. "To Pappy Starr," she says, toes hanging off the ledge of the cliff.

Wyatt makes a face of revulsion. "What do you want with that prick?"

Fallon cocks a shoulder. "I'm taking up with him."

A scoff pops out of Wyatt. "He doesn't rep girls."

"I think the statement you're searching for is he doesn't rep *you*."

"Wouldn't want him to," Wyatt grumbles, snapping a twig in half and tossing it over the cliff.

The disgusted look on his face echoes my own. Pappy Starr is a sleazy rodeo agent who worries more about what his clients can do for him than what he can do for his clients. He treats the rodeo like a game instead of the sport that it is.

"Besides," Fallon continues. "He will if I do something crazy enough." A sly grin crosses her face as she sticks a leg out over the cliff ledge. "Life number four, here I come."

Wyatt laughs, but his gaze is on her precarious balance. "Sounds like you need a therapist."

Fallon rounds on him, looking like she's ready to mow my brother down with her gunfire eyes. "Sounds like you need a muzzle," she snaps.

Ruby, watching the scene with great concentration, edges closer to me. "What'd he do?" she asks softly.

"Who?"

"Wyatt." She arches a brow, wags a finger between Wyatt and Fallon. The glares they're giving each other could melt steel. "To make Fallon's face look like that?"

I consider my brother. Ruby's right.

That's a goddamn great question.

I can't tell if Wyatt wants to fuck Fallon or fight her. Maybe both. Which is strange because Wyatt usually tells me everything, but he's never told me what he did to piss her off.

"You wanna feel alive," Ford says, intercepting the argument with a wicked grin. "Let's climb these cliffs, cowgirl."

Taking the dare, Fallon wiggles her brows and grabs Ford's pack. "You got chalk on you?"

"Christ," I groan. Beside me, Ruby lets out a panicked squeak. The last thing we need is these two idiots plunging to their deaths.

"Y'all need to chill the fuck out," Davis growls, stomping forward. In one swift motion, he hooks a finger through Fallon's belt loop, lifts her into the air and sticks her back on solid ground. I watch the tension melt out of Wyatt's lean frame.

Sticking her tongue out at Davis, Fallon grabs a beer from the cooler. "I'm gonna do something that'll blow y'all's mind, then get the hell out of this town."

Ford holds up the last lantern. "Y'all get in here."

Chuckling, Stede ambles forward and takes the lantern from Ford. A flash of silver shows in his smile. "I've had a pretty good life, but I sure would like some more."

A small intake of breath beside has me glancing down at Ruby. She looks faraway, her light dimmed.

Fallon goes to her father. "That's perfect, Daddy," she says, her face the softest I've seen in a long time.

As Stede releases the lantern, I reach out and cup Ruby's cheek in my hand. We watch as the glowing lantern floats in the dusky sky. "Your turn, Sunflower," I tell her.

She shakes her head, stiffening at my words. "I don't need a wish," she says. And then she looks up, a gorgeous smile overtaking her face. The storm cloud in her eyes disappears, her sunshine glow restored. "I have you."

How much I love this girl.

It vibrates through me like an electric shock.

Stays in my bones. Ashes my heart. Caves in my chest.

"Goddamn, baby." I pull her closer into my arms.

That mouth is mine. I claim it in front of everyone, drinking her in deep.

When I release Ruby, all eyes are on us.

"Take a damn picture," I growl.

Ruby blushes and ducks her head against my chest.

Everyone laughs and the night goes on. The stars come out. The cooler is emptied. We build a fire. Ford launches into a story about the fish he caught this summer and the bear he swears stalked him for a mile before he offered it the trout in exchange for his life.

Stede appears at my side. He looks healthy as hell. "Charlie, Davis, think I can bend your ear a second?"

Davis and I catch each other's eye and slip away from

the group. Stede takes a seat in one of the campfire chairs we brought, while my brother and I sit across from him on a log bench Ford whittled over five years ago.

"What's goin' on, Stede?" Davis asks.

"Listen, son, I'm an old man and I do things like stick my nose in spots where it might not be wanted." He lifts a hand when I open my mouth. "I'm your elder and you respect your goddamn elders, you hear me?"

I chuckle. "We hear you."

Stede leans forward. "Charlie, son, I'm afraid to tell you, but you got yellow-bellied grunkles on your property."

I rub my jaw, my gaze flicking to Davis. "What the fuck's a grunkle?"

A raspy chuckle comes from Stede. "Hell, if I know." A mischievous grin appears on his weathered face. "I've been trying to find a way out of your problem, and I think I've done it. You know I have that friend at the Fish and Wildlife Service. Well, I went down there a couple of weeks ago. It took some time, and I cashed in some favors, but Runaway Ranch is officially designated as a wildlife preserve."

Davis and I stare at each other in stunned silence, then look at Stede.

Emotion has me in a stranglehold, and I have to clear my throat to get the next words out. "Jesus," I say hoarsely.

No one can take Runaway Ranch from us now.

Davis still looks stunned. "Must have been a lot of fucking favors."

Stede grunts. "Don't ask."

Blowing out a slow breath, I shake my head. "Why'd you do this? We have it covered. We have dirt on DVL."

"And what about next time? When someone else

comes calling? This way, even if you sell the land, it's protected." He lifts his Stetson and smooths a hand over his bald head. "I got money, son, a little power, some respect. Let me put it to good use. I'm the damn fool who didn't think of the solution earlier."

Davis covers his face and barks a laugh of disbelief into his palms.

"Charlie, you being on the deed, you're due down at the courthouse to sign paperwork tomorrow," Stede says. "It's all set up. No one can touch your ranch now."

I smear a hand down my beard, overwhelmed. "Stede. It's too much."

"It's not." He straightens up, his gray eyes flicking to Fallon. "I admit, it wasn't from the goodness of my small-town heart. I want you to do something for me."

"Name it."

"I want you to protect my daughters."

More silence. Davis sits straighter.

"Call me old-fashioned, but my daughters are my everything. I won't be around forever. When I'm gone, I want you to look out for them."

Davis lets out a sharp breath. "You didn't have to do this. We'd protect Dakota and Fallon, no matter what. All you have to do is ask. And no disrespect to you, sir, but I'm not so sure your daughters need our help." He glances over his shoulder at Fallon, who's currently howling at the sky.

"Fallon can't be tamed," Stede says, pride in his eyes. "My fault I suppose. Wild as the wind, that girl. Ever since her mother . . ." Stede trails off, his hand turning to a fist. He takes a beat, clears his throat, and says, "And Dakota, well . . . she's a mystery to all of us."

Davis flinches.

Somewhere across the ridge, a coyote joins in with Fallon.

Stede raises his hand, cutting off any further discussion. "You all are like sons to me. I trust you. With the land. With my daughters."

"We'd be glad to help, sir. Anything you ever need." Davis glances down, knuckles going white around his beer can. Something in his expression, in his tone, is soft. Unreadable.

Stede stretches out, searching his pockets. He comes up with a hard candy and pops it in his mouth. "I love being alive, man. I know I did something good with the time I got left."

My throat clogs. "You got lots of time."

"Time is the one thing we're not guaranteed, kid." Stede's voice is steady. "We have to make our time. We have to make every second count. You can't miss out on your life trying to get it together."

I freeze at his words.

Stede looks out over the ridge, gesturing at the landscape. "This is what it's all about." Davis and I both rotate, following his eyeline.

In the distance, the splash and crash of Crybaby falls. The spires and cliffs of Meadow Mountain. Darkness breaking over the trees.

He's right.

The dirt. The earth. Family. The girl in front of me dancing in the firelight.

I'd be a damn fool if I didn't make her mine forever.

"Fuck." I open my hands. Let out a breath. It's like a weight's been released. "Thank you, Stede."

Stede stands and raises a hand without looking back.

"Out here, it's all about the people you know," he replies. "And you know me, and that's all you need to know."

Davis nods, but his eyes are distant, his mind elsewhere.

With that, I leave Davis to brood on whatever it is eating him while I head back toward the group. Laughter rings out. And there's Ruby, shining like a diamond in the firelight.

Too beautiful for words.

And she's fucking mine.

I need to tell her about the ranch, but first I need to tell her something else. I go to her and take her hand, pulling her away from the others.

"What's up, Cowboy?" she asks brightly, turning her magnificent blue eyes on me.

I touch the brim of her cowboy hat. Stars freckle her cheeks. "Thinkin' about things."

Ruby lifts on her toes and presses her lips to mine. "What kind of things?"

"Thinkin' about the sunrise."

She tilts her head. "Try tonight?"

"Goddamn right we do." My palms ride over her shoulders. Her body arcs toward mine, the beat of her heart pulsing against my chest. "Thinkin' about you and me and what's next."

She wiggles her eyebrows playfully. "And what's that?"

"Thinkin' about how I'm plannin' to marry you."

She gasps. Her eyes widen and she sucks in a shaky breath. "Oh, Charlie."

"Soon, Sunflower," I warn, taking her face in my hands. "I'm gonna put a ring on your finger and pray like hell you take my last name. Because you own me. For the rest of your life, Ruby, I'm yours."

The days of wondering what I want, of walking around like a broken man, are gone.

I'm building a future with Ruby. A family. A garden. Her in my bed. Rocking chairs and whiskey and flowers and sunshine.

Until the end of goddamn time.

"Will you be my wife, Ruby? I'll love you well, Sunflower. I'll make you happy."

She's crying now, nodding into my chest. Tears streak over her cheeks, soaking the front of my shirt. "Shhh, baby. Don't cry." I kiss the top of her head, inhaling her strawberry scent. Then, lifting her face, I swipe her tears away with my thumb. "Happy or sad tears?"

"Happy." She's smiling so brightly that my own lips rise. "This is without a doubt the very best sunflower day."

"Sunflower days for the rest of your life," I vow. "I'll give them all to you, baby."

"You have me," she says on a sob and my chest heaves in relief. "You have my heart, Cowboy."

I lean down, sweeping my mouth against her lips. And that final dark part of me that's hidden in shadows finally slips into the sun.

42

Ruby

SWEATY AND NIGHTMARISH, I JOLT UP IN BED, gasping for air. A brilliant burst of gold peeks beyond the horizon.

The sunrise.

We missed it.

But I don't miss the beat of my heart.

It's hammering, some insane fist of rage knocking on the inside of my chest.

Charlie sleeps beside me, his broad chest rising and falling in a steady rhythm. Dark hair mussed, handsome face peaceful, sheets tangled around his legs. His tense muscles all soft and relaxed in sleep.

I reach out to touch him and the entire room moves.

Oh no.

Panic sets in. I scramble out of bed and rush to the bathroom. I slam the door shut and lock it.

Gripping the sink, I gasp at my reflection in the mirror. My face is pale, dark circles beneath my eyes. Haunted. I look haunted.

With trembling fingers, I massage my chest, trying to force some calm into my distressed heart.

Not now. Not here.

Not when last night was so perfect.

Charlie wants to marry me.

Having him in my life—it's been a miracle.

He's been worth every secret, every flutter, every risk, every crazy, heart stopping moment that's happened this summer.

I want love. I want Charlie. A bone-splitting ache tears through me, and my eyes blur with hot tears. Because I can't have any of it.

My heart won't let me.

The reality of what I've been doing settles over me like a blanket of doom. My flutters are happening more and more. My heart's getting worse. This summer, I've asked for too much from my patchwork body.

I've pushed myself to my limit.

I've been so obsessed with finding a new life, but what I need is a new body.

A new heart.

I sob-gasp, then slap a hand over my mouth to smother the sound.

It's hard to breathe. Tears fill my eyes and I blink fast to ward them off.

What am I doing lying to him?

I scramble for my pills, knocking the soap and Charlie's razor off the sink and onto the floor. I shake out a pill and swallow it, even when I know it doesn't matter.

It doesn't matter anymore.

I'm not fooling anyone.

Least of all Charlie.

He'll find out.

Soon, he'll know I lied to him.

God. All the stupid lies I've hidden behind.

It's all my fault. I set out on this trip with boundaries, with rules, and I broke every single one of them. I chose this life with Charlie. I made it ours because I wanted it so much I ached.

If I had run weeks ago, if I had left him none the wiser, I wouldn't be in this situation.

But I am. And now I'm trapped by my own heart.

Maybe he will understand.

Maybe he'll forgive me.

And then I think of Maggie and I burst into tears.

No. I can't do that to him.

Except I can't keep going like this. I'm sick and my heart is compromised.

It terrifies me.

I could die.

I could leave this life I've come to love.

"Idiot," I say with a heavy breath. My heart feels like it's coming apart at the seams. Tears slide out of the corner of my eyes, and I'm too tired to fight them any longer. "Idiot."

I touch my heart, its rapid beat disorienting me.

The world spins. Black spots dance in my eyes.

A knock at the door. "Ruby?" comes Charlie's concerned voice. "Sunflower?"

"Charlie." My voice trembles.

I try to answer him, try to open the door, to croak out a response, but even that tires me out.

"Charlie," I whisper, resting my hot cheek on the cool wood of the bathroom door.

The doorknob jiggles.

"Ruby. Open the door." He's worried now, stern.

Lifting my chin, I meet my pale reflection in the mirror. "Don't you dare," I beg my body. Another tear slips down my cheek. "Please. *Don't.*"

But my heart isn't taking any more requests.

It won't let me hide.

My heart skips.

Stops.

Resumes its beat.

The room tilts and I go down.

43

Charlie

"**R**UBY!" I GRIP THE DOORKNOB, TRY TO SLAM open the door, but it's locked.

I can't get to her.

I can't get to my girl.

A thud on the other side of the door has me absolutely losing it.

"*Ruby!*" I slam my shoulder into the wood. In two quick tries, I knock the door off its hinges.

My gaze instantly finds her, slumped face-down on the floor.

The air leaves my lungs.

I rush to her, falling to my knees beside her. "Ruby?" Gently, I turn her over, lifting her onto my lap.

Her eyes flutter. "Charlie?" She attempts to push herself up but can't. Her face lolls into my chest, obscuring my view.

"What happened?" Automatically, my fingers find her pulse. Her heartbeat feels like wild horses in her chest, and my panic deepens.

"Nothing." She moans softly. "I'm fine."

"Bullshit. You're not fine. Baby, talk to me."

"I don't feel good." Her whisper ends in a choked sob.

"Shhh. That's all right," I say, gathering her against my chest. "Come here. We're gonna get you better."

"You can't," she croaks. Dried tear marks waterfall her cheeks. "You can't get me better."

I lift her tiny body in my arms and stand. Once I carry her into the bedroom, I place her on the bed and peel off her sweat-soaked T-shirt. She trembles as I cover her with the sheet. After bringing her a glass of water, I sit beside her and wipe the sweat from her brow with a soft cloth. "You fainted?"

She nods. "I'm sorry." Her voice is soft, pained.

"For what?" I stroke her tangled damp mess of rose-gold hair.

"For everything." Her eyes glass over. "I'm bad for you, Charlie. I am."

Over and over, I shake my head. "You're not bad for me. You're mine."

"I shouldn't be," she says under her breath, tears still slipping down her cheeks. "I'm a thorn. I hurt people."

"Shhh." I grip her hand, lacing her fingers with mine as if I can bring her back from whatever grim ledge she's on. "Don't say that."

I wait for her to say more, but she doesn't.

Her eyes flutter closed, and soon she's asleep.

A buzz of warning sounds in my head.

I stand from the bed and lean over her.

I've never noticed the rhythm of a heart. But tonight, in my bedroom, with Ruby sleeping naked in the sheets, I do. Reaching out, I fan my fingers over her rapidly rising chest.

Her heartbeat is fast. Unnatural.

Christ.

Worry blazes inside of me as I press two fingers to her slender white throat. Clock the blood thrumming in her veins, the frenetic pump of her pulse.

Then I move them to mine, noting the difference.

I go cold.

The sunrise outside dims as my vision blurs.

"Ruby," I whisper, keeping watch on her pale face. "What the fuck's wrong with you?"

44

Ruby

WORSE. IT'S GETTING WORSE.

My hands hold the steering wheel in a death grip as I drive back to Runaway Ranch from town.

The doctor's words play over in my head on a loop.

Get back to your cardiologist.

Slow down. Stop pushing yourself too hard.

If you're not careful, you could die. The likelihood of a severe cardiac arrest is a certain possibility.

I woke early this morning, barely an hour after my flutter and snuck out of the cabin. I left Charlie sleeping beside me. He's headed to Bozeman today to finalize the ranch's protected habitat status, but that hasn't stopped him from leaving me numerous voicemails and texts. I spent five hours talking to the doctor in Resurrection, with my cardiologist on Zoom, telling them about my heart, and listening to their advice. And it's all the same.

Go home to get better.

But how? How do I go home after this summer?

Sadness pours into me.

I love this life. I don't want to go back to my old one, but at what cost?

Is that the risk I take?

Live while accepting my fate?

Or go back to being quiet, knowing I had a cowboy who loved me and that was good enough?

What is enough?

My whole life I've never been afraid of dying. I've been afraid of not living, but now that I have lived, the thought of losing everything, the thought of a life without Charlie, is too painful.

Wasted. Everything seems wasted. This entire summer, all the miles on this old Skylark, all the checks off my bucket list, all the love I have for Charlie—wasted.

I imagine his future as I drive. He'll meet someone else. A guest, a tourist, a local. Someone alive and healthy. They'll have babies, a family, a long life together—everything I can't give him. He'll forget me.

And he should.

I let out a strangled cry. The thought of a life without Charlie has me feeling sick inside.

My gaze tracks the storm clouds rolling down off Meadow Mountain and over Resurrection proper. I punch the accelerator, steering through my tears.

It feels ominous. A sign I need to decide before it's too late.

I inhale a steeling breath.

How can I leave? How can I go back to anything other than this heartbreaking, wild life?

For a split second, I'm back at that gas station in Winslow, a cool Coke bottle in my hand and a map spread in front of me. Would I change it if I could? Point my heart in a different direction?

No.

The answer is no.

I wouldn't change it. Not for the world. Not for my life.

After this summer, I will never go back to living half-asleep. Of experiencing the world through my bedroom window, or on my computer screen.

All these miles, all these years, my heart was leading me to Charlie.

I have to give him the choice to accept it, to forgive me or not. To love me . . .or not.

If he doesn't, I'll understand. I'll move on.

It's my mistake.

I have to own it.

I have to come clean.

Tell Charlie the truth.

Tame my heart.

My phone buzzes, and I sigh when I see Max's name on the caller ID.

Why does he have to pick this moment to call? Still, I've been avoiding his calls ever since I decided to stay in Resurrection. I can't ignore him anymore.

With trembling hands, I pull the car over to the side of the road, because I don't trust myself to have this conversation and drive safely.

I put the phone to my ear. "Hi."

Max exhales in relief. "So, you're alive."

"Barely," I whisper, glancing at the storm clouds again. My heart beats crazily, an echo to my mind.

"What's that supposed to mean?"

"Nothing."

Max swears. "You had a flutter."

I almost drop the phone. "What? No."

"I can tell, Ruby."

He's right. He can. My brother has been a part of my heart as long as I have had it.

"How many? How many flutters, Ruby?" Max's panicked voice cuts through my muddled mind.

"Too many," I say flatly.

"Fuck. I'll come get you."

I shake my head, over and over. "Don't. Don't bother."

I feel my life slipping between my fingers.

I want to marry Charlie.

I want to live at the ranch.

I want so many things, but it feels like my time's up.

"I know where you are."

My eyes flash open, big as saucers. Dread caves in my chest. "What?"

"You're in Resurrection, Montana. I called Molly. I found the Instagram you've been running."

I let out a bitter laugh. "Congrats, Max. Detective big brother for the win."

"I'm coming to get you."

Oxygen rushes out of my lungs. "No," I blurt. "You can't."

"Why not?" A heavy silence, then, "Don't tell me you're staying."

"Fine. I won't."

"Does he know?"

"Does who know?"

"The cowboy who loves you?"

I pinch my eyes. They're leaking again. "He doesn't love me."

A big rig zooms by, shaking the car.

Max chuckles, a dry, hysterical sound. "Did you see that photo of you two by the creek? Because I did. He loves you, you idiot." His voice breaks. "What's it gonna do to the guy, Rubes?"

A shuddery breath rockets out of me. "I'm going to tell him."

"Does it even matter?" Max asks, and I wonder if he means for me or for Charlie. Either way, he's right.

"You're an asshole, Max."

"And you're a liar, Ruby."

It feels like I've been slapped. As I sit here, collecting myself, trying to be strong, I hear it. The worst sound.

Max is crying.

"You're pushing yourself too hard."

I swallow down the bitter lump in my throat. A tear slips down my cheek. "Max. Please. Stop."

The last thing I need is an earful from my big brother about how I screwed up. I already feel like shit.

I feel broken. Wilted. Like a flower without petals.

"You are *sick*, Ruby!" he shouts, causing me to jump. "Life isn't a fucking fairy tale. Start caring. And stop falling in goddamn love."

I stare at the phone, wide-eyed and wounded.

It's the cruelest cut.

But I deserve it. Deserve it for leading Charlie on. For putting my brother and my father and my heart through hell.

"Maybe you're right, Max. Maybe I don't deserve love." I screw my eyes shut, a sob escaping my mouth. My tears keep coming, a steady stream of pain. "I don't deserve anything. Or anyone. Because you want me to live my life like I'm in a cage."

Max inhales, sharp. "That's not what I—"

"Fuck you, Max."

I hang up. My heart pounds so hard it hurts.

Numb, I watch a flock of birds sail across the sky.

Free.

They keep going and going and going.

They keep going.

If a heart stops beating, did it ever exist?

If I fall in love, does it even matter?

If everyone says no, why do I only hear yes?

I inhale a breath.

Then I turn off my phone, squeeze my eyes shut, and scream.

I need to feel alive. One last explosion of life that settles your soul. One last hurrah before I tell Charlie the truth.

I park my car in Charlie's driveway and walk across the gravel drive that leads to the barn. Though it fights with the clouds, the bright sunlight above fills me with energy, with electricity. Max screaming at me was like a foreign shadow settling in my heart. I don't know how to process it. I'm angry and upset and I don't like myself.

I want my sunflower back. I want my sun.

I need calm. I need to ride.

Ford, replacing a saddle in the tack room, blinks as I storm into the barn.

Charlie must have told him what happened this morning because he straightens up and says, "You're supposed to be resting." His light brown eyes scour my face, concern in his typically easy-going expression.

I know what he sees. Tears. Rage. Recklessness.

"Fuck rest," I say breathlessly.

Ford stares, reaching for the radio on his hip. "Ruby . . ."

I ignore him. "Leave me alone, Ford."

After Max, I'm not in the mood to be told what to do.

I go to Arrow's stall and let him out. He comes to me easily, knowing me by now. I see Ford disappear as I saddle up Arrow the western way. My mind goes over the instructions Charlie taught me. Pad first, next the saddle, secure the straps, then bridle.

There's a tightness in my chest. My heart pumps out a warning for me to slow down.

Never.

I have too much to lose.

My home. My ranch. My cowboy.

When I'm finished, I reach up, my fingers skimming Arrow's muzzle. "Hey," I whisper, a wobbly smile tipping my lips. "We're gonna do this, okay? Then I'm going to talk to Charlie. What do you think about that, you sweet, beautiful boy?"

Serious black eyes stare back at me. I press my face against his cheek, inhaling his hay and horse scent.

Then I swing myself up on Arrow's hulking black back. My mother's face flashes in my mind, and I touch the bracelet on my wrist.

Honor your heart until you become it.

This wild heart knows the answer.

One last ride.

45

Charlie

IT'S FIVE P.M. BY THE TIME I MAKE IT HOME FROM Bozeman.

This morning when I woke up, Ruby was gone. She left a note when she should have been in goddamn bed. All day I've been on edge. Not even signing the paperwork that declares Runaway Ranch safe has eased the ache in my gut. All day my mind's been on her and it's no different when I storm through the front door and toss my keys and wallet on the counter, growling at the empty house.

The ranch without Ruby is like the sky without the sun.

Unnatural.

"Ruby!" I call out, my pulse quickening. I feel like every vein in my neck is about to pop.

I scan the kitchen, the living room, bathroom, before sprinting upstairs.

She's not here.

"Fuck." I tear a hand through my hair, returning to the kitchen.

She's avoiding me, avoiding what happened this morning.

I pace the kitchen, dragging a hand over my beard. Except for a text that told me she went into town, my calls have gone straight to voicemail. Her laptop's on the kitchen counter, her car's in the driveway, but the worry about her taking off still eats at me. Where the fuck is she?

I eye her bucket list on the fridge. Something I once chalked up to an excitable girl's dreams, but now . . .

The entire summer plays back in my head. Her refusal to tell me why she's running away. Hand to her heart. Pills at midnight. Fainting in my bed. Ford's words: *What do you know about this girl?*

And her list.

That goddamn bucket list.

"Fuck," I blast out. I brace my hands on the kitchen island and bow my head.

Ruby's sick.

Something's wrong with her.

My gut is lined with shards of glass. She's been good about keeping her secret, whatever it is, but it ends today. I need to find her, and when I do, I'm going to sit her beautiful, stubborn ass down and make her tell me the truth. I've gone easy on her, but not anymore.

If it is anemia, I plan to drag her to every doctor in the state of Montana.

I twist around at the clatter of the screen door.

Ford stands there, wild-eyed. "Charlie, Ruby saddled up Arrow."

I go cold, then I get pissed. He knows as well as I do she isn't supposed to ride without me.

"Shit." I tear a hand through my hair, keep it there. "When?"

"Ten minutes ago. She's in the pasture." He hesitates, then says, "She doesn't look so good, man."

"Fuck," I swear before sprinting out of the house at a dead run. Ford's right behind me as we clear the gravel road, picking up speed when I'm within eyesight of Ruby sitting atop Arrow.

Behind her, Wyatt comes up on Pepita.

Thank Christ for my brother.

I storm toward her, but when Ruby glances down at me, my entire body locks. My heart drops to my boots.

She looks beaten down. There's no other word for it. Her face is pale, her rose-gold hair in a wild tangle, and red rims her blue eyes.

But it's her spirit dulled, broken that scares the shit out of me.

"Hi, Cowboy." She says it so casually, like she hasn't been avoiding me and my calls for the last eight hours.

"Ruby," I say, fighting the urge to growl at her and instead channeling a gentle calm I don't feel right now. "Get down from there." I grab the bit, stilling her and Arrow, but he snorts, stomping his feet and backing up.

She stares at my hard gaze. "You're going to yell." Her lower lip trembles.

"I won't yell." I blow out a frustrated breath. "Baby, I'm worried."

Tears well in her eyes and she shakes her head. "Don't be."

I take hold of the saddle horn. "Give me your hand. Let me get you down."

"No. Not yet."

I edge closer, my hand moving to grip her thigh. "We need to talk. Right the hell now." My voice is rougher than I've ever used to talk to Ruby, but I need her to hear me. To listen.

She flinches. "I know we do. I just need to ride first. Please. Let me do this, Charlie." The tremor in her voice nearly knocks me off-balance.

With a gentle nudge, she leads Arrow into a slow trot.

I hustle beside her to keep up. "Your list. What's it really for, Ruby?"

Fear flickers in her eyes, and her voice turns to a whisper. "Charlie, it is what it is."

"Bullshit," I growl, and then my stomach drops when I see it.

Instead of letting the rein lay across her palm, she has it wrapped around her left hand. A motion that tells me she's distracted, her mind elsewhere.

She should not be on a horse right now.

Worry rips a hole through me. "Ruby—"

I go to grab the back of the saddle and pull myself up behind her, to force her down, but she's quick. With a graceful movement, she squeezes her legs, moving Arrow into a bouncy trot across the pasture and away from me.

She's a fast learner and I'm the fucking idiot who taught her to ride.

Worried eyes meeting mine, Wyatt follows behind as I head after her.

Shoulders tense, Ruby closes her eyes as she tilts her head back and lets the sunshine warm her face. Like she's trying to charge herself back up.

The thought hits me like a sucker punch.

She's had a thorn stuck in her this entire time and I've been too blind to see it.

I was right.

All this time Ruby's been running, but she's not running from me.

Not anymore.

Ruby and Arrow come to a complete and abrupt stop in the middle of the pasture.

My body goes cold.

Muscles tensing, I jog over to her. "Ruby?"

For a few seconds, she sits still, swaying slightly. And then her glassy gaze flickers from Arrow to me.

She breathes heavily. "Something's going to happen," she tells me.

My question's a panicked growl. "What?" I reach out and grip the back of the saddle. "What's going to happen, Sunflower?"

"Cowboy," she whispers, her long lashes fluttering. "Catch me."

Before I can process her words, I watch in horror as her eyes roll back and she goes limp, her tiny body slumping to the side. But she doesn't fall.

Unconscious, she hangs in suspended motion.

"Ruby!" My stomach is a black hole of panic, my heart lurching into my throat. I reach up to catch her, to pull her safely into my arms, but I can't.

She's held tight, unable to be moved.

And then Wyatt screams out, "Charlie, her wrist! Her goddamn wrist!"

No. God, no.

Her slender wrist is tangled in the reins.

Spooked by the yelling, Arrow bucks, ragged hooves

flying. The rough motion jerks Ruby's small frame like a rag doll. Her head falls back for a moment, and then comes forward again.

"No! Wyatt!" I bellow, trying to still Arrow, but the frightened horse jolts, trying to shake us loose, to bolt for the stables.

Somehow, I manage to move Ruby so she's slumped forward over Arrow's neck.

The ground thundering beneath him, Wyatt pulls Pepita up alongside Arrow. He reaches for Ruby's arm, his shaky hand running along the length of rein, attempting to free her.

"I can't get it," Wyatt breathes. "Fuck. *Fuck.*"

Ford's there too.

On his horse, Eephus, he bookends Ruby's other side, blocking Arrow in so he can't get away. "Hold on tight," Ford bellows at Wyatt. "Don't you let her go."

Christ. My legs almost go out from under me.

It's my worst nightmare happening in slow motion.

If Arrow takes off, Ruby will fall.

He'll drag her, trample her.

My heart is in my throat. Unable to breathe, to think logically, when she's in danger.

This isn't happening.

Not again.

Not to her.

Nostrils flaring, Arrow rears back, fighting my hold on his bridle, readying to run.

Ruby jerks, slips, sags lower toward the hard-packed grass.

Ford swears.

"*No!*" My left hand clamps around her free wrist and I hold her tighter.

The soft hiss of leather.

Suddenly, Wyatt's bowie knife is in his hands. Eyes wild with panic, he saws frantically through the leather strap of the rein. The steel blade shimmers in the sunlight.

"Cut her loose!" I holler at Wyatt, my blood pumping. "*Now!*"

"I'm trying, man!"

Wyatt continues to saw at the strap. He swears viciously as it refuses to break, and then, after a few terrifying seconds, it snaps.

Ruby's free.

I pull her limp body into my arms.

And then I run like hell for the house.

46

Ruby

I BLINK, MY VISION BLURRING AS I TRY TO ORIENT myself. I'm in bed. The room is dim and cool. A burning sensation sears my left wrist. Thunder rumbles, the sky outside dark and stormy. Rolling my head across the pillow, I see Charlie's dusty Stetson on a chair pulled close to my bed. A glass of whiskey is on the nightstand.

When I push myself up on my elbows, a figure comes out of the shadows, towering over me.

"Charlie," I whisper.

The bed shifts as he sits beside me. "Sunflower." His voice—deep, rough—washes over me like a familiar song. He pushes a strand of hair behind my hair and cups my face with a big, calloused palm. I lean into his beautiful touch.

"Do you remember what happened?" he asks.

"I fainted on Arrow," I whisper.

He shakes his head, his expression dark, pained. "I never should have let you on that fucking horse."

Blinking back tears, I focus on Charlie's haggard face. "It's not your fault. It's mine."

The last thing I want him to do is blame himself.

Tears spill down my cheeks. "I'm sorry, Charlie. I'm so sorry."

"Don't be sorry," he says in a stern voice, pushing my chin up so I look into those fierce blue eyes of his. "Baby, if there's something I should know, go ahead and tell me now. Tell me before I lose my damn mind." His voice tears, splits. "Don't make me guess."

"Okay," I say. "I'll tell you."

My throat burns and I keep my gaze on his face, gathering courage.

I touch my chest, tracking my heartbeat.

We're almost there.

No more running.

I don't want to be cynical or angry or hate my heart.

Or myself.

I have to tell him the truth.

Even if I lose him.

Inhaling a steadying breath, I sit up straighter and say, "I have a heart thing."

Charlie closes his eyes like he's been expecting this. "What kind of heart thing?"

I swallow, pressing on. "It's called supraventricular tachycardia or SVT for short," I say. And then I take a deep breath and release all of it. How my brother and father shielded me. All the medical jargon. My triggers.

"Stress is tricky," I explain to Charlie. "It's like the electrical charge in my heart gets disconnected and when it does, I faint. I call it a flutter."

Charlie stares at me like every interaction we've had

this summer is running through that beautiful brain of his. His broad chest rises and falls.

"And your pills?" The words wrench from his mouth. "Is that the treatment?"

I nod. "I have medicine and techniques to ward it off if I feel it coming, but . . .it's getting worse." I take a shuddery breath. "I went to the doctor today. They want me to go home and see my cardiologist. The pills aren't working anymore."

"Then what will?"

I shake my head, wanting him to understand. "It's not something you can fix, Charlie. I won't ever get better. And one day, my heart will stop, and it will never start again, and I will die."

Charlie makes a kind of tortured sound in the back of his throat.

I go on.

"It could be two years, or it could be twenty. My mother had a heart attack. My aunt died at twenty-eight. Our life expectancy isn't great." I bite my lip and keep my gaze on my hands as I admit the hard truth. "I shouldn't have been here this summer. I made it worse. I was reckless with my heart." I meet his eyes. "With yours."

Turning away from me, he sets his head in his hands and breathes deeply.

"Charlie . . ." I press a palm against his muscled back, but he rips up off the bed and crosses the room.

At the distance he puts between us, I burst into tears. "You're mad. I understand."

He makes a fist, sets it on the wall, squeezes his eyes shut, and rests his brow beside it. "I'm not mad, Ruby. Hell, I'm—"

Devastated. Broken.

I see it on his face, the sensation of being completely knocked off his axis.

Heartbroken.

I did this to him.

"Why didn't you tell me?" he asks, pushing off the wall and pacing the room like a caged animal. Confusion creases his handsome features.

I rub my weary eyes. "I never thought I'd see you again, let alone work for you. And then we made the deal about Runaway Ranch." A weak, tearful laugh shakes my body. "We were supposed to be temporary. And I didn't want you to treat me like I was broken or fragile. I wanted to live for once in my life. If you knew . . .that's all you'd see."

Charlie's eyes soften.

I sniffle, reining back more tears. "I didn't think it mattered. That I'd be gone by the end of the summer. But then I fell in love with you, Charlie, and I found out about Maggie and Ford said—" Charlie swears. "I tried to leave. I didn't want to put you through any more pain. But I . . .I couldn't." I choke on a sob. "I love you too much."

Charlie stands by the door, his large frame tensed and locked, processing what I've just told him. "You should have told me," he growls, his gruff voice laced with pain.

I nod. "I know. I tried. Every day I told myself I'd tell you, and every day, I chickened out. I was selfish. I didn't want to hurt you or lose you."

His jaw hardens, and he stomps toward me. "You went through it all alone. All this time you were hurting and in pain and sick, and I didn't know a goddamn thing about it."

A hot tear rolls down my cheek. My heart hurts. I

deserve every bit of his anger, his frustration. I have no excuse, no rebuttal.

Charlie sighs, his dark brows furrowing as he closes his eyes. "You put me through hell, Ruby."

My lower lip trembles. "I know. I'm sorry. I can't tell you how sorry I am."

Silence. Awful, awful silence.

Weakly, I scoot to the edge of the bed. The drop of my bare feet on cool hardwood is like an anchor. "I want to tell you I love you. I want to tell you that I've never lived as much as I have this summer because of you. I want to tell you that you have my heart even when it stops beating."

His large frame sags and his face screws up. "Ruby, don't."

I touch my chest, the beat of my heart calm, and urge myself to go on.

We're almost there.

Sniffling, I shake my head, wiping tears off my cheeks. "I don't regret this summer, Charlie. I'd do it all over again, even if it ends like this."

Charlie turns his head, his hard expression morphing into shock. "Ends?"

"It has to end."

I make a decision.

God, it will hurt, but I have to let him go.

"I'm getting worse, Charlie. I thought I could do it, but I don't want you to go through it."

He freezes, stops breathing.

My tears overflow.

I push myself up to stand on shaky legs and glance around the room for my things.

Gaze narrowed, he turns to me, smearing a hand down his dark beard. "What're you doing?"

"Making it easier for you." I sniffle. "I lied to you and your family. I could die, Charlie. I can't give you children. I'll go, okay? I'll—"

Suddenly, Charlie's not by the door anymore. In one swift motion, he's hauling me into his muscled chest. "Go?" he asks in disbelief, his voice breaking. "I stopped you once. Why in the hell would I let you run away now?"

"I lied to you," I gasp. The sudden feeling of being in his arms once more has my legs giving out. Gripping his shirt to stay steady, I press my face to his chest and weep. "You should hate me."

He chuckles. The vibration rolls through his body and into mine.

Then he takes my face in his big hands and stares into my eyes. "Am I pissed? Am I worried? I won't lie to you. Yeah, I'm both of those things. But Ruby, baby, as long as your love keeps rushing through my lungs, I am yours and you're mine. You're still my sunflower."

I'm crying so hard, big, wet sopping tears that streak my cheeks. I'm so relieved it's out. Charlie knows my truth, knows every little piece of my heart. And still . . .

He won't let me go.

How could I ever have doubted this man?

Charlie wipes away my tears with his thumbs. "There is no question I love you, no question about us," he rasps, pressing his warm lips to my brow. His voice shakes with emotion. "I'm not walking away. I can't. I won't. So don't ask."

"Okay, Cowboy." I smile wide. Tears sparkle on my lashes. "I won't."

In answer, Charlie kisses me with such force I gasp into his mouth. My fingers dive into his thick head of dark hair. His lips are full, soft, drinking me in, telling me everything will be okay. My body curls into him. And then he's lifting me off my feet and I'm back in his arms.

Where I've always belonged.

47

Charlie

H ER HEART COULD STOP BEATING.

Her beautiful, pure, courageous heart.

How the fuck did I miss that?

I don't miss things. On a ranch, missing things means a horse gets sick. People get hurt. Crops die. You lose an entire working day because you fucked up.

I plan to rectify that fast.

Seated at my kitchen table, Ruby's laptop in front of me, I research my questions about SVT to fill in the blanks. Everything I've learned about her heart in the last week isn't enough. I have to do more. Stock the ranch with heart-healthy foods. Order a top-rated heart tracker. Find her the best doctor so she can get a real checkup. If anyone smokes around her, they're a dead man. Most importantly, no fucking stress.

I wouldn't be the man she deserves if I didn't do everything in my power to learn about her condition. Not to fix her. To be there when she needs it. To protect her.

I click on an article and read.

I read another.

The heart will suddenly start racing, then stop racing or slow down abruptly. Episodes can last for seconds, minutes, hours.

A muscle pulses in my jaw. It explains so much about this summer. The racing of her heart. Her fainting spells. Her small sips of coffee, of alcohol. Everything about it terrifies me. It haunts me that every beat of her heart is tentative.

But even as worried as I am, I am in this. Walking away from this sweet, kind, fearless woman will never happen.

Even now, the memory stings. I hate she thought I'd reject her. That I'd give her up. That I could do anything but love her when she is the only thing I've ever wanted.

She's continuously putting me on my ass.

For ten years, I walked around this world in a daze, breathing the same stale air when Ruby was gasping for it. And what did I do with my life? Drank it away, brooded while Ruby fought for hers.

My girl's a goddamn force. Strong as hell. As worried and as pissed as I was, I'm also in awe. Ruby didn't let fear stop her from living.

My gaze ticks to the screen door. The sky is dark with clouds, signaling thunderstorms are on the horizon. The empty ranch is silent except for the faraway clash of thunder.

I check the time on the kitchen clock. It'll be evening soon.

Ruby left an hour ago to feed Winslow, and her absence has me desperate to see her. Worry lances through me. Worry that she fainted. That I'm not there.

I drag a hand down my beard, shaking off the grim thoughts that have taken root.

It's something I have to work on.

Before my thoughts can get away from me, the screen door clatters open and Ruby stands in the doorway, her lips parted and a flower crown on her head.

I straighten in my chair, the tension immediately leaving my shoulders at the sight of her.

"Hey, Cowboy," she breathes.

My lips curve. "Hey, Sunflower."

She kicks off her shoes, wind-blown hair falling around her shoulders. The hem of her pink sundress flips up, fluttering around her thighs and highlighting her long, lean legs.

"I thought you'd be out on the ranch," she says. The scent of sunshine and pine follow her in.

"Took the day off," I rumble, reaching for her.

"Another day off?" She laughs and arches a brow. "Your brothers will think I'm a bad influence."

With a growl, I catch her around the waist and tug her onto my lap. Press a kiss to her lips. "The best bad influence around."

I told my brothers about Ruby's condition. Instead of voicing their doubt or trying to change my mind, they understood. As always, they had my back.

Ruby and I—we're doing this. *Us.* We got the entire fucking world laid out in front of us. I'm living my life with this woman. I love her heart, her soul, and her wild dreams.

I love *her*.

She's mine, and I won't give her up for anything or anyone.

Ruby tilts her head back for a kiss, then turns to face

the table. "This is new. Charlie Montgomery on a computer." Eyes curious, her small hand slides over my shoulder. "What're you doing?"

"Researching." I tuck a lock of hair behind her ear. "Getting you the foods you should be eating. Checked out some cardiologists in Washington. We can head out there whenever you need to."

Ruby's bright blue eyes widen. "Charlie, you did all this?"

I flash a crooked grin. Don't even bother to hide it. "Damn right. My girl gets the best."

Her breath hitches. Silently, she slips off my lap and walks to the kitchen island.

I frown. The faint trace of sadness on her face makes my stomach lurch.

She stands there, palms on the counter, head bowed. After a second, she closes her eyes. "I love that you're doing all this," she says quietly. "But you can't fix me, Charlie. I don't want you to have false hope or try to change what you can't. This is my heart. This is me."

Not fucking happening.

I rip out of the chair and go to her, hauling her to my chest. "I'm sorry." I frame her face with my hands. "I love *you*. Just like this. And you're right. You're not something to be fixed, but I will keep you safe. Long as I live, I will always fucking protect you."

"I know you will." A weak smile flits across her face, then disappears. Color flames her cheeks. "You just . . . can't treat me different. You can't think I'm weak or worry all the time or stop me from doing things I need to do."

That's it. Her fear. Why she didn't tell me after I told her about Runaway Ranch.

She's been so sheltered her entire life she's used to people keeping her back.

I want her to see herself how I see her.

Perfect.

"Ruby," I say her name forcefully, so she looks at me. "I didn't see someone weak this summer. I saw a fierce girl who pushed me to be a better man. Who made me fucking live. Who helped people when she didn't have to. That's you. Golden, just like your heart, and nothing about you is ever bad or broken."

"Really?" she whispers, hope in her voice.

"Really. And this heart?" I press my palm against her chest. "I'm gonna learn everything about this because it's mine now, you hear me? Your beat is my beat."

Her eyes sparkle.

"You're gonna keep on livin', baby. I'm just gonna be the one to rope you."

Blood rushes into her cheeks. She lifts her chin, the teasing smile on her face like a shock to my system. "You think you can, Cowboy?"

Dragging her closer, I growl against her mouth. "Sunflower, I know I can." I slide a hand up the slope of her breast to curve around her slender throat. Her pulse hammers beneath my fingers. I track it like she's taught me this last week.

This heartbeat is mine.

Mine to memorize.

Mine to love.

Every beat precious.

Powerful.

"What is it?" My hand lingers on her throat. "About 150?"

Her long lashes lower and she feels her wrist. "130."

Worry twists my insides. "Does it hurt? Are you in pain?"

"No," she says. "It feels fluttery. Like a butterfly. When it beats faster . . .it feels like pressure." She laughs, a melodic little chime that sets my soul on fire. "Here. I'll show you."

Lifting on tiptoes, she kisses me, slipping her tongue into my mouth. Her nails dig into my shoulder, and a tortured groan emerges from my throat.

Beneath my fingertips, her pulse speeds up.

With a growl, I jerk back from her. "Ruby," I warn, not wanting to hurt her.

A smile tugs at her mouth. She steps into me, slipping a slender leg between mine. "This is how you start a heart," she says, her gorgeous blue eyes darkening with lust. "You just kiss me, Cowboy."

Fuck it.

I do.

My lips crash against hers. Ruby melts into me, the fast pulse of her breath syncing with her heartbeats. Each one I feel. Treasure. I hook my hands under her legs and lift her off the floor. She kisses me deeper, wrapping her legs around my waist. My hold on her tightens as I carry her into the living room.

"Slow," she whispers breathlessly.

"Slow," I mouth gruffly against her lips.

Her slender arms lift to the ceiling so I can strip her bare. I toss her dress, her panties, onto the floor while I maneuver us to the couch.

A desperate, animalistic need overtakes me. To hold her. To fuck her. To feel her heartbeat crash against mine and know she's here.

I unzip my jeans and sit down, Ruby straddling me. When she sinks onto my thick length, I groan, bathing my cock in her sweet heat. She's slick and tight and I growl my approval. I guide her hips up and down, burying myself so goddamn deep that we both cry out.

"Don't know how I fucking survived without you, Ruby," I rasp into her wild hair, tangled with flowers. "Don't know. Don't wanna know."

The air around us is electric, neon in a way only Ruby can make me feel. Alive and buzzing. It's all for her. What my girl needs to feel good. My thrusts are slow and controlled, dismantling all my dark parts so there's only the man she loves. The man she deserves.

Too much, too much, Ruby's too much.

She will never be enough.

"Charlie . . ." Ruby gasps as her back arches. Her long lashes fan against her smooth skin. Her mouth parts in a perfect O.

I bury my face in her neck. "I fucking love you."

She whimpers, kissing my jawline. The heat from her mouth warms my cheek. Her slender arms wind around my neck. "I love you, Cowboy."

My chest heaves faster as I match the rhythm of her hips, her heart. Slow, fast. Slow, fast. Slow, fast until she's crying my name, her small form trembling in my arms, shaking from her release.

My ragged moan fills the house as my orgasm hits me like a sledgehammer. I come inside of her, pressing soft kisses to her throat, her cheek, her lips.

When our bodies stop quaking, I pull her back onto the couch, keeping her in my arms. I grab a blanket and drape it over her body.

Outside, thunder cracks across the sky.

"Try for the sunrise?" I skim my knuckles against her flushed cheek.

She laughs, rolls her eyes. "We'll never make it, Cowboy. Let's face it."

I chuckle.

Sighing, Ruby burrows against me, resting her head on my chest.

I stare at her as she's curled up in my arms.

Sometimes I can't believe she's real. That she's mine.

"There was a trial," she says in a soft voice.

I lift my head to hear her better. "A what?"

"A clinical trial for SVT. Some new medications. Surgeries." Biting her lip, she looks up at me. "I missed it."

"Baby," I say, my breath knocked out of my chest. "Where?"

"California." Her pretty face hardens. "It would have meant leaving the ranch. Being trapped in some hospital for a month. And I couldn't." She slides her hand up my chest. "I couldn't leave you, Charlie."

"Is there another one? A study." If I have to bang down their door, I'll do it.

"Charlie." Her gorgeous blue eyes shutter. "I'd have to leave."

"I'd go with you."

"What?"

"I'll take you to California. Maybe we won't make the sunrise, but I can do a sunset."

I'm rewarded with a smile so bright the sun ceases to exist.

"Oh, Charlie," she whispers.

No doubt about this woman.

Nothing could make me love her less.

I'm opening my mouth to tell her that when a loud shout sounds from outside.

Tensing, I shoot up straight, a primal protective instinct chilling my blood.

Ruby's wide blue eyes dart to mine.

Footsteps pound on the porch stairs.

I scoot forward, placing my body in front of her.

"Baby, stay—"

And then the front door bursts open.

I yank the blanket up to cover Ruby. "What the fuck?" I roar.

Wyatt stands in the living room, every ounce of color drained from his face. "Charlie. The barn's on fire."

48

Ruby

"THE HORSES?" CHARLIE SHOUTS AS HE AND Wyatt run out of the house. They sprint across gravel and grass, and I'm right behind them, rushing to keep up in my bare feet. My legs are numb and wobbly but my stride is fast.

"Ford and Davis are there now, trying to get 'em out." In his panic, Wyatt trips, and Charlie grabs his brother's arm to keep him from face planting. "We got the fire department on the way."

"Lightning?" Charlie asks.

"Not lightning. Someone started it. The door's nailed shut. The horses are trapped."

Wyatt's words chill my blood.

A dark curse blasts from Charlie's mouth.

My entire body trembles as I race after Charlie. Smoke coats my nostrils and floods the dusky sky.

The horses. Please let them be okay.

Horrified, we all skid to a stop in front of the barn. The fire's small, the light rain dousing most of the flames, but it creeps with a low blaze, spreading slowly. Flame licks up the wood and over the front door.

My hands fly to my mouth. "No, oh no."

Some of the horses have already smashed through, kicking down the stall doors to escape the flame and smoke. Wild eyes, nostrils flaring, they race across the pasture. Ford and Davis swing the axes in their hands, smashing holes in the wall to evacuate the rest of the trapped horses.

Terror floods my body.

Charlie grabs my arms, pushing me back, away from the blaze. "Stay here," he shouts, fear on his face.

I fight against him. "No. I can help. They're our horses. This is our ranch, Charlie."

He kisses me hard. His eyes molten, frantic. "Use the rope. Lead 'em to the pasture. Tie 'em up so they don't run back into the barn." Chest heaving, he levels a big finger at me. "That's your fucking job, Ruby. Nothing else."

And then he and Wyatt rush off to help their brothers.

I snap into action.

Heart thumping in my chest, I grab a length of lead rope from the pasture fence. I work fast like Charlie showed me, looping the rope around the necks of the free horses and walking them calmly to a fence post where I tie them up. I round up Arrow and Pepita and Eephus. I don't see Winslow or the demon horse that Wyatt broke over the summer.

I count seven horses, which means there are eight still trapped.

The tight knot in my stomach turns into a gaping hole. My hands shake. I feel so helpless. Everything's commotion as the crackle of fire snaps in the evening air. Davis,

Ford, and Wyatt work together, smashing wood, tearing down the front of the barn.

I do a fast sweep of the ranch, looking for Charlie. I don't find him. Ice freezes my bloodstream.

Oh god. Where is he? I squeeze my eyes shut, praying he didn't run into the barn.

That's when I hear a familiar, terrified whinny.

My head whips around.

Winslow.

He's trying to kick his way through the back of the barn, a section of hallway not yet engulfed in flames.

Rage has me running.

I can help. I can do something.

Spying one of the small axes used during the campfire dinner stuck in the woodpile, I grab it up. I edge closer to the burning barn. The flames sear, and I hiss out a breath. But I steel my shoulders and hammer away at a small hole Winslow's already kicked in the side.

The small hole becomes bigger.

Biggest.

My muscles burn, and I cough, choking as the smoke engulfs my lungs, nostrils, and eyes.

I drop the axe.

This time, I use my hands, tearing at the already broken sections of barn wood. My pulse pounds in my ears and my vision pinpricks. I ignore the pain in my fingertips. My chest.

My body tells me to stop. My heart tells me to keep going.

Shouts carry across the pasture—maybe Wyatt, maybe Ford—but I keep my focus on the task in front of me.

The tips of my fingers are bleeding and blackened, but

all I can think about is getting the horses out. I wrap my hands around a huge chunk of wood, and bracing one foot on the barn, I pull.

The wood gives.

I tear it away, big enough for a body.

A scream of victory rips out of me when Winslow lurches out like he's been waiting for me all his life. He comes to my side.

"Good boy," I sob, stroking him on his withers.

Dizzy, I manage to walk him to the pasture. I tie him up with the other horses and listen for sirens, but there are none.

That's when I double over into a violent coughing fit. The smoke curls deep into my lungs like gnarled fingers taking root. Panicked, I take large gulps of air. It feels like I can't get enough oxygen, like my heart is starving.

There's a clap of thunder and the skies unleash. Rain pours down in earnest.

The rain.

It'll save us.

Gasping, I straighten up and stand in the darkness, shivering, smoke swirling around me, staring at the ranch that saved my soul this summer. The ranch Charlie and his brothers love. The land that let me live.

Wyatt watches, wide-eyed, hands on his head, as the rest of the barn burns. An insane rush of relief hits me when I spy Charlie, dirty but unharmed, loping out from behind the burning barn.

Blinking back tears, I take a step toward him, but the world spins.

"Oh," I whisper, licking my dry lips. "Oh, no."

My entire body thumps. Pulse points. Chest. Temples.

A low-frequency throb fills my ears. Blackness creeps around the edge of my vision.

That's when I see my mother standing in the pasture. *Mom.*

She reaches toward me, one graceful hand outstretched toward my heart. I can hear her whispering to me. *Come, come with me.* I want to run. I want to scream *no.* But all I can do is feel my heart race.

This isn't just a flutter.

This feels different.

Suddenly, I'm so very scared.

I shake my head and turn away, trying harder to breathe, to think a clear thought, to find a way away from my mother's sight. I grab the tall fence post for balance and gasp for air.

Help. I need to tell someone I need help.

Once again, my vision blurs as I search for Charlie in the smoke.

My cowboy.

The minute my eyes land on him, a sense of calm fills my soul.

Beating or still, my heart belongs to Charlie.

I look up at the stars and inhale one last breath.

49

Charlie

WE ALL WATCH AS THE BARN GOES UP IN flames.

"No!" Wyatt cries, lunging toward the fire.

I get to him first and pull him away because he's this close to losing it. I know the feeling.

Everything's gone. All our equipment. Our tack. Medical supplies.

Gone.

But the horses . . .

A dirtied hand clamps down on my shoulder and I glance over. "You okay?" Davis rumbles, his face streaked with soot. He glances down, checking me for injuries.

I nod. "How many?" I scan the pasture and run a hand through my sweaty hair. All I care about is the horses. "How many did we lose?"

"None." My oldest brother's voice is stunned. "We got 'em all."

"Thank God," Wyatt chokes out, swiping at his eyes.

I'm nearly felled with relief.

Thank fuck, the barn was a new building. Old wood and we wouldn't have had a chance in hell of getting any horses out. We'll have to get a vet down here to check them all over, but it's a miracle they all survived.

"DVL," Davis bites out.

A vein pulses in my temple, and rage blurs the edge of my vision. Someone will pay for this.

But later.

First, I have to find Ruby.

Chest heaving, I scan the ranch. Rainwater soaks everything, and the fire slows to a sputter. Ford's on his phone, pacing back and forth on the gravel drive, trying to get a signal.

That's when I see her.

Her body lies limp and motionless, collapsed into a dead faint on the grass.

My entire world crashes around me, and I break into a run. When I reach her, I fall to my knees beside her. Fear grabs me by the throat as I take in her pale face. She's unconscious, lips parted, soot streaking her face and clothes.

She fainted. She never should have been out here. She's done more for the ranch than she ever should have.

"Ruby." My voice comes out harsher than I want, harsher than I'd ever speak to her, but the tightness in my gut twists. I cradle her slack face in my hands, trying to rouse her. "Baby, wake up."

No response.

My frantic fingers move straight to her throat. I check her pulse, waiting for that wild, hammering beat.

But there isn't one.

"This isn't fucking funny," I grit out hoarsely. "Ruby. Come on, baby, get up. Get up."

I don't feel her heartbeat. I don't feel anything.

Panic turns to all-consuming terror as I stare down at her still form. A buzzing static fills my head and my blood turns to ice.

I hover a palm above her lips. Dip my head to her chest and listen.

For life.

For her beautiful beat.

Nothing.

Her chest isn't moving.

She isn't breathing.

That little light that shined inside since I met her— it's gone. I can't feel it. Her sun. Her glow. My sunflower.

That connection that tethered her to me.

I can't reach her.

The thought sends me to the fucking grave.

A keening, protective cry rises out of me. "No. No!" I shake her. "Ruby!"

I lift her petite frame into my arms, clinging to her, burying my face in her neck. Her head falls backward over my elbow. She feels broken and fragile and so fucking lifeless that I lose my goddamn mind.

"Don't do this," I whisper, rocking her against me. "Don't fucking leave me." I stroke her damp hair, dark from the rain. "Baby, please. Come back to me. Wake up. Wake the fuck up."

"Charlie." Davis grabs my shoulder. He's on his knees beside me. There's sorrow and fear in Davis's eyes and it terrifies me. He's always composed.

When he isn't, it means—

"She's not breathing," I scream.

Ford has his phone to his ear, his face grave. "We need an ambulance!" he barks. "Now! Get here now!"

"Put her down," Davis instructs. "Put her down, Charlie."

My skin turns to ice. The world has shut off. Tears burn my eyelids. My fucking heart has stopped beating.

How do you start a heart?

You just kiss me, Cowboy.

Words from a lifetime ago.

Words that jumpstart me.

I lay her tiny body down on the grass and start chest compressions.

Tipping her head back, I lock my lips over hers.

All of my air, all of my life, she can have it.

"Breathe, *breathe*," I demand against her already cold lips. "Don't do this to me. Don't you fucking leave me. Please, Ruby. *Please*."

Time slows down.

Stops.

I can't stop. I can't.

Not when she needs me.

Her beautiful heart—I won't let it go.

Sweat drips down my brow, into my eyes. The crack of her rib doesn't register, neither does Ford screaming into the phone, the rain soaking my shirt or the ache in my arms, the burn in my chest.

All I see is Ruby. Her pale face tipped toward the sky, rose-gold hair spread out across the grass. Blue moonlight on her face.

Ruby at my kitchen island, barefoot, laughing. Her

sweet, smiling face burned bright in my memory. My sunflower. My heart and soul.

The woman I love.

The woman I need.

Stopping compressions, I check her wrist for a pulse. Nothing.

"No," I choke out.

Grief capsizes me. I collapse on top of her, cradling her tiny frame in my arms. My beating heart, my precious girl. "Take it," I tell her hoarsely. "My breath, my soul. Take it." A sob rips through me. "Breathe, baby. Just fucking breathe."

Lifting my face, I wait for her chest to rise. For her lips to draw air.

Instead—nothing.

"Sunflower." My voice breaks.

I bury my face in her neck and cry. "I am begging you, come back to me. I need you. I need you so goddamn much."

I sob and plead. Anything. Anything to bring her back to me.

"Charlie." Davis's voice is tight. "Stop."

Sounds distort. The heavy hands of my brothers clamp down on my shoulders, wrestling me away from Ruby.

"No!" I shout desperately, swinging a fist as I'm pulled backward, punching nothing but air. No one's taking me from her. "Don't fucking touch her!"

Wyatt locks his arms around my chest, holds tight. "Calm your ass down," he hisses.

"It's been ten minutes," comes Davis's grim reply. His eyes intense, he positions himself over Ruby and tips her head back. "You have to rest, man. Let me take a turn."

It takes me a second to realize Davis isn't trying to take her from me. He's trying to help.

Panting, I nod.

Davis locks his fierce gaze on mine. "We'll switch off until she's breathing."

Numb, I watch as my brother begins CPR.

Breathe.

Breathe, Ruby. Come back to me.

50

Charlie

MY WORST FUCKING NIGHTMARE—STARING at a closed hospital room door. Behind it, the woman I love fights for her life.

Making a fist, I look down at my hands, torn apart, covered in soot. I can still feel Ruby's pulse beneath my fingertips. We got her heart beating minutes before the ambulance showed up. I told them all I could about her condition, then they took her away from me.

I screamed out everything I had left to the sky.

Numbness gives way to grief, to rage, as I pace the carpeted waiting room of Bozeman's cardiac ICU, twisting a hand through my hair. I wonder if my eyes look as deranged as my brothers.

We've been here for six hours. My soul feels like it's been through a shredder.

The doctors haven't told us anything. If she's brain dead, if she'll wake up. If my heart should plan to keep on beating or just follow Ruby's down.

Thirty minutes earlier, Ruby's father and brother

arrived. They barely paid me a passing glance before they rushed into her room. They must hate me. I hate myself.

Unable to take it any longer, I slam a fist against the wall. "Why aren't they telling us anything?" I growl.

Davis's head snaps to me, a snarl of warning on his lips. I'm on thin ice as it is.

I lost it when we got to the hospital. When the nurses refused to let me see her, I started yelling. Security showed up. Then someone stuck me in the ass with a sedative, and my brothers manhandled me into a chair, and now we wait.

A security guard—the same one I tried to put a fist through hours ago for blocking me from Ruby's room— turns in the hallway.

I glare at the guy. They'll have to break every bone in my body and chop me up piecemeal if they think they're going to get me to leave this hospital.

Sprawled out across two chairs, Wyatt sighs. "Charlie. Shut up."

In two hard stomps, Davis is in front of me. "If you get your ass kicked outta here, how's that going to help Ruby, huh?" My brother shoves me against the wall, staring fiercely into my eyes. He worked just as hard as I did to breathe life into Ruby. "Sit the fuck down."

"If you fight in this goddamn hospital," Ford says, eyes closed, pinching the bridge of his nose. An empty coffee cup balances on the thigh of his blue jeans. "I will disembowel you fuckers."

Too exhausted to argue, I drop into a chair beside Ford. I smear my face in my hands, keep them there.

My eyes and throat burn. Regret grates my insides. I didn't protect her. I kept her on the ranch. I put her in danger. If I had let her go, she wouldn't have been in the middle of this war with DVL. Ruby would be in California watching her sunset.

Instead, the woman I love the woman I need, my reason to keep breathing is hurt because I failed her.

A tear rolls down my cheek.

She can't die. Something this pure, this good can't go out.

It feels like the sun has been erased from the sky. From my heart. My entire fucking world. Gone.

Without her, I'm gone.

I lift my head, my eyes burning again as I stare at Ruby's closed door. Everything that matters is in there. Nothing will calm me until I see her. The longer I'm kept from her the more I feel like some desperate, deranged man. I need to hear her voice, to hold her hand, to see her sweet smile. Christ. If she wakes up and I'm not there . . .

If she wakes up.

My eyes land on the white ribbon tied around my wrist.

If.

An image of Ruby on the ground, cold and lifeless, smashes through my brain. Only there's more. Vivid memories of this summer. Ruby. My sunflower. Her breathless laugh at night, her small hands on my beard, her murmured *I love you* like the softest prayer. Her wide-eyed wonder at the simplest things in life. The small gasps she made at night right before I devoured her mouth and held her tiny and warm in my arms.

Alive.

I can feel that hole inside of me, the one Ruby filled with her laughter and her smiles and her heart, emptying.

Emptying.

I don't know who I'll be without her. Happiness will become a fucking memory.

I could lose her.

Panic scrambles my brain.

Ruby died. She *died*.

Christ.

I can't do it again. I can't.

My gut clenches.

I must make a sound because Wyatt looks up at me. "Charlie, you okay?"

"No," I grit out.

There's a gaping hole in my chest.

"Fuck." I spear a hand through my hair, keep it there. My voice cracks. "Fuck."

"Breathe, Charlie," Davis says sharply. His hand lands on my shoulder.

But I can't.

I can't breathe. Can't think.

The need for her nearly strangles me.

"It's not your fault, C," Ford says, reading my thoughts.

"I need some fucking air," I gasp and rocket out of my chair. I take off down the hall, not stopping until I reach the automatic doors that lead out of the hospital.

I do exactly what I promised Ruby I wouldn't do.

I run.

I make it as far as the parking lot before I remember Davis has the keys to my truck.

I tilt my head back to the early morning sky. "Fuck."

A sharp, familiar floats across the air. "I know you're not leavin.'"

"Fuck off, Wyatt."

"Get your ass back to the hospital. Now."

I bend over, hands on my thighs, and gulp air. "I can't."

I am a cowboy. I am a man, I am a tough son of a bitch, but goddamn if this pint-sized girl has the power to tear out my soul and rip out my heart.

Wyatt stalks toward me, his stride lethal. "You're my brother and my best friend, Charlie, but you're acting like an idiot. What if she wakes up and you're gone?"

I squeeze my eyes shut. "Stop."

One step closer. His voice is like a drill bit in my brain stem. "What if she needs you, and you're not there because you're out here having a pity party for yourself?"

I straighten up. My jaw locks. My muscles tense.

"She doesn't need me," I shout, whipping around. "I'm the one who got her hurt. I put her right in the middle of everything this summer. She's better off without me."

"You're a coward," Wyatt says, pointing a finger at me. Anger flashes in his blue eyes, and he shoves me backward. "Asshole."

"Fuck you," I growl, balling a fist.

The automatic door slides open, and Ford steps through it. He stands with his arms crossed, watching us. A long-suffering sigh makes its way out of him. "Christ," he complains. "Y'all aren't doin' this."

But we are.

"Yeah, you want to punch me, try it," Wyatt sneers, flexing his fingers. "It wouldn't be the first time you lost."

"That wasn't losing, that was giving you practice," I snarl.

Then I explode.

Nostrils flaring, red blurring my vision, I charge my

brother, grabbing a fistful of his T-shirt. My fist jerks back, and I hold him tight, inches from me. Sadness and rage scream for me to beat the hell out of him.

But I can't. It's not him I'm pissed at.

I'm pissed at myself, at DVL, at everything that's happened.

My hand bobs in the air.

Before I can let him loose, Wyatt slams a fist in my stomach. No hesitation.

The air leaves my lungs. I stumble, doubling over, then find my balance.

"Cheap ass punch," I say through gritted teeth.

Wyatt scoffs. "If I have to beat your grumpy ass to wake you the fuck up, so be it."

He stares at me and I stare at him, tension breaking between us.

Wyatt walks away from me, taking shallow breaths, then he turns and says, "Maggie's dead, you know, but you're not. And neither is Ruby."

I flinch, his words like a knife in my jugular.

A hiss from Ford. "You're actin' like a dickhead, Wyatt."

"Someone's gotta say it," he snaps back.

I shove my hands through my hair, scrape them down my beard. "She deserves someone else." Admitting it out loud rips my heart in half. Hot tears sting my eyes. "I never should have—"

"What, loved her?" Wyatt cuts in. "Charlie, this girl woke you up." Eyes red, Wyatt shakes his head. Raw emotion crosses his face. "She deserves you. You fought for her, man. You worked on her for over twenty minutes. She has a pulse, she's breathing, because of you."

I freeze to the spot. Unable to breathe. Unable to think.

Hope and hopelessness war within me. I've been so afraid of loving again that I waited to take that risk, to admit how I felt about Ruby. I almost lost her once. I could lose her now. But if I had to do it all over again—I would.

In a fucking heartbeat.

My eyes move to the sun rising in the east, momentarily robbing me of breath. Bright, brilliant gold. Pops of purples and pinks. As bright as my sunflower girl.

Ruby would love it.

I need to get back there. I need to stay strong for her. I won't help her by crumbling.

I exhale and turn to Wyatt. "You're right."

"I always goddamn am." He flashes a cocky half-smile. Because that's Wyatt. My younger brother never lets me off the hook, has followed my ass halfway around the world to keep me from losing my shit, and for that I'm fucking grateful.

"Wyatt, shut up," Ford orders. "Charlie, get your head on straight." Then, in a low voice, he says, "The doctor's here."

51

Charlie

THE DOCTOR STANDS IN THE WAITING ROOM, surrounded by Ruby's father and brother, who talk in low tones. I recognize the resemblance. Ruby's father and brother share her bright blue eyes. They have the same fierce, stubborn lift of her chin.

With Ford and Wyatt flanking me, I don't slow my stride, and when the doctor looks at me, a knot of tension loosens in my chest.

Damn straight, he looks at me.

"Are you the husband?" he asks.

I settle in front of them, cross my arms. "Not yet."

Ruby's brother, Max, glares. His hands are fisted at his side like he plans to beat the shit out of me.

Let him.

I have something more important to worry about.

Heart in my throat, I rasp, "How is she?"

Hesitating, the doctor looks at Ruby's father. When he gets a quick nod of confirmation from the man, he says, "Ruby's breathing on her own, which is all we can ask for right now. She's currently sedated and in critical condition. She has an elevated heart rate and a cracked rib."

I flinch.

My fault. I hate myself for hurting her.

As if reading my mind, the doctor says, "A broken rib will heal. You did the right thing. Getting her proper treatment was the most important."

I swallow, blowing out a breath. "How—what happened to her?"

"Cardiac arrest. With her underlying heart condition combined with adrenaline, the emotional stress and smoke inhalation, her heart gave out." His eyes scour my dirty clothes, his face twisting in sympathy. "I understand you had quite a night, Mr. Montgomery."

For a brief second, I close my eyes, rage and pain sweeping over me.

DVL is fucking done.

"Will she be okay?" I ask, my voice breaking.

"If she makes it through the night, we'll worry about the rest. Right now, we're completing all the testing for brain activity while she's out. But we won't fully comment on her neurological function until she wakes up." The doctor offers an apologetic smile. "A full recovery . . . it'd be a miracle, Mr. Montgomery."

I give a tight nod. "Good thing you got a girl in there who is one."

The doctor considers this. "We'll keep you updated."

"Thank you." I shake his hand.

The doctor walks down the hall, leaving us alone with Ruby's father and brother. An uncomfortable tension falls over the waiting room.

Ruby's father turns to me. "You."

Behind me, Wyatt hitches a breath.

I meet his eyes. "Sir?"

I steel myself, terrified they'll blame me when I already blame myself. Terrified they won't let me see her. But I'll fight them. I would love to see anyone try to stop me or even suggest I shouldn't be by her side.

Tears sparkle in his eyes. "You're Charlie? The cowboy my Ruby loves."

"I am." I tilt my head toward Ruby's room. "She's my entire life," I tell her father. "Please. Don't keep me from her."

An eternity passes before he nods.

I'm already moving, but before I can enter Ruby's room, Max blocks my path.

My hands flex into fists.

This close.

This close to ripping down the goddamn door to get to my girl.

I lower my voice so only Max can hear me. "Say whatever the fuck you mean, then get out of my way."

"You know about her condition?" Max asks, a muscle jerking in his jaw.

"She told me."

"And you're ready to take that on?" His blue eyes, as tenacious Ruby's, pin me in place. "You ready to be there for my sister? To take care of her when she's sick? To never have kids? To watch her die in your arms again if it comes to that?"

I want to punch the bastard. But then I remember Emmy Lou. I'd do the same damn thing. Hell, I have. If it means I have to take her brother's shit to get to Ruby, I'll do it.

I'm coming for you, baby.

I step up to the kid, toe to toe. My hard gaze never wavers. "I choose her. I love her. Whatever she takes on, I take on. I'll be there when she's sick. Catch her when she faints. And I'll never *ever* leave her."

Sudden tears spring to Max's eyes. "You mean it?"

"On my life."

Max looks at his father, and an unspoken conversation passes between them. Then he jerks his chin in a nod and moves aside. "Go," he says, his tone resigned.

With that, I step inside Ruby's room.

There she is.

There's my girl.

Heart tripping, I stand rooted to the spot, feverishly taking her in. Ruby looks breakable, delicate, so fucking small in the hospital bed. Her face and lips are bloodless, dark circles beneath her eyes. Tubes and wires feed into her. Machines beep a steady rhythm.

Finally, I force myself to move. In two large strides, I claim the seat beside her bed. Already I'm breathing easier in Ruby's calming presence. I take her slack hand, nestling her small, soft palm in my rougher one.

She has a heart too big for this world, but goddamn if I'm not keeping her here.

I need her.

"Baby, I made it." My lips sweep over her knuckles. "I'm here."

Her heartbeat pulses against my palm.

Faint, but it's there.

She came back to me once.

Now she has to hold on.

She has to fight.

"Wake up, Ruby," I whisper, pressing her hand to my cheek. "You need to come back to me. Open those beautiful blue eyes and wake up." I lean over and cup her colorless face. "Please, Sunflower. You're not leavin' me yet."

Silence.

The heart monitor beeps.

I close my eyes, resting a hand over her chest, letting the beautiful beat of her heart reassure me that she's still here.

And I settle in to wait.

As long as I have to.

52

Charlie

FIVE DAYS.

Five days and Ruby still hasn't woken up.

Every ounce of her little body is fighting. Her breathing's evened out, and her vitals are strong. She just won't wake up.

I beg, I pray, I even yell because if breaking my promise has her opening those gorgeous baby blues, I'll apologize to her for the rest of my days.

"Stubborn," I growl, but Ruby's eyes stay closed to the world. I sweep her rose-gold hair back from her pale face, holding onto her hand for dear life. "You want to put me through hell, baby, this ain't the way to do it."

I clock the monitors that track her vitals. Her heart rate stays steady at eighty. Every ounce of her little body is fighting to survive.

Sunlight streams through her window. Her hospital's room's overflowing with vases of roses, pots of sunflowers, white daisies in vases. Every day, I bring her flowers. And I'll keep bringing them until she wakes up.

She belongs in the light, not the darkness.

"I brought you violets today. They remind me of you. Small. Pretty. Feisty." I drag a hand down my beard, then rest it over Ruby's heart. I don't trust the machines. I trust her. I'm going to become a pro at knowing my girl's heartbeat.

When there's no response, I sigh and bow my head. I haven't left her side. The chair beside her bed is mine. To hell with everyone else.

Her hand is small and cold. I rub it between my fingers like a piece of kindling, giving her my warmth. "Winslow misses you. We've been keeping the horses at the Wolfingtons' place, if you can believe that." I close my eyes and exhale, hoping she can hear me, even though she's unconscious. "There's so much I have to tell you, baby. So much we still need to do. We got a sunrise in our plans. California. But you have to wake up, Ruby. You have to come back to me."

Straightening up, I press my lips to Ruby's cool forehead. Tears burn the backs of my eyes. "I am not built to be here without you," I whisper against her brow. "I'll go on if have to. Live some piss-poor life that won't make either of us happy. But Ruby, darlin', I am not built for life without you."

More silence.

It's agony.

"Charlie."

I glance over my shoulder. Davis stands in the threshold of Ruby's hospital room, keeping a respectful distance. "I need to talk to you."

Waving him in, I rotate in the chair, keeping Ruby's hand in mine. I won't let go of it. I'm attached to her like the cords and tubes feeding into her body. Every second I'm away from her, not touching her, has me on edge.

Davis stops at the foot of the bed and stares at Ruby. "How is she?" he asks in a low voice.

"The same." I glance at Ruby, her long lashes resting against her pale cheek, and my chest tightens. "Strong. Stubborn."

He gives a grunt of a chuckle. "She took up with you. She's gotta be."

I drag a hand over my beard, eyeing my older brother in suspicion. "What do you want, Davis?"

He's the only one who stuck around. Wyatt and Ford both went back to the ranch to deal with the horses and the barn. Things are a mess, but I'm grateful I have my brothers to handle it. "If you're here to tell me to leave, save your breath."

"Would it make a difference?" he asks, raising a wry brow. "Telling you to leave."

I grunt.

"That's what I thought." He snorts and passes me the coffee in his hands. "I'm here to keep you awake."

Gratefully, I take it, drinking the lukewarm liquid in one long slug.

"Brought you a fresh shirt too." Davis tosses a bag on the chair. "Mom and dad are worried."

"I know." My phone has fifty texts messages I haven't returned. "I'll get back to the land of the living when she does."

"Charlie." Davis's voice is dangerous. Cold. His gaze flicks to Ruby, to me. "I'm going to Resurrection. I'll handle the ranch. Valiante."

I try to control my rise of anger, not wanting an ounce of my rage to transfer to Ruby.

A muscle jerks in my jaw. Fuck the photo. I want to kill the bastard. Wrap my hands around Valiante's throat and squeeze. Because he did this. He's the reason Ruby's lying lifeless and dim in a hospital bed.

"That's my job," I grit out. "Leave him for me."

"What're you gonna do, Charlie?" Davis asks evenly. "Drive to his house and kill the guy?"

"The thought's crossed my mind," I growl.

"Leave Ruby?"

I glare at him. Damn dirty bastard playing that card.

Davis steps closer and squeezes my shoulder. "No. You focus on your girl. I got you."

A memory of me and Davis from long ago creeps in my mind. We were hunting, and Davis was in front of me, leading the way. I tripped in the thick brush. My gun went off, a horrific mistake, but I remember the terrifying moment of seeing my oldest brother in the way of that bullet. He picked me up, brushed sticks and grass from my hands. "This is between us," he said. "Mom and Dad don't need to know." His voice was low, serious for a ten-year-old. "I got you, Charlie."

"I almost shot you," I gasped. I fell to my knees, and tears streamed down my face. I was just a kid, but even then, I knew I had almost killed my brother.

It was an accident.

But he forgave me.

He protected me.

And he's still doing it.

I inhale a breath, accepting it for what it is, grateful my brother has my back. "You have the photo?"

"Yeah," Davis says. "But if we put this out . . .it might mean retaliation. We don't know."

"I don't give a shit," I snap. "Put it out there, put Valiante's ass on the line. Let everyone see what dirty shit he's done. Let them see what he did to Ruby."

Face softening, Davis stares at Ruby. "This is for her."

I nod. "Thank you," I tell my brother. "For not giving up. For helping bring her back to me."

Davis's brown eyes lock on mine and hold. "I had to. I know what it would have meant, Charlie."

My throat constricts as I watch Davis walk to the door. He stops in the doorway, his broad back rigid, a hand moving to rub his shoulder.

"Your scar hurt?" I ask.

"No," he says, his deep voice steely with resolve. "Just reminding myself who I am."

I frown. "Davis . . ."

"Don't worry about me. I got Valiante handled."

I hold my oldest brother's hard stare. "Destroy his fucking life," I tell him, and then I get back to my girl.

53

Ruby

SHADOW TO LIGHT. EVERYTHING'S MUDDLED, LIKE I'm swimming through the swamp to break the surface of the ocean.

But as disoriented as I am, there's warmth on my legs. Sunlight. A thin blanket tucked over my body.

Exhaustion settles over me. The faraway beeps of machines sound in my ears, and there's a strange tightness across my chest. I feel like I've been hit by a truck. Or a very, very hard fist.

Blinking, I roll my head across the pillow. A happy glow unfurls in my chest at the sight of Charlie. My cowboy has the corner chair pulled up to the edge of my bed, his boots propped up on the metal footboard. A too-small blanket is draped over him.

"Charlie." I whisper, raspy. The words stick in my dry throat, but somehow, he hears me and stirs.

And then explodes out of his chair so fast he rocks my hospital bed.

"Ruby," he says hoarsely. Wild and haunted blue eyes

meet mine, but he doesn't come to me like I ache for him to do.

He stands there, breathing hard, chest heaving. He keeps his gaze on me, and there's so much weight in it. So much fear, pain, and desperation, I feel it all.

And I remember.

Everything.

The fire, Winslow, adrenaline, pain, rain falling from the sky.

My mother.

Dying with Charlie's name on my lips.

I died.

I press my shaky hand against my chest. My heart rate is normal—my normal.

I'm alive.

I lived.

I stare at Charlie. Sadness surrounds him. That same sadness I sensed back at the ranch all those lifetimes ago. So unlike the man I know now, the brooding rancher I first met in that bar. His eyes are tortured, his beard unkempt, his muscles tense. A man unhinged. It looks like he hasn't slept in days.

With tubes and wires wrapped around my wrist, I extend a trembling hand, like I'm coaxing a bear forward.

He flinches.

"Charlie?" I say quietly, worried. "Come here, Cowboy."

His eyes flare at my words, and then his face cracks, shatters into a thousand emotions I can't name. With a wild roar, he's storming toward me, towering over my hospital bed.

He sits himself at the edge of my bed, near my hips,

and gently gathers me into his huge body. His arms surround me like the home they've always been.

"You came back to me," he mutters desperately. His deep, rumbling voice is like heaven to my ears. "Ruby. Thank God, thank God. You're alive." He kisses my cheek, my throat, locking us together tight, like we're tethered by our hearts.

The relief in his eyes, his frantic touch, shatters my control.

I burst into tears.

"Yes," I whisper. I weep against his warm, solid chest, gripping his shaking shoulders. Grateful to be with him, to be alive.

The sound that leaves Charlie is a sob. "I love you," he says raggedly against my ear. "I fucking love you, Sunflower."

With those words, he kisses me. Soft, slow. I relish the sensation of his coarse beard against my lips. He holds my wrist in his fingers and my heart breaks. He's not okay.

"Feel," I whisper against his lips. "Feel me. I'm okay, Cowboy. I'm alive."

A shudder wrenches his body. "Ruby," he rasps, burying his face in my hair and hanging on for dear life. For a long time, he doesn't let me go. He holds me, making sure I'm here, alive and in his arms.

When we pull away, Charlie gently lowers me back onto my pillow. The bed creaks as he hits the remote to bring it to a sitting position.

"Do you remember what happened?" he asks. He keeps his eyes on me, dark with concern.

"I died," I whisper.

His face almost shatters. His breath is a harsh exhale. "Ruby."

My eyes widen. "The horses—"

"Are fine." He clasps my wrist, his fingers tracking my pulse. "All of them, baby. They're safe. We saved them all."

I smile weakly, relieved. "Superheroes."

Charlie kisses my knuckles. "They're safe because of you. Because of what you did."

"How long have I been here?" I glance at the heart monitor, pumping out a steady rhythm.

"Nine days."

I gasp.

His Adam's apple bobs. "I've been out of my mind, waiting for you to wake up."

And then I gasp again.

Because that's when I see them.

Flowers.

Everywhere.

Vases and vases of bold color and bright blooms and vines and trembling petals. Asters and hydrangeas and peonies. Any free space is covered with flowers. And the best sight—sunflowers. My sunflowers from Charlie's cabin have been brought here.

It's like waking up and seeing my heart up in the sky.

"Charlie," I breathe, my voice uneven. "You did this?"

"I said you'd always have sunflower days," he grates, reaching out to cup my cheek.

His words have me in a chokehold. Honest, gruff, and pure. *Mine.* Sheer joy sweeps over me and I reach for him, but the motion has me yelping in pain.

"Careful," he growls, stopping me immediately with loving hands on my shoulders. "Enough, baby." He tucks me against a fluffy pillow.

I press a hand against my side, feeling the scratch of

a bandage, and lean my head back. Exhale through the pain. "It hurts."

Charlie's jaw clenches. Gaze haunted, he says, "I broke your rib."

Realization dawns. I freeze, forgetting how to breathe. My eyes get as big as saucers as I look up at him. "You saved me," I whisper.

His eyes flare at my words, a hard breath shuddering out of him. "You took me down, Sunflower. Hell, I was gonna follow you if I couldn't bring you back to me."

I shake my head, the thought too terrible to contemplate. "Don't say that, Charlie."

"It's true," he says, gruffly.

I cover my mouth, unable to speak. Stunned by what he's done. How is it this man has never given up on me? How is it he can claim my heart like it's the first time over and over again? A rush of emotion has fresh tears hitting my eyes.

"Kiss me, Cowboy."

He does, soft and slow. His rough hand slides up to curve around my throat. At his touch, my heart rate speeds up, and the monitors beep wildly.

He breaks the kiss and freezes.

"It's okay, Charlie." I murmur, my lips sweeping over his beard. "Again. Kiss me again."

With a heated gaze, he cups my face in his hands. His tongue slides against mine, my core warming with sunshine, his calloused thumbs skimming the pulse in my throat.

"I love you, Ruby," he says when he pulls back. Visibly overcome, he presses my hand over his heart, and his piercing blue eyes stare into mine. "From this heartbeat until the last, I am yours."

The seriousness on his handsome face has me losing it all over again. I sniffle and bring my hands to my face. Charlie gathers me in his arms.

We sit here in the quiet. The kind of quiet that speaks volumes. I can hear it in the rumble of Charlie's breath. Feel it in the curve of his kiss. Our fears. Our pasts. Our future.

And then I start to cry again, but I smile through my tears, because I know what we have, and I know what we are.

Lucky.

The luckiest hearts alive.

54

Ruby

"You okay?" Charlie asks as he helps me out of his truck.

"I'm okay." I give him a bright smile. "I'm ready."

So ready.

For a long second, I stand in his gravel drive, hands clasped to my chest. The sight of the ranch, of his cabin, brings tears to my eyes. Sunlight streams over the pasture, but the air is cooler than when I first arrived back in June. Closing my eyes, I inhale. I drink it in. I let the sunlight bathe my skin. After being in the hospital for so long, even just walking on my own two feet is heaven.

I feel reborn.

Resurrected.

Home.

I am home.

"Sunflower?"

I look up at Charlie. His intent gaze hasn't left my face. "Yeah, Cowboy?"

"C'mon, baby. Let's get you inside."

He offers me his hand and I take it. Slowly, side by side, we walk up the porch to the front door of his cabin. A riotous cheer goes up the second we step inside the kitchen. My mouth drops.

"Out," Charlie thunders.

"Shhh," I giggle, slapping his bicep.

Everyone's here. Fallon and Stede with pies from The Corner Store and a growler of beer from Nowhere. My father and brother, their bags packed and ready to head to the airport later. Tina and Chef Silas. And, of course, Charlie's brothers. They pour out whiskey and coffee in Styrofoam cups.

My flowers from the hospital have been rescued. They sit on the counter, on top of the fridge, in the hallway. Daisies, sunflowers, peonies, violets.

My heart feels so airy, so light.

My family.

My favorite sides of my life, getting along with each other.

Charlie stares at the surprise intruders, looking like he wants to boot them out on their ass. He hasn't let me out of my sight since I woke up.

"Welcome home," Fallon says, tackling me with her hug. When she pulls back, she scowls at Charlie. "Relax, big guy."

Davis kisses my cheek. "Welcome home."

I blush.

Wyatt slings an arm around my shoulder. "You know you're like a ghost now, Fairy Tale."

"Wyatt," Charlie growls.

I place a palm on his ridged chest. "You're yelling."

Charlie blows out a frustrated breath and scowls. "I said no parties."

"It's not a party. It's a homecoming," Ford rebuts, giving me a wink. "You're back, aren't you? To stay."

My lips rise into a smile. "I am." I glance at my father. "Sorry, Daddy."

The pride in his eyes fills my soul. "Don't be." He claps Charlie on the back. "I'd tell you to take care of her, but you already did."

Hard emotion crosses Charlie's face, but he says nothing, just clears his throat and shakes my father's hand. The sight has my heart close to exploding. After I woke up, I was in the hospital for a week of midnights and mornings. My father and Charlie spent some time together. Dad saw how much Charlie loves me and protects me, so it's easier for him to let me go.

My father turns to me. "Looks like you got a real wild life here, Ruby Jane."

I beam. "I do, Daddy."

From the kitchen island, Stede's voice cracks. "Get Charlie a whiskey. Boy could use a drink."

I glance at my cowboy. Face pained, shoulders slumped, Charlie looks like having everyone in his house is wreaking havoc on his patience.

Palming the small of my back, Charlie guides me to an island stool. "You should sit down."

"I'm okay," I tell him. "I sat enough in the hospital."

He doesn't press, but he grunts unhappily, and hangs back near my side, arms crossed, brow furrowed.

He's angry. *He's* not okay.

I'm worried about him.

Shifting his weight, he tears a hand through his hair.

"I'll get your bags." He kisses my temple, then turns on his boot and strides out of the kitchen, slamming the screen door with an iron grip.

Wyatt shoots a worried glance at Davis and follows.

I chew my lip. The hospital was always chaotic, so we never had time to talk about what's happened. And Charlie needs to talk. I can see the rage eating him up, the pain on his face when he looks at me. I don't want pain for him. I want his grumpy smile. I miss him.

My brother hands me a bottle of water. "How are you feeling?" he asks.

"I feel good."

I've been ordered to take it easy for the next three weeks. No stress. No exercise. But each day, I get stronger. I have better medications. Machines to monitor my heart. All the doctors concluded they've seen nothing like it.

Like me.

I'm miraculous.

I run my gaze over the cabin, my friends and family, and smile at my brother. "I lived, Max."

Unshed tears line his eyes. "I know you did." He shoves a lock of hair out of his face and takes my hand. "I'm sorry for what I said to you that day on the phone, Rubes. I tried too hard to protect you."

"You just love me," I say with a big smile.

"I do. And he does too."

I follow Max's nod, my eyes landing on Charlie's massive figure in the doorway, talking to Stede.

Max chuckles. "I still don't think life is a fairy tale, but you sure are a goddamn miracle."

Smiling, I lock eyes with Charlie. I make a move to go to him, but I shift too fast and the sudden movement wrenches my healing rib. I try to keep my face neutral, but Charlie's quick. At the sight of my wince, he immediately breaks conversation and heads my way.

He reaches me and takes my arm. "You're sitting down," he says, voice tight. "Now."

Max waves his beer. "He's right. Onward, Rubes."

I roll my eyes but let them herd me into the living room. Two hours later, after a lunch of apple pie and whiskey, the house clears out. Stede and Fallon leave after hard hugs all around. Tina drives my father and brother to the airport. Which leaves me, Charlie, and his brothers sitting around the living room.

I curl up next to Charlie on the couch and smile at the sunlight streaming through the windows. "Today was the best day."

Tracing slow lines over my bare thigh, Charlie presses a kiss to my temple. "Sunflower status?"

"Most definitely." I scan my eyes around the room, happiness blooming inside of me. "Everyone I love confined to one impossibly small space. Perfection."

"Gonna get even better," Wyatt cackles, kicking a boot up on his knee. "Wait until you see what I got here." He waves his phone and leans over Charlie to hand it to me.

I gasp and rocket to sitting. "Oh my god. You used the photo."

On the front page of the *Billings Gazette* is the photo I took of Declan Valiante with the headline: DEVELOPER'S AFFAIR SCANDAL! RANCH SABOTAGE! VALIANTE CAUGHT IN THE ACT!

Eyes wide, I look up at Charlie. "When did you do this?"

A blanket of awkward silence fills the room. I see Ford and Davis communicating silently.

Finally, Davis speaks up from his spot in the recliner. "We put it out after you were hurt," he says, offering an explanation. "Valiante won't have a campaign after this."

"What'd I say?" Charlie snaps, grabbing Wyatt's phone like he could crush it. Anger hardens the line of his jaw. "No stress."

Wyatt blanches. "Shit. Sorry."

"Charlie." I lay a hand on his clenched forearm. Anger comes off him in waves. "Let's take a walk."

His piercing blue eyes snap to me. "You should rest," he says on a rocky exhale.

Ignoring him, I stand. Charlie's immediately on his feet.

"Ten minutes," I tell him, getting a nod of agreement from Davis.

"Ruby."

"Please."

He stares at me, then nods, slips his Stetson on his head.

We don't talk about where we're headed, we just drift there. Automatically.

Intrinsically.

Charlie and I come to a stop in the pasture, our gazes on the charred remains of the barn. Rubble litters the blackened earth of the pasture, and the scent of smoke still lingers. The memories of the destruction of that night, the sight of an empty field of horses, has hot tears filling my eyes.

"I'm so sorry about the barn," I whisper.

"We'll rebuild," Charlie says, gruffly. "It's all replaceable, Ruby. You're not."

I link my fingers with Charlie's. He makes a noise in his throat, pulls me closer.

"Charlie," I say. "Are you okay?"

"I just . . ." Shoulders tensing, then crumpling, he shakes his head.

"Where are you?" I whisper to him. My hand slides to his muscled back. "Don't pull away from me. Please."

Flinching, he turns, tucking me carefully into his arms. "Never."

I shift to look up at him. "Then talk to me."

He blows out a breath. "I can't unsee it, Ruby." His chest collapses, giving in. Letting me tug the truth out of him, even if it hurts. He points to a spot on the pasture. "I see you there." His handsome face twists. "You were dead, baby. It wrecked me, always will."

"I know," I whisper to him. "I feel it too."

Strange words, but Charlie nods like he understands.

That's my fate and Charlie's heartbreak.

To live it. To remember.

It's fitting. Resurrection. Sometimes I feel like I can still remember the way it felt. To die. To come back. Charlie's mouth on mine, his fingers tangled in my hair, his tears on my cheek.

I can't, really. But I feel like I can.

Immortal because Charlie will never let me go.

My cowboy restarted my heart and brought me back to life.

I'm the person I wanted to be, the heart I had to find in this big world, the voice of my mother. That night is a part of me and it will never let either of us loose.

Which means I have to live now. Every second Charlie and I have together is precious. And we plan to live every one of those seconds like it's our last.

"I'm okay," I tell him. "I'm here. Alive. Still yours, Charlie." I reach up to cup his cheek, running my hand over his beard. His blue eyes meet mine. An overwhelming amount of love shines in them. So much love. "You just feel my heart, and I'll feel yours, and we'll know where the other's going."

Charlie doesn't say anything. He just kisses me, his breath filling my body, his lips heating every inch of my skin. Our hearts beat a steady rhythm, powered up and pumping.

My lips rise into a smile against his and Charlie's lips do the same.

Matching me.

I break away from his kiss. I'm still smiling. "There"—I press up on tiptoes to poke his stern smile—"is my Cowboy. The man I love."

Charlie steals my fingers, brings them to his lips and kisses each fingertip. Then my wrist. My heartbeat.

Tears flood my eyes.

This man. He leaves me breathless.

"There," he rasps and points at the spot where I died. "That's where we put our garden. Right there, baby. And the first thing we plant . . ."

"What's that?"

He grins. "Sunflowers."

Epilogue

Charlie

THREE MONTHS LATER

"I'M GOING IN, CHARLIE," RUBY TELLS ME AS SHE dances in the surf. She wiggles her eyebrows. "Naked."

"Don't you dare," I growl. I walk across the beach and come to a stop, my boots at the edge of the ocean. The November sun drops in the sky, a golden glow rising out of the waves. "Baby, that water's cold as hell."

"Too late, Cowboy," she teases playfully, a gorgeous smile overtaking her face. And then she splashes into the water, squealing and laughing.

"Look at me!" she shouts, arms to the pink sky. "I'm alive!"

"Look at you," I marvel, softly. "Alive."

Alive. She's alive.

The thought rocks me to my very core.

My chant. My refrain.

My miracle of a wife.

Every reason *I* am fucking alive right now is standing in that ocean.

"C'mon, Cowboy!" Ruby shouts, peeling off her sundress.

I catch sight of her breasts before she disappears into another wave.

Thank Christ the beach is private.

I go to tug off my boots but freeze as the chime of my phone fills the air.

"Goddamn it," I groan, seeing Davis's name on my caller ID. The last thing I want to do is answer, but I need to talk to him. He's been avoiding my call for the last three days.

"How's California?" Davis says when I pick up. "Avocados change your world?"

I roll my eyes. "Dickhead," I mutter.

Every one of my brothers ragged on me relentlessly for setting foot in California, but they understand I have to do this.

Wherever Ruby goes, I go.

Davis chuckles. "I bet beach Charlie is a vibe."

"Won't get me outta my boots for long."

"Congratulations, by the way." Davis goes on. "Mama is talkin' about it like it's the end times. You elopin' and all."

"Thanks." I glance down at the band of gold on my left hand. Last week, Ruby and I were married in a small ceremony at the Resurrection courthouse. Wyatt was my best man. We had a small reception at the Neon Grizzly, and the next day, we hopped in my truck and took off for California.

Didn't want to waste another minute.

Sunflower days for the rest of our lives and we take them all.

We're spending our honeymoon at a small beach house

on the California coast. In two weeks, Ruby will undergo a clinical trial at Stanford. It keeps us in California until Christmas, puts us back at the ranch early next year, but if there's anything that can make her heart get stronger, I'll make it happen.

"Listen," I tell my brother in a low voice. "I gotta make this fast. I'm on the beach with Ruby and she's about to bounce into the Pacific." I keep my eyes on Ruby's slender silhouette, daring the waves to take her away from me. "Valiante. Where is he, Davis?"

A long silence. "I don't know what the hell you're talkin' about."

"Bullshit," I growl.

He released the photo months ago, creating a shitstorm for Valiante. His campaign, his marriage, his career over. But last week, Valiante never came home from an out-of-town business trip.

Missing, the news proclaimed.

I spear my fingers through my hair. "What's the fucking rule? If you're in it, I'm in it. No matter what."

"Not this time," Davis says evenly. "You don't need to know, brother. Start your life with Ruby. Forget about it. I got you."

I squeeze my eyes shut, processing what he's telling me.

"Enjoy your vacation, Charlie," Davis says before the rock in my throat can dislodge. "Then get your ass back here. Last year's gonna be hard to top. But we're damn sure about to try."

I laugh lightly. "Yeah."

We end the call.

I cast a glance at the water, catching sight of my wife's

bare ass as she trips in the waves and then sputters, standing, arms tossed to the sky.

And then I'm stripping off my boots, my jeans, my shirt and tossing them onto the sand beside our things.

I go in after her.

Like I always fucking will.

She's smiling, her mouth open in laughter as she spots me coming.

"Fucking cold," I rasp.

Ruby bounces into me, and I grab her around the waist. "Had to get you in somehow," she says, her blue eyes glittering with mischief.

My lips meet her soft ones, inhaling her saltwater and strawberry scent, those soft gasps I goddamn adore. Then my hand skims her jaw, letting my fingers gauge the pulse in her throat.

My bad habit.

My addiction.

Her heartbeat.

I know its pulse as well as my own.

Because it beats for me as much as it does for her.

On the ranch, I've always known you can't tame the wild. And I now know I can't tame Ruby's heart. All I can do is love it.

"C'mon, Sunflower," I tell her, staring into her bright blue eyes. "We're gonna miss the sunset."

She tilts her head. "You came all this way to tell me that?"

"I came to kiss you. Now I'm comin' to get you out before you fuckin' freeze."

I carry her onto the beach, naked and dripping wet. I grab the towel from the sand and drape it over her shoulders, my eyes trailing over her slender throat, her tan breasts. Beautiful beyond words.

"How was it?" I ask.

"C-cold," she says, wringing out her wet hair, her breath heavy in her chest.

I make sure she's warm, dry off and dress myself, and then we settle onto our blanket right in time for the sunset. She sits in my lap, leaning back against my chest,

I kiss her temple. "This is it. Last thing to check off on your list."

We caught the sunrise in Tahoe right after we were married.

A radiant smile overtakes her face. "Yep." She gestures toward the horizon. "It's my California sunset. And we have the very best seats in the world."

"A show just for you, darlin'."

For a long few minutes, Ruby's silent. Then she gasps. "It's beautiful."

"It is," I say, but I'm looking at her.

The sun disappears below the horizon in a brilliant burst of purples and oranges and pinks that only she can rival.

Her smile vanishes, her gaze faraway, on the setting sun.

I frown, stroking a hand over her silky hair. "What's wrong?" She told me last night she was nervous about the clinical trial. Even though it's not major surgery, I'm terrified. But I refuse to worry or entertain grief. I did enough of that in my last life.

Ruby shuts her eyes and takes a steadying breath. "I feel like everything is over, Charlie." Her eyes open at my growl. "But not in a bad way. I feel like I know who I am now. I came to do what I wanted to do and did it." She palms my cheek and I catch a flash of the yellow diamond on her hand. I went overboard, but I couldn't help it. It's as bright and as bold as Ruby herself.

"I came, and I found you." She smiles, tears glittering in her eyes. "My cowboy who yells."

I bust out in a rumble of a laugh. Then I clear the rock from my throat and kiss her roughly. She makes a small whimper, twisting in my arms. Her lips are hot, sweet, soft.

When we part, I gather my wife against me, so tight I can feel her heart beat against mine, and I bury my face in her hair. "Christ, I love you," I breathe into her neck. "I love you, Sunflower."

I can never tell her enough. The words don't mean enough. What this wild, gorgeous woman brought to my world, every heartbroken piece of me she put back together with her sunshine glow and her laughter. I'm the grateful fucking man who has Ruby in my life. And I'm never letting her go.

My sunflower that I will always keep blooming.

"I love you too." Beautiful blue eyes glassy with tears, she rests her forehead against mine. "Let's start a new list, Charlie. *Our* list. For our new beginning. For our life and our ranch."

My eyes close briefly. Goddamn.

There is not a day that passes where I stand in amazement at the power of my wife.

"I want everything," I tell her. I run a rough hand down her arm, relishing her pulse beneath my fingertips. She's mine and she's *alive*. "Every reason I love you will be on that list. And we'll do it together, baby. We'll fill it and cross it off and add to it until the end of our goddamn days."

"Yes," she says breathily. She nods and nods and nods. Her smile brightens everything around us. "Yes."

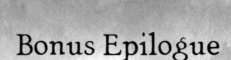

Bonus Epilogue

BLOOM'S BLOOMS IS BUSTLING.

Twinkle lights glow across the large walk-in coolers. Vases full of hydrangeas and purple roses dot the long plank table in the center of the room. Spring sunshine dapples a whitewashed wall of river rock. Cowboy boots crunch across the hardwood floor. I take a second to admire Charlie, standing at the counter, his big fingers tying twine around the ends of a custom-made bouquet of sunflowers.

The best sight in the world. My cowboy.

Amidst the chaos, my husband's piercing blue eyes find me. He gives me a wink and warmth curls through my stomach.

Today is the opening day for Bloom's Blooms. My little flower shop with white shutters is now a reality. Located in a charming former drugstore from 1920, the light-filled shop is like a secret garden on Main Street.

Between healing my heart and getting Runaway Ranch back to where it was after the fire, it's been a long journey to get here. It took many sunrises and sunsets, but we made it. Somehow, we did it.

And now all our family and friends are pitching in to get my flower shop open and off the ground.

I've never been so loved.

Wyatt lifts a circular vase of peonies. The ends of his fingers are dyed bright pink from the florist dip dye. "Where do you want these, Fairy Tale?"

I point across the room. "Cooler."

Davis's wife pops her dark head up behind a table and lifts a Mason jar filled with wildflowers. "Do we take pre-orders for these?"

I puff a lock of hair out of my eyes and squint. "We do now."

Charlie's sister, Emmy Lou, rushes across the room, followed by her husband Jace. Her pretty face is flustered as she scans the shop for her daughters. "Oh Lord, where'd those babies go?"

"Got 'em," Davis drawls, one giggling twin slung over his shoulder, the other carried under his arm like a baguette.

The day passes in a flash. I trim the ends of a bouquet of daisies, while taking a phone order for thirty centerpieces to be used at the National Finals Rodeo celebration dinner.

Tourists from Main Street stop in to see what the fuss is about. Husbands buy roses for their wives. Locals pop in and place orders. I unpack a box of vases handcrafted by local artisans. My father and Max FaceTime me and I give them the virtual tour of the shop. Fallon hands out flower crowns to each new customer. We sell out of ranunculus, then roselilies.

Finally, around six o'clock, the shop clears out. Charlie

locks the door and flips the sign to closed. He claps his hands, the sound loud and victorious, and the room erupts into cheers. "Fucking done," he announces, but he's smiling.

"You did an amazing job," Fallon says, coming up beside me. She hugs me to her, and I squeeze her tight. When I release her, she places a hand on my shoulder to steady herself. Still off-balance with her limp. A limp that has Wyatt watching with a blazing gaze from his spot across the room.

"Thank you," I whisper, smiling at the compliment.

Fallon swears. "Shit. Ruby, I swear to God if you cry . . ."

Giving a tearful laugh, I scan the flower shop. "Thank you to everyone." My voice trembles as I fight off the emotion and clasp my hands to my chest. "I couldn't have done this without you."

Grumbles and shrugs abound from this big, gruff family. By now I'm used to it.

My family.

"Hell, we're not done yet." Hearing Charlie's deep rumble of a voice, I turn, eyes locking with his. "I'm still looking for the brightest flower around."

My pulse soars and warmth curls in my stomach. It still boggles the mind how much I love him. How handsome he is with his dark beard and worn blue jeans. Those dusty boots, bright belt buckle, and black t-shirt just complete the fantasy.

My forever cowboy.

Falling in love with him has been the best risk my heart ever took.

I smile brightly. "I think we have some dahlias in the cooler."

"Nah," he says, planting his big hands on my shoulders and kissing my lips. "You, Sunflower, you're it."

"You see? I was right. Everyone needs flowers." I giggle, relishing the pride and love in his eyes. "I think this checks lucky number thirteen off our to-do list."

He tilts my head back, capturing my lips. I'm pulled into his muscled body, and he slides his hand over the curve of my hip to coast over my butt. His gaze darkens in that primal way I love. "We're not done celebratin'. Not yet."

"We have to clean up first," I whisper, wanting nothing more than to get naked with Charlie in the backroom.

Ford lifts the broom in victory. "Hell, let's order a pizza."

"Pizza?" Ford's wife suddenly sits up on the couch. Her sleepy eyes shoot open. Tangled within her blonde hair, baby's breath. I insisted everyone working today have a flower crown. "Please, pizza."

Charlie chuckles. "Feed your woman, Ford."

"Fuck you, fucker," Ford snarls at him before he dips to give his wife a kiss.

Davis heaves a carton of Miller High Life out of the cooler. Emmy Lou follows, two bottles of champagne in her hands, twins at her heels.

Corks are popped. Drinks are poured. Flowers are put away. Laughter rings out. Ford and Jace return with pizzas from Nowhere. Fallon slaps Wyatt in the face with a carnation, and instantly, the bickering begins.

With tears lining my eyes, I clasp hands to my thundering heart. My soul feels so bright, so airy, I could float into space.

This is what I'm supposed to do with my heart.

Joy and sunshine and flowers. I never expected this level of happiness.

But how could I doubt that with Charlie I'd have anything less? He's made every day of our life together a sunflower day. My wildest dreams exist because of him.

Taking my hand, my husband pulls me away from the crowd. Without words, I follow him as he leads me down the hall and into our back office. There's a mixture of pride and wonder on his face as he stares at me. I tilt my head. "What?"

"You're amazing." He pulls me toward him and I melt into him. "This. All this. You did it, baby."

"Not without you." I slide a hand up his warm, broad chest. "None of this would be possible if it weren't for you, Charlie."

He slides my wrist between his roughened palms. For a long second, silence. "120," he grunts, unhappily.

I thin my lips. "Cowboy."

I love him for taking care of me, for worrying about my heart. When I wake in the middle of the night, snuggled up safe and warm next to Charlie, it's always with his hand over my heart. Protecting me.

Ever since the clinical trial, the catheter ablation that restored my heart's rhythm, my flutters have been few and far between. Typically, I faint only twice a year, in overly stressful situations. There's still a chance my fast heartbeat may return permanently, but I take each day at a time. That doesn't mean I don't have moments of fear, but I'm fearless in my life with my heart. All I can do is follow its beat.

The frown on Charlie's brow deepens. "Today was a lot, darlin.'"

Standing on tiptoes, I kiss him. "Didn't you hear? Busy is who we are now. We have a lot more coming."

The stern expression on Charlie's face softens. "We do," he says.

We're pregnant. Only not in the traditional sense.

Charlie's brother's wife offered to be a surrogate for us. Putting my body and heart through childbirth is one risk Charlie and I aren't willing to take. It's the greatest act of selfless love, the greatest gift Charlie's family could ever give us.

With a grin, Charlie sets me on the edge of the desk. He kisses my lips, his coarse beard tickling my face. "We're busy as hell, but we'll get it all done."

My heart thuds in my chest. I grip Charlie's hand and hold on tight as it all sinks in. Nerves and exhilaration and anticipation. The future.

The past.

Even now, my mind still goes back there.

"Cowboy?"

"Yeah, Sunflower?"

"Do you still think about it?" I whisper. "The day I died?"

He looks at me, his handsome face clouding with pain. "Every day, every second of my life, I will remember that moment. I will never forget it, Ruby," he says, his voice thick with emotion. Stepping closer, he cups my face in his hands. "Why are you asking?"

"Because there was a time when I didn't care what happened to me. I just wanted to live. And now . . . we have so much." Hot tears blur my eyes. "Sometimes I'm so afraid of losing it all."

He exhales, the tremor rocking his massive frame.

"Don't be. We found our way back. And nothing's taking it from us now." Brushing a lock of hair from my face, he kisses me, then says, "It's okay to be sad on happy days, Sunflower."

"You're right," I say with a soft smile. His words make me feel like I'm floating, but he's always my anchor. The steady beat of my heart.

In his rugged face, I see home. Comfort. Hope. Endless possibilities. One heartbeat at a time.

"Are you scared?" I ask him softly, running a finger over his forearm. "For the baby?"

"No," he rasps. "Never." A muscle clenches in his jaw as his throat works. "When our daughter comes, she will light up my life exactly the way you did. With a happiness I never thought possible." He leans down and looks me in the eye with such fierce love I'm breathless. "My Sunflower."

This time, the tears come ruthlessly.

And I think of the story I'll tell our daughter about her father. About our love.

Once upon a time there was a girl, and the girl was me, and the girl had a perfectly imperfect heart and she followed its beat. And the beat was loud and brash and brazen, but so was she. Then she met a cowboy who was true and kind and handsome. He gave her sunflowers meant just for her. Memorized the beat of her heart, made her feel like she wasn't an afterthought in someone's mind, and when he said "stay," she said "yes."

Sometimes love is as simple as that.

With a sob, I wind my arms around Charlie's neck and hug him to me. "Thank you. You made today one of the best days of my life. You've given me everything I've ever wanted."

"And I'll keep on keepin' on," he says with that reckless, adoring smile I love. His hands clasp the small of my back, rocking us from side to side. "You and me, we got more sunflower days comin' and they aren't gonna stop."

I kiss the tip of his nose. "I love us."

His dark blue eyes turn soft, his voice a deep rumble in his chest. "I love you, Ruby."

I smile widely. "I love you, Cowboy. With my whole heart."

The Runaway Ranch series continues with *Rope the Moon*.

Thank you for reading!

If you enjoyed the book, please consider leaving a review on Goodreads and the site you bought it from. Every review means the world to indie authors.

Don't miss out on Ava Hunter's upcoming books! Sign up at www.authoravahunter.com to be the first to get the latest book news and bonus content.

Acknowledgments

A huge thank you to the two who brought this book to life: Sarah at Okay Creations for designing an amazing cover to kickstart this new series, and Paula at Lilypad Lit for working magic on my words.

Anna P., Chelsea, Yolanda, and Rachel for being the best beta readers a girl could ask for. Thank you for your endless support and feedback.

Eve Kasey for always letting me bug and annoy her with random writing questions.

Jenny Bunting for letting me rant, rave, and always lending an ear. Thank you for kicking my ass to write in first person!

The Trauma Fiction group on Facebook for their generosity and expertise in all things medical and heart-related. Thank you for your knowledge on SVT. You inspired Ruby and made sure I had wonderful resources to craft her journey. I did not take her story lightly and I am always so grateful to you.

A special shout out to my husband for being a sounding board for all my wacky ideas and devious plot lines.

And lastly, my readers—thank you for reading my books. All your support, every post, every review means so much. I truly could not do this without you. Bottom of my heart, all my love and thanks to you.

About the Author

Ava Hunter is a strong believer in black coffee, red wine, and the there's-only-one-bed trope. She writes contemporary romance with healthy amounts of angst where the damsels are never quite damsels, but the men they love (good, bad and rugged) are always there for them. Married to her high school sweetheart, Ava loves crafting strong, stubborn women who only make their obsessive, overprotective men fall harder, adores all things pink, and can never ever get enough of protector romance.

CONNECT WITH AVA:

WEBSITE: www.authoravahunter.com
NEWSLETTER: www.authoravahunter.com
FACEBOOK: facebook.com/authoravahunter
INSTAGRAM: instagram.com/authoravahunter
TIKTOK: tiktok.com/@authoravahunter

Made in the USA
Las Vegas, NV
11 November 2024

11622482R00275